HILDA

WHATEVER HA
VICKY HOPE'S ~~BACK OF~~
MAN?

Laura Kemp

About *Whatever Happened to Vicky Hope's Back Up Man?*

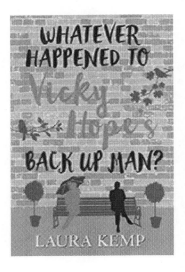

A tender, funny and haunting coming-of-age novel which asks if the past can ever be part of your future.

Twenty-one and insecure, Vicky Hope comes up with a plan on the eve of travelling the world with her high flying friend, Kat Lloyd: if she isn't married by the time she's thirty, she'll marry her geeky best mate Mikey Murphy.

Fast-forward eight-and-a-bit years, Vicky, now Vee wakes up on her thirtieth birthday in Brighton, expecting a proposal of marriage from her arty boyfriend Jez. Instead he tells her their relationship is over and she has no choice but to return to her parents' home.

Devastated and alone in her childhood bedroom, she decides she has nothing to lose and tracks down her two old mates.

With shock, she discovers Mikey, now Murphy, is a successful app designer driven by his tragic upbringing. Kat, or Kate, never made it – but she hides a devastating secret, which threatens the happiness of all three.

For LK, who has my unyielding devotion – in other words, I'm totes devotes

Prologue

Roath, Cardiff, September 2007

Lying flat on her back, Vicky Hope screwed up one eye and waited for the orangey night sky to stop spinning.

When it didn't, she groaned, reached out across her parents' manicured lawn for Mikey Murphy's hand and squeezed it hard.

'Ow! What in the name of Britney Spears was that for?' he said, yanking back his arm.

'Everything's whirling and I can't stop it,' she wailed as the street light in the top right of her vision pogoed up and down. This was not how she had wanted to look back on the farewell barbecue held in her honour for family and neighbours the night before she left home and travelled the world. She'd intended to behave seeing as Mum had pulled out the stops, having bought the posh burgers from the supermarket.

'That's five hours of sinking everything in your Dad's drinks cabinet, that is,' he smirked, splayed out beside her, blowing smoke rings into the for-once still Indian summer air. 'Maybe you shouldn't have had that last one. The green concoction that tasted of melon with an umbrella and a glacé cherry. That made you sick. That ended the party.'

'Not helping,' she gulped, panicking at the prospect of her six-month tour with their friend Kat Lloyd, beginning with boarding British Airways flight 548 from Heathrow to La Paz, Bolivia via Miami at 11.25 a.m. tomorrow. Twenty-one hours in transit – not including Dad's painfully sensible driving from Cardiff to the airport – was bad enough when you'd never gone further than the Mediterranean but with a hangover? Vicky felt panty and light-headed at the thought of Kat in bed already after a tame family supper. 'And I've got to get up in about four hours and Kat says she's taking far less than me and that I've overpacked. But I think five pairs of shoes is fine, don't you?'

Mikey gave a loud snort.

'What?' Vicky said, turning her head to face him.

Mikey, being Mikey, deliberately kept looking upwards, his face expressionless, the profile of his heavy brow, strong nose and defiant lips as inscrutable as Snowdon.

But having been best mates with him for eight years, Vicky knew exactly what he was thinking: she was ridiculous. So she elbowed his skinny ribcage.

'Oi!' he barked, making to sit up before giving in to gravity and collapsing alongside her. Vicky watched as he stretched to stub out the last burning embers of his fag on the edge of the patio. Knowing the drill, he pocketed the butt – funny how he followed the rules here at Mum and Dad's but nowhere else.

'It's not enough to leave me – yet again. Oh no, you have to go and duff me up,' he said, pouting for effect, which sent Vicky wild.

'You were invited!' she screeched. 'Me and Kat always said we'd go travelling after uni and we always asked you to come.'

Vicky's indignation evaporated then when she realized it was no longer an idea but an actual happening. She was frightened of the food, the toilets, the language barrier – and of being The Plain Friend. Vicky loved Kat dearly: they'd wished they were twins in primary and that the corridors would swallow them up in secondary. With Vicky's ginger hair and puppy fat and Kat's towering height and thick specs, they'd stood out in Cardiff High for all the wrong reasons. Then when Mikey had turned up from a rough estate in Llanedeyrn with long black hair in Year Nine he'd had no other choice but to join their gang.

Now though, Kat wasn't the square in glasses anymore. She had contact lenses, a thigh gap, perky boobs and glossy Angelina Jolie hair as well as a first-class degree and a career in banking waiting for her when they got back. With her pale podge, 'strawberry' blonde hair, a 2:2 and that clueless gawp if asked what she was going to do for a job, Vicky was still hoping to have her ta-da moment of transformation.

Whenever Vicky admired her friend's new looks, Kat would make sure she returned the compliment: Kat knew what it was like to feel unattractive. But that didn't change the fact that Vicky was going to spend the next six months in Kat's shadow.

If only Mikey was coming, he always made her feel special. Sort of interesting, funny, clever, kind and not the big idiot she considered herself to be. Oh, God, she thought, shutting her eyes, she was going to miss him madly. He was her constant, her ally and her teammate – even more so than Kat, who'd been put in a different form and was whisked off at home-time to her smart semi overlooking the park for after-school tuition, leaving Vicky and Mikey to deal with the bullies alone.

He'd been moved by his mum and dad from the 'interfering' catholic school at a time when she was having one of what Mikey called her 'mad attacks'. With drainpipe school trousers and both ears pierced, he stood out a mile and from day one he was 'a poof' and 'a queer'. A mouse of a student who, at best, was called a plodder, Vicky had no hope: hanging out with him meant she was tainted by association.

When everyone else had been sorting themselves into their tribes, whether they were indie kids or trendies, she and him had been on the periphery, united by not being like everyone else. They paired up because no one would sit next to them. That was when they bonded; over their pencil cases scrawled with Pulp and the Manic Street Preachers; class war; and their hatred of Tony 'Tory' Blair. Being singled out as weird, they took it and turned it on its head, thriving on their otherness: there was comfort in their in-jokes, secret codes, latest activist causes and understanding that they were different. Kat, or Katherine back then, flitted in and out of their world when she had a second away from her heavily scheduled 'free' time of music and maths. Everyone else followed the crowd: the girls all had Rachel from *Friends* haircuts while the boys tried to look like *Baywatch* extras with blond highlights.

Those clones had no hope: Mikey and Vicky however were destined to make it, whatever 'it' was. Vicky would listen enraptured, her heart beating wildly, as Mikey talked of the future, desperate to get away from his drunk of a dad: how he'd tread the roofs of the identical new-build estates like stepping stones and pick his way to London, paving the way for a better life. The others, he'd scoffed, could only see as far as ten minutes up the A48.

Vicky didn't have the same motivation – unlike Mikey, her family was boringly normal. The weekly shop was always done on a Wednesday. Dad drove an executive Ford. Mum dreamed of having a side-return extension to their Victorian terrace round the corner from Roath Park. And her big brother Gavin was scaling the grades in the finance department of the National Assembly for Wales.

But that was precisely why Vicky yearned to fly. Because she was so ordinary, she had an emotional need to make herself stand out, be accepted, be someone. To be interesting.

Disappointingly, Reading Uni hadn't done that for her. Mikey was supposed to have gone with her – she was going to do sociology while he did computer science, Kat, of course, was going to Oxford – but he'd spectacularly failed his A Levels after yet another bout of 'trouble at home' and as soon as she left home, he started working nine to five at the phone shop. It was a horrible first in Vicky's life, leaving him behind and going it alone.

She'd felt on the back foot right from the start. There'd been plenty of going out and all that, the girls in her house 'loved a giggle' and 'I Will Survive' by Gloria Gaynor, but there was no one she clicked with on such a level as Mikey. When she'd pop back home for the weekend to see him, people would ask her why they weren't together as a couple. But it was never like that: they were best mates, she'd explain, they didn't fancy each other. Boyfriends and girlfriends let you down – bezzies didn't. They'd seen it first-hand with each other's rubbish relationships, which generally lasted a fortnight, much to their relief: for who would the other hang out with? And while Vicky had never admitted it, she didn't like his attention going elsewhere - it wasn't out of jealousy, definitely not, it was his choice of heavy eye-linered girls who she thought looked 'tarty'.

When Kat came home for the holidays, it was obvious to Vicky and Mikey that she had blossomed at Oxford, where she was reading maths. She was out of her mother's control and so she began to learn her own likes and dislikes. Here was a girl who'd only known set bed times and curfews and then discovered she could stay up as late as she liked. While she didn't go the whole sex, drugs and rock 'n' roll route, Vicky saw when she visited her that she was dabbling a bit with boys, booze and gigs. Her work didn't suffer though because she was conditioned to study, she had an innate thirst for knowledge, it was just that she'd found her own voice.

When they'd graduated in July, Vicky had got swept up in

Kat's desire to see the world: it was her reward for getting a first and having a job in the City lined up.

But Vicky had no plans – she would go because she had nothing better to do. Neither a career nor a calling; not even a pleading boyfriend asking her to stay. Unlike Kat who'd ditched the sporty spunk, who'd ruined it all by getting needy, a few weeks before their departure.

Vicky had got caught up in the excitement of reading up on their route during quiet times at the bar at Dad's golf club where she'd worked to save up. She hadn't really thought about the consequence of being thousands of miles away in a different time zone from Mikey. She'd assumed he'd get swept along in their travelling chatter, jack in his job and come for the ride. But he never cracked.

Now, Vicky was overwhelmed by the realization of not being able to pop home to see Mikey until March. For he was, and always would be, the most awesome person in the world.

'It's not too late, you know. You can get a ticket and join us. Go on, please come,' she begged.

This time he turned to her. In the warmth of Mum's new garden pathway lights, bought especially for Vicky's farewell barbecue, she saw his eyes flicker with emotion.

'No, ta,' he said, covering it up with his bored voice as his fingertips fiddled with the sweep of his thick black bob.

'Come on, Mikey, this is our chance to escape!' she implored, 'Like we always said we would. To get away from suburbia. To cheat death by conservatory. To beat everything we've always raged against – crisp packets on the pavements, grey multi-storey car parks, people washing their cars on Sundays, anonymous shopping centres, beer guts, gravy with a wrinkled skin, service stations, people talking about the weather.'

'Don't. I'm still going to have to live with all of that.' He spread his sarcasm thick but she knew he was speaking from his heart.

'Exactly, so come! You hate working in the phone shop! Think of that stupid corporate red tie they make you wear. And hey, guess what? You might not die if you swap your Doc Martens for flip-flops. We'll find ourselves. Together.'

'I can't think of anything worse,' he spat, still the rebellious teenager. 'Toffee-nosed kids having experiences when all they're doing is going on an extended package holiday, conforming. Plus I hate the sun.'

Vicky clamped her mouth shut into a thin line. He didn't have to make it sound quite so, well, conventional. But when his voice cracked she recognized his regret at snapping at her.

'My mam... my sister, I can't leave them with Dad.' His eyes blinked slowly, protectively.

'I know,' she said, laying a reassuring hand on him but feeling terrible that she'd forced him to admit what she already understood. There, that tug between them then was what only they had.

'It's just...' Vicky said, 'I'll have never been so far away from you, for so long, and I wish I could take you away from all of this.'

'When I leave here I don't want to be running away.' His glassy stare had focused on something behind her left ear. It was his 'thinking things' face.

Then he fixed his eyes on her: the excitement, a rarity these days, made them glow like conkers. 'I've got plans. There's this thing called an iPhone,' he said, waving his hands. 'It's just come out, and it's going to change the world. Mobile applications. The Internet. And I want to be in on it, I think that might be the way for me to get out.'

Vicky hadn't a bloody clue what he was on about. She had a pay-as-you-go phone and was the only person apparently in the world not on Facebook. But he definitely had enough intelligence, wit and techie skills to make a go of whatever it was – he'd been stripping and reassembling computers ever since she'd known him. And the dark techy side of things gave him camouflage: it was somewhere he could hide, create, be anonymous or anybody. She just hoped this iPhone thingy worked out and was worth it.

'God, I wish I had the same ambition as you,' she said. All she'd ever desired was to find something that inspired her, but she didn't know what. She suspected that the something might actually turn out to be a someone and babies, but she would never admit it, what with her being a feminist and all. 'That's why I'm going. Because I've got nothing else. No direction. That's what... Pete said when he dumped me.'

Tears came to her eyes then and her shoulders began to shake.

Pete. The so-called dependable scientific boyfriend she'd spent her final year with at uni. They were going to live together. She'd come home from some job or other to find him cooking a wholesome meal after he'd spent the day examining hamster populations in the Sahara or whatever it was he was going to be researching for his Masters. Then they'd get married and have kids. But unfortunately she hadn't discussed any of that with him. And now he was going to a university in Scotland. And she wasn't invited. He loved her but he wasn't sure they'd make it when real life started.

She'd been crushed. It wasn't because she was convinced he was The One. It was because he was her only chance of a relationship. He'd been her first proper boyfriend after two rubbish blokes, one of whom had treated her mean while the other had been overkeen, in a suffocating, clammy palms kind of way.

Now the worry that she'd never find anyone, that most private thought which haunted her, which she wasn't supposed to feel because she was young and carefree, came dashing to the surface.

'I'm going to be alone forever, Mikey,' she blubbed into his shoulder, her tongue loosened by the drinks cabinet.

'Pete was one boring fucker, Vicky,' he said into her hair as he put an arm around her. 'He did you a favour.'

Mikey had disliked him from the off - an awkward introduction when she brought him home at Easter ended up with both of the men in her life moaning about the other.

'But what if that's it? What if I never meet anyone else? That's what I'm scared of.' Loneliness – or being left out – was what she wanted to run from: she'd had enough of it through school, always the last-but-one to be picked for anything (thank God for Terri 'Smelly' Matthews). It was made worse because her parents were so loved up: they did everything together, from popping out for a few bits of shopping to going upstairs to bed. It made her feel in the way at times, which she knew was dumb, because as twee as they were, it was sweet how they followed each other around. But it set the bar too high on relationships and some days seeing her parents smooching made her feel that she would never find her perfect fit.

'It's better to be single than in a shit relationship.'

'You say that but what about Sundays? The worst day of the

week. Everyone else is coupled up and you're in your pyjamas in front of *Hollyoaks* with no one to talk to.'

'What? So you'd rather be like my mam and dad, would you? Fighting over how much he spends in the pub and the bookies? Bringing out the worst in each other?'

Vicky shuddered and, with it, blades of grass poked her where they touched her skin, emphasizing Mikey's point.

'Course not. But imagine getting really old, like thirty, and being on the scrapheap.'

She could see it now: having a meal out at the Harvester with just her biological clock for company while happy paired-up strangers gave her pitying looks.

'Fucking hell, Vicky. You're being irrational now. You want to be in love, that's all this is. We've got years ahead of us.'

Vicky hummed a concession into his armpit – this was the trouble with someone knowing you back to front, they always called you out on dramatics. But still she felt the grip of fear.

Sensing it, he added softly, 'Look, believe me, there is no way you'll end up on your tod. You're too amazing for that. If anyone's going to be all alone, it'll be me, all right?'

His compliment bounced off her: her natural reaction was to big him up instead.

'Oh hardly! You get asked out, which is more than can be said for me!'

This was true. Not that he bothered with most girls, which pleased Vicky - none of them were good enough for him. His clouded eyes and jagged cheekbones were more tortured than boy band, he loved gaming rather than *Match of the Day* and he drank Guinness not premium wife-beating lager – but he got away with it because girls read him as brooding and mysterious.

But Vicky's equivalent wonkiness of 'interesting' clothes, wishing she'd gone to Hogwarts, lusting after David Tennant as Doctor Who and preferring Stop The War marches to Saturday shopping trips just wasn't sexy.

'Alone by choice, I meant. Girlfriends are too high-maintenance. Whatever mood I'm in, you're about the only person I can hang out with. I couldn't be bothered to have to explain myself to someone.'

This time, his words hugged her.

'Aw, me too. At least we've got each other.'

'Yeah, defo. Although don't think you can get away with

making me listen to Coldplay when we're in the old people's home together, sipping hot cocoa.'

'I do NOT like Coldplay! That CD was Pete's, not mine.' Then she realized what he'd said and a ping went off in her head. 'But it's a good call, that.'

'What is, like?'

'Well, why don't we make a pact? You know, if both of us are still single by the time we're thirty and ancient, we get together.' This could be the solution, she thought, suddenly feeling sober, the security she needed to get on with the rest of her life.

'You must be joking! I am never getting married. Not to you nor anyone. Not even Lara Croft.'

Oh, he was so infuriating.

'Can't you just say yes, because I'm really worrying about this,' she said, heaving herself onto an elbow so he could see how much this meant to her.

'We're mates. Being girlfriend-boyfriend would be… odd.'

'Right,' Vicky said, whispering now as she lay back down. All of the breath inside her had been punched out by his definitive refusal. She hadn't meant it. Not really. Not much. It was just a bit of insurance; to know if it all went tits up, they'd at least have each other.

'Tidy. Glad we've cleared that up,' he said, putting an arm behind his neck. 'Sometimes, Vicky, you are mental.'

But she was stewing now: it wasn't such a bad offer, was it? She began to feel offended then, that he considered the idea of her as his partner so ridiculous.

'Fine,' she said, sternly, inching away from his body, defensively pulling down the hem of her slightly too-tight Barbie T-shirt, on which she'd written in fabric sharpies 'Screw you, Ken'.

'Vicky?' Mikey shifted his head to work out what was going on inside hers.

'What?' she said, prickling from his rejection.

'Are you in a strop?' he said. Vicky could hear his eyebrows shifting like tectonic plates.

'No,' she said, bristling, looking away from him.

'Oh dear God,' he said, amused. 'You are in a strop. You. Are. A. Nutter.'

'Well. For feck's sake…' she huffed.

'What?' he said, his voice arcing.

'I thought we were best friends. We'd do anything for each other.'

'Are you Meatloaf?' he said, flicking his fingers against her arm, singing 'I'd Do Anything For Love (But I Won't Do That)'.

'Go on then, have a laugh, take the piss. I'm off tomorrow, you better make the most of it.'

She felt his chest rise then as he took a breath. He held it as though he was weighing it up. Finally, he blew out of his cheeks and squeezed her tight.

'All right,' he surrendered, 'all right. Have it your way, you ludicrous person, you. If we're both single when we're thirty, I'll be your back-up man. Okay?'

At first, she was annoyed because he'd practically yawned it. But then, that was his way: he was guarded with his emotions because it was always a risk to him, to show he cared. Hadn't he always been like this? Reserved and self-sufficient because no one had really looked after him. This was the closest she was going to get to an agreement. Bite his hand off, she told herself.

'Really?' she said, staying very still to make sure she'd hear his confirmation.

'Really. I swear on Jarvis Cocker's life.' Again he delivered it in a fatigued voice.

Vicky had a little wiggle to celebrate, not even caring about the wobble it set off down her body.

'You're mad, you know that don't you?' he said.

Vicky giggled: he was bound to be rolling his eyes at her. 'But don't you feel better knowing that whatever happens now, we've got a plan B? I know I do. I feel all secure now.'

'Good, good. You looney.'

'See, this is why I love you, Michael Patrick Murphy. You know what it means to me.'

'I do, Victoria Anwen Hope, I do,' he said wearily, but she could tell he'd spoken with a grin. Her snow globe of worries began to settle: having Mikey in reserve steadied her.

'You've just got to pray I meet someone now!' she laughed.

'Our Father, who art in heaven…' he began.

'Cheeky git,' she said, letting him pull her in, which moved her towards his neck. She smiled as she anticipated breathing in the boyish salty smell she'd known forever. But in its place, and to her surprise, there was a musky manly scent.

Just then, Vicky had a moment. A shivery split-second thing which seized her and made her reach out and place her hand on his chest. Beneath his ripped Pulp T-shirt, she felt his heart thumping as fast as her own. She had actual butterflies.

A question appeared in her head… but it was one which she dismissed before it had even fully formed.

Because Vicky had her plan B. If it all went wrong, then this time in nine years if neither her nor Mikey were in a relationship, he would be there for her.

Right now though, I'm twenty-one and the world is waiting, she told herself as she tried to imagine a place where the sky hadn't been fake-tanned by the lights from the M4.

Eight-and-a-bit years later...

Chapter One

V

Brighton, February

This was it, Vee thought waking up on her thirtieth birthday, the day that Jez would propose.

This was the moment she'd been waiting for and had not just hinted heavily and repeatedly at but explicitly spelled out over the last few years.

Jez knew what was expected of him: to ask for her hand in marriage.

This was the one concession to their avant-garde living: after all, hadn't she always supported his art and gone along with his lifestyle in this freezing rattily windowed warehouse flat in Brighton and the dismantled bicycles in the hallway and veganism? Indeed, she'd even thrown herself into it because she found it all quite entertaining. Apart from the secret cheese she had behind his back. By doing what he did, it gave her some purpose and concealed her own jellyfish act of floating here and there, unable to find any sort of calling in her work life or hobbies or anything.

Once, he'd tried to argue against marriage: we are all masters of our own fate and no one was forcing anyone to do anything, he'd said. Besides, he'd disagreed with it on the grounds that property was theft. But as far as this matter was concerned, she had refused point blank to even address his view. For this was the one and only condition she had placed on their relationship – and she was putting her foot down. It was non-negotiable. End of. And anyway, who said a proposal had to be predictable or naff? You're an artist, Jez, she'd said, think outside the paintbox!

It was only when Vee had spied her slippers that she darted out of bed, which was a mattress on a floor of concrete. Carpets and floorboards were out of the question – 'too bourgeois' – so for warmth she relied on a pair of grey alpaca wool booties which dated from her travels in Peru. Sometimes, when she put them on, she'd wonder whatever had happened to Kat, but today her past was far from her mind: it was all about the future.

Sticking on one of Jez's holey jumpers, Vee dashed in to the loo then nipped down the spiral metal staircase to their open-plan lounge-kitchen-diner which was bathed in sun during the spring and summer but murky as a mine now in winter, even at 11am.

'Hello?' she shouted, her voice echoing off naked brick walls, hoping he'd have taken the day off because it was important to her. Surely, he knew? She swallowed her disappointment at the silence, telling herself that he had had to go to the studio as soon as the sun was up to make the most of the daylight. With his exhibition coming up, he'd been working really long hours. Instead, yes, instead, he'd have left her something, a teaser of his intention.

Weaving her way through sculptures and tyres, casts and tools, she looked around the room for a sign of her surprise. What form would it take, her proposal? Perhaps there'd be a treasure hunt of clues? Or maybe he'd have made her something like he usually did, which wasn't because he'd forgotten her birthday – no, it was a heartfelt and unique personal expression of his adoration.

Lost in thought, she banged backwards into a six-foot iron tor, a piece entitled 'The Angst of Man', which on the quiet she thought resembled a penis, and it tottered dangerously from one edge to another.

'You clumsy cow,' she said aloud, holding out her arms to catch it should it fall. Oh Christ, she thought, imagine being cheated out of a proposal because she'd been squashed to death by a metal cock.

Thankfully, the structure settled down and Vee continued past the brown cord retro sofa and the beach driftwood coffee table towards the table, which was an old door balanced on four metal beer kegs – her present had to be there! Because he wouldn't have forgotten. Would he?

Could there be a little sparkly box on it? she wondered

before berating herself for being so dull and uninspired. As if Jez would go to H Samuel! As if she'd want a rock from H Samuel! Well, she wouldn't refuse it if there was one.

But Jez was far too imaginative for that. A diamond nose stud would be much more up his street! Now that would be both edgy and romantic. Bugger, she thought, why hadn't she asked for that? Not that Jez liked her suggestions a great deal. God knows how she was going to get him to agree to all the bits and pieces that she wanted for their wedding.

But she had it all planned: it'd be traditional with a twist. The sort of wedding the artist Banksy would approve of, that's how she'd sell it to Jez. Their ushers would tell people to sit wherever the hell they fancied, the photos would be Victorian-style with no smiling, they'd ride to the reception on a tandem, guests would pick their favours out of lucky dip boxes and the centrepieces on the tables wouldn't be flowers but collection boxes for their favourite charities. She'd just have to present it to him as an installation, that's all.

Just then, in amongst the detritus of his breakfast, she saw an envelope marked 'V'.

Here it was! She hugged herself, wanting to savour the moment because within an hour she'd be slaving away at work. If she had a wedding to plan it would distract her from that awful bloody place.

She was sick of *Hello Daaling*, the budget veggie bistro where she was supposed to be a member of the waiting staff but had been the de facto manager for two years, ten hours a day, five days a week on shit money. It was damp and cramped and the student waiters and waitresses were completely unreliable. How had she ever thought that slogging it in that cafe was The Answer? It was just the latest in a long line of dubious 'career' choices she'd made since returning to the UK with Jez from Thailand seven years ago. Her six months of travelling had turned into eighteen when life - and love - got in the way. She'd come back with a nose piercing, an empty bank account and a 6ft blond dreadlocked artist boyfriend, but no clearer sense of direction.

There'd been the yogi course which she'd had to quit because she couldn't get her leg behind her neck. She'd tried jewellery making, but she was too heavy-handed with the pliers. Having a stab at training to be a counsellor, she'd realized it

4

wasn't for her when she kept drifting off during the classes, too busy thinking about her destiny or whether she was going to cook falafels or puy lentil parsnip risotto for tea. If only she'd become a teacher as she'd wanted to when they moved back. But it was too late.

Now, she realized, in terms of her working life she was no better off than years before when she'd paid for her simple and uncomplicated existence of food, bed and fun by handing out beach party flyers to backpackers on Koh Samui.

Thank God then for Jez. Her relationship was the one thing she'd invested in.

And this proposal would prove it: it'd be a signpost to the security of a soulmate, to move from the stinking North Laines to Hove where they'd get a dog, then have kids, loads of them. They'd start trying as soon as they were married for a child called Star - his choice but she'd work on that. He'd be such a great dad, she knew it, all hands on and playful: theirs would be one big beautiful scene of chaos and love. She'd home educate and never have to go back to honking of onions courtesy of *Hello Daaling*. And that future was waiting for her in this envelope.

Her fingers trembled as she reached out to pick up the envelope, which stood against Jez's bowl of chilli avocado porridge. Shaking drops of almond milk off it, she anticipated some act of ingenuity: he was all about making memories. Even though he was thirty-three, he never let life suck him dry. His inner child brimmed over: his big brown eyes were often hopping boyishly with excitement. In fact he looked a bit like a jester with his spongey dreads and colourful clothes! But then he could afford to be, thanks to mummy and daddy who, out of guilt for nobbing off to the South of France to be near his sister and their grandchildren, had bought him this place and signed over two of their London flats to him so he could live off the rent - justified by him as a sacrifice he had to make so he could create rather than work for *The Man*.

At least it meant minimal contact with his plummy parents, who had neither a microwave nor telly in the kitchen.

But Jez's spirit, his joie de vivre, his refusal to let the details get him down were what attracted Vee to him in the first place on the night they met on a Cambodian beach. Kat had long gone – and this was Vee's last hurrah before heading home. She couldn't believe that the handsome topless double-barrelled public-schooled fire juggler liked her back. But by then she had buried her suburban self: Vicky had become Vee after she got in with a bohemian crowd. Her hair was long and bleached by the sun; she'd finally got a healthy colour; she had a fake tattoo of a Buddha on her lower back which she religiously had reapplied because the real thing would be too painful; and she was skinny after a persistent bout of Thai tummy (which still troubled her, probably irritated by all the lentils they ate). Jez had been impressed with her voluntary work at a children's home and taken with what he called her quirky Welsh ways. The way she spoke in reverse, like Yoda, 'Coffee, I need', and celebrated St David's Day wherever she was. She had been his 'sweet little rarebit'. Six years on, it had come down to this moment.

Tearing open the envelope, she saw the card inside wasn't birthday-related, which didn't surprise Vee. A golden 3 and 0 was not his style. Instead, the card was one of the promos he'd got made up of his works of art to sell at the exhibition, which Vee did think was a little bit 'me, me', me'. But she was prepared to overlook it... until she read inside.

> Vee,
> I'm so, so sorry but it's not working. We've had an amazing time, AMAZING, but recently I've felt there's something missing. It's not you, I just need to be free. I need some authenticity, to find meaning. Existence precedes essence – I've forgotten that I'm an individual and I need to throw off the labels that have defined me for too long.
> The absurdity of it all though is that my quest will not be done alone – there is someone else, a sort of soulmate, like I had no say in it. I never wanted to hurt you.
> Do not be sad, rarebit. Fly, like me, and embrace the beauty of the world.
> Jez

The shock was like a blow to her head with a cast-iron Welsh cake-baking stone, robbing her of breath and balance.

Vee followed her stomach and dropped to the floor, taking a spoon and a hammer with her. In slow motion, they somersaulted down and clanged and clattered at a deafening volume as they hit the dank concrete.

Holding her ears, Vee's head exploded and she began to fight for air. He was ending it, he'd met someone else. But no, it couldn't be. She refused to believe it.

The card had fallen from her hands and she scrabbled at it desperately, her fingers numb and clumsy. Reading and rereading it again, she raged at his crass employment of existentialism to justify his philandering – had he forgotten she'd done sociology at uni? That she was damn sure Sartre and Camus hadn't wrestled with what it was to be human to assist spineless men dumping their girlfriends?

The lively black swoop of his handwriting came alive, swimming at first then crawling, threatening to suffocate her. Terrified, she threw the snakes across the room.

On her hands and knees, she began to heave from the pit of her insides. It's over, her brain said, he's leaving you, there's someone else, that's why he's hardly been here. For his 'soulmate', a word he had always mocked for its suggestion of perfect love. There was no such thing, he'd always said. What he'd meant, Vee knew now, was he hadn't felt a perfect love for her.

Delirium told her to talk him round – that's what she'd do. He was just having a bit of a crisis, he was an artist, for heaven's sake. And with all her talk of marriage, maybe it wasn't the be all and end all. They could go for a walk on the beach and she could get him to throw his worries into the sea like stones. She had to, because after seven years of him, there was nothing else in her life.

Her surroundings drained to grey as she blinked hard to focus on a spot of paint on a chair leg, which squirmed until she could bear it no more. She slumped down into the foetal position as the blow to her heart infected her bloodstream and poisoned her all over.

She wanted Jez. But it was useless, she realized. He didn't love her. It was over. Her plans incinerated, she wanted to die. Paralyzed by agony, she lay still for she didn't know how long, listening to the stampede of terror of how things would now be. She tried to shut it out, but with eyes closed the frenzy became louder, hotter, sharper. Then the shakes came. Still alive but it was a living death as the tremors rattled her body.

Lurching up to her knees, she had to get out. She had to do something. But what?

Go to the studio and confront him? A blurry movie of screams and recriminations played out before her. She didn't have the strength nor the desire to be humiliated in person. His artist friends would close ranks, tell her to chill out, cool it, babe, which would make her want to beat Jez in the chest until she was dragged off. Instinctively, she knew whoever 'she' was would be there too – she searched her mind for who she'd be. But these muses, these young up-and-coming artists, they were all the same, lithe and fresh, and Vee couldn't bear facing up to a new model: she would forever have her face scalded into her mind.

She could wait here until he returned. But her hurt would be a million times worse. Because it would expose what she understood now was a complete daydream of their togetherness: this was his home not hers – they owned nothing jointly. They each had their possessions, there was no TV and their ornaments were cheap trinkets from their travels. Jez had always said 'who wanted stuff when you had everything?'. Vee gave a strangled howl at the broken mess of her naive delusion.

She needed to go to a friend's. Yes, that was it, that was she had to do.

But who? She mentally ransacked her list of contacts on her phone but most of them were old work colleagues or those she'd lost touch with, not people you could spill your guts on. As for trusted friends, well, her best friend had been Jez, she'd had no need for anyone else. There was Bex, who used to work at *Hello Daaling*, but had she said she was moving to Devon or somewhere? Vicky had meant to respond to her texts to meet up three times before Christmas but she never got round to it because of her life with Jez. Jemima? But she was Jez's best mate's wife and they had a baby and, oh no, she'd have known all about his betrayal. Jem would feel compromised, Vee would be mortified. Unmistakably, she had no one to turn to. There was not one person 'on her side': their friends were either mutual or his, she thought, ashamed of her stupidity. All her eggs, and ovaries, were in one basket – she had nothing of her own. It had been all she wanted, to be allowed into his gang. She was stripped of dignity, naked and needy.

Thirty and dumped. No money, no home and no mates. And it was all of her own doing. She'd nearly got away with it – but he'd found out she was still that chubby ginger kid.

She needed to leave. And quickly because the panic was giving her palpitations, which she needed to outrun.

Burning all over, she forced herself up to standing.

She groped her way up the stairs and saw an old crone in the broken mirror glue-gunned on the landing wall. The beginnings of wrinkles, a mess of pink strands in her bleached hair, a red nose with a tiny ring piercing and two swollen eyes: It was a far cry from how she thought she'd look the next time she saw Mum and Dad, all sparkling and engaged.

That was how she admitted to herself that she had nowhere else to go but to her parents', the house she'd grown up in, aged thirty. What a birthday this had turned out to be.

She threw off his jumper and found her rucksack at the back of the wardrobe and began to chuck in anything that seemed essential, like knickers, bras, clothes, make-up and her craptop, her battered old laptop. Surveying the messy room, guttural gasps rose from her chest as she saw how one-sided their so-called love nest was. His paintings and arty prints were up, the standard lamp was angular and male, even the grey duvet covers were masculine: what little of hers there was, such as postcards and books, were laced with his influence as if she had been following a guidebook on How To Be Jez's Girlfriend.

In her attempt to be accepted and to feel like a somebody she had sinfully subverted her very self. She had no idea who the real her was. She'd been a parasite, that was clear.

Looking down, the only thing that remained of life before Jez was the fraying Jarvis Cocker T-shirt she was wearing as a nightie. Gazing down on his black and white pixellated face of specs and beard, she thought of Mikey. What she'd give to see him but it was impossible – the Mikey she'd adored was a memory. She hadn't thought of him in yonks. She hadn't needed to. When she had it'd been with an 'oh well that's life' smile, thinking back to her crazy innocence, when she'd asked him to be her back-up man: yet now she realized she was no more grown up than she had been then. Humiliating herself, she imagined arriving at his door, telling him that she needed him now after all. But he wouldn't be the same: he'd obviously changed when she'd gone travelling. The old Mikey would've at least replied to her heartfelt letter from Thailand, made a joke of it or soothed her. Oh, she'd got over the fact he didn't feel the same way as her, when she'd said that perhaps her feelings towards him weren't just platonic. But she'd never understood why he hadn't responded. Not even when she'd tried to friend him on Facebook when she'd got back from travelling even with

Jez in tow – she'd been ready to forget things – he clearly hadn't. Anyway, she thought, wiping her eyes, people grow apart, they change and harking back was not the answer.

Vee threw a hoodie over her T-shirt, pulled on leggings and boots then galloped downstairs to throw on her fake-fur lapelled three-quarter-length coat. She tied the belt tight to stop herself falling apart and scraped her hair back into a bun.

She took out her petite nose stud, letting it drop from her hand onto the table, and then she hoisted her backpack up onto one shoulder.

Looking round the vast cluttered room, which seemed the emptiest place in the world right now, she had a surge of pure fury and she kicked out at 'The Angst of Man', which rocked on its feet before toppling to the floor with several metallic bangs as it broke up. The destruction made absolutely no difference to how she felt.

Defeated, she opened the door and stepped outside, not feeling the icy sting of the February downpour.

Oblivious to the puddles and car spray, she was able to cry unnoticed, protected by the veil of rain which merged with the tears rolling down her cheeks, all the way to the coach station.

'Cardiff, please,' she said to the ticket lady who didn't bother to look up at her.

'Return?'

Vee shook her head. Then remembered she was invisible.

'One way,' she croaked, 'I'm going home.'

Chapter Two

M

Tignes, France

Murphy flinched in his seat even though the gunshot of the cork came nowhere near his body.

Dodging the spill of the fizz, some of the lads shouted 'wahey' above the thud of tunes which filled the huge luxury chalet right up to its snow-lined windows.

'Wahey nothing, lovely boys,' he called from the leather sofa and jerked his head to the side to get someone to bring the bottle over.

His body was pounding with the after-effects of too much… well, too much everything in the last couple of days – make that the last six years. But this was what he was here to do – there was no point calling it an early night, if it was in fact early.

He had no idea of the time: it was dark outside but that didn't mean anything because the night fell fast here in the wintry mountains. It seemed like hours ago that they'd eaten, yet he had no hunger. It could be 7 p.m. or 2 a.m. and, to be honest, who gave a shit? Only when they were too trashed to walk would they crawl to their beds.

Savouring the warmth from the heated wooden floor which rose up through his naked feet, the only bit of him which ached in a good way were his thighs: the snowboarding here was immense. The trouble was, the après-ski was even larger.

The bottle banged as it made contact with the coffee table and again Murphy felt the impact.

He paused his trembling hands, catching sight of the scar on his ring finger, always there, inescapable, and poured himself a drink. Then put the bottle on the table for Hugo, who was chopping charlie for champagne supernovas.

It's all okay, he told himself, *you're with your mates in this fuck-off fantastic log cabin in the French Alps and you've earned it.* He nodded in time to the dance track to confirm this was gospel and slowed it right down, scanning the spoils of his success.

On the right, the glass doors were indecently flung open onto the steaming patio, where Beats and Flo were neck-deep in the hot tub.

Dave and Jonesy were in the high-gloss kitchen, knocking back a single malt whisky. Shell and Orla were Tomb Raiding on the PlayStation lying in sheepskin-rug gaming chairs right next to a roaring fire. And on the left, Potts was on the climbing wall – whoever had designed this place had known just what would give international playboys a hard-on.

But Murphy silenced his sneers because he was here, wasn't he? If he listened, he'd have to admit he was a sell-out and that was the worst thing he could be. He hated the irritating whine of his conscience that mocked him. Hated it because it always asked what on earth would Vicky make of him? *Whatever happened to your politics, Mikey, to your compassion, to your sense of injustice?*

He answered it back: *she's not here so do one.*

He watched Hugo run half a lemon around the rim of some champagne saucers, dip them in coke then pour the bubbles. Murphy got up and took one outside.

'Not having one?' Beats said from the hot tub as Murphy handed it over then lit a fag and rested on the glass balcony wall.

'Nah,' he said, his breath smoking skywards as snowflakes started to fall. Not his scene, he wasn't some posh boy even though his surroundings suggested it.

He turned around and stared out at the twinkling magical cabins dotted around the valley. With a pang in his heart, he thought how much Mam would've loved it here. The air, which was so cold it hurt to breathe after a while, was the definition of clean and fresh. As for Dad, Mikey would be tempted to push him down a slope.

At least Orla was here to witness how beautiful it was: his little sister who'd come along for the ride when one of the squad dropped out. She knew everyone anyway: they all hung out together in Hackney in London and he had no trouble paying for her. It was nice to be able to treat her when so much of her life had been shit. He liked having her here: it kept him grounded. Ish.

'Don't stay in that hot tub too long,' he said, suppressing the desire to flick his fag into the blackness to watch it Catherine wheel into nowhere, 'it'll make your dick shrink.'

It was a crap joke but Beats laughed because he was off his tits. As usual.

He chucked his butt into a bursting ashtray and went back inside, realizing what a tip they'd made of the place. The surfaces were littered with glasses, cups and wrappers. Magazines and a set of massacred playing cards were spread over one of the settees. Snowboots, bits of outdoor clothing and wet towels covered the hall.

How could eight adults make such a mess in the few hours since maid service? He doubted anyone but him and Orla noticed – the rest of them had been brought up on hotel holidays and privilege. It wasn't their fault: you only understood about tidying up after yourself if you'd had to share a minute caravan in Tenby in the pissing rain for a week.

He'd do a whip-round for the chalet girl later, wait until they were all a bit mashed so they'd give more. They could afford it anyway: apart from Orla, this rabble were all techie geeks who were coining it in.

Murphy started to have one of his out-of-body feelings: nothing to do with drugs, that wasn't his bag, but because he never really felt as if he belonged. Floating up on the ceiling, he looked down on himself, seeing his left hand rub his severely short dark hair as he decided what to do next. Having a stretch so his green Atari T-shirt lifted to reveal a yawn of his trim waist. Padding towards the table where he'd left his iPhone. Scrolling through messages vacantly, not taking anything in, waiting for inspiration. From on high, Murphy was amazed that he was actually here. The rest had all come up through IT degrees – but he was the only self-taught one. But to them, incredibly, it gave him kudos and added to his reputation as one of the best corporate app developers in the business. That so-called advantage had been his way in to Kode, the company where he worked. Everyone here had design, programming and computing skills, which usually dated back to sitting in their teenage bedrooms trying to make their Myspace look cool. But they didn't have the motive he had: the rocket fuel of grief when he lost his mam and the neglect of a drunk of a dad who lived off crap from Iceland. Nor the loss of the one person in his life, Vicky, who understood what he meant without having to say a word.

That was what had made the difference for this geek to inherit the earth.

So here he was, on another break. It didn't matter where he was: he could work remotely. He was always on the move, splitting his time between his two flats. The one he shared with Orla in Hackney was small but smart, reflecting how far your pound went in London. His city centre Cardiff apartment was an opulent high-ceilinged Victorian duplex which had a balcony overlooking the hallowed rugby ground, the old Arms Park. Out of everything he'd achieved, he suspected this was all his sports-mad Dad was proud of – not that he'd ever said 'well done, son'. Murphy still wondered if on a sub-conscious level he'd only bought it to show he'd made it when his father hadn't. Mud and scrums left Murphy cold – he loved the apartment because it was close to everything but far enough from Dad's damp sheltered flat.

It certainly helped him to relax when he was attending to one of Dad's benders.

Murphy could see his lips thinning: how easy it always was to sink into that lava pit of anger. He looked at his sister and the red hot turned white. They'd both been robbed of their childhood. Their father was still apparently in his – never growing up, never taking responsibility. How many times had Murphy had to sort him out since Mam died? How had he survived when Steve Jobs, his idol who co-created Apple, the man who changed the world, hadn't? The urge to leave the bastard to it was overwhelming. Yet so was the feeling of resistance.

Dad had no one else, having isolated the rest of his family. Mam's side had never been part of their lives: she'd left Ireland after some kind of ruck aged eighteen. Conflict, it was always there, threatening. Orla had dealt with it through counselling and was evangelical about it: she'd caught him on the dark side too many times: it had worked for her.

'You've got issues,' she'd told him again and again and she was right. But the sour taste of puke when he'd had to clean up

Dad after he'd soiled himself was punishment for the choices Murphy had made. The way he betrayed himself for taking the corporate dollar rather than doing some good as he'd always intended.

To feel he was dirtied with his father's genes let him get away with looking a smug bastard in his expensive trainers, headphones and manbag, slurping a ludicrous bowl of edamame miso ramen noodle soup after weights in the gym. What the hell would Vicky think of the man who used to be Mikey?

There again was the voice which he desperately wanted to silence.

Suddenly his body was back on the sofa: an arm was around his neck and a mouth on his, rescued him.

'Fancy a swim?'

Shell. His hot girlfriend of three months. Long straight black hair, green eyes beneath a savage fringe and scarlet lips; they were all red herrings, hiding her sweetness, Murphy thought. Shell was too good for him, he would hurt her, he just knew it.

'Yep,' he said, kissing her freckled nose, trying to make amends for those things she was unaware of. Including the fact that he'd wiped out in a powdery bowl of snow yesterday when he'd remembered it was Vicky's thirtieth birthday, his heart jolting as if he'd been tasered by electrodes of an emotion he couldn't describe: shocking yet with an inescapable inevitability.

He knocked back a large shot of tequila to anaesthetize his writhing intestines, which were refusing to settle quietly. Then bang. Beyond the grimace of the taste, he felt the wallop of elation which disarmed his hurt. Euphoria wasn't a bad option, he thought, slamming another tequila before jumping up, preparing to race her to the inside pool lit from above by blue and red fluorescent tubes.

What did he have to moan about, really? Oblivion was Murphy's idea of the ultimate escape.

*

Vicky's house, Roath, Cardiff, November 2000

Vicky hears banging at the door and curses her hand for jumping.

The eyeliner flick she's been practising looks like it's been done by a toddler with a crayon, she thinks, as the knocking comes again. God, it's like the filling in the Pulp and Who Wants To Be A Millionaire? *sandwich of sound going on between the music in her bedroom and the shit telly Mum and Dad are watching downstairs. The walls are so thin in this stupid house. Sometimes she hears them doing it and it's the most revolting thing ever.*

She throws her handheld mirror and Rimmel liquid eyeliner on to her faded and bobbly pony duvet, which dates from her ninth birthday when she was into horses, but it's the softest thing and it smells safe.

She holds her breath, irritated, ignoring the rumble in her stomach: she pretended she wasn't hungry at tea because she felt humongous in netball today. Isn't someone going to answer it? Checking her Nokia for the time, she refuses to budge because it's late and it won't be for her. It never is, mind. Probably one of Gavin's mates: she'll know if she starts gagging on a waft of CK One.

Gav thunders down the stairs. Vicky waiting, she watches the red wax rise and fall dreamily inside her purple lava lamp. If it's Dylan, his fit friend, she'll go and get a bag of crisps so she can have a perv – he's worth breaking the diet for.

He's clearly out of her league but no harm in window-shopping, like.

Thank God I haven't got my pyjamas on yet, *she thinks, pulling at a fraying thread on her ripped combats. She fluffs her fringe just in case and strains her ears, craning her neck towards the crack in her door.*

'Shit... Mum,' *Gav says, piquing Vicky's interest. Nothing exciting happens round here.*

'Fetch your sister,' *Mum says.*

Her heart stops. She leaps off the bed, checks her nose for whiteheads – all clear – and considers whether to change out of her pink Hello Kitty T-shirt. It's ironic, obviously, but will this visitor get it?

'Victoria!' her mum calls.

Too late to do anything, *she thinks, sucking in her stomach, although why she bothers she doesn't know because she still feels so fat. If she doesn't go now, it'll look like she's made an effort and that'd be tragic.*

At the top of the landing, she sees Mum's arm guiding someone's back through the hall. 'You poor dab.' *Her voice trails into the kitchen and Vicky follows the coos of concern.*

'Your boyfriend's here,' *Gav says, sarkily, crossing her on the stairs, still with one of his dumbbells in his hand, completely uninterested now that it's nothing to do with him.*

'Mikey? He's not my boyfriend,' *she says, giving him evils, trying to cover up that he's here so late, before chucking him a* 'dickhead'.

She swings round the banister, catching Dad, who is hovering by the lounge door in one of his hideous nylon golf shirts to see if it's men's business. 'Give me a shout if you need me, bun,' *he says.*

For God's sake, Dad, she thinks, rolling her eyes at his brown bank manager hair and leathery face, is it really appropriate to call Mum by her pet name 'bunny' when something's clearly up? What's wrong with calling her Mo? He's so embarrassing.

'Mum? Mikey?' *Vicky says as she breaks into a trot, catching her right arm on the door frame.* 'Ow,' *she says, rubbing herself. Then,* 'Oh, Mike…'

He looks up from where he's sat on one of the steel breakfast bar stools and he's nursing a bad hand. It looks all mangled, bits of skin are hanging off and it's grazed. His eyes are red and he's sniffing into the sleeve of his flimsy army jacket. Her stomach flips at his injuries and because he looks not normal. It's weird him being here like this. Dad would never let any old boy come calling for her in the house at this time of night. Not that that has ever happened, but she just knows he'd make up some humiliating excuse at the door, just to shame her, like she was playing with her toys.

But then Mikey isn't a boy – he's her best friend. Somehow Dad can tell the difference, or more likely Mum has explained it to him that members of the opposite sex can be friends. Like, der, Dad.

'Let me take your coat off, love,' *Mum says softly and she helps* him jiggle out of it with shared winces. 'Brave thing,' she says, ruffling his hair which is all messy like Nicky Wire from the Manic Street Preachers. Amazing how Mikey lets her do that.

He looks really skinny, even more so than before. His chest has sort of caved in.

'Can you get me the first aid kit, Victoria?'

'What's happened, Mikey?' she says, ignoring Mum. She thinks about giving him a giant cwtch of a hug but she's a bit stunned. If anyone's hurt him, she swears she's going to kill them. Or go so mad at them or whatever.

'I need the Savlon, cotton wool and bandages, Victoria.'

She chews a nail and nods, feeling stressed and sick because there might be blood and Mikey still hasn't said anything.

'Where is it?' she asks, frightened.

Mum keeps her eyes on Mikey as she says 'Far right top cupboard, bottom shelf, next to the emergency torch and batteries.'

She's doing her nothing-to-worry-about smile which makes the tip of her nose move. That really gets on Vicky's nerves, the way the tip of her nose moves. That's one of her greatest fears, that she'll turn into her mum, along with her habit of wearing sad comfy tracksuit bottoms which save her clothes and crap middle-aged newsreader hair. Then she feels bad because Mum is being really kind and she's like a second mother to Mikey. His is weird and mental, a bit OCD. But she doesn't bake cakes or fuss about uniform or drive him anywhere or give him lectures. She doesn't even care that he goes into Queen Street on a Saturday to man the anti-vivisection campaign stall without a coat.

Vicky unzips the kit and lays it down next to her mother. Then she slips onto the stool next to Mikey. He smells of fried food and it makes her gulp. It's not often she feels lucky. Most of the time she hates everything about this family: the way Mum and Dad always sit next to each other on the settee holding hands while they watch the telly. When she catches them slow-dancing in the kitchen to Steve Wright's Sunday Love Songs. Or when Dad turns up Simply Red in the car and gives Mum that look. That every day she knows what they're having for tea: fish on a Friday, Dad's curry on a Saturday, Monday is rissoles from Sunday's roast and tonight was Mum's spag bol. No one ever takes her vegetarianism seriously. They're so institutionalized, she thinks. Then she feels terrible when Mum asks if Mikey's eaten and he shakes his head.

'I sort of missed tea,' he says, trying to hide the tremor in his *voice.*

'Got plenty here for you,' Mum says. 'Micro the Tupperware in the fridge, Victoria. And grate some cheese for on top.'

Vicky does as she's told without a word, knowing the leftovers were for Nanna Tupperware, that's how they distinguish her from their other Nanna, which Mum takes her every Wednesday when she helps her get her large-print books at the library.

She sees her give him a lovely warm smile and, for a second, Vicky feels really bad that she can be a bit harsh on Mum.

'My God, you're freezing, Michael,' she says, cleaning the cuts. It's his left hand, he's one of those cool left-handed people who can write upside down, and there's like a gross gouged bit on his ring finger. He'll be made up that he can get out of PE. 'We'll warm you up, love.'

How come Mum hasn't asked him what's happened? If Vicky walked in like that she'd get an interrogation.

The beep goes, so Vicky pops the bowl in front of him and gets him an apple juice. She knows for a fact there's only ever corner shop fizzy pop at his, which at first she thought was great but that was before she started counting calories.

Mum quickly safety pins the bandage so he can eat.

'There we are, all done. Tuck in,' she says, tidying up. Somehow, she knows to give him space, that he'll talk when he's ready. Vicky watches him eat. He's like a dog, the way he shovels it in just in case someone else tries to nick it off him. Her appetite is gone now – she still feels a bit funny, like she's seeing this as a child, not really getting what's going on. But Mikey is getting his colour back. Vicky feels a flush of relief: she didn't like him looking all grey and scared. It worried her in a way she can't explain.

'Lush, Mrs. H,' he says, relaxing a bit, letting Mum fuss over him. 'I needed that.'

Mikey lets Vicky in then, meeting her eyes with a smile. And just like that, like a snap of the fingers, it's the two of them again, like normal as Mum goes back to tidying up.

He holds up his hand which looks part-mummy part-boxer.

'Got caught in The Matrix,' he says, grinning.

It's his favourite film – computer hacker doing bendy shit in an alternative reality. Vicky likes it too but mainly because she really fancies Keanu Reeves.

'You defo need to get one of those long coats,' she says, with a grin, relieved to get back the Mikey she recognizes. 'You'd look *proper awesome.'*

'*I'd look a goth twat, I would,'* he says, thinking it's out of Mum's earshot but she hears everything. Although she doesn't flinch tonight because of the situation.

'*A cybergoth twat.'* Vicky swears, feeling bolder.

They both laugh at that. Then Mikey looks tired all of a sudden. He takes a wobbly breath. Vicky is really glad Mum is still in the room because she's not sure she can cope with hearing what's coming by herself.

His eyes dart from his hand to a bit of fluff on his jumper. Then he starts talking quietly. '*So… Cardiff were losing and Dad was pissed up, listening to it on the radio and he was getting his hair off. I was just ignoring him, playing Grand Theft Auto, and he started on me. Asked why I didn't give a fucking shit.'*

He glances up at Mum. Vicky feels a bubbling up of hatred for his dad, talking to him like that.

'*Sorry, Mrs. Hope, 'scuse my French. So, he kept on, asking what was wrong with me, was I a poof and all that, not liking sport. The usual. Then Mam brought in tea but I didn't see her because I thought she was doing one of her office cleaning jobs and I told Dad to eff off and he went mad that she'd heard me swearing. I lost it then.'*

Dropping his chin, his eyelashes mask his eyes. All she wants to do is to protect him, Vicky thinks.

'*I punched him,'* he murmurs.

'*You punched your dad?'* Vicky says, horrified by the violence because she's never seen anything like that apart from on the telly. '*Was he hurt? Did he hit you back? What did your mam do?'*

'*It was a crap punch, he moved at the last minute, I got his shoulder, didn't actually hurt him. I did my hand in punching the brick wall outside when I'd legged it. He tried to take a swing but Mam got in the way with the ketchup and stopped him.'*

'*Your Mam? But she's only five foot!'* The image of Bernadette breaking them up takes the wind out of her angry sails.

'*Irish blood,'* he says, shrugging.

'*What about Orla?'* Mum says, from over her shoulder, pausing as she wipes her prized worktop for the millionth time today. Mikey's little sister is the sweetest thing, she's part of the package, always hanging out with them. *My God, if she'd been there…*

'*She'd gone over to a friend's after school. Wasn't back yet.'*

20

Vicky sees Mum's shoulders drop with relief and feels it too.

'But that must've been ages ago. Where've you been?' Vicky says because it's arctic out there and he only lives ten minutes away.

'Just about. The park, walked round the lake for a bit.'

Mum switches off the main kitchen light so the room goes cosy from the fancy spotlights which sit under the wall cabinets.

'Right, well I'll ring your mother, tell her you're here. You can stay tonight. Better to let the dust settle.' She says it like fact and Mikey doesn't even argue, he just nods. It's no biggie - him and Orla have stayed over a few times before when things have been heavy at home.

'Victoria, go and get some of Gavin's clothes, please. Then give me your uniform, Michael, and I'll wash it for the morning.'

She picks up the cordless phone from the side and calls to Dad in the lounge. 'Can you come and help me make the bed, Bob?' she says.

This is just an excuse to fill him in – the spare room is always ready. It's really confusing seeing Mum take charge of all of this. Dad's the one who carves the meat and makes the official complaints. Usually Mum is all 'I'll have to ask my husband', but tonight she's wearing the trousers. Really bad saggy-kneed trousers. It's troubling and unnerving because Mum can flap a bit. Like when the potatoes boil over, she acts like it's a disaster, as if the kitchen's going to get flooded. So why is she mega-calm now?

Then Vicky gets it: Mum is scared, because this is a proper emergency, but she doesn't want Mikey to know it. Vicky feels really worried now – as if she's crossed a line into adulthood. She'd rather not know that Mum is concerned because if she is then it must be really bad. Vicky scrambles around in her head for something to say. Food. That's the best comfort. So she goes with that.

'You know where everything is,' she says to Mikey, pointing at the treats cupboard. 'There's cake, Mum's done a Delia thing. And stick the kettle on. We can go up to my room, listen to "Common People" if you like. Or watch a Buffy *or an* X-Files *before bed.'*

Hiding it behind a big smile, she can't stand the thought of him sitting there alone while the rest of the house bustles around, fixing things and making him feel safe. He'll be thinking how different his house is to this, she can see it in his eyes. They're all watery and he's swallowing hard too. And she feels so desperately sorry for him, because what's the solution? He can't move in here because he's only fourteen. And he'd never leave his sister or his

21

mam.

She wants to save him, but how? Then she feels helpless and ashamed that her problems revolve around deciding what ringtone to have, whether she can afford some new face scrub at the Body Shop when she goes into Cardiff with Katherine on Saturday and working out if there's any way she can reconcile her hatred of NSync with her thing for Justin Timberlake.

Vicky doesn't want to leave Mikey by himself. Ever.

But still she hops down from her stool, gives him a quick hug then dashes out of the room.

Because she doesn't want him to see her cry.

Chapter Three

K

Pontcanna, Cardiff

This was supposed to be one of those precious mother and daughter moments, Kate thought as she prepared to try on her eighth wedding dress.

But not even the soft lighting, chaise longues and beautiful fabrics could mask that what was happening today was happening to the woman her mum wanted her to be: what had been happening to her her entire life.

Behind the curtain, she couldn't hide from the reflection of her gaunt face, which was momentarily permitted to show her strain. Her blue eyes in public were bright and inquisitive, but here, in private, they were brittle, like glass, owing to her guilt, shame, sorrow and regret at the life she'd formerly led as Kat.

Her body, in precise white pants and matching strapless bra, never lied: taut, muscly and lean, it was punished daily in a finely tuned exercise regime which trained her mind to stay focused rather than wander into the darkness.

Here, she teetered on the edge, knowing it would take one step to plummet into the mess which was always threatening. *Do not go there*, she warned herself, forcing her ears to tune into the classical bridal compilation CD which played in the background.

Smoothing her straightened brunette long bob, Kate took a deep breath and stepped into the gown, which this time, thank God, wasn't so fussy. How apt, she thought, hearing her mother Pam's voice in her head telling her sharply 'Don't make a fuss.'

Had she followed The Plan, then it would've been a different story. Her mother would've been shouting her success for all to hear. Now it was about containing the failure, putting on a brave face, pretending nothing had happened even though her 'mistake' was right in front of them, day in, day out. Nobody but immediate family knew. And that was how it would stay, right, girls?

That was why Kate was in a designer boutique in Pontcanna across town from the family home, sticking to the formula her mother had devised to save them. Why didn't she rail against her? her heart whispered: her head answered that she'd tried it before and look where it had ended up. It was easier to submit: easier to do what was expected of her once more. To be the princess.

Yet Kate felt like a mannequin: stiff, one-dimensional and frozen. How could people not see she was a screaming shambles inside? Luckily for her, as Mum said, people judge on appearances and 'you have it in spades, darling'; as close to a complement her tiger mother could make.

'God knows why she's left it to the last minute to choose a dress!'

Her mum was on the phone to Kate's big sister, sorting out childcare arrangements for Charlotte's seven-year-old son Griff, but not letting an opportunity go to hiss a barbed sneer. Good old Charlie, who'd saved her when she needed her, would be trying to stick up for her, Kate knew, telling Mum that five months is plenty of time to get one fitted. Older than Kate by six years, she had a different relationship with Mum – she was more her own woman, permitted to be because she'd never let herself down.

'Why doesn't Katherine listen to me? It'll be a last-minute panic job as usual with her.'

Tears wouldn't come to Kate: she was trained enough to internalize the blows. Instead, she absorbed that which went unsaid: if you swim against the tide, disobey the rules, you will muck it up, just as you did before. And who sorted it out for you last time?

'Need a hand in there?' the assistant asked, hovering at the damask divide.

'Not just yet,' Kate said, as the sleek ivory dress sat on her hips. 'I'll give you a shout when I do.'

'Okay. I'll get some accessories, so you can see the whole package.'

Hearing her mother bellow her approval at the assistant's suggestion in her telephone voice, Kate mouthed a thank you to the heavens – this would buy her some more time before she fell under her critical eye, which could singe her wings with a glance.

Her eyes glazed, unable to avoid the temptation of going back in time; Kate remembered once that her feathers had been full and glorious, flying her high into the sky. Not knowing any different, she had been ferried from school to clubs, tutors and music lessons, subscribing to the belief it would all be worth it in the end. And it was, for a few wonderful years, when her A* A Levels earned her a place at Oxford to read maths. There she had her first metamorphosis from Katherine, the ugly braced duckling, to Kat, with bold beautiful brains, who tasted fun for the first time in parties, girlfriends and blokes. Still in love with learning though, still able to balance her studies with her social life, she buckled down to score a first which led to a fast-tracked job in the City. She'd take six months off to travel then throw herself into her career, a decision supported by the banking giant which had taken her on. It would be good for her to get it out of her system, they said.

But in spite of all of that, it apparently wasn't enough to win her her freedom. Her mother had raged at her stupidity. She hadn't pushed her and made all those sacrifices for Katherine to go off on a jolly. She was a woman, she wasn't from a public school – she needed to work twice as hard as the entitled ones. But Kat insisted, her confidence still brimming. She could have it all and she would.

Kate's heartbeat raced with excitement at the recollection of all the possibilities she'd once contemplated and then, inevitably, it began to canter: she should've known it would be futile to revisit half the story. She pushed her palms into her eye sockets to try to make the other half go away, but her recklessness of the past thundered around her. The ensuing collapse, a protracted and painful domino run, had demolished her mind, body and spirit.

The walls of the cubicle began to contract as her breathing quickened.

Had she been allowed to deal with it her own way, to delve for the independence and self-belief she'd once had, things might have turned out differently. But Mum had swept in with gritted teeth and bright lipstick to take charge: damage-limitation, she'd called it. The career and prospects had disappeared overnight. And now here she was once again, being supervised.

Think positive, she commanded herself now, leaving sweaty palm marks on the mirror. *Reframe your thoughts with positivity*, citing the words she'd learned from all the secret self-help books she'd devoured.

Her job, which Dad had arranged in whispers through his chartered surveying contacts, had steered her towards safety. It had been his last real input in her life: once they had shared a bond so strong, he would put her to bed when he came in from work, cut her fingernails and brush her wet hair. When she was ill, he would sit with her and chat, but on her recovery he had pulled away so painfully: mother had laid the blame for her downfall at his feet, his mollycoddling had never done her any good. Now he took a back-seat in her life, making small talk at mealtimes then withdrawing to his study.

Mother insisted on saying Kate was 'in property', but life as an estate agent suited Kate. She'd quickly found her feet and performed negotiations and valuations with ease. It was also a joy to spend time away from the emotional vacuum of the family home and have it confirmed that not everyone kept house in such a controlled, static way. Her soul sang when she walked into a property with chipped staircases, bumpy walls and cluttered hallways because it reflected how she felt inside.

And it was the reason she was standing here. Feeling calmer, Kate saw her face relax as she thought of Jack, her hulking wholesome man bear who was so good and patient and understanding. The total opposite of the chinless wonders her university friends fell in love with, he wore a smile, blobs of paint on his biceps and sawdust in his messy blond curls thanks to his job as a period house restoration craftsman.

Kate pulled the bodice up over her chest and imagined Jack's reaction if this was the dress? It wouldn't be suitable if he had it his way – they were both in agreement about what they wanted: to tie the knot on Brighton's beautiful bandstand, where Jack had proposed on a weekend away, with just their flatulent Golden Retriever Boris.

But he'd given up trying to persuade her to follow her heart. The consequences of disobeying Mum were too exhausting to contemplate. She might be a capable thirty-year-old everywhere else but when her Mum was involved she forever felt like a child.

This big wedding was subtitled She Cocked Up Her Career But She's Not Going To Die Alone – unlike some of her mother's friends' daughters who had everything but a man, which she spitefully considered the ultimate flop. That was how Mum had rewritten Kate's life. Once it had been about breaking through the glass ceiling with rock-hard manicured fingernails but Kate's downfall meant Mum had had to change the script.

Marriage and homemaking would do now – it had been good enough for me, her mother had said, adding in her charity work to show her 'goodness'. 'Husbands require support, just as I have done for your father.' She made that clear when Kate introduced her to Jack for the first time, months into their relationship so she was sure he wouldn't run a mile when he met her Machiavellian mother. On that day, Mum had practically begged Jack to marry Kate on the spot. 'She's only ever wanted a family,' she'd said as Kate choked back tears. That was when she could still cry.

And so, having found herself a respectable husband-to-be – second best to a good career for herself but it would do – she was permitted to pursue her little life. Mother at least had Charlie's GP career to brag about.

In a warped way, this was exactly how Kate needed it to be to survive: if she stayed low on the radar then she could be happy with Jack.

But in her mother's company, the straitjacket remained. It was just something she had to live with. Which was why she was here trying on her eighth wedding dress.

Taking a deep breath, she threaded her arms through cap sleeves and called: 'I just need to be done up at the back.'

The petite rosebud of an assistant passed noiselessly through the curtain. Kate gave an inner groan at the gentle way she did up the tiny line of buttons; she was going to be no match for her mother.

The dress wasn't immediately Kate's first choice but it was certainly better than the other intricately over-boned strapless lot which her mother had picked but dismissed on the grounds of them showing up Kate's physical short-comings such as her 'boyish hips' and 'flat chest'. She liked its sheer lace scooped neckline because it didn't make her feel exposed. Below the bodice, a long tie began at her hips and then fell to the floor with the body of the gown in a picture of understated elegance. She felt like a flapper girl from the 1920s: a simple corsage on her wrist would finish it off.

Making sure to blur out the onlookers, Kate could just about imagine herself walking up the aisle to meet Jack in this. It was as close as she would get to her dream gown of simplicity.

Her mirage was disturbed then by the metal screech of eyelets against pole as her mother tugged back the curtain.

'Let's see you, then,' she ordered.

Kate turned her body round, her head trailing behind, bracing herself for the sharp intake of breath, narrowed eyes and pursing of lips.

Let this be over, I just want to go back home on my day off and make supper, Kate thought, although she made sure she presented a serene bridal face.

'Hmm, do you think it's got enough presence, you know, to make it stand out amongst all the guests? Because we've got an awful lot of people coming.'

The question wasn't directed at Kate: for she wouldn't be asked what she thought. That was irrelevant. Kate couldn't care less about the numbers coming anyway – very few of them mattered to her, being mostly her parents' friends. She was more affected by those not coming: namely Vicky.

Growing up, they had always promised they'd be one another's bridesmaids and even though it had been years since they'd been mates, it still played on Kate's mind that her oldest friend wouldn't be there. It wasn't as though she'd ever found a replacement for her either. Not that she'd known that when she'd deleted every one of Vicky's emails, which had begun as chatty updates on her travels after Kat had returned, then had become awkward pleas of 'is this the right address?' and 'if you're getting these, please answer me' before they eventually stopped when Vicky had informed her she'd come home.

Where would she be now? Just thirty, she'd undoubtedly be married with kids, three or four, because she had a way with them. With a pang that she'd never made it to be bridesmaid after all, Kat recalled how Vicky had given out pens to the street children in South America, and made them laugh even though she didn't speak Spanish. The last day she'd seen her, Vicky had said she wanted to volunteer to teach English at a kids' charity in Cambodia. The way she'd blossomed on their travels, wide-eyed with excitement, quickened by the size of the world when Kate had been overwhelmed. How many times had she wanted to find her, say sorry, start over: she would do anything to put things straight. But Kate had been such a liability, Vicky would never want to see her again and that was without knowing what Kate had done when she'd returned home from backpacking.

As for Mikey, when she thought of him she felt the bile rising. She was facing an impossible dilemma: if she could go back and undo her wrongs then she would deny part of her very self. That's why she could never work this through, that's why she didn't discuss it with Jack. He didn't know all of it – if he did it might ruin everything.

'Kate looks stunning, Mrs. Lloyd,' the assistant said. 'Absolutely breathtaking.' Her tone was warm but authoritative: Kate had got her all wrong, she clearly did have her mother's number.

Kate shot her a grateful smile.

'Such a pity she's not in white…' As if ivory meant Kate was a fallen woman!

'Perhaps a veil would elevate it…' the assistant suggested prettily, skillfully diverting her mother's attention.

Yes! That would be brilliant – she'd have something to hide behind. What's more, Kate had been praying, Anything But a Tiara.

The lady got onto her tiptoes to arrange a headdress of embroidered tulle around her shoulders and Kate felt a swell of happiness: it was perfect, just like Harry Potter's invisibility cloak.

'Oh, yes,' Mum said, clasping her hands together, 'that really does make a difference. It would be lovely to have some sort of detail on there. Swarovski crystals, that sort of thing.'

In one tiny act of rebellion, Kate would make sure it had nothing of the sort.

'Right. Good,' Mother said, beginning to prepare for her exit. It was always the same routine: find handbag, reapply lipstick, pat hairdo and then look around for someone to put on her coat, who was usually Dad. But the assistant played along, probably wanting to get rid of her as much as Kate did.

'She might need some padding around the breasts,' Mother trilled. 'And don't let her change her mind!'

Then she bent in to air-kiss Kate and announced she had to go.

'My grandson needs picking up from school,' her mother said, throwing the words happily into the air like confetti. But in the chill of the gust which whistled through the open door, they turned to hail and stung Kate's heart.

Chapter Four

V

Roath, Cardiff

'We're just going to take the dog for a walk, Victoria, if you'd like to come?'

Her groggy flat-lining daze of despair interrupted, Vee turned her head towards Mum, who stood at the mouth of her bedroom zipping up her purple fleece. Her smile was as warm as a cup of tea, her kind, forgiving eyes lined like a well-worn sofa.

Another piece of what little was left of Vee's heart shattered onto the carpet beside her where she was hugging her knees against her old single bed.

The invitation was loaded with concern: it said, 'a bit of fresh air would do you some good, you've hardly left your room since you've been here, you've picked at your food, you haven't had a shower and me and your Dad, we're worried.'

Already suffocating from Jez's cruelty, Vee felt an avalanche of guilt at causing them such anguish. She was thirty years old, a grown woman; she should be the one looking after them, not the other way round.

But if she was dissected at this very moment, they'd find she was one hundred per cent No Use To Anybody, a composite of devastation, grief, self-loathing, failure and fear. And they'd find no evidence of water because she'd cried it all out.

Her eyes felt tight and swollen, her lips pulsed and her nose was blocked from three days of sorrow.

On the long nauseous coach journey home, Vee had watched her phone illuminating with her parents' calls. Their first message just past Crawley had been a joint chorus of 'happy birthday to you'. Then they'd followed that up at Swindon with 'expect you're having a fablas time... too busy to talk to your Mum and Dad! You go for it, love!' and then on the Severn Bridge 'Still trying to get hold of you!'. By the time she got to Cardiff, only three people had texted her happy birthday – her brother Gav, a waitress at work who was also trying to find out where the hell she was and Jemima, Jez's best mate's wife, who said she was 'really sorry, sweetheart'. What a way to learn the sum of her life's work so far: losing touch with everyone she'd cared for and throwing her need to belong at a circle who didn't give a shit.

Even her parents weren't there when she'd let herself in, they were on a 'date night' at the cinema. So she'd sat beaten and numb in the darkness of their new side return extension until Mum and Dad came in and told her she'd given them the fright of their lives.

Since then, she'd either been in bed or slumped on the sofa – new from Next apparently – with daytime telly on a high definition drip. She hadn't watched this much in years because they hadn't had what Jez called a 'brain rot box' in their flat. He'd been wrong about it rotting her mind - he'd been the one to do that. Every few hours, tea and cake or squash and sandwiches would appear on the bedside or nest of tables. She'd had a bit, to show she was so grateful, but every mouthful was a battle.

From the landing, Dad popped his head round the door and gave her a wink. 'Oh, love,' he said, his face crumpled with compassion, 'Arthur is desperate for you to come.' Arthur the Cocker Spaniel didn't look very desperate. He was more interested in sniffing his own backside. 'It's stopped raining and I'll treat you to tea and cake. That right, Bun?'

Mum rubbed his arm, acknowledging his lovely gentle nature, which only made Vee feel even more tragic. 'Fancy it?' she said, going through her pockets for gloves. 'We're going to Castell Coch.'

The fairy-tale Gothic castle just outside of Cardiff where Gav had got married five years ago. Where Vee had adored the horse and carriage and six bridesmaids: it wasn't what she'd have chosen, but she understood it had been her sister-in-law Claire's dream. Jez, of course, had called it hackneyed. In a stripy crusty jumper, looking every bit a cliché himself, she could see now.

Vee didn't want to be reminded of that. She shook her head: it was the only part of her body she could move. She couldn't face getting changed out of her T-shirt and leggings, brushing her hair or cleaning her teeth.

'Okay, love, we'll try again tomorrow. Just maybe instead have a nice bath then, perhaps?'

Vee did a half-hearted nod which said 'yeah, I won't but thanks for the suggestion.'

'Right, we won't be long. Fish and chips for tea tonight!' Dad said, rubbing his hands, trying to make everything all right as was his way.

Their unconditional love was overwhelming: it kept coming even though she'd been largely absent from their lives for eight-and-a-bit years. During her travels, she'd rung once a week and sent postcards. Then when she was in Brighton, she'd kept up the phone calls, popping home for a quick weekend here and there, for Christmas or when she had to come back, like for Nanna Tupperware's funeral. She'd hated leaving Brighton because it was the centre of the world as far as she was concerned. Mum and Dad's was just drab and quiet by comparison. Losing touch with Kat and Mikey meant she didn't know anyone local anymore anyway. There was also the fear of missing out on something when she was away – it was hard enough to keep track of the latest thing even when she was there! It didn't matter anyway, Mum and Dad had religiously visited her twice a year, rejecting her offer of a sofa bed, preferring to stay in a posh seafront hotel, which suited Vee. Mum would treat her to afternoon tea and one night her and Jez would go to their hotel for dinner. And then they'd go back home and would slip to the back of her mind, until the next visit

As the front door slammed, Vee felt ashamed at how self-centred she'd been. How violently desperate to keep up with Jez that she'd stayed by his side, no matter what. Mum and Dad had never said she'd neglected them: they were really busy people. Always had been, ever since they'd retired a few years ago: Dad had gone early from the bank because he'd invested wisely and Mum followed suit from her part-time receptionist's job at the dentist's. Not that Vee had a clue what they did most of the time apart from, probably, Dad's golf and Mum's coffee mornings.

It was just another failing of hers that had come to light in this seventy-two-hour period of self-assassination which would wake her at 5 a.m. and remind her she had nothing to show for her life.

At that time of day all there was to do was run through every sign that things had been going wrong with Jez. There was nothing massive, no one indication. Apart from what she'd spent years trying to deny: they were from different worlds, she didn't belong in his. How had she made it last so long?

The rage she felt at all of that wasted time. Marriage and motherhood had been imminent with him, or so she'd thought: now she was years away from it, if ever. Then there was the sense of loss: not just his physical presence in bed but the glow of knowing she had someone there who'd worry if she'd gone missing. It was the little things: he'd make enough granola for both of them and always buy her vegan Percy Pigs if he stopped at the mini M&S on his way home.

All right, perhaps it hadn't ended up as the world's greatest love story. They'd last had sex a month ago and she'd put that down to his exhibition stress, and that wasn't so bad if you'd been together seven years. But she'd been happy.

Vee's brain would run through the two calls she'd made to Jez since she'd come home. Her brave 'hellos' soon buckled into desperate sobs of 'why didn't you say anything?' and 'we could've worked it out', which led to deranged and repeated questions of 'who is she?'.

Through his waffle, the bottom line was she'd come along at a time when Vee's 'marry me or else' had felt like an ultimatum. They met at the studio - Vee had been right – and he couldn't help falling in love with her. Then it rounded off with him saying he would always love Vee, but not in 'that way'. The calls would dry out soon, she knew that, and it frightened her. As if her drug supply was going to be cut off. No girlfriend would stand for her bloke spending hours on the phone to his ex, which was all she was now. And he was just going through the motions, she knew, out of guilt. She'd done him the biggest favour, leaving Brighton like that, he could love again without the fear of an hysterical ex-girlfriend turning up. And he knew it – why else hadn't he had a go at her for breaking up 'The Angst of Man' sculpture? She felt embarrassed about that now: it had been petty and pointless. It merely confirmed that there was nothing she could do to change his mind. Unless it all went wrong with the bitch who'd stolen her man and her life. Yet even then he wouldn't come back to her: he was a propeller, always flying forward, looking for the next thing. She was starting to accept this: she couldn't make him love her. Yet still she had waves of empty hope that he would come back.

She felt as if she was at the bottom of a canyon, trying to climb up but the rocks kept slipping underfoot. She needed a hand to pull her up. But there was no one.

Apart from Mum, who had been a comforting, non-judgmental ear, rubbing her back and cooing 'there, there' when the agony tore her in two. And Dad's arms around her, telling her it wouldn't be forever and perhaps she'd like to come to the club one night because there was one chap who'd just got divorced and while he didn't have much hair he was an excellent golfer, which had made her howl with laughter rather than sorrow.

Mum had suggested getting back in touch with her old friends. 'Times have changed, people grow up, the past is forgotten,' she'd said. 'There might be a school reunion coming up or a group who go out regularly for a coffee.' But the words felt naive: 'It's not the 1950s, Mum,' she'd said. 'They'll have moved away.'

The guilt came again: that was the trouble with being here. It was a refuge, dear God it was the safest place in the world, but it made her feel a child again with its soul-destroying reminders of how far she hadn't actually come.

Gav's room had been redecorated and stripped of all traces of him: there was no need to preserve anything because he was happily married with kids and a people carrier, commuting to Cardiff Bay for work from a new-build estate off the A470.

Why had Mum and Dad kept her room as it was? Had they always known her relationship with Jez was doomed? If so, how, because, in the nicest possible way, weren't they the tamest and least insightful people on the planet? For God's sake, they gave each other running commentaries on which birds were eating the fat balls in the garden.

Vee heaved herself up to switch on her lava lamp: the gloom was setting in and she couldn't see the point of drawing open her curtains.

Her eyes took in the scrapbook of her room: a line of

ancient Beanie Babies on her shelf beside her Judy Blume, *Harry Potter* and *Flowers In The Attic* books. Kat had secretly borrowed them because her mother only let her read the classics. *Oh, Kat,* Vee thought, aching for her, *why did we let one row ruin years of friendship?* If only Vee had known that proper mates were so hard to come by, but in those days you took it for granted that life would be full of opportunities, not dead ends.

She shivered, feeling haunted, as she looked at her *American Beauty* poster. It was a reminder of the yearning she'd had to escape middle-class suburbia when everyone else was into *American Pie.* Then Mikey came to her again. The one who had meant so much but had disappeared without a trace. Where was he now?

And where did she go from here? Brighton was a lifetime away and her job was gone. Maybe Mum was right about finding her friends. But why, if she was only going to be here for a bit until she'd pieced herself back together and decided where she would go next? Yet she needed allies. For the first time in days, she felt a quickening.

Her fingers began to tingle and they reached out for her craptop. This was an emotional risk – she remembered how she had checked her emails with apprehension and a bit of excitement in the days after Mikey would've read her letter in which had said she might feel more for him than she'd thought. Her confession hadn't come from nowhere – he'd written how much he missed her, he was coming to visit her in Cambodia and he was feeling that something good was about to happen. But then the days of waiting to hear back from him stretched into weeks. His silence had made it obvious that she had freaked him out and he wasn't feeling it. Despite the intense sadness, she was by herself in Thailand then, Kat had gone, and she'd had to survive. Believing enough time had passed for them to reconnect and forget the weirdness that had gone on, Vee had sent him a Facebook friend request when she had settled in Brighton. But it had never been accepted.

Over time, she'd come to terms with her loss: it just hadn't been meant to be. Yet always there were moments which reminded her of him. Hearing a song they'd loved or an opinion they'd hated had reminded her he was no longer there to dance or do snorty laughs with. It was all water under the bridge yet that didn't mean she wouldn't be affected if she found him now in exactly the same dire straits. Because how would he have air-lifted himself out when everything was against him? She'd feel sorry for him. And what if she saw his face and her heart leapt? What if deep down she still had feelings for him?

It was unlikely though: people and music and books meant things at particular moments in your life, meeting whatever need you had at that time. Like, if she sat down now to read *Sweet Valley High*, it would only ring a very distant bell.

Then there was Kat, who was bound to be sharp-suited and into luxury handbags, her life organized on a spreadsheet. Kids in Mini Boden and a home straight out of an interiors mag. It would drag Vee down. But down to where? For fuck's sake, she couldn't fall any further.

With that, she flipped the lid, her heart fluttering to life. You couldn't go back, people said, but what choice did she have...

On Facebook, she went for Kat first – her story would be easier to stomach. They might not have anything in common, but could the bond they'd had count for something?

Unless she'd got a taste for blood after what happened in Thailand... Vee was afraid now – she had sent Kat loads of emails after she'd gone home, all of which had gone unanswered. Clearly, she hadn't wanted to know her.

But it was too late, curiosity had got the better of her as the returns of her search threw up plenty of Katherine Lloyds. Scrolling down, down, down, she saw her face: instantly, she recognized Kat. The profile picture was of her with a lovely looking man, of course he would be: they were opposites, his light curly hair against her dark swishy locks. Both smiling, they were outdoors somewhere, not abroad because they were in matching Christmas jumpers with a background of green hills, probably taken as a selfie judging by the close-up. Scanning down, she saw the words 'engaged', which set off a stab of self-pity.

And then the blood in her veins sped up because she was in Cowbridge, half an hour from Cardiff. And because she was an estate agent. And not an exclusive high-end one for Toffs but a company Vicky recognized from years ago, which was part of the area's fabric. Maybe she was the boss? But it didn't say so. It was as far away as you could get from banking or bonuses. It was ordinary. Spectacularly so.

It completely blew Vee's mind. She had to know more: how her life had turned out so... normal. It was bewildering. And yes, slightly comforting that Kat, now Kate, which sounded so ordinary, wasn't a high-flyer, albeit at a higher altitude than Vee. She clicked on 'message'.

But how did you make up for eight years of no contact when they'd fallen out on such bad terms? She needed to think a bit first. So she started looking for Michael Murphy.

Her beating pulse pounded with worry. He'd been intelligent and creative and smart enough to be anywhere but circumstances had conspired against him, what if he was trapped at the bottom of the heap in a bedsit? Even though he'd been the one who'd decided to drop her from his life, that would still be upsetting.

A fruitless list of Michael Murphys and no sign of him on Kat/Kate's list of friends. And there were too many Michaels and Murphys to scroll through.

Just as she was beginning to give up and her legs were feeling stiff in the pre-heating chill of the afternoon, there was an entry for someone simply called Murphy. She almost clicked away when she saw the profile picture: a pumped-up hipster in neon pink shades lying on a sun lounger with a Las Vegas sign in the background.

It couldn't be him, she thought. Then she took a second look, gasping aloud, knowing it absolutely was him. Those thick eyebrows, the defiant mouth, the jut of his chin – what the heck had happened to him? What had happened to his hair? His lush bob of brown waves had been shaved to his scalp. Her breathing galloped as she saw his location – everywhere – and job title of Pro Geek.

She was racing to take in all of this information about him – this person she thought she'd known better than anyone who had become someone she didn't recognize.

He had hundreds, thousands, of friends. And his latest post, from two days ago, was astounding: he had been snapped mid-bomb, frozen in the air above an indoor pool, watched by a laughing leggy tattooed stunner in a yellow bandeau bikini. His girlfriend. It had to be – this was the profile of a man who had everything.

Shocked, thrilled and even a tad envious, she went down the rabbit hole, necking shots of him living it large all over the place. Drinks in New York, doing the samba at Rio carnival, a healthy shake lunch in LA, skateboarding in Rome, scuba diving in Cuba, bungee jumping in New Zealand, sailing in Hong Kong, clubbing it in Ibiza...

Deeper she went, drunk on his check-ins at a beard convention in London, a tech conference in Amsterdam and on and on.

Vee came up for air. Here was the most private introverted person she'd ever known hanging it all out on display.

'Oh my good God,' she said to the ceiling, as she held her cheeks. Mikey, the person who'd hidden behind his hair, who'd shunned anything trendy, who'd wanted to make the world a better place, had turned into a humble brag tosser. Actually, drop the humble, he was as flashy as a footballer's wife's jewellery box. A capitalist prick, in fact.

There's no way he'd remember her at all. And if she got in touch with him, then he'd see her limp Facebook page with its dated entries from travelling. She'd let it lie dormant for years. 'The me-me-me sore of celebrity culture,' Jez had called Facebook, so she'd stopped looking. It wasn't as if she had anything to update it with now, being thirty and dumped and living back at home with the parents.

Now though, having gorged on the detail, Vee was consumed by wanting to know how Mikey had ended up as Murphy who was dining out on his success. It had to be tech-related, but she'd always thought IT types were nerds. Clearly not, she thought.

And what did she have to lose? She was pared back to the bone now. There was nothing left of her to hurt. Nosiness, curiosity, and a strong sense of having a right to know pushed her. They'd been so close, so so close, that she felt he owed her an explanation for dropping her and moving on. Vee felt an overwhelming sense of injustice, on behalf of herself and no doubt the many he would've trampled over to get where he was.

Only then could she rebuild herself. How could she be frightened to ask someone why he'd ignored her when he'd promised to bloody marry her if they were both single at the age of thirty?

A bolt of madness came to her then, why the hell not message him? She'd never see him again. She was a crazy dumped woman and she seethed with a bitterness that life had dealt her lemons – she wanted to squeeze the juice in his eyes. Remind him of where he'd come from…

No. Her spine shrivelled. That wasn't the way. She wasn't like that.

Sighing, she faced up to it: she had come online because she was lonely. She had discovered she was still hurting too, eight years later.

The urge she had, the most basic desire, was wanting to reconnect with him and Kat. In her very soul, she felt a love for them both still. To correct the wrongs, to provide a bridge from then to now, to heal the damage she still felt when she thought of losing them both. If she heard back, she'd get some kind of closure – they'd been young when it had all gone pear-shaped: it was possible to get over that. If she didn't hear from them, she'd know they weren't worth it.

At this moment when she felt such a loser, when the music in her head was sad and melancholy, she needed to know if she still mattered. To prove that whatever had passed, you could go back and not feel only failure.

She scrolled through her photos to find a half-decent one – if she was going to make a comeback she needed to change her profile pic. But all of them were selfies with Jez. The only one she could post was of the two of them at a festival in Spain in the summer: she looked all right in it because the sun was behind her and, with a bit of a filter change and a crop, cutting out Jez, she looked okay. Her pinky bleached hair was lit up like a halo and she was laughing. She liked her teeth, they were straight and even, and her make-up hadn't melted off yet.

She wrote the same light message to both: Hi, long time no see! I know it's out of the blue but just wondering how you are. Would be great to catch up.

And she signed both as Vee – she wasn't Vicky anymore.

Then she snapped the lid shut and got a waft of armpit.

It was time to have a bath and get her life back.

*

La Paz, Bolivia, September 2007

What the hell have I done? *Kat panics, her chest heaving from the altitude.*

On the ripped back seat of a dilapidated cab, she takes a sly look at Vicky because surely she's thinking the same thing. Because she's never been anywhere outside Europe. But Kat? She's been to America, Canada and South Africa, where she even did tours of the Soweto township and Robben Island. That, though, means nothing to where she finds herself now.

Incredibly, though, Vicky's face is actually illuminated with excitement. 'This. Is. Mental,' she mouths at Kat, her eyes wide and bright.

Desperate to contain her fear, not daring to speak in case she screams, alarmed that she is terrified about where she is but Vicky isn't, Kat nods frantically which, thank God, doesn't let her down: Vicky beams at her then turns back to the window to gawk at the view of La Paz.

How the heck is she so not frightened? She can't be hiding it because Vicky lets it all out: the way she deals with stress is to reveal it immediately, as if she's thrown it up. Kat really thought Vicky was going to be a wreck. But apart from a wobble when they said bye to their parents, Vicky seems to have left her scaredy-cat at home. Kat's though has jumped up from her rucksack and is currently scratching her face off.

The ride to the city is bumpy – the gaudy Virgin Mary relic swinging from the rear-view mirror makes her feel sick. It's just the comedown of the adrenalin rush, she tells herself, still stunned by their birth from the airport's womb into a shoving and pushing crowd thick with hawkers crying 'taxi' and 'hotel', trying to hijack them en route to the official taxi rank. It's bizarre how getting into a car with a strange man suddenly felt like the pinnacle of safety. Then there's the tiredness of twenty-odd hours in transit on hardly any sleep and the fact her brain, which believes it to be night-time, blanches at the severity of the afternoon sun.

The red digital numbers of the fare, accelerating wildly because there's loads of Bolivianos to the pound, begin to jump around then bleed, leaving a trail as she looks away to take in La Paz.

She'd crammed the Lonely Planet, but nothing, nothing, prepares you for the sight of the highest city in the world at three thousand, six hundred and fifty metres above sea level. It is all laid out before them in a bowl of a valley, surrounded by snow-capped mountains even though it is technically spring. This place is challenging all her senses: the sky is the truest blue she's ever seen and while the sun seared her cheeks the second she stepped out into its cruel rays, there's a creeping coldness. But then she wore completely the wrong clothes – she's in a cardie, flip-flops, vest top and jeans. She feels stupid now for laughing at Vicky's fleece and utility trousers which zip off into shorts.

The landscape doesn't seem real: millions of tiny makeshift buildings which look as if God has dropped brown sugar cubes from the sky. There are no neat lines, it's haphazard, confusing. Roofs of blue, red and yellow chaotically break up the mass of the canyon, which is centred by old-fashioned white skyscrapers, none of which are the same height or size.

Disorientated, she feels a cold sweat now, wishing the taxi driver would slow down, stop beeping and turn off the radio which bellows pan pipes and a tongue she knows is Spanish but might as well be the national language of Mars.

She blinks hard, her contact lenses as dry as the air here. Her breathing still hasn't recovered – she did think it was just the buzz of landing and having to think on her feet. But it's the altitude and panic which is making her lungs strain.

Kat needs to find some sort of common denominator, something she can relate to. So she switches her attention to the blurred scrubland through which they're passing. But she recognizes nothing.

Rusting cars which look abandoned suddenly lurch into life like the undead.

By the side of the road, the odd stall here and there selling dusty wares, mainly bottles and packets of unfamiliar stuff, sits unmanned.

Stray dogs snooze while llamas – or are they vicuñas or alpacas – graze on... what exactly? Because there's no grass, just small thorny-looking bushes.

And there are kids in rags out walking, but where have they

come from and where are they going? There is only miles of flat and sparse plain.

The women, wearing bowler hats, long black plaits and full colourful skirts, are carrying loads in bulging sacks tied on their backs. A glimpse of a face makes her gasp: they are transporting their young inside those wraps of fabric – there are no trendy pushchairs or designer baby slings here.

Vans stuffed with men, women and babes in arms overtake: every now and then she makes eye contact with one of the passengers and they both stare. With her long face, loose hair and upturned nose, she must look as exotic to them as their high cheekbones, dark skin and heart-shaped faces do to her.

What had she been thinking, demanding of Vicky that they start their travels here? They should have acclimatized first with some beach time in Ecuador or Brazil. Or forgotten South America altogether. Headed straight for the east coast of Australia with its backpacker party culture.

But no, Kat wanted to come here, to soar like a bird on the thermals of confidence. To show everyone, perhaps herself too, that coming out of her shell wasn't a temporary thing but for life. But Bolivia isn't Oxford: Kat can hardly believe she thought La Paz was the next logical step after three years of hockey, entz, gowns and grace before supper at Mansfield College. She shakes her head, feeling nothing but self-contempt for her stupidity at thinking she was a woman about town just because everyone made a fuss out of her for being one of a few females studying maths. Her leap from her mother's control was no more than jumping into a cocoon. She has been kidding herself, and what a time to discover it. How easily self-esteem can become vanity, she thinks. And they are in South America for a month, booked onto tours of salt flats, Lake Titicaca and Machu Picchu and signed up for thirty-hour coach journeys and tango classes in Buenos Aires.

Bewildered, her tongue feels fat and her breathing is laboured: the air is thin and she can feel it. Inhaling as deeply as she can doesn't draw in enough oxygen and it makes her feel uneasy because she's used to being healthy and in control.

'Here we go,' Vicky says, again radiating that smile, that indecently genuine smile, as they begin their descent into the city.

But Kat is still suffocating because the volume of people and buildings expands, crushing her inside. It's all traffic fumes now and stop-start: people don't wait at zebra crossings but weave in between cars and there's a toothless woman squatting on the pavement selling what looks like chewing gum.

But then as they get deeper into La Paz there are some signs of civilization in which she finds comfort: women in high heels and business suits, men carrying briefcases, billboards for McDonald's and Inca Kola and the grand colonial buildings which she's read up on.

Up a winding alley and down a cobbled street, the cab finally pulls up outside a battered metal door. This can't be it. They've booked a nice hotel to start with, just to settle them in, with a courtyard and proper duvets. Kat was against it but thank God Vicky insisted – she could kiss her she's so grateful.

Kat is about to whisper 'this can't be it' to Vicky, but she's already double-checking the address with the guide book.

'We're here!' she says and Kat's disappointment is quickly joined by fear. On alert, adrenalin pumping, Kat grips her hand to prevent a rookie mistake – always wait until the driver has left the vehicle before exiting to get your bags or he could drive off with all your stuff.

Wanting to look on top of things, faking it in the hope she'll make it, Kat goes to pay him a ludicrous amount of notes but he asks for dollars instead and she fluffs around in her money belt, feeling a fool for showing how much cash she's got on her. Vicky is struggling under the weight of her rucksack and Kat feels a jab of irritation that she packed the kitchen sink. Kat's is lighter, leaner, but she can bet she'll end up having to carry Vicky's because she's not as strong as her.

'This is beyond!' Vicky says, banging away until a member of staff opens up to reveal a glorious square of quiet. It's not the height of luxury but it's better than she'd expected. Cafe-style tables are on the left by the bar-restaurant and a heated pool is on the right. No one is actually in, the backpackers are either on or queuing to use the computers, reading guidebooks or drinking cans of Taquiña beer. Kat feels slightly easier now, but only until Vicky grabs her, making her jump.

But Vicky isn't warning of a threat – she's beside herself with glee, hugging Kat then herself, looking around, wanting to get stuck in.

'Let's go out and explore!' she says. 'Right now!'

This was how Kat had imagined she herself would react. But how she feels in reality is the total opposite as it dawns on her that

44

*her previous five-star structured travels had just been her mother's
sanitized, controlled version. She wants to organize her bedside
table, curl up and sleep. She wants to regroup, make sense of where
she is. Anger spikes inside at how easily Vicky is taking this.*

*'Shall we check-in first?' she says in a clipped voice, which she
knows Vicky catches. She sounded patronizing and she feels bad,
but why isn't Vicky finding this weird? She's a right home-bird,
she's already said she misses Mikey a thousand times, which made
Kat wonder if she's second-best. This self-doubt, this thin skin is
how she used to be. When mum would tell her ninety-eight per cent
wasn't good enough or she was 'a piggy-wiggy' if she ate all her tea.
It has taken a lot of self-help books plus a course of counselling at
uni to see that she can switch off her mother's critical narrative
inside her head. She doesn't want it back.*

'You all right?' Vicky says, warily.

*'Yep, just want to, you know...' Kat tries to soften her voice,
'dump my stuff.' She manages a smile which Vicky gobbles up.*

*'Phew, thought you were having a bit of a freak-out there,
Kat!'*

*The nail hammers into her head and she feels a surge of
attrition: she's the one who's supposed to be brave, she's the one who
landed a first and a job and fought her mother to be here. Vicky
has always had it good; supported and cuddled and mollycoddled.
She should be the one feeling vulnerable.*

*Kat stalks off to reception and has a word with herself as she
fills out forms.* You're under stress, she thinks, don't take it out
on Vicky, she's your best friend and it'd be so cruel to piss on
her parade. Her enthusiasm is infectious, it always has been, so
relax and lap it up.

*Kat gives Vicky a squeeze when she returns with the key, to
show she's sorry. Then they walk arm-in-arm as a porter carries
their bags to their room.*

Oh my wow, it's gorgeous, *Kat thinks, as she inspects the white
walls, shuttered window, animal-skin rug and Andean textiles
draped over a small sofa. A calm begins to emerge on the horizon –
if she can come back to this, she might just be okay!*

*Kat laughs as Vicky bounces up and down on the edge of the
big bed, saying:* 'Bagsy the left side!'

But then she reminds Kat that this is a one-off – 'Make the
most of it, after this it's dorms all the way' *– and she begins to
shrink again.*

45

Her temples begin to pulse to the rhythm of her heartbeat which is still fast.

'Have you got any paracetamol?' she asks Vicky, who gives her a look.

'Ha! I was waiting for you to need something from my overpacked bag!' Vicky sings it in victory.

Kat pokes out her tongue and holds out her hand as Vicky finds her Boots kit of lotions and potions and chucks her a box of painkillers.

'You all right?' Vicky asks Kat's back as she goes to the loo to get her shit together.

Inside, she splashes water on her face – then panics as some goes in her mouth. It's not safe to drink, *she thinks, spitting it out then gulping back two pills with the last of her mineral water.*

'Kat? You feeling rough?' Vicky says through the door.

She can't admit she feels shaky and grey and baggy.

'Nope,' she calls, 'just a bit of a headache.'

'Cool,' Vicky whoops as Kat steps out into the room, finding it an enormous effort to breathe.

'Fab, because the first place I want to go to is the witches' market, where they sell llama foetuses and amulets and dried frogs. Then we could go to one of those canteens, the ones that do salteñas, those spicy pasty things, or we could eat "cuy", that's what they call guinea pig here, it's a delicacy apparently. And maybe we could get a pisco sour after! Have a few drinks!'

The room is whirling, Kat feels nauseous and she just shakes her head. 'I just need a lie down.' She doesn't care now that she's shown herself up. 'You go out there, have a bit of a fact-finding mission, I'll be fine, honestly.'

'Oh God, I can't leave you. Is it the altitude? Shit, I thought I'd get that not you.'

Kat mentally agrees with her because she is fit as a fiddle whereas Vicky gets every bug going and she's... Her head hits the pillow and she shuts her eyes, disgusted that the next words that she was thinking were 'a bit of a slob'. She feels ashamed that one test, one blip, has made her spiteful and mean. She begins to backtrack: she didn't mean it nastily, it's just that she's read somewhere that fitter people have more – or is it fewer? – red blood cells and require more oxygen or something? Her mind is jumbled and dizzy.

'I just need a quick nap. Go and check out the hotel, get some water and snacks and stuff. I'll come and find you in a bit. Meet

you in the bar.'

'Right, okay, if you're sure, but say if not because—'

'Go, honest.'

And then as Vicky leaves the room, Kat sinks with her regret into the covers wishing she was anywhere but here, accusing herself of the utmost stupidity for thinking this up.

A blackness pulls her under for God knows how long until a sound of metal saws in her ears. She sits up and can see Vicky with her key in a kind of twilight.

'Hey! How you doin'?' she whispers in their Joey Tribbiani-style greeting, born of a mutual teenage obsession with Friends. Usually, Kat says it back to her, but it feels foreign, inappropriate. *'Sorry, did I wake you?'* Vicky stumbles. *'I've been in twice but you were doggo so I've just been in the bar. Bit pissed actually. You okay?'*

'What time is it?' Kat says, feeling out of sync, suddenly starving hungry.

'Ten. I've brought you some water and there's a toastie, sorry it's cold but...'

Kat couldn't care less. She glugs the water greedily and polishes off the cheese sandwich, feeling slightly better. Here in the dark, she can finally say it out loud. *'Christ, I felt terrible earlier. What a wash-out, I bet you must think I'm a right weakling. I just felt overwhelmed. I'm sorry for being a cow.'*

'That's all right, mate, you weren't,' she says, joining her in bed. *'It is mega mental here. Just the strangest place on earth. Apart from Mikey's house! I mean, the furthest I've been before this was Turkey with Mum and Dad.'*

Kat grabs on to Vicky's acknowledgement like a life raft.

'Hey, I've been talking to some of the people out there, they're just like us, taking gap years or whatever and they've got loads of tips and suggestions. Oh, and most were affected by the altitude when they got here too so don't worry.'

This was music to Kat's ears – perhaps she'd fallen apart because she was ill not naive.

'Flic, this girl I spoke to, who was really nice, said it'll take a few days to acclimatize. The trick, she says, is coca tea, apparently. It's not drugs or anything, although it is related to cocaine but just distantly, like. A herbal infusion which alleviates the effects of being so high up. We'll get some tomorrow for you, they sell it everywhere.'

'Brill,' Kat breathed, relieved this shortness of breath and

anxiety wasn't her but being two point two eight miles above sea level.

'God, do you know, I was so scared before we got on the plane. But the weirdest thing happened when we took off. I just had this feeling that my life starts now: that this is what I've been after the whole time. New things, different faces, like. You read books to change your reality, but for the first time I'm living it. I'm free! And so are you! We're going to have the most epic adventure, Kat!'

Kat lays back down and reaches out for Vicky's hand.

'Thanks, mate,' she says. It was exactly what she needed to hear: why hadn't she talked to Vicky when she began to feel bad? Next time she'd tell her straight up. 'I don't know what I'd do without you, do you know that?'

'You too, Kat. Now let's get some sleep, breakfast is from 8 a.m. to 10 a.m. We can plan our stay then over tea and toast, they do that here! Although I might try the Bolivian breakfast, they do a kind of doughnut thing and you know I can't resist a doughnut.'

Kat giggles because that's typical of Vicky. Not just the thinking of her stomach bit but that she's embracing everything. Vicky sees herself as a struggler, as a nobody, no matter how many times Kat has told her she isn't. Instead she is blessed with magnetism and positivity and flexibility and there is no one she'd rather have by her side.

'Best friends forever, Vicky,' she murmurs.

'Word, Kat,' Vicky says, sighing sweetly into the night.

Chapter Five

V

Cowbridge, March

Vee pulled up in Mum's car outside Fromage, a deli Kate had suggested for their 9.30 a.m. rendezvous.

Set in the smart – or what Vee read as smug – town of Cowbridge nestled between Waitrose and what could only be described as a designer charity shop, it looked the part with its swirly French font, dark wooden cellar door and battered cafe-style shutters. A chalkboard outside declared: 'When one is tired of cheese, one is tired of life', which reflected there was zero sign of life here.

She inhaled a shaky breath, bracing herself for this meeting of past and present. What was she going to find? Vee had learned nothing from the brief exchange of messages with Kate – Wow, what a surprise! Yes, I'd love to catch up.

Ever since, she'd been doubting herself. Only this morning, she'd consulted the dog-eared poster of Jarvis Cocker Blu-tacked inside the left hand door of her white MFI chipboard wardrobe, just as she'd done as a teenager. He'd been a good agony uncle through the years, although his advice could be a bit negative.

'Should I cancel?' she'd asked him as she got dressed into skinny jeans and her A Woman's Place Is In The Revolution T-shirt. He'd pointed out that she was going to be here for a while because she was skint, therefore she had to get a job and if she was going to sort herself out, she needed a friend.

Mikey hadn't replied, but then wherever he was, it'd be so flash and futuristic, they probably communicated through robot beeps. That was obviously that – he was off living his life.

Jarvis was right: the fact was, meeting Kate was important. While Kate had never replied to Vee's emails, Vee wasn't after an apology, that wasn't what this was about. Instead, at the very least, she wanted to make peace, show that the past was in the past.

Still, in her heart of hearts she hoped it would lead to more: to have someone in her life now who 'got' her. To laugh at how obsessed they were with *Titanic*, how they used to squabble over who got to sing Robbie Williams' part when they'd listen to Take That in her bedroom. To have a bit of support too: as much as Vee loved Mum and Dad, they didn't know what it was to be thirty in the twenty-first century.

Understanding she had to be mild rather than mustard, Vee had taken off her statement T-shirt and opted for a navy one instead. No Brighton green eyeshadow either: round here it'd make her look like a mad old lady who still thought it was 1940. A bit of talc on her hair had diluted the pink bits – getting rid of them would be the first thing she'd do when she had some cash.

Vee checked her watch: it was time. She stepped out into the sunshine, which was doing a decent trailer for spring, and felt waves of apprehension. Bats circled her head, kangaroos thumped in her tummy and gorillas fisted her chest. But she could leave if she had nothing in common anymore with Kate, which was a possibility. Kate was a country girl now, living in a hamlet with a very Welsh name of just consonants. Such isolation was an appalling thought for Vee, who'd die if she didn't have a Spar up the road. And it fitted in with her theory that Kate had made millions in London, moved into a posh pile and got herself a little job to keep her busy.

Standing outside the deli, she ran through her opening line. Their old Joey from *Friends* 'how you doin'?' – which used to set them off laughing – wasn't right for two thirty-year-old women. Neither was 'so… what the blinking hell made you come back to live in the back of beyond?'. A frightened 'it's been a while' plus an observation on how fantastic Kate looked was more like it.

With false gusto, Vee went in expecting to come face to face with her – Kate had been brought up on punctuality. Instead, through the murky air, she saw a harassed-looking man with a battered brown leather apron round his waist shouting into the phone.

The tinkle of the door had announced her arrival and she waited for him to do the usual embarrassed awkward grin of the proprietor who'd been caught being anything but the convivial host. But he stared at her as if she had just walked into his own lounge rather than a public place.

'Yes?' he said, irritated, his green eyes flaring in a ray of sun which had broken into the dingy deli.

'I'm meeting someone for—'

'Right, sit down then,' he directed, waving at her to one of the empty wrought-iron table and chairs before he launched back into his conversation.

Bewildered but intrigued, she took in the sight of stacks of sacks on the floor, rambling shelves, a large American fridge and a massive gleaming stainless-steel counter stocked with all sorts of cheeses and meats. The smell in here was deliciously earthy and salty, like a giant wheel of Brie, tinged with ground coffee, expensive bitter chocolate and the sweet scent of basil.

'Food hygiene regulations stipulate the implementation of food management safety procedures. One of which is the control of hazards. The law says I must have adequate lighting. The lighting you were supposed to have fixed... Lack of staff? My heart bleeds! New member of the team, you say? You'll be here within the hour? Oh, excellent! Finally. Goodbye.'

Then he turned to Vee's astonished face.

'What a cretin. Twenty-four-hour call-out, my arse. Can't see a bloody thing.'

Vee didn't know whether to laugh or leg it, but she was hypnotized by this man's behaviour. Had he ever heard of customer service? She'd have got up and left had he not been so... well, unbelievably attractive. Tall, dark, broad and tanned, he looked like he was out of *Game of Thrones*. All that was missing was an animal skin robe and a sword.

'You could open the door? That might help?' she said, wondering why he hadn't thought of this already.

He pulled in exasperation at handfuls of curly brown hair. 'You see? That's why I can't run this place by myself. My brother, who is supposed to be front of house, has decided cheese isn't for him. I mean, how preposterous! It's what the sign says, tired of cheese, tired of life.'

Vee was clearly expected to share his look of disbelief.

'He's left me in the dark. Literally. Coffee?'

51

'Er, yes, black, please.'

'Excellent.' He rubbed his palms and then gave her a dashing smile.

She couldn't take her eyes off him as he stalked about behind the counter, fiddling with the machine, creating steam and swearing all the while. What a bizarre place this was, what a beguiling man and she'd almost forgotten...

A tinkle broke the spell and there Kate was, her smile timid, apprehensive. Still beautiful, but her looks were no longer indecently stunning, they were more modest and grown-up. Perhaps because they were tempered by an uncharacteristically unstylish old jumper, muddy jeans and wellies, . Eight years since she'd seen her, eight years ago when Kat had been on the edge. Now she appeared worn-in and experienced.

The sight of Kate, her eyes mirroring Vee's emotion, was as if someone had shouted 'clear' and pulsed her heart back to life. She couldn't help it – she jumped up, flapping her arms.

'It's you,' Vee said, moving towards her then stopping awkwardly just in case she had read it all wrong.

'I can't believe...' Kate said softly, her eyes creasing from a teary sob which escaped her mouth. She squeaked a Joey 'How you doin'?' and that olive branch of familiarity and recognition was all it took to send Vee into her arms. She was still as skinny as she ever was, but Vee could feel a tautness to her body, which made her think of armour.

'You look...' Vee said, pulling back, holding a hand over her gob, then sitting down as her knees gave way.

'I know, I'm sorry,' Kate said, joining her at the table. 'I was walking the dog in the woods and he ran off after a squirrel and by the time I'd got him back I had no time to change.'

'I meant, you look the same but different.' The way she moved with grace. Her gait so upright and measured. Yet her eyes, now she was up close, hinted at something sombre.

'So do you. You're...'

'In a bad way,' Vee said, already strangely comfortable.

Vee saw it in Kate's face then, a concerned and curious admission that yes, indeed, Vee wasn't at her best. But Kate stuck to the script, their old mutual fan club script of reassurance.

'Rubbish! You look great! Not a day older than—'

And there was the moment, the reference to their past, when

the trust had been broken and they'd parted relieved to see the back of one another. It was a fact they couldn't deny but which they had to acknowledge if they were going to rebuild their relationship. And magically, that possibility was in the air. Vee had assumed she'd be the one to bring it up in some goofy way, for she was the one who couldn't contain herself. So for Kate to do it within minutes of meeting, whether she'd meant to deliberately or she'd stumbled across it, it nearly knocked her off her chair. If you'd wronged someone, then wasn't sorry the hardest word?

This, Vee knew instinctively, was her chance to let bygones be bygones.

'I just wanted to say, you know…' Vee bit her lip then went for it.

But Kate was already in there, holding her palms to her chest. 'It was my fault. All of it. I'm sorry and I hope you can forgive me.'

There in Kate's gaunt and haunted face, Vee saw how time had affected her friend. What journey had she been on? she wondered. Overwhelmed by Kate's apology, it was time for Vee to show her own hand. Literally. She reached out for Kate's and began.

'It was a long time ago, Kate. I'd like nothing better than to get past it. Life hasn't quite turned out how I wanted it to. It's a bit pants actually. That's why I'm at home. I just got dumped after seven years with this bloke, we were living together in Brighton,' she said, her chin wobbling. It felt terrible to say it out loud but it felt fantastic to share it. In that moment, it was just like old times, talking boy trouble, not needing anyone to provide a quick fix solution but simply an ear. 'My parents are driving me up the wall with their talk of draught excluders and bulbs in the garden. I've pretty much got… nothing. But it's my own doing though, so, you know, no violins.'

'Oh, Vicky, sorry Vee, I didn't expect that at all. I thought… anyway, it doesn't matter what I… you must feel crappy.'

Kate's eyes caressed Vee's face but then the lights went out as she opened up.

'I've had a funny time of it myself. I'm fine, now,' she said, making it clear she wasn't after sympathy, 'I never made it into banking. It all went a bit wobbly when I got back from travelling.'

Kate grimaced and Vee shook her head, not understanding.

'I'm forever condemned to be known as the family disappointment. My mother is still the same. No, actually, she's worse.'

Vee had a hint of comprehension – was it that Kate had been a forecasted whirlwind only to change direction or had she blown herself out?

Their sniffles were the soundtrack then as they digested the headlines of their lives.

A giant set of knuckles appeared before Vee's face then and she looked at its owner. It was the *Game of Thrones* guy who was holding out a box of tissues with a bored look on his face.

'And here's your coffee. Rwandan beans, the finest,' he said, letting it slop over the lid of the cup onto the saucer.

'Pierre,' Kate said, recovering herself. 'What ever happened to service with a smile?'

Ah, so they knew each other! That would be why Kate suggested here.

'It's not my job to be customer-friendly, as you well know, Kate. That bastard brother of mine has walked out on me. Hence why I'm the face of Fromage.'

By way of explanation, he spoke to Vee. 'I'm the cheese man. I deal with the cheese. And the meats. The olives. All of it. I look after the deliveries and the imports and the orders. I make sure there is no pre-cut shrink-wrapped cheese, that our salami is succulent, that our bascaiola sauce has never seen the inside of a factory. I search out the very best wares, which you will never see on a supermarket shelf.' Then to Kate, as he strode back to his counter, he said, 'Your usual, my dear? Ecuadorian green tea?'

'Please!' she said, just as a strikingly beautiful woman in dungarees and workmen's boots strode in and clattered a toolbox on the floor.

Pierre's broad shoulders hunched at the sound and whipped round with a face of thunder, demanding to know, 'What in God's na—'

His thunder became a dreamy rainbow as his brow collapsed into a mega-watt smile, which took Vee's breathe away. This place was so intriguing.

'The sparky,' she stated, fiddling around for something in her breast pocket.

'I say! I beg your pardon?' he simpered, gazing at her almost eye-to-eye she was that tall. 'Is that some sort of cheese I've never heard of?' He had become breathy and excited.

'Ee-lec-treesh-an,' she elongated in a European purr for his benefit, her eyebrows arched. 'In British culture, electricians are commonly referred to as sparkies. I am here to fix your lights.'

Pierre's jaw clunked open and he cleared his throat to assert his manliness. 'Yes, yes, of course, I was just joshing,' he said, scratching his chin.

'Yes, yes, of course,' she repeated, looking unamused. 'Is hilarious, yes, that a woman come here to do your electricity. And she is foreign.'

'No. NO! God, no. Perish the thought,' he said, horrified. 'I... I love women electricians. Particularly the... er... foreign ones... absolutely smashing people. My friend here, Kate, she will testify that I am actually a feminist, isn't that so?'

'Never mind. Give me coffee and I fix you,' the woman said, picking up her bag as Pierre agreed absolutely with her and led her inside.

It was all too much for Vee, who released a giggle. 'What the hell was that about?'

Kate shrugged. 'That is classic Pierre. You'll get used to it.'

Vee went to speak then stopped as the intention behind Kate's words sank in: it may have been just one of those phrases people said, but 'you'll get used to it' gave her a warm fuzzy feeling that she was welcome around here.

It made her heart bloom that someone she'd once cherished was as pleased to see her as she was. But how could she say that out loud without looking like she was Billy No Mates? Well, she couldn't. Instead, she nodded at her coffee – she wanted to show her appreciation of the deli, their meeting and the hope of beginning again.

'Now this... this shits all over Mum's Nescafé,' Vee said.

Kate creased up. Then they made a start on catching up where they'd let each other go.

Chapter Six

M

Barry Island

'It's gorgeous here, Murphy,' Shell said, her face peeking out of the hood of her furry parka as she held her arms out wide to embrace the wide empty expanse of beach.

In the crisp midday sunshine, he almost felt warm.

'If you ignore that dog over there taking a dump,' he said, digging his chin into the throat of his coat.

'It's a blue flag beach! You've got no soul.'

Then she took off, running towards the sea, careering left then right in loops, like a child.

This was the trouble with Londoners. Take them out of there and they became all doe-eyed about nature and views: it was a superiority act, one which said, 'I am urban, I am more sophisticated because I appreciate that which you do not.'

Well, if it's so good here then why are you living there? Let's see you leave your skinny decaf latte and take-out sushi for full-fat-or-nothing and a pasty.

Murphy kicked out at an abandoned lopsided sandcastle and pushed himself off the edge of the concrete promenade wall. If he couldn't hear the tinny tunes on loop of the kiddy rides, then he could imagine he was anywhere but Barry Island.

Barrybados they called it now, this vast crescent of a bay which marketeers were trying to brand as Wales' answer to Bondi Beach, half an hour from Cardiff.

But he'd always found it hard to see it as anything but a desperate day out: he'd only come here to play on the slotties then have a cone of fat soggy chips when there was nothing else to do. With the old Butlins replaced by a housing development on the headland, the businesses were now left to trade on that BBC show *Gavin and Stacey* from a few years ago, which over three series told the tale of an Essex boy falling for a Welsh girl, now confined to the glorious heights of the Dave Channel.

Fair play to them, though, he thought, trudging towards the shoreline, they had to make a living. And better to brag 'this is where Nessa works' than 'this is where Fred West's ashes were scattered' while flogging serial killer memorabilia. Day-trippers were their bread and butter. So he tried looking at it through Shell's eyes. He could hear her whooping on the wind; she was drawing something in the sand with her feet.

Begrudgingly, he admitted it was pretty cool that apart from him and her, the only other person on the beach was that crapping dog and its owner. The water was actually really clean too, he thought, and the sand was Rapunzel gold.

He turned to watch Shell now, her black hair swirling and knotty from the sea air. She was taking pictures of her work with her phone. Curious, he went over.

'What you doing?'

'Just…' She smiled bashfully and her eyelashes dropped. Murphy saw she'd sketched out a heart and written their initials inside.

'M&S?' he teased. 'We can pop in on the way back if you love it that much.'

She lifted her face to his and he was struck by her beauty: she was minus make-up today and as much as he loved the juxtaposition of red lips against porcelain skin and olive hair, she was radiant when she went natural. His stomach flipped at her fresh symmetry, the feline curve of her eyes and the dots of freckles on her nose, which he found so sexy. In bed, they were absolutely epic. She'd been here for three days now, visiting him at his maisonette in Cardiff's grand Westgate Street while he was clearing up after his dad's latest suicide mission. If only he would top himself and get it over and done with.

Once a month he came down to sort Dad out: his nostrils were still full of the damp in his flat, mouldy Value sausage rolls and his sweet and sour sweat of alcohol that never left his system. Mikey never told Orla the bones of it, about Dad's piss-stained trousers and mountain of bottles, only that he was here on business. Mam would be horrified: she'd been so house-proud. But the family home was long gone, sold up so Dad could live off the money, he'd retired early, did his back in and he spent what little pension he had on booze. For once, this visit hadn't been all bad.

Him and Shell had cooked together, walked in Bute Park in the centre of the city, sampled extreme cornets at the liquid nitrogen ice-cream parlour in the arcade near his flat, had a coffee in a cat cafe where she cooed over some tabby moggy, watched Netflix and hung out, working a few hours here and there. It'd been good: actually, it had been great. A laugh and relaxed, no pressure. They understood each other's work and chatted easily about it. Shell was thinking about leaving IT to lecture instead, to inspire women to code. He admired her for that – what had happened to his intentions to do good in the world? They'd been shelved while he enjoyed the spoils of being on the team that had created the blueprint for every major shopping app in 2010. Still, being here allowed him to tune out a bit. From the London scene - and from that projectile message from Vicky: the bloody cheek of her, invading his space like a pixelated alien. Orla, knowing nothing in detail about how their friendship had ended, remembering how Vicky had been like her big sister, had thought it was a good idea to meet her. She'd got it out of him that Vicky had got in touch as only she, the caring sharing social worker, could. He'd been scornful that Vicky – or now Vee – wanted to know how he was and what he was up to. Orla had scoffed at him - hadn't he changed his name too? He ignored that - it would only make him chase his tail with questions. The issue was this: what the hell did she want? It could only be to apologize after what he assumed had happened - after weeks of emails pleading with him to come to see her abroad, he'd caved in and said he'd go out but then nothing. She obviously hadn't want him out there to crash her party. After that Facebook friend request, he never heard from her again. What good would an apology do? You couldn't turn back the clock to the good old days with a 'sorry' and expect to be best buds again. She'd been the one to cut him off, dicking off with her scrotey backpacking mates, choosing them over him. Too much had happened. Besides, one minute in her company and he'd defrost.

That was the trouble. When he thought of Vicky – when hadn't he? – he felt weak. It made him question why he'd never settled down, why he was afraid of commitment. Vicky mugging him via messenger had set off a load of alarms, which he didn't understand. Things, feelings, he thought he'd forgotten about. Her big smile, her laugh. It felt like he was self-harming.

As the years passed, he'd never searched for her online. Ever. Nor Kat, definitely not Kat after what she did, who lost it, big time. When he needed to be, he was as disciplined as a kid in a convent. Why would he throw himself at her mercy? He needed to move on. He needed to swim not tread water: his personal life and his sanity depended on it. There was no point harking back: Vicky was thirty now and milestones made people nostalgic. He had no desire to look at her happy selfies with her kids. Surely she'd know they'd have no mutual interests anymore? His Facebook pix would've spelled that out – as much as he hated himself for it, he couldn't resist sticking everything up to show the doubters he'd done something with his life. Nah, he just wasn't interested.

With Shell, here, now, he could maybe start afresh. A snapshot of her dark nipples, pricked up on perfect breasts, flashed in his head and he felt his cock stiffen. For God's sake, he thought, disgusted with himself, he was an absolute animal to think like this when she was talking of love. For that's what the heart in the sand was about, wasn't it?

He readied himself to begin shutting down, as he always did when they started the preamble to the L-word. Recently, he'd noticed a parade of engagements, births and marriages and it had astounded him because he had never been anywhere near that.

But ever since Vicky's message, hadn't he lain awake the last few nights as she'd slept, watching the perfect even pulse in her neck, and wondered if he could love her? That was, if he could ever love anyone, truly?

'It's just so nice to be here with you without everyone else,' she said, simply, tilting her head to the side, squinting an eye in the sun and holding up a rainbow mittened hand to shade herself.

Shell was the sweetest thing, he thought, not a player, bang on the money straightforward and she was honest. He liked her because she was everything he wasn't.

Could he be better by proxy? He'd only know if he tried, he thought.

He drew her into his arms and, not wanting to let her go, used his teeth to pull her scarf down away from her mouth. Then he kissed her from deep inside, eating up the salt on her lips.

'My mam, she would've liked you.'

He was shaken then, taken aback by the surprise of how freely he'd spoken these words. Where had it come from? he wondered, because he never talked about his mother to anyone but Orla. What did it mean? That he was subliminally comfortable with Shell on a level he hadn't realized? Was this a sign that he might allow himself to be happy?

'Tell me about her,' Shell said into his chest of Puffa jacket.

He rubbed the base of her back instead, because where did you begin to tell the story of the person you worshipped yet knew was flawed? How did he explain that she loved him and Orla, Dad even, fiercely but had this way of withdrawing, shutting them all out. He didn't want anyone's pity or judgement – Mam couldn't help her depression, whatever had set it off he didn't know, but not everyone was so forgiving. He had grown up hearing other mams whispering she was 'strange' and his guts had twisted in anger and shame and love. Dad, the arsehole, hadn't wanted to see it – that's why his drinking worsened when she was going through it, not that that was an excuse.

She was also stupidly proud, moving him and Orla out of St Joseph's because someone at the church had discreetly asked if she had any problems at home. It was about the time he'd had to pretend he'd lost his blazer because there was no money to buy a new one. She refused all offers of second-hand uniform because she didn't want her kids 'looking like paupers'.

'Those interfering, nosey types sticking their oar in, where it's not wanted,' she'd said. If only she'd shown her face occasionally, to prove things weren't too bad. But she never went to parents' evenings or concerts, which was the one thing he liked about that school because he got to play guitar in a band. But she wouldn't take a day off cleaning the offices. Looking back, Murphy realized she'd done that out of fear: if Dad drank the wages then she had to work all hours so she could feed her family. If only he'd told her just once that actually he'd loved moving to Cardiff High because he'd met a kindred spirit.

Yet at that time it taught Mikey that turning your back rather than asking for help was the way to deal with a problem. Still, he could forgive her that – she had no one else.

But then she could be the most amazing person, like on their birthdays, no matter how she was feeling, she'd always put up balloons the night before. You'd come down and she'd be there in her pink waffled dressing gown cutting up a cake, which she'd let you eat as a treat for breakfast. Never home-made, she couldn't bake to save her life, it'd be one of those synthetic sponges with an inch of white icing all over but they loved it. And then as you shovelled it in in case she changed her mind, she'd tell you the story of your birth. 'Mikey was a long skinny thing, so he was, furious at being born, but Orla, she was awful gorgeous and mewed like a kitten.' And then she'd say how they'd made her so happy and the pain had been worth every second.

Six years she'd been gone – if only she could see him now. He'd have got her help, if she was still alive. Why hadn't God taken Dad first? he wanted to ask the sky: no one would've missed him, but no, cancer stole his mum, robbed her of the chance to see how well her kids had turned out in spite of everything.

It was too soon to let this out. But still, he felt himself thawing from Shell's love: because, he knew, she loved him, she just hadn't said it yet. It was on the horizon and he wished he had those words building up inside of him. Maybe he just had to try harder.

'ARTHUR! Do not shake yourself there,' a voice shouted urgently from behind his left shoulder. 'Oh God, he's going to cover you, quick, mooove!'

But it was too late, as Murphy turned round to see what was going on, he got a face full of sand and saltwater which stung his eyes and splattered his new Howies organic jeans.

'Oh for fuck's sake,' he said, jumping back, temporarily blinded. 'Can't you control your dog?'

Then his eyes started watering and in the blur he saw pink on blonde. His heart shuddered, the hairs on his arms jumped up, his empty stomach cramped.

Just stop it, he told himself, *just stop looking for her*. He didn't want to see Vicky, his brain was playing tricks on him. It had been the same ever since he'd checked her out on Facebook:

he'd had to, just quickly, see her face. And ever since, in the street, on the periphery of his vision, when he closed his eyes, hues of pink kept appearing whether they were real or not. He had resolved this, so why was she still lingering?

It couldn't be her, he thought, blinking at speed, needing to prove it was a fantasy. All this is, he thought, was the last dying embers of his old life. He rubbed his eyes and felt them clearing.

'I'm so sorry. Arthur! Come here, you utter fool of a...'

Then everything went slo-mo as he saw Vicky in front of him, open-mouthed, confused, agog.

His heartbeat dropped to a heavy bassline as his lungs rose, expanding his ribcage millimetre by millimetre. The blood moved around him like a lazy river, bubbling in his ears as his blinking eyes caught up. His brain, lagging behind, was writing the programming language of the situation: is it really Vicky? It looks like Vicky, a slighter version of her, but all the hallmarks are there: the chickenpox scar from when she was three is above her right eyebrow, the same shade of early deep blue dawn is in her eyes and her lips are slicked with something shiny just as they were when she had a different fruit balm every week. Conclusion: it is Vicky.

The shake of his breath rattled up his throat and rushed out of his mouth. How many times had he wished he'd been in *The Matrix*, but why did it have to be now, like this?

'Fuck,' he said as her eyes skipped around his face, no doubt confirming that he too really was who she thought he was.

'Mikey?' she said, shaking her head and the hair which tumbled around her face, bleached and pink, like Orla's punked-up Girl's World styling head from their childhood. Her voice was parched, strained as if she hadn't spoken yet today. Highly unlikely, he caught himself thinking, because she never used to shut up. She held up her hands in shock then self-consciously put them down. His reflexes leapt into action as he saw her trying to work out if physical contact was expected.

He stepped back and put out an arm to protect Shell, who he now remembered was beside him. She was looking intrigued at his reaction, he just knew it. He was unravelling and he had to pretend he wasn't. He stroked his palm down his face, apprehensive, and began.

'Shell, this is Vicky, from school. Vicky, this is Shell, my...'

He hated himself because he faltered then. Did he have it in him to label her as his? He had to or he'd fall apart.

'…girlfriend.'

Shell looked relieved and he wanted to punch himself for having that power: for making her happy when he wasn't sure he could handle that responsibility now or ever. Waving a small hello, Vicky nodded back with a 'hi, there'. Not a flash of anything insincere about it. Or, and he reprimanded himself as he thought it, a flicker of resentment at Shell being here by his side.

So awkward at his past meeting his present, and possibly his future, if the sand could've parted to reveal jaws, then he'd have taken his chances and somersaulted in. Instead he had to contend with it – plus an anger that Vicky had walked in on him just when he had blocked her out again.

'What are you doing here?' she said, wearing her disbelief like a flaming Blue Peter badge.

At least she had the decency to blush now that the initial astonishment was over: no doubt she was trying to work out what you said to someone if you'd disappeared, just like that, from someone's life. Tasting it as if it had just happened, he remembered her silence: when, finally, he'd emailed to say he wanted to come and visit her when she was away. That possibly there was stuff he needed to say to her. He felt her neglect again. Then the warning which had come from Kat that awful night they met when she'd got back from travelling: 'She's changed.' That's why he'd never accepted her Facebook request which appeared one day out of the blue in 2009, around Christmas. And why he'd never accepted her request to catch up this time round either.

'Just showing Shell the sights,' he said, tartly, expecting her to get the message to cut this short and go. But of course they were British and they would have to play this out and only then could they leave. God, he hated this! Why couldn't he just announce there was no way back and walk away?

'Right,' she said, guardedly, 'I'm walking the dog… Obviously.'

Then her cringe took him all the way back to the classroom, the discos, the parties, the pubs where she'd known straight away when she'd said something stupid.

'It's my mum and dad's. Not mine.'

Murphy raised his eyebrows then looked down at his feet where his toes were curling. *Please, just go,* he thought. He saw her DMs shuffling – still in DMs, like a teenager. He met her stare then, challenging her to go. She chewed on a nail – Christ, she always used to do that when she was upset – and took in a deep breath.

Murphy pulled himself back up, making his posture tall to show this was how it was.

She put the dog back on the lead and turned to leave. But then she stopped and lifted her eyes to his: they were stormy with hurt. And he saw now she had a trace of a blotch on her neck, which meant she'd been crying recently. He felt the weakness of knowing her inside out.

'Did you, um, get my message, the other day?' she said, as if she was giving it one last chance. 'I wondered because I'm back here for a bit and I thought it'd be nice to catch up. If you're around, at all?'

As much as he wanted to hiss that yes he had and couldn't she read between the lines, he was wavering from her gabbling.

'It's just, the other day for the first time since… in years, I saw Kat.' His innards writhed at the sound of Kat's name. What did Vicky know? Had Kat said anything? She couldn't have, otherwise her reception would've been colder than a polar bear's arse.

'She's Kate now. Like I'm Vee… and you're Murphy.' She shook her head at her awkwardness and pushed on. 'Anyway, it was like old times.' She tried to smile. A limp wet fish of a smile. 'But better. Like, we're older now.'

He wanted to give her a sarky round of applause for having the gall to attempt a sickeningly saccharine Disney-style moral of the story: that people make mistakes, that forgiveness is possible, that we all grow up.

But then a sob escaped from her and she turned away and blinked into the wind to compose herself. Fuck it, he thought, he was softening seeing her in black and white rather than her old technicolour. He dipped his head and shut his eyes in a pathetic last line of defence.

She must've seen then it was worth one final attempt.

'…it was all so long ago and we decided to just put everything behind us. So, if you change your mind…'

Then without finishing the thought or waiting for a reply,

she walked away towards the prom, leaving him humbled and sorry and with something in his eye as he watched her retreat. For someone who had a degree in making a pig's ear out of something, she'd mastered dignity.

'Blast from the past?' Shell said, tugging his arm, pulling him back to her. 'Don't worry, we all have them.'

'No, it wasn't like that,' he said, tightly. 'She's not an ex.'

Shell shifted her head backwards – she didn't understand what he meant.

He gulped as he gave in to what he wanted to say.

'My best mate,' he said, realizing that once he'd said that, without putting it into the past tense, he would absolutely one hundred per cent see her again.

*

Mikey's parents' house, Llanedeyrn, Cardiff, Christmas 2007

Stuffed. Well and truly.

But Mikey still rifles through the Quality Street for a green triangle, locates one, unwraps it and lets the chocolate melt in his mouth. He savours it, just like he savours Christmas. It's the one time of year Mam and Dad call a truce. Weird how everyone else gets wrecked this time of year but Dad reigns it in to redeem himself. 'Christmas is for amateurs,' he says, with the contorted pride of a professional boozer. Mikey looks at him on the other sofa, his bald patch shining red, green and blue, reflecting the fairy lights on the fake tree. His craggy head lolls beneath his gold tilted paper hat, supported by the roll of chin on his chest. To anyone else he'd look like he was sleeping off a skinful. But he's only had a couple of cans, like he knows this is Mam's special day. As if she's saying sorry for the way she hibernates and doesn't eat even when Mikey's made her favourite, pie and mash.

He watches her still in her Christmas pinny, entranced by Strictly, *cuddled up with her mini-me Orla, who's in the middle. Mam's going grey, but Orla's curls of bluey-black hair are identical to the photos of Mam when she was her age. Their eyes are on the amber side of brown, like a lion, which is pretty apt seeing their hearts are as big. He got Dad's looks, big rugged features – a dream for those artists who do crap caricatures by Spanish beaches – but that's as far as the analysis goes because he doesn't want to find anything else in common with him. Even though he's been like a proper Dad today with rubbish jokes and chit-chat. That must've been what Mam fell for...*

So he listens to Mam and Orla's running commentary on the outfits and dances as if they're bloody pros. It's all feathers, feet positions and technique.

They've already seen Doctor Who *– he was happy with that* seeing as Kylie was in it – and EastEnders, *a bit of a cracker when Bradley Branning found out his wife was banging his old man. He's sat through all of that because it's rare to have everyone in the same room at the same time. Mam has earned this, he thinks, she always throws everything into Christmas, saves all her money from her £5-an-hour jobs to make sure no one goes short. And he hasn't. He can't move he's so full.*

He checks his watch: there's only an hour and a bit to go. Mikey has bagsied the late film, The Motorcycle Diaries, *because he loves Che Guevara. And he wants to see what South America is like, see the landscape where Vicky has been. She's in Australia now and still on at him in her emails to visit. For one thing, he couldn't handle people talking in fake Aussie accents and ending their sentences with a higher inflection.*

And another, well, he'd be mad to go.

Life is on the up here: he's applied for a job at the Apple shop in Regent Street in London. It's a Specialist position, which is a fancy word for salesman, but imagine going to work every day there – it's a flagship store, which was Europe's first and the world's largest branch when it opened in 2004. He's been up there for a recce – he stood outside for ages just taking it in. It's the grandest building, a listed one built in 1898, all arches and windows. Inside, he couldn't believe how airy it was compared to the rabbit hutch of his shop. The Genius Bar alone is fourteen metres long! There's a theatre there, a kids' area and workshops. It's like a religion, but a cool one.

That's where he wants to end up because the iPhone is incredible. One million were sold within seventy-four days of it going on sale in June. And it wasn't even launched in the UK until November. Mikey reaches for his to give it some love. His manager still calls them carphones, the prick. God, it's beautiful, *he thinks, smoothing its rounded edges. He was one of those saddoes who queued up at midnight to get his hands on one when it first came out. Totally worth that. It can't connect to the Internet without wifi – yet – and it's a bit slow but it's incredible enough to have an entire computer in your hand. Steve Jobs somehow managed to shrink Apple's desktop system and put it in people's palms. It's the design too: like, there's no buttons. It's just a screen which you can pinch and zoom and double-tap. It's so simple, intuitive. Being able to touch the screen directly: it makes it feel part of you. But the thing that excites him the most is that, last month, Apple took the decision to allow anyone, not just their employees, to develop* software for it. Some clever bastards had managed to jailbreak it within days of the iPhone's release so people could install software not approved by Apple. It means anyone, even him, could come up with a game or business or entertainment application and they can be sold from an online shop.

Mikey feels an electricity inside him, as if he's plugged in, recharging.

But hold tight, he thinks, because there's other stuff happening. Like if he leaves here, he'll never know how Mam really is because she'd tell him nothing. She gets these tummy aches which make her double up, he's seen it, but she won't go to the doctor. Dad is oblivious. And Orla's just started uni in London so he can't worry her. She is loved up with a bloke she met on the first night at a freshers' party: she's been texting him non-stop and he's not playing it cool either. It's amazing to see how she can love without fear.

The only person he can behave like that with is Vicky. Not that it's 'love' love, just the safety of knowing she won't blow him out or go hot and cold. God, he misses her. He thought he'd be okay, having coped with her going off to university. But then she was on the end of a phone or would come back to see him. Now he depends on her emails for contact. He has found a new openness through the written word: like he can say things he couldn't say so boldly to her face.

They're like little confessions: how he feels about Mam and Dad, his job, the people he's hanging out with, the band he's sort of joined and the girl he's seeing, who's a bit like you, he'd said, but not as funny. She's all right, a friend of the drummer, not like the last bird who started asking how many kids he wanted on their third date. But there's still this empty space where Vicky should be. When she says she misses him, and wishes he was there with her, his jumpy insides are soothed into a calm: feeling wanted and anchored is what she does to him.

It was weird having to find some new people to go out with. He got talking to someone at a gig soon after Vicky went and he ended up having a jamming session with his band. He had nothing else happening so he started going to their practice nights regular, like. It's tidy because there's no real talking, just playing. Their name is quite good too: Going To The Dogs sounds like something Jarvis Cocker would sing. They should try writing their own stuff though rather than do shit Oasis covers. But then he's not a proper member and it serves a purpose so he's not going to get into an argument *about it. The rest of the time he's upstairs in his room teaching himself how to code. It's sort of taken over his head. Like, ever since he started programming, he sees algorithms everywhere. When you cook, say, you have a starting point, with the ingredients, you follow steps in a sequential order, then you have an end product. It's really satisfying because nothing else in his life runs according to any bloody rules.*

As Dad starts to snore, he wonders what Vicky is doing now. Probably still asleep as it's Boxing Day morning in Australia. She emailed on her Christmas Day, they did the whole 'chuck a prawn on the barbie' on Bondi. It's so naff, but somehow she can get away with it. He wonders what's up with Kat – what a fucking state she's in. She never emails him, lets Vicky do it and so he only gets her version of things. It sounds like Kat's going a bit funny, like she's trying to prove she's wild and crazy. Vicky hasn't said as much but there are lots of exclamation marks following her antics. Probably all that freedom. They've had a couple of rows too. Vicky said she went mad when they arrived in Australia because she'd hated South America: she's gone off with blokes and left Vicky in clubs by herself. That's not good. He'd try to talk some sense into Kat if he was there – or take Vicky away from it all, make her feel good. As for blokes, she doesn't say if there is anyone but he hopes not, which he knows is tight and double-standards, it's just he doesn't want her to be taken for a ride. That's all.

He sent an email this morning, told her about Midnight Mass, when he nodded off because he'd been to an indie night with Orla and they'd got wrecked. He smiles remembering Mam tutting with a 'what would the baby Jesus think?'. Then he hears Orla going on at him last night to get together with Vicky: he had to spell it out. They've got a platonic friendship, he doesn't think of her that way. She's cute, very, but he couldn't snog her. Orla asked if it was more like she was a sister. But that isn't it – the way he feels towards Orla is protective, like she's little, and they had blood in common. But Vicky is his equal and it's special because they chose, and choose, to be mates. Orla just slurred that she didn't get it and then bounced off to the dance floor. People didn't – they never had done, that a boy and a girl could get on without sex being involved. But hand on heart he'd never seen her as female. He couldn't even tell you if she had big boobs or not. Why did people have to reduce everything to a poke? Although this girl, Nadia, she was fit, and they were building up to it. That's how he liked it, which apparently was weird for a bloke: he didn't trust anyone enough to give them one from the off.

'Anyone for a turkey sandwich?' Mam says, getting up.

Obviously Dad suddenly wakes up and says, 'Yes, with salt and lots of butter.'

'I'll do it, Mam,' Mikey says, 'you've been on your feet all day.'

'Brown sauce on mine, Mike.' He sticks two fingers up at Orla's cheeky chops.

'Nothing for me. I'm full as an egg,' Mam says, patting her stomach. He hopes that's because she's eaten too much and not that she feels poorly. Her face is bright though, so he takes her word for it. 'Use the nice bread. That's what it's there for.'

He loves his Mam for thinking Mother's Pride is posh. He bends down to give her a kiss.

'Today's been magic, Mam,' he says, then he jumps into a boxer's stance. 'Fancy more of this tomorrow?'

She was brilliant on the old Wii Sports earlier, she's got a massive right hook. He'd got it for Christmas from all of them. He never thought he'd get them to join in a bit of gaming, but fair dos, they all had a go. Even Dad, he had to do the football, didn't he? He couldn't help but have a dig at why Mikey would want to play sport on the computer but not the real thing. But Mikey let it go.

'No, love, I've taken early retirement. Like your father should do,' she says, digging her elbow into him. 'Eh, Bryn?'

There's a voluntary redundancy deal at the railway where he's an engineer and she wants him to give it up. She thinks he'll stop boozing if he gets out of there, because he drinks with his workmates.

It'll take a fuck load more than that, Mikey thinks, as Dad just tells her to 'give it a break, Bernadette, today of all days'.

'Is there enough for me to make some sandwiches to take to work tomorrow?' Mikey asks, shaking his head that he has to go in and open up at 6 a.m. for some sad fuckers to buy a phone with £20 off. He offered to do the shift because some of the staff have kids. And he needs the money. He doesn't know what for yet, maybe for his first month's rent if he gets the job in London. Maybe Vicky could flat-share with him?

'Of course, love, I did an extra leg for sandwiches,' Mam says, taking a sip of her Irish coffee, then she tuts. 'It's not right, the shops opening tomorrow. What have we become?'

Mikey shrugs because he can't show her he's as pissed off as her.

70

'I've got New Year off so it's all right.'

Into the tiny kitchen, he flicks the switch and as the fluorescent tube flickers into life, he hopes it's the start of a new dawn. That 2008 will be his year. It has to be, he thinks, because it's about time he had one.

Chapter Seven

K

Penllyn, just outside Cowbridge

Kate was more nervous tonight than before her reunion with Vee, who was coming for dinner.

While they'd hugged spontaneously last week, out of the sheer dramatics of their first face-to-face in years, this was different: the initial surprise had gone. Wary now, Kate was fearful that there may not be anything deeper, the art of friendship was about sustaining it when the fireworks had finished.

There were colleagues at work, such as fifty-something Lowri, who was more like a substitute mother, and of course her sister Charlie, but never again had she found a replacement for Vee. She wouldn't allow herself that pleasure after what she had done. So this was her chance for atonement.

That was Jack's influence: once she'd read Vee's message, she had panicked, taking it out on her body with a crucifying hilly run in the winding country lanes, slipping on mud, lacerated by the rain. What if Vee had wanted a scene? What if it threw up all the old pain? What if she had found out what had happened between her and Mikey?

But as she soaked in the antique tub of their old cottage, Jack had taken his ever-present pencil from behind his ear and challenged her cons with a pretend list of pros on his palm. What, on the other hand, if she had missed you and wanted to be friends again? More buts, but inside her head: she'd have to explain how she went off the rails, sleeping around, the night that changed her life, the diagnosis, the aftermath. Waves of self-loathing had descended as hard as they'd come so frequently years before. The memory of the lights in the unit, the gulping for air, serrated, bleeding. Jack had pulled her from the bath and folded her naked into his heart.

'I can live with how you are forever and a day, but I'm worried you won't be able to,' he'd said as her tears merged with the bathwater from her dripping body, the smell of turps and woodstain on his old T-shirt calming her. Filling in for her father's lack of support, which still hurt her. The prospect of letting light in on the old ravaged twisted roots of wretchedness had been horrifying: for so long she'd covered them up. But that hadn't stopped their thorns from piercing her skin. Perhaps the only way she could hack them down would be to confront them. She knew as she lay in Jack's arms she couldn't carry on like this. She needed to come to terms with her past. She needed to prove that in her stoic silence she wasn't becoming her mother.

Taking that with her to their meeting in Fromage, Kate's worry had evaporated when she'd found Vee as warm and sunny as she'd always been. It had felt so natural to invite her over for a kitchen supper, which was where she was now.

Wringing her hands, Kate made a final check of the creaking house. Griffy was here on his weekly sleepover so her sister and brother-in-law could have a quiet night to themselves which meant her earlier tidying had been for nothing. But she wouldn't have it any other way – this was her inner sanctum, this reflected who she was.

Then, above the cries from upstairs where Jack was getting covered in bathwater by Griff, she heard a car mush the gravel on the overgrown drive.

Her heart beating, she rushed to open the door and was confronted by a row of knuckles.

'Well, that would've been a good start,' Vee said, laughing as she retrieved her fist, 'battering the host in the face.'

Kate was still clutching her chest. 'Lucky we've got such a ferocious guard dog.' Boris was lying on his back and wagging his tail.

'Aw, look at him,' Vee said, bending down to tickle his tummy. Kate watched her make a fuss: it was uncomplicated with a dog, everyone knew what to do with an exposed belly. But human beings were far more complex.

Vee presented a bottle – 'Hope it's okay, Dad forced it on

73

me so...' – and they worked out what sort of physical contact would be appropriate. They settled on a kiss on the cheek: they had to proceed with caution.

She hung up Vee's tweed cape, learning it was a charity shop find, a skill Vicky had held onto when she became Vee, and headed towards the kitchen down the narrow hallway.

'Is it shoes on or shoes off?' Vee asked, still on the mat in boots. Kate felt a stab of sorrow that her oldest friend had to ask the house rules, so long had they been apart.

'Whatever you fancy. In here, you can even sit on the sofa in jeans,' she said, referring to her mother's strict no-denim on the upholstery policy of their childhood.

'I like your top,' Kate said, following the rules of female engagement with compliments.

'Oh, this old thing,' Vee said, chucking her DMs, playing along as she pulled on the baggy zebra-print T-shirt which she wore over leggings and woolly knee-high socks. It felt good to know they were both laying the foundations together. 'You look in such good shape. Do you go jogging or go to the gym or...?'

'Bits and pieces, whatever I feel like, really,' Kate said, hiding that she ran and ran and ran until she out-sprinted the demons.

'Red or white?'

'Whatever's open. I thought about driving but Dad gave me a lift and a tenner for a cab, bless him. Called it pocket money, as if I'm ten!'

Kate took three glasses off the Welsh dresser and poured red all round. 'Jack'll be down in a minute,' she said. Then at the sound of a stampede of feet, she said, 'Talk of the devil.'

First to enter the kitchen though was Griffy, the sight of whom never failed to melt Kate. At each stage of his development, she never thought perfection could be topped. Yet she was wrong, as his delicious newborn smell gave way to adorable podgy wrists and his delightful first steps were trumped by his toddler pot belly. Now seven and skinny as a rake, in spite of his never-ending appetite, his ribbed chest and puny arms took her absolute hostage. 'Where's your pyjama top, you rascal?' she said, grabbing and kissing him over and over.

'Aunty Katieeee, stop it!' he said, giggling as he tried to wriggle out of her grasp.

'Never!' she said, smiling, thanking God for this boy's spirit which had rescued her.

Banging his head on a beam as ever, Jack filled the room as he appeared, panting and ruddy-cheeked from the chase.

He threw Griff's *Star Wars* top at Kate, then his Hagrid hand, a broad grin and a booming 'hello' at Vee.

'Pleased to meet you! And who's this?' Vee asked, gazing at Griff.

Suddenly shy, he covered his blue eyes with luxurious lashes and ruffled his beautiful shaggy brown hair.

'My nephew. Charlie's little one,' Kate said, bursting with pride.

'I'm the tenth oldest in the class,' he said, wrapping his arm around her thigh. She loved the randomness of his reply.

'Runs in the family, doesn't it?' Vee's acknowledgements of the little boy's DNA caught Kate right in the throat.

Hoarsely, she directed Griffy to the lounge for milk and biscuits. Jack would put him to bed while she got dinner ready.

He skipped off still topless and Jack pursued him, mimicking his light steps.

'He's a cutie,' Vee said, then adding with embarrassment that she meant Griff not Jack.

Kate smiled. 'They're pretty much on the same wavelength.'

She wanted to brag about Griff: his reading, football trophies, his adventurous palette but she stopped herself because she didn't want Vee to say what people always said when they'd seen her with Griff: 'You'd make such a good mum.'

Kate took a big glug of wine instead.

Vee then swept her arm around the kitchen and sighed with pleasure. 'It's lovely here, Kate. So... rustic.'

'In estate agency speak, rustic means dilapidated and full of cobwebs! That's how this place was before we did it up. That's not to say it's finished, because it isn't. But I like it like this.' Not perfect, a work in progress, a symbol of how she felt inside. 'Oh God, I've completely forgotten to ask if you're still a vegetarian?' She racked her brains to work out what she could rustle up if Vee was. It was another reminder of their separation and Kate inwardly cringed.

'Nope. I started eating meat again when I got back to Mum and Dad's. It was bad enough turning up at theirs needing some

TLC, imagine if I'd started banging on about beans and nut cutlets? I'd had enough of that anyway. I was vegan for years because of Jez, well, apart from my secret cheese stash. I used to feel terrible about that, but now, well, I wish I'd shoved a salami up his arse.'

Vee's honesty combined with the wine began to warm Kate up.

'Ha! Well, I've made a cawl, Jack's mum's recipe, lamb shanks, swedes, carrots, spuds. It'll be about half an hour.'

'Oh, I haven't had a proper Welsh cawl in forever. It smells amazing.'

Vee took a seat at the table and Kate joined her, happy she felt relaxed enough to make herself at home. There was something she wanted to say to her before she got tipsy: to show she meant it sincerely.

'Any news on the job front?' Kate asked to test the ground.

'Yeah, not great. I've applied for loads of stuff but not heard anything yet. It'll take time, I suppose.'

Kate took a deep breath and began. 'Well, say if you think this is a bad idea, but I've had a word with Pierre...'

She waited to see Vee's reaction – and bingo, her eyes opened wide with interest.

'Go on.'

'He's looking for an assistant. He needs someone very quickly, as you could probably tell from your visit! I asked if there was any way he would have a chat about it with you. Only if you fancied it? I mean, I know it's not mega-bucks and it's a drive from yours, but it could tide you over.'

Vee took a long drink and Kate teetered in the middle of not knowing if she would see her as interfering or kind. Her soul didn't just jump but flick-flacked disproportionately for joy when Vee gave her a thumbs up. This was the start of Kate making amends. She needed to do this – to come to terms with her past in her own way, to find peace and resolution.

'That would be brilliant! Oh, Kate, that's exactly what I need. A quick buck is all I'm after at the moment. I'm still a bit all over the place.'

'I'll give you Pierre's number so you can call him.'

Vee pumped her left fist. 'All that cheese!'

'He did say he'd throw in lunch every day.'

'How do you know Pierre, then? What's he doing in Wales?

He seems very… British for a bloke with a French name.'

'He's Jack's best mate. They met doing some kind of survival boy scout thing, you know, a weekend in the Brecon Beacons being shouted at by an ex-SAS bloke. Skinning rabbits and hedgehogs. His father is English, his mum is French, she was some bigwig at the embassy so he was brought up in London, hence his cut-glass British accent. No one has ever heard him even speak French. He did the whole privileged kid wanting to get back to basics, that's why he moved here. Cheese is his passion, as you might have noticed. He's just eccentric. In a nice way.'

'Shit. Talking of bonkers,' Vee said, half-choking on her wine, 'I saw Mikey the other day.'

Hearing his name out loud was like a clatter of thunder. She had to get up. Couldn't risk Vee seeing her panic.

'Really?' Kate said from behind the safety of the fridge door. What the hell was he doing here?

'Yes! It was so weird. Just after I'd messaged him, same as I'd messaged you.'

The shelves began to swirl before her eyes. She should never have got involved in this. How did she think she could do this without him coming into it? Why did she believe she deserved to have Vee back? 'I actually bumped into him and his girlfriend on the beach at Barry Island. Like, not seen him in yonks, then boom. This is Wales, mind, you can't leave the house for seeing someone you recognize. Anyway, I was walking the dog and having a bit of a cry into the wind. Standard at the moment.'

Kate picked up the mayo jar and held it up against her hot forehead, glad Vee couldn't see her.

'I tell you what though, he was so incredibly rude. Made it clear he wasn't interested in catching up.'

Thank God he didn't say anything, Kate thought, feeling the tension draining from her body, taking out some basil for the garnish.

'It was really disappointing. How much he'd changed.'

Arrogant, bullish, wild. In a black cloud.

'To think I used to idolize him. Well, you know how I felt about him, you were there. He never did answer my letter.'

Kate's heart stopped. The letter. She could still see it in her hand, creased from the travelling, shaking as she retrieved it from her bag. She dug a fingernail into her wrist to drown her shame with pain. Searching to make sense of it all, she needed to know why he was in Wales. That night, he'd said that he'd had enough. He was leaving and would never come back. She had made double sure she wouldn't see him again even by accident by moving here into the sticks. And it had worked until now. Please, let it not be karma bringing them both back on the scene...

'What was he doing? Being here?' she asked, over her shoulder, the words like razor blades.

'Said he was showing his girlfriend the sights. Who, by the way, was stunning. Obviously.'

Was that envy, Kate wondered, fearing Vee still held a flame for him because where would that lead? Panicking, she reasoned that no, she couldn't have, not after all this time, especially as she'd said he was up himself. Oblivious, Vee carried on.

'Maybe he was just visiting? Who knows? Oh well, I guess it just wasn't meant to be. The. End.'

Only now with Vee's verbal white flag could Kate's defences stand down.

'Life moves on, people change. That's the way it is.'

Kate shut her eyes with relief: it was the full stop on the subject of Mikey.

Jack arrived at the right moment, asking for his drink.

'You ladies been talking about the wedding then? Favours and colour schemes and flowers?' He pulled a simpering face.

'He's being funny,' Kate told Vee. 'We'd rather not have a big day, would we?'

'I'm saying nothing,' Jack said, looking at Kate but hissing 'her mother' out of the corner of his mouth to Vee.

'When is it?' Vee asked, sitting up, amused.

'July the first.'

'So how did you two meet?' Vee was generously all ears and Kate relaxed, relieved the Mikey talk had passed.

Jack told their love story: how they'd met at an auction three years ago, he was buying furniture and she was representing a client. Their first date was afternoon tea – 'Jack's from the nineteenth century, even though he's three years younger than me,' Kate chipped in – and then twelve months later, they'd moved into a rented place in Cowbridge. But when this ivy-clad cottage came up, Kate and Jack had pounced. He'd proposed in Brighton – yes, how strange that they'd both been there– and the rest was history. Vee gave a little round of applause but Kate sighed.

'I wish we could run away and elope. But, you know...'

Jack put his arm around her in solidarity. Kate wrapped herself in him then, loving him so very deeply, from his emotional intelligence and sense of humour to his perennial combat shorts come rain or shine and his fair eyelashes. And then she felt sorry because Vee was looking serious. It had been insensitive of them to rub her nose in their love.

But when she spoke, Kate realized she'd read her wrong.

'Well, for what it's worth, I reckon you should do what you want to do, the two of you. What I've learned from the whole mess of Jez and Brighton and all of that is that you need to be true to yourself. That's where I went wrong. Like, losing Jez was hard but realizing I'd lost myself was harder.'

Loss. Kate knew all about that. But she felt as if she was on the brink of some kind of recovery. So as Jack rattled around finding plates and swore at the pot of cawl which seared through an old tea towel into his finger, Kate found a stillness, a serenity.

For what Vee had dared to offer was an opinion on her life which showed she cared. It represented a breakthrough: that they could forge a new kind of friendship.

And they had crossed a hurdle, surviving the tempest which had threatened with talk of Mikey.

The past was gone. Thank God for Vee for being so uncomplicated and forgiving: now they had a second roll of the dice at friendship. Now she and Vee had a future together.

Chapter Eight

V

Cardiff City Centre

Vee hadn't even set eyes on him but she was already cross with Mikey-Murphy, whoever he was for choosing this wanky bar.

With her tragic duffle coat and bobble hat, she stuck out like a sore thumb in this painfully hipster place, which was called Work Life Balance. Yes, really.

He hadn't even warned her that it didn't have a sign on the door, so she'd been up and down the low-lit dingy road in the arse end of the city centre until she saw some activity halfway up and deduced this was it. Why choose this pretentious out-of-the-way place? What was wrong with a bloody local?

She surveyed the bar, which had two graffitied arrows pronouncing this area was 'Work' while downstairs was 'Life', and it sent her heckles supersonic.

The stern-looking staff were dressed in shiny grey shoulder-padded eighties suits and ties. Eye-roll. The bar was a long desk decorated with awful beige plastic telephones and synthetic pot plants and there was a water cooler in the corner. How conceptual. Swivelling office chairs were coupled with filing cabinets for tables, framed briefcases were on the walls, a screen played footage of office life through the ages and the windows were covered by ugly metal blinds. Über sigh.

Oh, it was so clever and so ironic. God, Brighton was never this try-hard. Why would anyone come here after a nine-to-five? Yet it was rammed with some too-cool-for-school characters who were checking her out like she was the freak show.

What was she doing here? Okay, Mikey had clearly had a

change of heart, pinging her this week to see if she wanted a drink. It was only polite for her to agree, seeing as she'd started the whole thing off. But really, it was obvious they weren't going to get on. His Facebook feed was full of showboating, he'd been rude on the beach and this place joined all the dots: he wasn't who he had been. She couldn't deny she was curious though. And she conceded she still had the tiniest hope that maybe they'd have a connection: her heart needed a reconnection out of sheer loneliness. Because she'd once shared everything with him. And it had worked out with Kate – lovely Kate, who was proving to be an anchor for her. They messaged regularly, Vee had an interview lined up at Fromage and Kate, although jaded perhaps from life, was willing to listen to her misery. What if Mikey...

Stop it, she commanded herself. Dear God, she was an optimistic fool sometimes.

More likely, she'd get some closure today: see that she was better off without him.

She'd stay for one, then go. The irony didn't escape her that the alternative of being back on the sofa with Mum for the second half of the Corrie double bill was more attractive than being in this place.

There were no seats here so she went downstairs, stomping every step, dreading whatever preposterous the cellar had in store. But when she got there, she saw, in actual fact, that 'Life' was beautiful.

Quiet and cosy, battered leather love seats and wing-back chairs looking inviting in the cosy glow of light which came from lamps sat on ornate iron tables A log burner glowed in one of three walls papered with black and white velvet flowers. The end wall was a sea of white bricks and swirled with a projection of the Northern Lights. Hanging baskets of shiny green leaves edged the room, while the sound of the sea accompanied the murmur of voices. Less busy and more chilled, it was such a contrast to the clinical vibe upstairs. No wonder he'd picked this place: Mikey's life was beautiful and he wanted her to know it.

'What can I get you?' a man in black said. 'A Gintini?'

'A what-ini?'

'Like a Martini, but with gin. We're famous for them.'

A cocktail wasn't her style – she was a pint of cider or a glass of white kind of person – but it could be thrown down the hatch quickly.

'Right, yes, go on then. Please. Thanks.'

'I'll bring it over to you. Where are you sit—'

'Here,' said a voice. 'With me, butt. My usual table.'

The voice belonged to Mikey, still rich with an accent and unpolished with slang. He had come up from behind her. Probably with a swagger.

'Hi,' she said, turning round, forcing a smile, something she'd never had to do with him before.

'All right?' he said. His hair was just a little bit longer than when she saw him on the beach. But the regrowth had changed him, making him look less skinhead, more approachable.

Then he moved his weight from one foot to another and rubbed his hands. Christ, talk about awkward.

'Yeah, so, this is nice…' she said, approaching the table and taking a seat. Right on top of his coat, which had probably cost a squillion quid. 'Sorry,' she muttered, switching to the opposite seat and messing about with her duffle and bag.

He was looking at her in the most uncomfortable way. She panicked and started talking.

'Lush in here, isn't it? Makes me feel, like, all Christmassy even though it's March and—'

Slowly, he raised both of his hands to stop her, his almost-black eyes wide. 'I'm sorry. I was a total dick.'

'You what?' She felt her forehead scrumple up like a pug's. This was not how she'd thought this rendezvous would go.

'I said I'm sorry and I was a total dick.' He looked pained by his admission. He clearly wasn't used to rolling over in defeat.

'Oh, right. Okay,' she said, 'I didn't expect that.' She gave a small laugh because she'd just made the understatement of the year. He was supposed to be an arsehole not asking her forgiveness. Her drink appeared – in a cocking jam jar – so she slugged back a very alcoholic mouthful. She needed time to process this before she spoke.

'It was just a bit weird… to see you on Barry Island the other day,' he said, looking to her to give him some slack.

A bit weird? It had been insane. Like, you didn't see someone for eight years then within days of messaging him your dog covers him in wet sand. It was almost fate – not that she'd say it because he'd spit his drink all over her. She took another swig and felt her stunned rictus expression relax as the gin entered her blood stream.

'And I wanted to apologize to you for being a bit off. You know.' He shifted an eyebrow: she knew of old that this meant he needed some help here. They used to call it his SOS Eyebrow. Vee could only give him a stuttering nod.

'So I'm sorry.' He heaved a breath and added: 'I swear on Jarvis Cocker's life.'

And there it was: the pledge they used to make when they were sharing a bit of gossip from school. He was trying to communicate that inside the man standing before her was the boy who'd been her best friend. Then as if he needed to show he meant it, he made a sign of the cross and kissed his fingers like the Pope. It was exactly what he used to do when he did an impression of his mother. The scar from the night he tried to punch his dad, my God, it was still there, she noticed, seeing the faded jagged edge on his left hand. He wanted to make peace, she realized, and he was saying that he was still the same. How she wanted to believe it.

Lost for words, she touched his arm to convey she was on board. But that made her flap because he had a muscly bulge where there used to be a snowman's stick. The surprise leapt out of her mouth before she'd had time to process it.

'Don't tell me you work out!' she said, at once feeling a right idiot. Because it revealed she'd noticed his physique. But she had to make it clear that she hadn't done so in a pervy way. Oh God, he was going to think she was crushing on him. And she wasn't. That was all in the past, those feelings she thought she might've had. 'What I meant was, you used to hate PE!'

'These guns,' he said, pointing to his biceps which peeked out from his nicely cut black V-neck T-shirt, 'are actually from years of playing pool.'

She laughed naturally: his deadpan had always tickled her. A chink of familiarity crept in. And it was then she decided to meet him halfway because she had to be a grown-up. She was exhausted with carrying all these emotions on top of her despair about Jez. It was time not to sweep the past under the carpet but to let it go. Free herself of the questions of why he'd dropped her and accept you couldn't lug suitcases of history around with you – what was the point of harking back all those years to when they were still kids? It wasn't as if they would recover their friendship. This felt more like a handshake and a let's move on.

'Look, shall we just forget all the stuff that happened before...' She bit her lip wondering if this would be enough for him to understand what she was referring to. 'Because it doesn't really matter now, does it?'

He opened his mouth, paused, gave a small neat nod and then took a long mouthful of what was left of his pint, some sort of craft beer judging by the fancy glass: he'd been here a while, she realized, probably needing a run-up and some courage.

A weight toppled off her shoulders. It was as if she'd been freed from the past: sometimes, she now realized, you didn't need to dig over old ground. Part of being an adult was to know when to acquiesce, to settle for a ceasefire. She couldn't picture them as close friends ever again – they lived in different worlds now. But they could finish this moment on good terms.

'You look really well,' he said, crossing his legs, settling back into his chair.

'Hardly,' she scoffed because the upheaval with Jez had brought her out in spots. 'But I'll be getting rid of these as soon as I can afford it,' she said, pulling at the pink in her hair. 'They're a bit too Brighton.'

'That's where you've been?'

'Yep. Not going back though. Long story.' There was no need to elaborate: they were simply following a procedure now of pleasant small talk before they parted ways. She slurped her drink but kept a little bit at the bottom because it would be a bit premature to up and go now. But he saw and signalled to the barman for two more.

'Oh God, no,' she said, holding up a palm. 'Not for me.' She only had twenty quid to last her. The drinks were a bit pricey in here.

'I insist. Mate, here's my card for the tab.'

Vee watched him hand a black bit of plastic to the barman. From her years on a till, she recognized it as an exclusive one. He wasn't going places, he was already there. But he'd caught her 'there's posh' face.

'I do loads of travelling,' he said. 'It's a company card, gives me access to airport lounges and upgrades and stuff.'

'Oh, right, yes, I saw on your Facebook that you get about a bit. What do you do?'

'App development. I write code for apps people use on their

phones.'

'Like Angry Birds?' She felt stupid but that was about the breadth of her knowledge.

'Sort of. I did a game once, Smash The Suburbs. That did okay. But corporate stuff is my bag. The apps you use to shop on your phone, that kind of thing.'

'Wow!' Another Gintini landed before her. 'It sounds so...' She didn't know what because she wasn't up on technology. She had an old cracked iPhone which she used for calls and texts and not much else. Not knowing what to say, she went for a joke. '...I mean, you've done so well. You've even got your own table here!'

But his face went tight. 'My mate owns this place. He's been struggling a bit, there are so many places to drink in Cardiff now, so when I'm here I try to bring him a bit of business.'

'So you don't live here full-time?' she asked, surprisingly deflated. 'With your girlfriend?' She gave an inner wince as she said it because she had promised herself she wouldn't ask about his love life - she didn't care. It was just nosiness.

'Er, no. We've not been together long.' He looked uncomfortable at that, which had made the question worthwhile to wipe the smug off him. And he wasn't gushing about her, which would've made her want to vom. 'I'm based in London. But I can work anywhere really so I come here to check in on Dad. He's still a pisshead.'

'Oh, I'm sorry. How's your mam?'

He dipped his chin a millimetre. Shit. Something was up.

'She died six years ago. Cancer. Wish the old man had got it instead. But...' He blinked quickly a few times and she saw it still hurt.

'Oh, God, that's awful. I didn't realize,' she said, her hands to her heart, genuinely upset because she knew how much he'd adored her. And then she felt the sorrow of not having been in his life when he'd lost her. Then the confirmation, again, that their relationship was over. How could it recover when you'd missed a life-shattering event that once you'd have always assumed you'd be there for?

'And Orla?' she said, deliberately upbeat, because it felt inappropriate to try to share his grief.

'Yeah, good. Loved up. Saving up for a flat with her fella so she's living with me for now.'

'Here?' Vee's heart leapt because she would love to see her. They'd got on like sisters: she often tagged along when Mikey and Vee were out and about or round her house. Mum had had a soft spot for her and would invite her for tea when Mikey came over. And Vee would always give her her old clothes.

'No. In London.'

'Oh, that's a shame.'

'Well, there's nothing to stop you from getting in touch with her.' There was a hint of spite in there: she felt accused of something somehow. But she wouldn't chase Orla up; this had put her right off jumping out of any more cakes. She looked at her watch: if she could wrap this up in five minutes, then she'd be able to get the next bus.

'Well, you seem to be doing well, which is good.'

'Yep,' he said, again drinking but not taking his eyes off her.

Again she panicked and put her foot in it.

'So how did that happen then?'

He laughed out loud and she felt the embarrassment of it coming out a bit too cynically.

'Taught myself. Worked hard. University of Life.' It was a jab at her, the privileged one whose mummy and daddy had paid for her to go. He waited to see if she'd bite. Annoyed, she said nothing and held his stare.

'What you up to then?' he asked.

'Oh, stuff. You know.' She felt a right flop. It was time to go: she'd rather leave before she had to pretend life was rosy. 'Look, I'm really sorry but I'm going to have to go.' She began to drain her glass.

'Right, yep,' he said, playing with the strap of one of those heart rate fitness steps a day things. 'Kids, eh?'

She coughed on her gin.

'Kids? You mean, as in me?' The irony of it. She'd never been further away from having kids. And then she felt even worse because clearly she must look mumsy for him to say that.

'I thought that's what you meant.' He took his lighter off the table which had been on top of a pack of fags and began to play with it, making sparks.

'No. God, no. I haven't got any. Only nieces. Gav's got two. Sweet but knackering.'

'Where are you now then?' he said.

It was the question she'd been dreading. She considered

making something up: some kind of elaborate story which put her here, there and everywhere. It was far too embarrassing to fess up. The temptation to tell him anything loomed. She was going to leave in three slurps' time and she'd never see him again. They hadn't had that spark they'd once had: there were no common denominators upon which to build any relationship. But then he looked at his phone – he didn't mean to be rude but he was waiting for a business call from the States. He was telling her his time was precious, that he was worldwide, baby. The prick. That was it: why should she lie? Why should she try to impress him?

'I'm in my old bedroom, under my pony duvet, remember? I have no house, no job, no money, no mates. I've been dumped by the love of my life, or at least I thought he was but he turned out to be a spineless shitbag.' She held her chin high to show she was unafraid.

'Oh, harsh,' he said, pursing his lips, as if he'd just heard someone smash a glass rather than she had messed up her entire life.

'Yep. I'm a loser. It says so on my CV.'

'That's too bad, like.' He was expressionless: he couldn't even offer her fake concern.

'You know, it is. In many, many ways.' But faced with his superiority act, she found some self-respect. She took a slurp. 'But actually it's also very liberating. Having nothing makes me realize how much shit people carry around with them. I sort of feel freer.'

He swallowed, taking the dig. She took a second slurp.

'I'm in the position where I can start again.'

He gave her a sarky nod. Only a leaden hand-clap was missing.

Slurp three. 'It's terrifying but it's also life-affirming.'

Now he tilted his head to the side as if she was talking utter crap.

Fuck you, she thought, taking a fourth slurp. She had nothing to be ashamed of. In fact she was pleased with herself because she hadn't realized until now that that was the way to look at her situation. She might have spouted it out, fuelled by two Gintinis and years of reading *Psychologies* mag, but incredibly it made sense. This was a turning point and she felt like thanking Mikey for bringing it to the fore. Okay, their friendship was done and she felt sad and sour, but she was fine with it. This meeting had ended her mourning period for Mikey. He didn't exist anymore. This new version, this mark II named Murphy was sharp and stuck-up and dull. That was why he grandstanded on Facebook. And she was better off without him.

Vee buttoned up the toggles on her coat and pulled down her hat. She didn't care how she looked now: no, that was wrong. She did care actually: it was a revelation but she liked being in her own skin.

'Really good to see you,' he said as she got up, in the tone people used when they were glad an ordeal was over. There would be no hug: she didn't want to touch him again. Even though he'd transformed into a bit of a looker. His personality spoiled it all.

Then she chucked a fiver on the table and felt the release of being free from the hold he'd once had over her.

Heading upstairs and pushing her way through the crowds, she remembered the night she'd asked him to be her back-up man. As much as she hated being alone and as much as she could cope with being loaded, she'd have died a death living in his world. She would've been just as out of place in his as she was in Jez's. What she needed to do, she realized as she emerged into the night, was to find her own path.

Chapter Nine

M

Hackney, April

Murphy heaved himself out of the water onto the paving slabs then shivered as streams ran down his back and chest.

He imagined them traversing thousands of goosebumps, which were like minuscule erections, before seeping into his shorts, then gathering at his thighs to plummet through the forest of hair on his legs. Walking through the steamy air into the cold on his way to the changing rooms, he felt so clean and alive for taking on the elements so early. The sun had been rising when he got in. The last thought he had before he dived in was that the sky had been streaked pink just like Vee's hair. He'd buried his face in the water then and thanked the Lord the sky had turned blue by the time he'd finished. It was going to be a beautiful spring day.

As he showered, dried off and got into his clothes, he swore he could hear the *Rocky* theme tune playing: for it did feel heroic to have swum thirty Olympic lengths at dawn in London Fields' heated lido. It was victorious to be here, smack bang in the greatest city in the world. The losers would only just now be groping for the snooze button. But he was already dressed, wide awake and on it.

He went into the cafe, scanning the tables for Orla. She was in the queue, so he called her name and ordered scrambled eggs and a skinny cap. 'It's on me,' he mouthed but she waved his offer away, then when she approached with a tray, she told him it was her treat.

'You always pay,' she said, her slicked back black wet hair still dripping onto her shoulders. 'And I'm chuffed to bits you came with me.'

'Chuffed to bits?' he said. It was just a swim. Granted, she'd persuaded him to lose his lido virginity and he'd always refused before now. But steady on, like.

'Yes because we don't do much, just us.'

'Whaddyamean? We live together!'

'I mean as in hanging out by ourselves, with no one else around,' she said, slowly, as if he was five years old. 'Like we used to when we were small.'

'That's because no one else would play with us because they thought we were weird.'

Orla laughed. 'They were right! Anyway, you know what I mean, Mikey.'

She was the only one in their group who called him that. Most of the time he was Murphy the free agent and that was how he wanted it, but she made him feel like he belonged to her. That she was the only one now that really knew and accepted him for who he really was.

He took a slurp of his coffee: it was lush, like swallowing a woman in a silk negligee, all sensuous and voluptuous. It was because it was full-fat, he realized, Orla must've forgotten or they didn't have skimmed. He was going to ask but dropped it: she looked so happy.

'It's good here,' he said, to compensate, warming his hands on his cup.

Orla's smile widened, she had a little gap between her two front teeth, just like Mam had had. It made her look eternally childlike, fresh, free of worries, soaking up everything good that life had to offer.

'It's like being on holiday!' she said.

It fucking well wasn't, he thought, not the kind he was used to, but she hadn't been away for a fortnight for years. The snow break in Tignes had only been a few days and whenever he'd tried to coax her abroad with him she refused to be apart for longer than a week from the kids on her client list 'because they had no one else'.

'Tell you what, when you get married, I'll pay for your honeymoon.'

'What? Where did that come from?' she said, eyes agog.

How could he explain that he wanted to make life better for her, that the way she planned meals to the last penny using

90

Value ingredients broke his heart?

'Just been thinking it for a while,' he lied.

'We haven't even thought about a wedding. Phil and I have to get a place first. I reckon we'll still be engaged when we've got grandchildren. He sometimes says we'll go down the aisle on Zimmer frames!'

Orla's eyes creased up at the joke, which wasn't that funny to be honest. But if Phil still made her happy after eight years that's all he cared about. Even if the thought of meeting someone on your first night at uni, sticking with them all the way through that and then staying together when there was temptation and distraction at every corner made him feel queasy.

Then when she'd stopped laughing, she looked at him really intently.

'What?' he said, feeling to see if he had any snot under his nose.

'You. Like, I can see you feel sorry for me.'

'I don't!' he scoffed, glad to see their food coming. 'What you having?'

'Porridge, fruit, jam and toast. On a load of case visits today, so God knows when I'll eat again.'

He closed his eyes and inhaled the thick eggy smell then opened one eye to see she was still looking at him with her eyebrows raised to the roof.

'You don't have to, you know,' she said, stirring in blueberries and kiwi which muddied her bowl.

'Have to what?' he said, remembering the best eggs he'd ever had, at a hotel in Berlin, scrambled ones, tarted up with pancetta and maille hollandaise.

'Feel sorry for me.'

'Don't talk soft.' He rolled his eyes at her and picked up his phone to check the news. He'd subscribed to a techie feed in Japan and it was about now it'd drop. Nah, not there yet. Which made him feel like he was ahead of the game.

She tucked in and he was stabbed with a memory of her dividing up a pittance of own-brand Frosties into two bowls one morning before school. Mum had been having one of her episodes and Dad had already left for work.

'Do you know why I come here?' she said, changing the subject, thank God.

'They do nice eggs?' he said, through a mouthful, to show he appreciated her buying his brekkie.

'Because,' she said, pointedly, 'it was where I learned to swim. Two years ago.'

He looked up. He didn't know she hadn't been able to swim.

'Serious?'

'Yep. We never had lessons, did we? Too expensive. Mam and Dad never took us either. When we used to go to the caravan in Tenby, they'd never get out of their clothes at the beach, do you remember? Everyone else was in their bathers and Mam would be in her blouse and skirt and Dad would roll his jeans up to his knees. I'd splash about at the edge, but it made me scared to go in. Then when I met Phil, well, he's a real water baby and I'd watch him and think I was missing out. So he helped me. I did something for me even though I was scared.'

'I can't remember how I learned,' he said, ferreting around in his head for a memory of armbands. 'Shit, yes I can. Vicky's dad taught me. When I went camping with them in France that time.' He must've been fifteen. He'd felt a right idiot when Vicky had morphed from a moody teenager like him this side of the channel into a mermaid over there. He'd insisted on wearing his jeans by the pool even though it was boiling, but Bob took him aside that second day and sort of pulled rank on him. 'Now, boy, we haven't come all this way for you to sulk on the side. Your swimmers, get them on.' For some reason, he'd done as he was told; he was all right was Bob. Then when he'd got in and almost drowned, making an utter cock of himself, he'd swallowed his pride and asked Bob to teach him. By the end of the two weeks, he'd practically had gills.

'God, when you went away, that was the longest fortnight of my life. I lived off bread, marg and cold baked beans because Mum was in bed. Dad didn't notice, of course.'

She laughed it off. But it made him feel bitter. Orla would only have been twelve or so. He gripped his knife and fork so hard his knuckles turned white.

'But what I'm trying to say, Mikey, is that it doesn't matter, any of that. I sorted it out myself and Phil got me some lessons for my birthday one year and here I am. Like a bloody sardine, mun.'

'Tidy. There we go then,' he said, impressed.

'So… what I'm trying to say is…'

He stopped mid-munch. Oh my God. He'd wondered what she was going on about and now it finally clicked!

'Do you feel sorry for me?' he said, spraying specks of yellow into the air. 'You do, don't you!'

Orla conceded: 'A bit.' Then she buttered her toast as if she hadn't just said the most fucking ridiculous thing in the world.

'For fuck's sake!' He went to laugh but it came out all plastic.

She looked up at him, took a bite of her toast and started chewing without breaking eye contact. It turned the tables on their birth order: she seemed the older one now.

'That is the single most stupid thing I've ever heard. You feeling sorry for me.' He couldn't get his head round it. He had a charmed life. She was talking crap. Big steaming shovels of it.

'You don't need to protect me, Mikey,' she said. 'That's what I'm trying to say. You should look after yourself a bit more instead.'

'What? My body's a temple.' He flexed his pecs under his hoodie because he had to show her he was happy as.

'Temple of Doom, more like,' she said, poking out her tongue. 'I'm not on about your body or health and you know it!'

'I've got a decent job, two homes. What more would I want?'

'You're not happy though are you? Not really. Yes, materially and professionally, but personally, it's a mess, like you're missing something, like a loose wire or a connection.'

Orla kept eating as bold as you like. She was being a bit cheeky considering. He looked after her, didn't charge her rent, shared everything with her.

He finished off his eggs, feeling her eyes on him all the time, then he put down his knife and fork and pushed his plate to the side.

'Will you cut it out?' he said, lifting his eyes to hers.

'Hashtag just saying, that's all.'

He swirled the dregs of his coffee in his cup. 'Hashtag fuck off, that's all. No offence.'

'None taken,' she said, shrugging. 'It's you who's in denial not me.'

'What do you mean?'

'Look, you're a good person, Mikey, a really good person, but you can't see it. You're a success, definitely, but you've got a deficit of that in your personal life. Your friends aren't really friends, are they? I mean, they all look up to you, but there's no one you really trust, is there? And your love life, well, you just go from one girl to the next for no reason. Like Shell, she was lovely, but as soon as she got close you ended it. It's like you're punishing yourself for dad being a pisshead, Mum dying and Vicky going away.'

'Hang on, that's called drive. If it wasn't for that I wouldn't have what I have. Shell and I are on a break, that's all.'

He hadn't told her that he'd got scared by her sending him a fourth-month anniversary card shortly after their trip to Cardiff. Nor that he was now seeing a bird called Ruby, who he got talking to in a bar after work. She was a bit mad, a posh curator at a gallery, who'd worked in New York and seemed to have a lot going on. That was a perfect combo, because she wouldn't be needy.

'And anyway,' he added, 'what's Vicky go to do with it?'

'That's what you've got to work out for yourself. If I say it, then you'll only think it's bullshit. But you aren't happy. You met your oldest friend and you couldn't be yourself. That's weird, isn't it?'

'Now hang on, I told you why – it was awkward. We had nothing in common. She hadn't changed one bit and I felt sorry for her. Time to move on. End of.'

What he hadn't said was, well, pretty much everything. How hard he'd tried to be decent, to apologize from the off for losing the plot on the beach. He'd even rolled out the Jarvis Cocker pledge and his impression of his Mam, for fuck's sake. But he'd registered her shock as if she had thought he was incapable of humility. He, of all people, who had had his nose up against the windows of everyone else's good fortune. She'd completely failed to understand where he was going with it; that he was willing to forgive her for walking out on him when he was twenty-one. When she hadn't emailed him back with the details of where to meet her in Cambodia. She'd turned her back on him, not the other way round.

Then in the bar, when she'd suggested they let the past go, he'd thought about asking her why she'd just vanished from his life but he'd wanted to be a man about it. He'd even bitten his tongue when she'd taken the piss about 'his table', but it had only been a figure of speech. He didn't think he was King Henry the Eighth. And her chippiness about his credit card – some people had to go out to work to earn a living and not rely on The Bank of Mam and Dad.

Basically, for her, he'd bent over backwards, but rather than appreciate this, she'd shafted him.

She was full of attitude, she was, judging him for having two flats and a cracking job. And that show of sadness when he told her about Mam dying, he was this close to pointing out that he'd gone to her mam's six years ago, the day she'd died, to get her number. He'd been desperate to talk to the one person who understood. He'd got as far as the door but at the last minute he'd bottled it.

That memory sent him off on one: that was why he'd said feel free to get in touch with Orla – he'd implied she'd been the one to do the abandoning not his sister.

Then she did what he thought she would be incapable of – asking how come he'd done so well for himself in that tone, like he was scum. He couldn't help but pass her the shitty stick – he'd worked hard, he hadn't needed uni to make something of himself. Not that she had. She'd got in a right strop when he asked her if she had kids; what was wrong with assuming she had it all now? He was basically giving her the chance to bang on about how happy she was.

When she'd told him the state she was in, he was straight-up sorry. Her ex sounded a right wanker, she didn't deserve that. His face had said it all, he thought, he'd gone serious and offered her commiserations but she'd took it all wrong. Couldn't wait to tell him that the accumulation of stuff and success was false and he was in corporate chains. The little speech she did before she left about her freedom was as if she was trying to convince herself.

It was as if she was saying she saw right through him – that he had taken the capitalist coin in exchange for his soul. The nerve of it. Her disappointment was written all over her face. Her lovely face.

At three o'clock in the morning, shitted and miserable, he'd admitted that it had been like losing her all over again. To have had her there within touching distance and not been able to connect as they had done. The door was firmly closed on it now.

He didn't want anything to do with this Vicky. With her boho chic thing going on. She'd looked good, really good, not awkward and teenage but all woman and quirky.

But she hadn't seemed to have grown up – who ran home to their mam and dad at their age? Maybe if you'd had a nice feathery nest of love and ironed uniforms then it made you a soft touch. No backbone, no standing on your own two feet.

That was what he'd held onto as he'd travelled back to London, happy as Larry to be in amongst it, away from the conservatories and front lawns. It hardened his belief that he was doing all right, the way he was living. That was why Shell had had to go.

'Maybe she came back into your life for a reason?' Orla said.

'To show me how lucky I am to have made something of myself, yeah, I know.'

'All right,' she said, holding up her hands, 'I was trying to do you a favour. That's all. It's just a massive shame. A waste. Because I'd love to see her. She was a really good part of growing up. I'd love to have had the chance to let her know that things have worked out for me. To say thank you.'

'Whatever. Do it. You'll just find out what I did: that she went all hippy in Brighton, lived in a bubble then it popped. Don't say I didn't warn you though.'

'You have no compassion,' Orla said.

He was no Mother Theresa, he knew that, but he did check up on Dad most days without Orla knowing, scrub his loo when he visited and pay for a cleaner – a service, he lied, provided by the sheltered flat complex. Yet he couldn't tell Orla that.

She sniffed and began to look for a tissue up her sleeve. He picked a serviette from the holder in the middle of the table and handed it over. She gave him daggers as she said thank you.

'This,' she said, taking it with her fingertips to make a point, 'is what is called accepting help. You should try it some time.'

'Yeah, yeah,' he said, picking up his man bag. 'I need a fag. Thanks for breakfast. I've got to go, mortgage to pay and all that.'

Then he wanted to punch himself because she'd know by his sarcasm that she'd well and truly hit a nerve and he felt a total arse.

*

Koh Pha Ngan, Thailand, January 2008

Dancing ankle-deep in the sea which is as warm as a bath, Vicky reckons this night out is one of her best ever.

She's in paradise, beneath a starry Thai sky on a beautiful beach with a bunch of brilliant people. Closer to dawn than midnight, the rabid techno has given way to blissed-out tunes. And, she feels the need to pinch herself, it looks as if she's going to pull Conor. Gorgeous Conor, who is smiling at her, just her, after a week of flirting and getting to know one another after they met at the backpacker bungalows where they're staying on the island of Koh Pha Ngan.

This sort of thing doesn't happen to girls like her — he's actually interested in her: who she is, where she's been. She didn't believe it at first, but she reckons he's manoeuvred the gang away from the heaving mass of thirty thousand ravers at the full moon party to the fringes of the water's edge so he can talk to her rather than yell. As if the main event is happening between them; like the craziness of the people literally playing with fire, limboing under flaming poles and skipping with ropes set alight, is just a sideshow.

In that sexy Irish accent, he asks her if she wants a drink. She says no, because after two whisky buckets, she's on the right side of pissed and she wants to be in control, to enjoy whatever's coming rather than it happening in a blur. He gives her a hug which lingers. She can feel an electricity between them. Watching his broad back and neat bum weave their way to the bar, she feels her rude bits racing. How she'd love to go to bed with Conor. To put air between her and her Reading uni ex Pete, who was her last. And for once she'd like to be the one — not Kat — with a walk of shame story to tell over a very late breakfast.

Her skin goosebumping in the humid caress of a light breeze, Vicky thinks they came close to snogging earlier when the smoke machine fogged out everyone else: it felt like it was just the two of them, their eyes locked together, their bodies touching. But the magic was broken when the strobe lights crashed in. Then Kat fell sideways into some people and became The Annoying Pissed Person. If Conor wasn't here, she would've dragged her back to the bungalows to sober up. But Vicky's not going to miss her chance with him: he is just so good-looking, like Johnny Depp with that goatee, his chocolate eyes and brown wavy hair which hangs just above his shoulders. In an odd way, he reminds her of Mikey, he's funny in a quirky way and sees things differently. He's into culture and stuff, like her, rather than just the craic. He's travelling in the opposite direction to her, so she's been able to tell him what to expect in Australia and South America. He's given her a load of cool tips for the rest of Asia too, recommending Cambodia because it's less commercial. As much as Vicky likes Thailand for its temples, turquoise sea and tigers, it's too druggy here. Why come all this way to neck some pills when you could do that at the Eclipse nightclub in Cardiff? She'd rather read the Lonely Planet than The Beach - and wherever you go, you always hear that Moby song from the soundtrack of the film. She's going to ask Kat if she wants to go to Cambodia, but she doubts she will: Kat only started enjoying their trip when she got to party. And party and party as if the fun was about to run out. Or at least her drug supply. Desperate, how she looks now. As for Vicky, she just looks like she's having a blast. She tidies her frizzy hair back into a ponytail. She can't do anything about her red face, that's the sun and the dancing, that is. And her skin is slick with sweat. But, as she takes in everyone around her, they all look like that. And to her credit, she can still use both eyes simultaneously – the majority of them have collapsed faces. She feels good too in her cute black beach romper: it hides her tummy but makes the most of her arms and legs which no longer resemble the blotchy texture of corned beef because of her kind of tan and they're more sculptured from carrying her rucksack and loads of walking.

Christ, maybe for once, she is a catch!

But she still needs to check with Kat: there are some things you can only ask a bestie – whether you've got something in your teeth, there's a spot that needs squeezing or if a boy fancies you.

She reaches for Kat, who's being chatted up by a queue of blokes. She looks stunning in a bikini top and micro shorts with day-glo moons and stars accentuating the sinew of her skinny, tanned body. Vicky interrupts without any apology to Kat's audience – she knows by the way their tongues are hanging out that *they'll wait for her attention.*

'I need to ask you something, Kat,' she says into her ear. 'Do you think Conor's flirting with me?'

Kat twirls round and gives her the biggest hug. 'I love you, Vickster!'

'Yeah, I love you too,' Vicky says, laughing as Kat tries to lift her up. 'Stop it! Put me down! Listen, listen! Conor's gone to the bar. So quick before he gets back, do you think he's into me?'

Kat starts whooping and clapping to the beat. Vicky grabs her wrists, trying to stop her moving because she needs to know. This is Kat's job, to big her up and give her some confidence: Vicky needs encouragement because she's no good at stuff like this.

'Ow!' Kat yelps and it's then Vicky sees her face properly. Her pupils are the size of space and she's chewing gum like a cheerleader.

'Oh, fuck, Kat, not again. What have you taken?'

Vicky is really pissed off because three days ago, Kat went paranoid on a magic mushroom milkshake and Vicky spent five hours talking her through it. Then, until this morning, she was a wreck. Jumping at shadows, refusing to leave the bungalows, being really weepy and depressed. 'Some people aren't meant to take drugs, Kat, and you're one of them,' Vicky had said, hoping that'd be the end.

Vicky doesn't bother with it – there are so many headcases here who've got caught up in the scene. You see them, dancing by themselves in fishermen's trousers at midday on the beach, still up from the night before.

'Just a pill. It's fine, not strong at all. Chill out, Vicky. You sound like my mum.'

Vicky suddenly feels angry. She's going to have to keep an eye on Kat now because she loses all her inhibitions and judgement when she's like this.

'Anyway, Conor, yeah?' Kat says, her hands in the air. 'Go for it!'

'Well, I can't now, because you look nutted...'

'So?'

'So, I'm not going to leave you.'

'I can look after myself!'

'Yeah, right. Look at you.'

Kat staggers and laughs, her body is wet with sweat.

'You haven't got any water. I'll go and get you some, you need *to keep hydrated.'*

Kat rolls her eyes at her. Or perhaps she's just rolling her eyes because she's off her tits. Vicky tells her not to wander off – she's heard of muggings and assaults on girls – and heads to the bar through the thickening crowd of idiots doing big fish, little fish, cardboard box with their hands. If she hurries up, she can reach Conor who is just being served. But no, he's paid and he's on his way back and he hasn't seen her. There's no point shouting because the music gets louder the closer you get to the bar and waving her arms will just make her look like she's copying one of those dancers with UV wings.

Vicky feels her irritation building. She thought Kat would pull herself together after Australia, where she was pissed out of her skull the entire time. Vicky could understand that in a way because it had been a release from South America, which Kat had hated. By the end she was having weird breathing moments, which she tried to blame on the altitude but they'd been there too long for it still to affect her. Vicky suspected they were panic attacks but Kat wouldn't have it. The things that had made Kat unhappy were precisely the things Vicky had loved it: the proper foreignness of it. The massive differences between climates, when it would be freezing at altitude and baking at sea level; the extreme poverty and wealth; the vast emptiness of the Andes and the heaving bus stations where you could go anywhere for a few quid. Kat had either clung to Vicky or been snappy, claiming it was 'so not what she'd signed up for'. Going to Oz, with its backpacker industry, happy hours and familiar Western food, was a dream for Kat by comparison. That's why she'd launched herself into the drink, it stopped the 'funny spells' she said.

But Kat had got into it alone. She'd been sort of cold, as if she was bored of Vicky, and at every opportunity she'd teased her in front of people, that she'd been forced to go on hikes, visit museums and look at monuments. Vicky had felt very small at times, just like at school – Kat knew she was sensitive about things like that. But she'd put it down to Kat trying to find herself after being so quiet in South America. Then Kat had fucked off with a bloke in Sydney, and again in Cape Tribulation, leaving Vicky to make her own way back to their hostels. Both times, she hadn't seen Kat for a couple of days and she'd been so worried. When she turned up, dishevelled and touchy, Kat had accused her of being controlling and a square, that she didn't know how to have a laugh. Vicky had sort of retreated then because she didn't want to fall out with her: she had been frightened of being alone.

Then came Christmas Day, when Kat threw up for hours on Bondi beach from the mix of the booze and sun. And New Year's Day, when they'd traipsed round the city to find a chemist so Kat could buy the morning-after pill.

Finally, on the flight to Bangkok, after staying up all night, Kat had apologized for everything. She said she'd get her act together, admitting she had been feeling anxious, and she did for a bit. Slowly though, she'd become undone again. Fed up of looking at statues of Buddha, she wanted to go island-hopping then stay somewhere for a couple of weeks or so in Thailand. Have a holiday was the way she'd put it, as if that wasn't what they'd been doing already! Vicky had relented because it'd be nice to have the chance to wash all her clothes and read up on Vietnam, Laos and, fingers crossed, Cambodia. But Kat had just used the opportunity to take as many drugs as she could. It was like being with a stranger: Vicky had never known her to be so wild.

It's really unsettled Vicky because she's starting to think Kat is a bit selfish and not the person she once knew so well. But if she carries on down that path, it'll lead somewhere really major and they only have six weeks left and Vicky doesn't want to spoil it. Besides, Kat says she's just making the most of things before she has to conform when she goes to work in the City.

With a bottle of water for Kat, Vicky heads back to find her. She didn't notice it before but there's a smell of BO and sour breath – she quickly checks it isn't her, it's not – and she feels sick as other people's arms slime against her.

Where the hell is Kat, she thinks, because she's not where she left her by that palm tree. Scanning the jumping heads, shading her eyes from the flashing lights atop towers of crates, her eyes go back and forth, and then thank God, Kat's over there with Conor.

A girl accidentally jostles Vicky then and she drops the water. She bends down to get it then comes back up, ready to wave to them that she's almost there. Then, the sound of the music drains from her ears, leaving just her roaring pulse, because she sees Kat hanging off Conor. He's looking really awkward and trying to peel her arms off him, but she's holding on tight. What the fuck is she doing? A strobe comes on and Vicky can only see chunks of action, as if she's watching a slideshow of stills. Kat has her hands on his face. The strobe flickers then it goes black. Conor pulls his head *back. Black. Kat's mouth is on his. Black. Conor pushes her away. Black. Kat is on the floor. Black. Oh my God, what's going on? Black. As the strobe lights the place up once more, Vicky legs it over to where Conor is standing – he's got his palms up as if to say he didn't touch her. 'She's fucking mental,' he says to Vicky, who is groping to understand. 'She just went for me. Tried to snog me, she's off her rocker.'*

Vicky is torn – should she help Kat up, because she's clearly mashed, or should she take Conor's side? Whatever she does, she knows she's lost him because he's backing off and shaking his head.

'I really like you, Vicky, but… she's a liability,' he says and that's it, he's walking backwards, away from her, then he's gone.

Kat is convulsing with laughter, still on the floor and Vicky is so cross, so sick of her.

'What the fuck have you done?' Vicky shouts, hating her for ruining her night and the thing with Conor when she expressly told her she liked him, and hating herself for not being able to desert Kat because what if something happened to her?

Vicky feels a storm of frustration and anger and hurt welling deep inside of her. Surely Kat sees she's fucked up. But she's on her feet now, looking the aggressor.

'I was only dancing with him, what a freak,' she says, as if she was the victim here, brushing the sand off her hands. She's still moving to the beat, which tells Vicky that she doesn't care.

'You tried to snog him. I saw you. Why would you do that?' Vicky screams as people begin to move away from them.

'Oh, for fuck's sake, Vicky, he wasn't all that. He totally overreacted, I was only having a laugh.'

'You could have anyone. Why would you go for the one I fancied?'

Kat looks hostile now, cornered, like a wild animal.

'Get over yourself, Vicky,' Kat sneers. 'It's not as though I've tried it on with Mikey, is it?' Kat gives her a look as if she's played some kind of trump card.

'What the fuck are you on about?' Vicky doesn't understand what she means. Why bring him into it? She feels her body stiffen, waiting for attack.

'Oh, come on, Vicky, you never stop going on about him.' And then in a whiny voice, she says: 'Mikey would've loved this, Mikey would've hated that. Mikey, oh Mikey, I miss him so much.'

Vicky gasps: Kat's impression is thick with contempt. She feels winded and then she's burning with fury.

'You total bitch,' she says, swallowing hard, and then embarrassment, does she really sound so pathetic?

Vicky turns her back on Kat, suddenly the sand has lost its warmth. She feels her body wanting to run, needing to move. Her flip-flops, she sees them by the water and jogs over to the shore, still confused by Kat's betrayal. Her octopus arms all over Conor were bad enough but the hateful edge in Kat's voice is more troubling: Kat has gone for the jugular, her weakest, most sensitive spot. She bends over and retches, fighting to breathe. To think of all the times she's protected Kat during this trip and she's been mocking her behind her back.

Kat bounds up by her side, like a boxer waiting to pounce. She hasn't had enough yet.

'Do you know something? I'm sick of hearing you banging on about Mikey. It's all you talk about.'

'I can't believe this,' Vicky says, standing up, struggling to comprehend how Kat can justify her treachery. 'You've just humiliated me and yourself and you're blaming me for it!'

'You've made me feel second best the entire time. Like you wish Mikey had been here not me.'

'When did I ever say that? You're warped, you are. Is that why you tried to snog Conor? To get me back?' The realization that Kat has been silently seething all this time, for days, weeks, months even, is like a slap on the face.

Kat lifts her chin defiantly.

'Oh my God, that's it isn't it? You're jealous. That is so twisted... I can't even begin to...' Vicky stares at her open-mouthed. She thought she knew Kat inside out, that they were best mates. But this changes everything.

Vicky begins to back off, frightened by where they go from here: even if they can find a way through this, their friendship will never be the same. She doesn't care about leaving Kat now, she can go to hell. Vicky marches off, sickened by Kat's viciousness. She steps between bottles and fag ends, then her stomach recoils when she sees a syringe. These people are disgusting, fucking over the locals, who have to put up with this self-indulgent shit. No wonder Kat loves it. Vicky stomps on, up the beach, not looking behind her.

That's what it takes for Kat to come to. She's by her side now, pulling at Vicky's arm with cold sticky fingers, trying to bring her to a standstill.

'Just leave me alone.' Vicky bellows it into her face. Her outburst is like taking a peg out of a grenade: her body begins to judder as the venom from Kat's violence spreads within.

Kat begins to wail and she drops to her knees. Her hands are covering her eyes and there's snot coming out between her fingers. When she comes up for air, her mascara is smudged all over her cheeks and she's grimacing, desperate. As if she's in a horror film.

'I'm... sorry... Vicky,' she says in shaky gulps. Her lips are misshapen, grotesque. 'I don't know what's happening to me...'

Vicky is trying to catch her breath. She wants to go for her, tell her it's always about her, that she's an insecure cow. But she's shocked by this falling apart before her.

How did they get this far together and Vicky didn't notice it was brewing? She's stung by the realization that Kat has been struggling the whole time. That's why she's been swinging from one emotion to the other. She's been quietly cracking up.

'I'm sorry,' Kat says, over and over, falling into the sand.

The adrenalin subsides and Vicky feels heavy with tiredness. A strip of light bleaches the horizon.

'I should never have come. I'm a fraud, I thought I could do this, but I can't. I've hated everything about it.'

She's crumbling and Vicky feels helpless.

'I'm a monster,' Kat says, looking pleadingly into Vicky's eyes. 'Help me.'

The anger has gone now: Vicky begins to feel pity instead. So she gets down beside her, takes her in her arms and tells her they'll sort it out.

'It's been so easy for you,' Kat says, her head tucked under Vicky's chin. 'Like, you just loved it from day one. I never thought I'd be like this. I thought I'd be the one who flourished. But I hate it: the cockroaches, the constant moving around, the anxiety about getting food poisoning or getting lost or the expectation to have the best time. I've realized I need routine, not this...'

'That's why you've been getting wrecked,' Vicky says.

'Yes and I've bottled it up, I've been so stupid. I haven't failed before...' She sounds weak, childlike. Vicky wonders how long it'll be before Kat leaves her. For this is the end of their journey, there's only one way forward for Kat and that's going home.

'You don't have to stay, you know,' Vicky says, realizing that she isn't ready to go back yet. She'll be fine by herself. She'll be scared, but she will be okay.

But Kat hasn't heard her. 'You've blossomed. I've been so envious of you, the way you've just got on with it.'

Vicky is knocked for six: jealous? Of her? When Kat has everything going for her.

'But why?'

'I dunno. I've always felt not good enough. Even with you and Mikey. Like, this was supposed to be our thing, but I've felt like you've just wanted Mikey here instead of me.'

'That's not true, no way,' Vicky says. But she understands the feeling of 'otherness', of not being included. 'Look, we've had some great times...' She quickly raids her memory to prove it. 'Ayres Rock was ace, wasn't it? And we had a ball in Buenos Aires. 'I do miss Mikey, madly, of course I do. But I've never wished you weren't here. Apart from that thing with Conor.'

She shakes Kat to make her see that last bit was a joke.

'Oh, don't,' Kat says, 'I feel terrible. I'm so sorry.'

Vicky thinks back to how she must've sounded, bringing up Mikey at moments when Kat wanted it to be special just for them.

'I'm sorry too for making you feel bad about Mikey. I do talk about him a lot, don't I?'

Kat sits up then and gives her a sad smile. 'Don't go mad...' she says, which makes Vicky clench her stomach muscles. What is she going to say next? She can't cope with any more drama right now. '...but I wonder if you're in love with Mikey, just a tiny bit.'

Vicky's heart stops. 'What?'

'I'm just putting it out there, that's all. No one compares to him.'

Her heart starts beating again. Very fast.

'That's crap!' Vicky says, 'He's just... Mikey. I don't see him like that.' But she hears her head and heart whisper in unison that there was that second when she lay beside him on her mum and dad's lawn, wondering... She shakes it away and then tries to pull Kat up to standing. It's getting late or early or whatever - it's time to sleep. The music is coming down like the people save for the odd casualty raving into the dawn.

'No, let's watch the sun come up,' Kat says, tugging her down. 'It's going to be a beautiful one.'

They sit in silence for a while admiring the wispy streaks of orange and pink and blue. Vicky senses this will be their last shared moment for a while.

'It's weird, coming all this way to find out stuff,' Kat says.

'How do you mean?'

'Well, we've come so many thousands of miles but what we want most of all is back home.'

Vicky goes to challenge her. In spite of all the arguments, she's had an amazing, eye-opener of a time. Yet how many emails has she sent to Mikey, asking him to visit?

As the sun crowns where the sky meets the sea, she wonders if Kat might just be right.

Chapter Ten

V

Cowbridge

'Right. Bollocks to it. That's enough. I'm closing up,' Pierre said, turning the open sign on the door of The Big Cheese.

'Right you are,' Vee called from the till and began to cash up. It was a typically rainy April Saturday afternoon, their last customer had come in an hour ago and the pair of them had already cleaned everything that didn't move. 'Anything you want me to do in particular because I've done the fridges, coffee machine, floors and—'

'We're having a team meeting,' he declared, clapping his hands together and rubbing them furiously.

In the five days since she'd started working for him, she'd found out Pierre was even more of a funny old bean than she'd thought.

He served her coffee and croissants every morning, insisting she sat down to eat, while he got the shop ready for the breakfast rush. There was a magnetic weather map on the wall on which he diligently stuck up the day's forecast. A basket of single-stem roses would arrive just before opening, which he'd hand out to ladies and gents with their brown paper packages of food and drink. And he'd make deliveries to local offices and businesses on his strange custom-built trike and trailer rather than via the chiller van parked out the back.

And now, even though there was just two of them, he was calling them a team. But she was comfy with it all.

'I hope it's Brie-f,' she said, waiting for a reaction which didn't come. 'Geddit?' she asked, as he cleared the tables of sugar bowls.

Pierre completely ignored her attempt at a joke. 'You require training.'

'Oh, give me a chance! I've not been here a week! I promise you, I will get... feta.' She tittered aloud as she counted the day's takings. The protracted silence made her look up.

He had crossed his arms and was examining her with curiosity. 'You've done very well this week. Very well indeed. You're excellent with the customers, punctual. Meticulous with hygiene. Enthusiastic. Willing to learn. In fact, you have a thirst for knowledge. And, unlike my bastard of a brother, you do not pinch the stock.'

Vee beamed and self-consciously patted her hairnet with her latex-gloved hands. Finally, after weeks of despair, it was all starting to come together. Less and less, she thought of Jez and she hardly thought of Mikey at all. Life was on the up! And it was all thanks to Kate who'd helped her out, and Pierre, who'd taken her on during a one-minute interview once he'd found out her catering background.

'But,' he boomed, 'you are not giving the cheese enough respect.'

She chuckled and sighed, he really was hilarious. And a bit scary. Mum and Dad had worried she might be a bit bored in a deli, but somehow this bizarre man's devotion to his trade, not to mention his quirkiness, turned it into a twinkly Aladdin's cave of treasures and belly laughs. It also helped that Pierre was astonishingly attractive although clearly she wasn't interested: with his thick shiny brown curls and permatan, he was definitely the result of good posh breeding. He was bound to be part of some Beautiful People set with his symmetrical chiselled features: his wide green eyes were exotic and mysterious, his Romanesque nose posed above perfect red lips, which sat above a nut-cracking jawline. The dimple in his chin looked as if it had been thumbed by God himself. Yes, all in all, Vee was very content in her job.

'I am telling you the exactitude of the matter,' he said sternly, which stopped Vee in her tracks. The comfiness she'd felt from the second he put her behind the counter drained away as she realized he was being serious.

'You're too rough with the cheese. It's understandable, a very common error among beginners, but I need you to think of every piece of cheese you handle as the last dodo's egg on earth.'

Vee nodded slowly at first, bemused by his obsessive words. But then when she remembered his distress after she'd dropped a wheel of some French variety on the floor on her first day, she started to get it.

'Be tender, reverent, humble, deferential,' he implored.

And then he tore off his black Big Cheese T-shirt and stood there topless, apparently unaware that undressing in public, in a deli, in front of your new employee wasn't the done thing. With his leather apron around his waist, he looked like he was in one of those saucy charity calendars. Vee was unsure what was going on: why did he have to strip down to make his point? There were worse ways of being given a lesson, she supposed, feeling all of a dither.

His body was magnificent: sculpted strong shoulders presented a clean, hairless muscular chest, two ripe nipples and a torso so taut you could use it to grate parmesan. Gulping, she tried to concentrate on his face. Because she kind of fancied him in a she-could-appreciate-his-hotness way. That didn't mean she wanted him to do an Orlando Bloom and get it all out though.

'The cheese we sell is artisan,' he said, holding his thumbs and fingers together, oblivious to Vee's cheeks, which were boiling out of embarrassment and awe at his physique, 'hand-made using the traditional craftsmanship of skilled cheesemakers. They are complex in taste, aged for textural characteristics, a product of intense chemistry. A change in the quality of grass eaten by the cow or goat or donkey can ruin everything. It is a delicate process, dating back five thousand years.'

She jumped as he leapt to the door leading to the storeroom and produced a starched white lab coat, which he threw on with aplomb. It ruined her view somewhat but at least Vee would be able to concentrate on his actual words a bit more. Then he got a pair of industrial goggles and rested them on top of his head.

'Cheesemakers know the precise amounts and types of ingredients used. It is a science,' he said, which explained the outfit. 'But it is also an art. Not...' he said, thumping the counter, 'that the world recognizes it. A sommelier is the term used for an expert in wine, there is a formal qualification, for heaven's sake. But while it is just as critical to pair cheese with other foods or to keep it at exact temperatures, there is no such equivalent term or training. It is a scandal.'

He stared at her and she realized he was waiting for her to agree. So she did, vigorously.

'Which is why we must serve cheese to the highest standards, to show our customers that we are not a supermarket and we do not deal with blocks of cheddar from a mass-produced mechanical process.'

He was right! She'd noticed how limp and processed the cheese was at home compared to Pierre's practically still-breathing produce. His face lit up when he saw the light bulb go on in her eyes.

'You understand?' he asked, heavy breathing with excitement.

Yes! Yes, she did. 'Yes! Yes, I do,' she breathed back, almost as entranced by his passion as she was by his torso.

'We, you and me, Vee, we are connoisseurs. We,' he sang, 'know our Bleu de Severac from our Pule.'

Vee panicked. 'Oh God, I don't, Pierre. What are they?'

'This is what today's training will teach you. Bleu de Severac, from ewe's milk from the Midi-Pyrénées, creamy, tangy, sublime, increasingly rare due to European Union bacteriological correctness. Pule is the world's most expensive cheese made from the milk of Balkan donkeys, fetching a thousand euros a kilogram.'

'Right, okay. But we haven't got them... have we?' What if they had and she was about to be sacked for her ignorance, for crimes against cheese?

'Non, my budding maître fromager. But... come with me...'

It was as if she was hypnotized: she followed him wordlessly into the back room where he rattled around in a bottom cupboard and pulled out half-full bottles of red then white wine from the fridge, which he claimed was making a clicky noise and, with a sigh and a glint in his eyes, he'd have to get that electrician in back again. Then he nipped into the deli and brought in a tray of goodies and invited Vee to sit at the table.

'And now, we taste...' he said, pouring out two glasses. 'I am going to teach you how to pair wine and cheese, to pay homage, to love cheese tender. Then you can pass it onto our beloved and noble clientele.'

An hour later, Vee knew that Shiraz went with asiago, sparkling accompanied Havarti and dessert and port coupled up nicely with blues. And she was as pickled as an onion thanks to Pierre's generous sloshing.

'Right,' he said, finishing his glass and wiping his mouth with gusto, 'would you be able to drive?'

'What? Now? Hardly! I'm going to have to get the bus.'

'No, no, no,' he said, shaking his head, as if she'd said something completely preposterous. 'A week Friday. I have a delivery coming from France. They drop off in London then head back. I'd go but I can't drive. My bastard of a brother used to take care of that. You can take the van. Refrigerated, sat nav. A joy to drive, apparently. But I never learned. We were driven around in embassy limos when we lived in London and I liked cycling so...' He gave a Gallic shrug and then a British nod.

'Yes, of course, that'll be good, a day out.' She was pleased that he'd thought she was trustworthy enough to get behind the wheel. And she understood he was putting her in a position of responsibility.

'Marvellous,' he said, putting the money away in the safe, switching off the lights then giving her a set of keys. 'I think you have real promise.'

'Aw, I'm so touched!' she said, heartened by his gesture.

As she locked up, she realized he was still dressed up.

'You not getting changed then?' she asked. 'Out of your lab coat thing?'

'It's for a fancy dress party. Doctors and nurses. I'm going as a surgeon,' he said as if she was thick. 'Fancy coming?' he said. 'Unless you're washing your hair, that is?'

Then his face went shy as if he was bashful because it sounded like he was asking her on a date.

'Actually, I am! But not like that. My Mum's friend, a hairdresser, is coming round to sort out this mess,' she said, pointing at her hair. And the truth was, while she saw he was attractive, there was no spark between them – he was her boss and too out there for her. 'Otherwise, I'd have loved to. Right, I think this is my bus coming now so—'

'Bus?' he roared, his eyes aflame. 'I won't hear of it. You're Team Fromage now. I'll drop you home in a cab. I'm going into Cardiff. The taxi rank is just up here.'

'That's so nice, thank you,' Vee said, her heart running not just from keeping up with his giant stride but from the simple acts of kindness that she had never expected to find here, in the place she now called home.

Chapter Eleven

K

Roath, Cardiff

The jaunty theme tune of *The Archers* taunted Kate as she sat at the gleaming marble breakfast bar at her parents' house.

Over-bright and forceful, the music perfectly summed up her mother's masquerade, who was humming along while she made coffee on her top-of-the-range machine. The omnibus edition of the serial was always on here of a Sunday morning; it was an essential box to be ticked on Mum's keeping up appearances checklist. Soaps on the TV were 'common', but this saga of country life was acceptable because it was on Radio Four. In Pam's world, in this well-to-do suburb of Cardiff, it was the perfect subject for small talk, along with tennis club gossip and the downturn of Marks and Spencer's ladies' wear.

Most of the time, Kate managed to get out of visiting – her excuses ranged from taking part in a 10km run somewhere to an outing with Jack to a waterfall or an antiques' market. But it was impossible to avoid every week. Thankfully, her big sister – her saviour – was here today too, which diluted the pain.

'Isn't it lovely, just us girls, together,' her mother said, which was code for her daughters being easier meat when the menfolk weren't there. Dad wasn't here – of course. Mother had seen to ruining their father-daughter bond, out of sheer spite, she suspected. The whispering harsh voices one night when Kate was recovering; Mother blaming Dad for pandering to her when what that girl needed was a stern word to pull herself together. Slammed doors and her father working longer hours, missing out on mealtimes. Jonathan had chosen his wife over his daughter, that was clear, and Kate had lost an ally. Mother had won again, and while she was angry at Dad for not standing up for himself or Kate, she too was guilty of rolling over because it was easier than to risk Pam's wrath.

Today, he was with Charlie's husband Tom, watching Griffy play in an end-of-season rugby tournament. Jack was whistling in his shed at home, delighted he had been excused by virtue of gender.

Delivered in her very best John Lewis mugs, Pam handed out the coffees – black for her and Kate, a latte for Charlie – then announced: 'No nibbles today, though, because we all need to be thinking of the big day, don't we, Charlotte? Not long to go now, only two and a half months.'

Behind the safety of a towering vase of lilies, Kate gave Charlie a look of sympathy; the comment was aimed at her sister because she had the cheek to not be a size eight. Voluptuous and womanly, Charlie was the opposite of Kate and their mother, who had more boyish straight-up-and-down figures, for genetic but also self-inflicted reasons. Kate thought Charlie was beautiful, like Nigella, with her creamy skin and tousled brown hair which rested on her incredible boob shelf. She'd worked out her own style, always wearing wrap dresses to accentuate her hourglass shape and it complemented her rounded, less angular features.

But Mum was threatened by her curves because it showed Charlie was beyond her authority. And happy. Which was a dangerous combination for a control freak. Kate felt a frisson of peril from just thinking about it.

'I think you'll look amazing as you are,' she dared to say, feeling a little braver beside her sister, who was less of a walkover. 'I love the dress you're going to wear, Charlie. Red is your colour.'

'Just so you can hide behind me! I know your game. "Don't look at me, look at her!" that's what you mean!'

'Yep, you got it.'

As Mum went to open the bifold floor-to-ceiling doors which looked out onto a landscaped garden to let in some of the glorious spring sunshine, Kate said quietly: 'I'm dreading being the centre of attention. If it was just one thing, the walking down the aisle bit, I could cope because that's the important part.' To have her father give her away, once again to be the apple of his eye. 'But there's the pictures, the cutting of the cake, the first dance…'

'I loved it, everyone looking at me! I felt like a celebrity!' Charlie shook her hair as if she was mid-photo shoot.

Her sister's wedding nine years ago had been a big do, so Mum and her had pretty much seen eye to eye - it had given Pam the chance to live out her own dreams. Kate could reel off her mother's speech about her own wedding: 'We didn't have two pennies to rub together. I had to make my own dress and your father wore his one work suit. So think yourselves lucky.'

Unlike Kate, Charlie had earned the right to have a say on the guest list and favours and all that because she'd done everything in the right order. Straight As at A-Level, a medical degree, post-grad then GP training. To top it off, she was marrying a surgeon. All by the age of twenty-seven. But Kate wasn't jealous: she admired her sister and had she not been in a stable position when Kate had needed her, well, it didn't bear thinking about.

Their mother announced her return with a cough: they needed to remember that she was in charge.

'Sorry, Mother,' Charlie said, her blue eyes dancing, 'back to the agenda. The Wedding of the Year.'

'Well, we haven't got long, Katherine has… what is it you have later?' Pam checked her highlighted feather cut was behaving. She was feeling for any disobedient strands that revealed either the deep slash of a frown on her forehead or chicken's feet at the side of her eyes. Any rebellion would be quashed with a whip of her fingers.

'We're seeing Jack's mum.' Thank God, because that meant she had a reason to leave soon. She needed to get ready, it would take an hour or so to get to Diana's place in Swansea where they'd have to walk Boris before their beachside brasserie booking at 1.30 p.m.

'She's very lucky to have such an attentive future daughter-in-law,' Mum said, playing with her pearls. This was a barbed reference to Kate's fab relationship with Di, whom she adored: Kate dreamed of telling her mum she preferred her to her own mother, that's why they saw her so often. Instead she went for something less incendiary.

'Di's by herself, she's got terrible arthritis and Jack's sister lives in America.' Which you well know, she added in her head.

Mum swept it aside, her platinum bangles crashing like

cymbals. 'We need to talk top table plans. Featuring, obviously, the usual suspects: bride, groom, mother-of-the-bride.' She stopped to smile at her own mention. 'But instead of being at the head of the banquet room, we could go in the centre, be in amongst it all. I read that it's becoming a thing in London and I don't know anyone here who's done that yet, it would cause quite a stir!' And give her the upper hand amongst her cronies, Kate thought.

She gave a dazzling smile then ran her tongue over her teeth in case her claret-coloured lipstick had revolted.

Charlie turned to Kate. 'What do you reckon?'

Kate considered it: she'd rather be tucked away in a cupboard if she had a choice. But she didn't. When it boiled down to it, she didn't really give a toss about where she was sitting: it would only be for a couple of hours before the band. But Mum's motive to set a trend was vulgar and if Kate didn't give a sniff of a fight then she'd look even weaker. Then again, was it worth arguing for the sake of it? There would be more important matters to contend – one of which she was preparing to raise this morning. She had to pick her battles. So she decided to let this go.

'Whatever you want, Mum,' she said, keeping her tone even, not wanting to provoke her.

'Oh that's wonderful!'

Kate registered her mother's surprise that she'd been so reasonable. Even though she'd been nothing but!

'I'm so proud of you, Katherine,' she said, her face relaxing into kindness, which was a rare event. Kate knew she was only getting praised for agreeing with her. But still, like a starved child, she would snap up anything vaguely resembling nourishment from her mother's hand. She hated herself for gobbling up her crumbs, but despite everything, Kate still needed her approval.

'I know we've had a few... contretemps,' her mum said, softly, 'but you've become a lovely young woman.'

Even a backhanded compliment like that, which hinted at her ugly past, was welcome because it wasn't a criticism of how she was now. It had taken a long time to get here. Kate couldn't change her mother, she'd learned that, so she had to take the positives where she could.

Charlie was the one to translate Mum's words into a hug:

that was one step too far for their mother, who shied away from physical contact unless it involved Griff. Kate loved a cuddle from her sister, it made her feel they were both on the same side, and with a six-year age gap, Kate had seen her more as the mother figure in her life.

It was then Kate decided that she was going to bring up Vee: while it would never be the perfect moment, this was as smooth as it would get.

Kate had found a new sense of hope from her friendship, which was budding again. Still they trod cautiously, aware a careless comment could set off a land mine. But dinner ten days ago had been a success, Vee was enjoying her job and slowly but surely their lives were being woven back together. They exchanged texts regularly, Vee coming to her with funny titbits about Pierre, invites for coffee and offers to come with her to do some wedding shopping. Soon, if things continued the way they were going, Kate would invite her to the wedding: at the very least, it would be churlish not to include her. Not that she was going to tell her mother any of this: she would limit it to the bare bones and go from there. Perhaps Mum just needed to be consulted, maybe that was how Kate needed to approach their relationship and, if so, she might be able to bring her round.

'Oh,' she started, as if it had just occurred to her, 'I've been in touch with an old friend.'

Her mother nodded. 'From Oxford? How lovely.' She took a sip of coffee without breaking eye contact.

Kate hesitated out of habit. But she was happier now than she'd been in a good while and her mother couldn't be upset with that, so she went on.

'No, from before,' she said, keeping her voice low to hide her emotion.

'Oh yes?' Mum's mask slipped an inch as one of her plucked-to-death eyebrows arched, straining for details now.

'You remember Vicky, don't you?' Kate directed it at both of them, not just her mother, because she couldn't take the icy blue stare for long.

Charlie, God bless her, jumped in. 'Oh, yes, I know, the one from school. How is she?'

'Okay. She contacted me through Facebook and we've caught up a bit. You know.'

Kate saw the muscles in her mother's cheeks clench. But she said nothing.

She carried on, sticking to the facts. 'She's back in Cardiff. Round the corner in fact. At her mum and dad's. Her relationship, in Brighton, didn't work out for her.'

'Oh, that's regrettable,' her mother said. The tip of her tongue touched her top lip. Kate knew this of old: she was working out her tactics. Kate prayed she would leave it be and see it as harmless. 'Is she here for long?' Mum said, lightly. Kate began to breathe again.

'I don't know. She's got to find her feet first, I should think.'

An encouraging smile came her way.

'And how are things between you?'

'Good. We're only just getting to know one another again really.'

Her mother's eyes narrowed. Then she hissed a long sigh as she splayed her hand and corrected her stack of engagement, wedding and eternity rings.

Kate understood then that she'd made a mistake by implying their friendship had a future. Like a cat swishing its tail as it prepared to strike, her mother tapped a nail against her cup. Kate's stomach began to tumble, waiting for the reprimand. The verbal slap came hard and fast as her mother snapped.

'You stupid, stupid girl.' Her fists were clenched as if she was trying to stop herself physically lashing out.

Kate's cheeks burned from the assault.

Her mother looked up to the ceiling. Kate tensed, preparing for more blows, trying to hold herself together. She felt Charlie's hand on hers. But she couldn't reciprocate the squeeze of solidarity – she was paralyzed.

Growling, Mum said: 'It's all going to come out now, you realize.'

'Well, no, it doesn't have to…' Kate's throat went dry as she saw an angry vein stick out on her mother's neck.

'How hard we've all worked to make sure you had a future and now you're going to throw it back in our faces.' Mum was getting louder now and her words were like freezing hailstones on her face.

'No, no,' Kate said weakly, trying to stop this from escalating. 'We agreed, to leave the past be.' Kate had believed that. Yet hearing it aloud, she knew her protest sounded hollow. This was typical: in her mother's company, under her scrutiny, she was a fool.

Mum gave a bitter laugh.

'This is going to ruin everything. You are going to lose it all. Unless you back off.' The last sentence was accompanied by a sickening smile – it was an instruction, not a request. 'You have only embarked on this… this sheer idiocy to lessen yourself of guilt. Nothing good ever comes from that.'

Kate was drowning in her own incompetence. Her mother was right – no matter that Vee had contacted her first, she should've let it go. But she had ended up trying to make amends: this was no friendship and there was no equality. It was simply an attempt to relieve Kate's disgrace.

A sob escaped from inside of her as she began to concede that she was risking everything by trying to start over - in her heart of hearts she suspected there was no way forward for her and Vee.

'Mum…' Charlie said, warily from the side.

'Mum, nothing.' She sucked her cheeks and began to massage her temples with her fingers. 'What on earth do you think you're doing, Katherine?' Then her voice softened, became persuasive. 'You have Jack, you have a job, you have a nice home. Do you think that's all going to be there when people find out? The one person we did this for, to protect and keep safe, will suffer. You don't want that, surely?'

No, no, no, of course not, she wanted to scream. But she felt mute from fright now. How was she going to undo herself from Vee? How could she have put herself in this position? The hope Kate had had in her grasp was slipping away.

'We have to be true at some point, Mum.' Charlie almost whispered her words: they were so dangerous, they had had to be delivered with kid gloves. Kate turned to her, astounded by her courage: for Charlie would lose out too.

Their mother shut her eyes.

Charlie went on: it was like a suicide mission. Kate couldn't bear it. 'We cannot put it off much longer. We've avoided it, ignored it for years. But it cannot remain a secret forever. We've always known this.'

Kate dropped her head, overwhelmed by the fact. She felt the shame coming in waves, just as they had done nearly eight years ago.

'I will not stand by and watch this family fall apart,' Mum shouted, smacking the worktop.

But Charlie stood up. Kate wanted to pull her back down, to tell her she didn't need to sacrifice herself.

'If we aren't upfront, then we will fall apart.'

Kate turned to her sister, incredulous, shocked that there was an alternative. She held her hand over her open mouth. What if Charlie was right and not Mum? What if owning the facts, releasing them before they tumbled out was possible?

Kate held onto the stainless steel of her stool as it dawned on her.

For the first time, Kate felt the potential for the tide to turn within her. Years and years of keeping quiet, padlocking the hurt and watching from the side might not have to be the way. Jack didn't know all of what she'd done, but he did know she had fallen from a great height. The sleeping around, the alcohol and drugs when she went travelling, it had been her way of blocking out her losing control. Yet he'd accepted it and helped to repair her with unconditional love: the thing she'd been chasing for so long which her mother had never given her.

She looked at Charlie and saw the love burning in her eyes: her sister wanted it out in the open. Her sister, who was prepared to ride the storm for her sake.

'You want to right the wrong,' Kate said, her eyes brimming with tears.

'No.' Charlie shook her head and grabbed Kate's hands. 'There was no wrong, Kate. Can't you see? We've been blessed by what happened to you. And we should celebrate it.'

Kate felt the revelation sweep through her: she felt her gut settling on the idea. She grabbed her sister and held on tight, rocking slowly, as a strange calm descended.

She'd forgotten her mother was there until she cried out.

'I've only ever wanted the best for you both. Your father and I, we came from nothing. Look at what we've given you. You cannot let this slip out.'

Kate turned to see her. She was trembling on the other side of the bar: it was a last attempt to bring the matter back under her selfish jurisdiction.

But empowered by her sister's support and insight, Kate had had enough.

'I've been living with this, this… anguish and sickness and misery and I need to rid myself of it. I can't stand the lies anymore.'

She began to step away, then picked up her bag and clutched it to her chest.

And then she blew a kiss at Charlie, who nodded, understanding she had to leave. To show there would be no more discussion.

Her mother was gasping for air: unable to believe she had lost. No doubt, Kate knew, she would be reloading her weapons the second she left.

But from now on, she believed love would protect her.

Chapter Twelve

M

Hackney, May

He hated himself for it, but every once in a while Murphy wanted to shout at the top of his voice: 'I love you, London!'

And, as he walked home from work, this was one of those moments.

May had exploded with one of those explicit heatwaves which sent everyone out onto the pavements, grass and riverbanks, knowing it could just as easily go cold next week. Cars passed him with their roofs down, tunes pumping out, and laughter exploded in his ears as he swerved to avoid pissed-up punters spilling out of the pubs. With their shoulders bare and legs out, people were seizing the day – that's what this city was all about and why he'd never leave.

The sun was right in his eyes as he headed through Hackney: he didn't mind because soon it'd dip behind the buildings and he'd been cooped up in offices and tubes since 7 a.m. On a high of seeing his home borough buzz like a pimp's phone, he planned his weekend: a Vietnamese coffee at the Saturday market, an artisan picnic in London Fields, maybe a dip in his new fave place, the lido, which he'd come to claim as his own much to Orla's amusement. A bit of shopping, a few pints and then dinner with Ruby. She'd cancelled tonight but he didn't mind: he liked a woman to have her own life. That's where it had gone wrong with Shell, she'd wanted to stay in and do couplie stuff and watch boxsets. Ruby, though, was different. Northern and cheeky, blonde and beautiful, she had loads going on and if he saw her twice a week he was happy. And she liked her food. She'd suggested the Argentinian cafe round the corner from his for tomorrow night, he was impressed she was into big fuck-off steaks. Too many women nibbled on a lettuce leaf.

He turned into his road, leaving behind the roaring buses and sirens, and checked out the multi-million-pound houses which led to his place. One day, he always thought, admiring the four-storey squeaky clean facades that protected immaculate insides and gardens as living spaces. One day. If he kept on going, then who knew? The app economy was now bigger than Hollywood and it wouldn't slow down: every company, every organization needed an app. Billions would give way to trillions. But it wouldn't just be confined to phones; cars, TVs, gyms, even fridges and clothes would become 'smart'. He imagined a world where watches checked blood pressure and ordered medication without a GP appointment, where heating systems adjusted automatically to the temperature.

Yet the problem was, more developers were flooding the industry. There were those free programming software kits, so anyone, literally anyone, could do it. Profit margins were going to fall. Soon the younger kids would be snapping at his heels and he needed to think about what he did next. Perhaps he should leave Kode and set up a consultancy to matchmake demand with supply. Remove himself from the actual doing. But that felt too far in the future. Jesus, he wasn't forty! And he still yearned to make an app which made it big. Some mad game-changer that set the world alight. But what? The World Peace app was out of the question.

He checked himself then: it was Friday night, he'd end up giving himself a headache with all this thinking. Park it there, brainstorm on Monday because now it's the weekend. What he'd do for a cold beer.

Coming up to his block of flats, he sniffed at a white van parked opposite. The residents' committee, made up of Lexus, BMW and Golf drivers, would have a fit if it wasn't gone by the morning. Forget the gunshots they sometimes heard from other boroughs, a drop in property prices was the biggest crime. Tapping in his security code, he got a nod from the concierge who handed him some post. He'd read it tomorrow: all he wanted to do was to sit on his west-facing balcony for a bit to catch the last rays. Then he might go to the gym in the basement, grab a premium lager, bit of PlayStation and make something fancy for dinner. Orla was out tonight so he had the place to himself.

Up the stairs, into his lobby, he let himself in and then stopped.

He could hear voices, a bit of laughter. Shit, he murmured, it was Orla and she was bashing around in the kitchen. He'd told her to go easy on the units – they'd cost a packet.

'Thought you were going somewhere?' he called, hanging up his bag, irritated enough to not notice the thrill from the cold tiled floor on his feet when he kicked off his stinking espadrilles.

'Thought you were too?' she said, appearing in the hall, looking behind her then at him.

'Ruby's got a private view, I'd forgotten.'

Then he noticed she looked a bit cagey, like. She'd wrapped a leg around another and was bobbing about, like she was a robin dying for a piss.

'What's your excuse?' he said, moving forward. But she blocked him by moving into the middle of the corridor.

'There was a change of plan,' she said, her eyes darting back to the kitchen. 'We've got a guest.'

'Oh Christ, it's not one of your neglected kids, is it?' She was always threatening to bring one back.

'No!' she said, actually looking at him as if he was the mad one.

Murphy groaned and ran his hands through his hair: he was growing it because he wanted to distance himself from the short-back-and-sides Yuccies, the Young Urban Creatives, who were still wearing beards and moustaches long after he'd shaved his off.

'Who then?' he said, going in to the loo. 'Please tell me no one I know,' he shouted out through the open door, his words echoing off the brick-effect white gloss tiles. If it was a mate of Orla's he could grunt hello then get on with stuff.

'It is, actually,' she whispered loudly, telling him off like he was being unwelcome. 'Don't kill me but...'

'Who?' He wiped his hands on a thick fluffy grey towel and came out to face her. She had her best Bambi eyes going on and he knew then that whoever it was equalled a nightmare.

'It's... Vee,' Orla said, looking as guilty as a BBC presenter from the seventies. She glanced over her shoulder to make sure Vee wasn't about to walk in on them.

'You. Are having. A giraffe,' he hissed, shaking his head and shutting his eyes. He'd managed to get over the embarrassment of their drink in Cardiff: it had taken a bit, but finally the stinging humiliation of it had faded. She was out of his life once and for all. Her being here made him feel hot and uncomfortable again.

'No. I'm not.'

'Jesus, Orla,' he said. 'Why?'

'Look, you said it was okay for me to get in touch with her.' That defensive look because he was apparently being unreasonable. 'We started messaging then she was up here, something to do with work, picking up a delivery, and her van broke down and she had to get the AA out, by which time it was too late to do the pick-up and while she had, from travelling, three numbers for people who lived in London, they were so old one had moved to Scotland, another had no space because they had three kids and the third was off his tits, and she doesn't know anyone else here and she didn't want to drive back empty-handed. She can do the pick-up first thing tomorrow. I'm sorry. You said you'd be out. What else could I do?' His first instinct was to run, but to where?

'Fuck, fuck, fuck,' he said. 'Why did you offer?'

'Because she needed help, Michael. Is it that difficult to understand?' she said, her hands jutting at him. 'You're a prick, you know that. She doesn't know anyone else in London. She couldn't afford a hotel and she has only just started this job and she doesn't want to let down her boss. She's upset. Thinks she's incapable of being a grown-up. Why are you so bothered anyway?'

'Because it's weird.'

Orla screwed her face up, making him feel a bit tight. All right, maybe he had gone a bit OTT, but seriously, why couldn't Vee just sort herself out?

'And anyway, she can't want to stay here, surely?'

Orla dropped her head then and he guessed.

'You told her I wouldn't be here, didn't you?'

She looked back up at him with dejected eyes.

'This is the problem with being helpful, Orla. Yeah?'

He crossed his arms and sighed.

'Well, she's not staying,' he said, 'Get rid of her.'

'No! Don't be so terrible.'

'You created this, you fix it.'

'Go and stay at Ruby's or someone else's…' Orla's eyes glinted with power. She knew he had nowhere else to go – he had mates, of course he did. But he'd never crash on them. He prided himself on being self-sufficient.

'Right. If you won't do it, I will.'

He brushed past Orla and marched into the flat. Vee couldn't stay here. No way. He'd make up an excuse. Even give her the money for a hotel if he had to. He wanted to chill not pretend it was all hunky-dory over a bottle of wine and dinner. This was his home, for fuck's… shit.

He stopped as he heard crying. Then Murphy could see her on the balcony, her bare shoulders shaking, the sound of tears coming in on the breeze through the French doors.

Her hair was wobbling – the pink was gone and it was cut into a long bob, which he knew was a lob because Orla once had one – she was sobbing her heart out.

He would have to be an absolute bastard to tell her to go. In fact, he couldn't believe he'd even considered evicting her: was this who he was now? Was he that much of a lowlife? Murphy felt the pressure then to prove he wasn't. And he bristled at the realization that whenever she tripped into his life, she made him reflect on himself and want to be a nicer person.

Murphy put his hands over his face and prayed she'd have disappeared by the time he took them down. But no. God didn't owe him anything.

Resigned to having to do the right thing, his heart in his mouth, he slipped outside and as he said her name he ran his thumb over the thickened skin of the scar on his finger.

'Vee.'

She jumped and turned around, her eyes on stalks. 'What are you doing here?' she gasped.

What was it with these two? First Orla and now Vee, making out he shouldn't be in his own flat.

'I live here,' he said, all sarky. Then he repeated it again, this time without an edge because she looked rough as, puffy and red. Tired and - Jesus, he was coming undone here - lost. His fingers tingled. Like something was changing in him, but he didn't know what.

'I was just popping in. To say hi to Orla. I'm on my way now,' she said, averting her eyes, moving to go past with her back to him, 'I'll get my bag and some loo roll to blow my nose, if that's okay, then I'll be gone.'

He said nothing, processing the sight of her desperate to get away from him. Like he was a serial killer. Asking for permission for bog roll.

She hugged herself, rubbed her face, tucked a tendril behind her ear and looked everywhere but at him.

'I would never have come if I'd known you were here. Honestly.'

It was like a kick in the bollocks – seeing her shrivel in his presence made him feel sick, disorientated. This person who'd been his best friend for years, who had been his right-hand woman, wanting nothing to do with him. Okay they hadn't got on when they'd met in Cardiff recently, it had been awkward, hideously awkward, but she didn't even want to look at him now. He swallowed hard, acknowledging the realization that she'd never wanted to see him again. Yes, he'd thought the same afterwards, but in all honesty that was because she'd been off with him: being rejected by her again was his overwhelming feeling rather than the embarrassment he'd claimed to have felt. He understood that now and he ached all over, dizzy with the distress of seeing her so distant. Because now he could admit it: he'd met up with her in the hope she would cure him of this sickness inside him, this inability to be close to someone. Her. That evening when he'd been humourless and nervous, she hadn't bothered to reach in to try to find him and he'd been rejected all over again.

Yet when he saw her just now, he'd felt protective, as if he'd been stripped of all the stuff he carried around with him. The anger and the bitterness. He'd only wanted to comfort her.

He couldn't bear it: he knew now he had one last chance. This was it.

'It's okay,' he said, stepping back, giving her space, 'you can stay. I'll let you two catch up.'

'It's fine. I'll look for a B&B,' she said, grabbing her phone out of her back pocket but clearly unable to see anything through those fat tears which were bowling down her face.

'You can have my room. I'll go on the sofa.'

He turned and left her in the evening sun which cast her long shadow into the lounge. Even when he wasn't looking at her he still saw her.

Orla came out from her room and he just nodded at her to go on through. Vee could tell her the news.

A strange sense of peace came over him: he had survived this moment and there was no bang, no explosion, no falling apart. It was the most unfamiliar feeling: warm and soothing. Like he'd crossed some line.

Dazed, he opened the fridge and stared in, seeing bottles but not really taking them in.

Then he felt a hand on his arm. 'I just wanted to say thank you.'

He looked to his side and Vee was there, her chin trembling, wisps of hair around her head like a halo. Her touch was... something else. Not electrifying but grounding, like home.

'I don't know London,' she said, quietly. 'Turns out I'm a bit of a bumpkin. With no buddies.'

'What? You? The international traveller?' Now he'd dropped the defences, it was surprisingly easy to slip back into their banter. How was that possible, he wondered? It was like they were seamlessly carrying on a conversation which had started sixteen years ago and that meeting in the bar had never happened.

She laughed through her nose which produced a huge bubble of snot. But, damn it, rather than disgust, he only found it sweet and nostalgic, this being the sort of care-free relationship they had, where they could expose all of themselves to the other and not feel judged.

'Oh, God!' she said, flapping her hands and wiping it away. 'What a state I am.'

'There's not exactly a line of mates at my door either.'

Vee looked unsure then, like she was weighing something up. But she decided to go for it.

'So... how about we become, you know, friends then?' she said shyly.

He played at sizing up her offer then shrugged.

'Might as well, eh,' he said, 'I'm Murphy. Bit of a prick. How do you do?'

He put out a hand. Then, oh shit, she was crying again.

'Happy tears,' she said, pointing a finger at them, having seen his face drop.

'I'm Vee. Bit of an idiot. Nice to meet you.'

Then she took his palm and they shared an emphatic but

brief shake. But the feel of her warm hand stayed with him and his eyes began to smart.

This was important, he wasn't sure why, it just felt seismic. Like he was transforming, doing exactly what Orla had said he should, to see if he could like himself, dare to open up to possible hurt, forgive Dad, make Mam proud. To move on. He didn't know what Vee's role in all of this would be, not specifically, but he sensed that forgiving and forgetting the reasons of the breakdown of their friendship and making it up with her could put him on the right path.

'Beer?' he said, quickly, as the word caught in his throat.

How were they going to start again? he wondered, as he fished one out and watched Vee use her teeth to twist off the top, as she'd always done. It was the oddest thing, seeing her here in his kitchen, pulling a move he'd seen a million times.

She took a long gulp and he considered asking about her job, her parents, her plans... but then that would all come naturally if it was meant to progress. When they'd met in that classroom all those years ago, they hadn't gone and had a deep and meaningful. They'd just had a chat about music and then it had all clicked. He had to trust it would be there again: because he felt it. Because he was being himself, letting her in. All he wanted to do was stick with this calm. It was obvious what to do.

'Want to listen to some vinyl?' he said, loping off into the lounge, where Orla was trying not to look over the moon about the way this had all panned out.

'Vinyl? As in records?' Vee said, padding in behind him and settling down on his corner sofa next to his sister as if they'd been doing this for years.

'Yeah, you know, as in a round thing. You stick a needle on it and music comes out.' He flicked through a stack of albums in a wave of déjà vu which fluttered around his heart.

'Oh God, don't tell me it's cool to like records again? Murphy, you are such a hipster!' Vee teased, making Orla snort.

'But there's something about the scratchy sound. And you can hold the record, feel the music, like you're part of it.' He stroked his Technics record player, enjoying the touch of its flawless walnut sheen. 'It's beautiful...'

Then self-conscious because he knew he sounded up himself, he added: 'I told you I was a bit of a prick.'

But where he expected to see mirth on Vee's face, she was

just nodding.

'No, I get it,' she said, softly. 'Like it's real. Not up in some cloud.'

He actually felt himself blush in appreciation. This simple exchange was natural: their minds still met. Like they'd come out of some fog and had reached out to one another.

He waited for his inner cynic to jump in. But there was silence. He knew then what he was going to play.

Without a word, he pulled out their favourite album as kids, *Different Class* by Pulp.

He slid out the vinyl, held it with his fingertips, blew on it to get rid of any dust then placed it down before carefully lowering the needle onto the grooves. He felt like a surgeon.

As the crackle gave way to the first song, he finally let his eyes rest on Vee for a second.

Her way of holding a bottle at the neck so as not to warm up the booze; her head nodding a fraction out of time to the beat; her eyes staring at nothing accompanied by an enigmatic smile. It was all the same.

He just hoped it would be different this time.

*

Bangkok, Thailand, February 2008

Seven a.m. on the Khao San Road but it could just as easily be the afternoon, Vicky thinks.

Even now, there's a grey fog at thigh level from the car fumes; virgin backpackers step wide-eyed out of taxis; old hands with hennaed wrists sit saucer-eyed in the bars, all fucked and laughing; horns beep, techno pumps and haggling hawkers offer 'nice price' between the steaming rubbish. It's a rotten, decaying place but Vicky is glad of it, this baking hot and sweaty morning.

It's a distraction from the fact that here, at a bus stop, her journey with Kat ends.

Vicky drops her dusty rucksack to the floor and takes a seat on it while Kat remains standing, strapped in unwilling to take hers off; she is primed to jump aboard her transfer to the airport, desperate to fly home. Her head strains to catch sight of it, which is due any minute. An enormous cockroach scuttles towards them, its terracotta shell gleaming brighter than Vicky's painted toenails. Usually she'd warn Kat because she's developed a massive phobia after one crawled into her bed through her mosquito net. Vicky doesn't like them either, but this is their home, she's the visitor not them. But she says nothing because Kat is wound so tightly she might snap. Ever since their row two weeks ago, things between them have been strained. Not because they weren't getting on, they sorted it, but because Kat has shut down. It's as if she's on sleep mode or like a telly on standby – there but not there. Quiet, refusing to go out and explore, counting down the days until she can leave. She's spent her days showering, complaining she feels dirty, so much so she won't risk using her 'filthy' hands to put in her lenses. With her glasses and severe French plait – to stop anything getting tangled in her hair – she resembles her schoolgirl self. To be honest, Vicky will feel relieved when Kat's gone: it's been really hard watching her suffer. She's tried to speak to her, help her, but Kat is stuck in a tight-lipped and drawn loop: Vicky gets that it's her way of keeping herself together. But it's meant that Vicky has been alone for a good while now and she's sort of felt responsible for her. At least when they part, Kat will feel safe.

Vicky isn't scared about being here by herself: backpackers travel like this all the time. She's had to make friends with people this last fortnight anyway and she's done well, considering she's not the most outgoing person.

Besides, she's got the absolutely best feeling about her last month away!

Mikey's got a week off coming up, just before he starts working for Apple. He got the job, sounds like a glorified salesman to her, but he's happy. So he's coming to see her! He finally caved in.

She got the email last night: Vicky is absolutely made up that that he'll be here, but she hasn't told Kat – that might tip her over the edge, make her think they've planned it behind her back. Vicky emailed back a million exclamation marks and said she'd tell him exactly what to book as soon as she knew where she was going to be. What he doesn't know is that he will hear from her the day after tomorrow – via a letter she's made Kat promise to give him in person!

She wants to surprise him but also she wants him to be able to hold it in his hand as if he's holding a piece of her. Emails are all right but a letter is concrete, like you can't delete it. And she's kind of opened up a bit to him. Not at first though because it begins with her plan for them: after Kat's departed, she's going to the bus station to catch an overland ride to the Cambodian border, from where she'll travel to Siem Reap. She'll wait for Mikey there before she goes to see the temples of Angkor: it's where they filmed Tomb Raider, *he's going to die when he sees it! Then they can go to the beach at Sihanoukville, followed by the Killing Fields in Phnom Penh and fly to Vietnam. It's going to be amazing, she just knows it: she's all shivery thinking about it because she's is pretty sure that something's going to happen. Like, after Kat said during their fight that Vicky might be a little bit in love with Mikey, she hasn't been able to stop her tummy somersaulting. Vicky thinks she might be a smidgeon right. Thinking about what she said has sort of shocked her: but in a heart-racing way, like what if he feels the same? She's re-read all his emails and he has been really nice – she's tried to be totally objective about them but, yes, there could be something there. Vicky has hardly slept since Kat suggested it, but she's not tired: she gets these pulses every time she imagines seeing him. She's even started to have rude dreams about him, which makes her* blush when she wakes up. *Oh God*, she thinks, *imagine if they did get it on - it'd be so mad! But it'd be perfect. Perfectly mad.*

At the end of her letter, she says that she has been longing to see him – she makes a joke that she might give him a promotion from back-up man. But then she gets serious and says the more people she's met and the more places she's been to have made her realize how special he is: she always knew he was, but being at home makes you think that's how it is in the big world. But it isn't – everyone pales in comparison to him. She doesn't exactly say that she wants to try getting together but she says 'if you're single then we could see what happens'. He'd have to be thick not to get that and that's one thing he isn't. Then she cracks another joke just in case: if she's got it all wrong, then feel free to never contact her again. It took her ages to put it in the proper tone – even though it felt completely right to do it – but she finished it off by head torch while Kat slept or at least jabbered fitfully. Had she done it by email, she wouldn't have had the chance to double-check this was what she wanted to do. But she still decided to go for it this morning as they packed up their bags and she gave Kat the envelope, telling her she had her to thank for this. Vicky had felt weepy and grateful, as she said it and she expected Kat to respond in the same way: a recognition that Kat had been the one to make Vicky admit her feelings. All she got back was a promise she'd deliver it. But things haven't been right since their row - there's a stiltedness where once there was intimacy.

Vicky hugs her knees at the prospect of hearing back from him. She examines her calves - for the first time ever she's got some definition there rather than big hefty cankles. She'd already lost a stone with all the walking, but another half has come off after a dodgy bowl of prawn noodles ten days ago. Her appetite has definitely gone down, she is a classic bored trougher, but here there's so much to do she can sometimes forget to eat. And there's not potatoes and bread and crap like that on offer, just healthy rice and stir-fries. Her hair is longer now too, a fraction below her shoulders, and it's bleached blonde by the sun. Vicky has never felt so good. But there's a horrid side to it too because Kat has never looked so awful. Her shoulders are bony and her skin has broken out in spots, poor love. Vicky sees a bead of perspiration run down Kat's left leg: Vicky looks up to see if she's noticed. She's been hypersensitive to anything relating to her body of late, flicking at invisible things on her arms and scratching at nothing, but she seems unaware now. Only her right leg jiggles, poised to scale the step of the bus as soon as it arrives and seal herself into the air-conditioned capsule of bus, airport and plane which will be her refuge.

'I think that's mine,' Kat says, pushing her glasses up her nose, craning her neck to confirm it. 'It is!'

For the first time in ages, she gives Vicky a big smile, a genuine one. Jesus, Vicky would be like 'kill me now', if she had to go home.

It takes an age for the bus to make its way down the street as tuk-tuks dart here and there and idiots walk out into its path without looking: Vicky will be glad to move on from here, get back to some real travelling.

She gets up and holds Kat's hand.

'Take care, okay?' she says, 'Make sure you see the doctor when you get back.'

'I just need to get home,' Kat says as her eyes settle on Vicky. 'I'm sorry. About everything. You can enjoy yourself now, eh?'

Kat tries to make it look like she's being funny.

'Don't be silly, I'm going to miss you.' Then, because she's her friend, she does a fake jolly add-on: 'We've had a great time! Seen loads and done all sorts, haven't we?'

It was true, definitely true in Vicky's case.

'Yeah,' Kat says, gulping. 'You go careful.'

Vicky nods and gives Kat a hug. Kat is stiff though and begins pulling away the second the bus pulls up. She's the first one in the queue and as she boards, Vicky says: 'See you in a month!'

Kat looks back at her blankly, as if she doesn't understand.

'When I get home!' Vicky says to explain. Blimey, she's a right sieve head.

'Okay' is all she says then she makes her way up the aisle to take a seat on Vicky's side. They wave a bit as everyone gets themselves seated for the journey, fussing with their bags and tickets and books.

And as the bus crawls off, Vicky picks up her rucksack then walks alongside Kat's window blowing kisses.

'Don't forget to give Mikey the letter!' she shouts, using her hands as a loudspeaker, as the bus picks up a little speed.

Vicky trots alongside, waiting to get the thumbs up, but Kat stares straight ahead and doesn't look back.

Chapter Thirteen

V

Cowbridge

'Mustard nuts?' Vee repeated, spinning around to see Pierre waiting for something.

'Well?' he said, his gigantic black eyebrows raised like two standing bears.

Her mind raced. She'd been miles away. Mustard nuts? What the hell? Was it a bad translation of some bizarre French term of endearment? Or, oh God, this wasn't one of his team-bonding things, was it, like he'd christened her Mustard Nuts? If so, why? She didn't own a pair of nuts, had no connection with mustard, and it sounded offensive, to be honest. If she smelled spicy it was because of his shop not her own fumes.

She decided to say nothing – she didn't want to give him ideas – and, with her best sad doggy eyes, got ready to apologize for being caught daydreaming in the store cupboard knee-deep in pasta, pickles and preserves.

'How are we doing? You know, stock-wise, with mustard and nuts?' he said, his hands on either side of the door frame as if he was holding up the entire room.

'Oh, I see! Right, well, er, I haven't got that far yet. I'm only on F.' She pointed at the capital letter she'd sharpied onto the shelf to show where she'd got up to on her alphabetical rehaul. Pierre had been astounded this morning when she'd suggested it. The room had been a higgledy-piggledy mess in which he couldn't find products or keep track of supplies. A bit of order would make a huge difference, she'd said. He'd behaved like she'd discovered penicillin. 'You are a genius. Marginal gains!' he'd shouted at her. 'Making small improvements add up to major improvements!'

'Does that mean I'll be Employee of the Month for May?' she'd asked, her tongue firmly in her cheek.

'You have a very good chance,' he'd said without an ounce of irony. The complete nutter.

The job had been slow, dusty and sneezy, but she'd felt like hiding away today. After a period of doing the badass strong woman thing – which had been down to picking herself up post-Jez with work and friends – the buzz had started to wane as the effects of flying solo and living with Mum and Dad kicked in. Vee felt flat. The tears had run out; the last time she'd cried was a fortnight ago when she'd been at Murphy's. Once she'd got over the horror of the van breaking down and Murphy's shock, the night she'd spent there had been brilliant. It had turned out to be the best night since she'd been dumped, maybe even before that. Over beers and some clean-eating thing he'd dished up, Murphy and her had connected effortlessly and Orla was absolutely lush. They'd stayed up until 2 a.m. reminiscing and catching up: Murphy had filled in a few gaps about his rise to success and Orla had revealed he'd made his way through half of London in pursuit of the perfect woman, which had made her feel a bit funny until she told herself he had a right just as she did to have a history.

But when she'd crept out early the next morning to do the cheese pick-up, she'd felt as if she was walking out of a life which could've been hers had Murphy and her ever got together. That thought had shaken her: imagining them as a couple hadn't occurred to her since Thailand when she'd written him that letter. And it wasn't as if she'd want to be with him now; there were little bits of the old him, his humour was still there, but Murphy was too shiny, too self-aware. She couldn't stand to live like that, worrying if she was cool enough, eating the right thing and wearing the uniform that such a life demanded. She'd done that with Jez and look where it had got her.

Going home to her teenage bedroom every night emphasized how little she had compared to Murphy and Kate. Mum was great at leaving her be and Dad had offered to decorate her room, giving her the choice of colour scheme and curtains, but she'd so far resisted: she couldn't bring herself to imagine she was back there for good. But where was she going? What was she aiming for? There was no money to retrain – yet –

and the thought of going on Tinder or Guardian Soulmates made her feel ill. But time was ticking: yes, she knew she was only thirty and in theory she could be in her forties before she started a family or found her professional calling, yet those things didn't fall in your lap the second you decided to go for them. It could be years before she felt ready to trust a man or an instinct again, and then how many attempts would it take for her to reach a place of contentment? This fear translated itself into late-night searches of 'freezing eggs' and 'adoption over the age of forty' which only made her freak out further.

The constant reminders that she was waiting for something were exhausting. Everywhere she looked, she saw what she was missing: the loved-up couples calling in the deli for brunch; sharing the bus with other losers rather than driving herself to a career in an executive set of wheels; and wondering what crazy Jez was doing while she was on the sofa with Mum and Dad watching their latest box set, out of bounds if one of them was out. One night, she'd been so desperate to talk to a friend, she'd messaged Jemima in Brighton: you couldn't ring her these days because she was always mid-feed or the baby was crying. She didn't want to lean on her – how could Jem console her when she had to be loyal to Jez? It had been a waste of time: the baby had a temperature, Jem was knackered and yes, Jez was still with 'her'.

Vee didn't want to overload on Kate – it was too early for that. Bottling things up was making her negative. She knew it was self-indulgent to consider 'why me?' and she fought against it most of the time. But sometimes, like today, she just needed to retreat from being in the audience of other people's lives. That was why she had offered to hole herself up in the store cupboard.

'We're out of banana flour,' she announced, to show she had been doing some work. 'Whatever that is.'

Pierre sighed. 'Banana flour is a superfood. Gluten-free. High in resistant starch which helps to protect against diabetes and colonic cancer. Controls blood sugar. Can substitute normal flour and be used in smoothies.'

Vee sneered a bit too wildly.

'We sell a lifestyle here, Vee. Humans believe poshing up their nosh makes them sophisticated. There are also health benefits too. Ergo, there is a market for it. That's what we do.'

Vee rolled her eyes: had she still been with Jez then she'd probably have known all of that. Food trends were his forte. Her move back home, where Mum bought Hovis and Heinz, was the extreme opposite of Brighton. She realized now that her dabbling in veganism and hot yoga had all been half-hearted, just to fit in. Just to be loved, approved of and feel special. With shame, Vee recalled how she'd been sniffy at first when she'd returned home, but now she actually preferred a nice spag bol and a weepy.

Doubt came along and stamped her on the forehead: what was she doing here? Peddling wares for idiots who lived off kale, used beard wax and juice cleansed their colons? She felt her skin prickling with irritation.

Pierre's forehead cracked like it was about to avalanche.

'I'm sensing something here. Are you in need of a camomile tea?'

'No, I'm bloody not. And what's wrong with PG Tips?'

'PG what?'

Vee shut her eyes and counted to ten. 'I think I just need to get on with this,' she said, knowing that if she didn't cool it, she'd be out of a job. She was entirely grateful to Pierre for giving her this opportunity and he wasn't to blame for her finding fault with tarty food.

'Would you like to play my anger drum?' he said, earnestly.

Her jaw dropped. He was weird, she knew that, but she'd never put him down as a pervert.

'Pierre!' she squeaked, 'that is completely inappropriate. You do realize that, don't you?'

'But it helps, having a good bang. It's a release. We can do it quick while the shop's quiet.' He nodded furiously at her. Then he nipped out of the doorway, leaving her to rip off her apron and throw it on the floor. There was no way she was standing for this.

Before she could run away, he was back with a huge smile... And a hand drum. A bloody instrument. That was what he'd meant! An actual drum, which made her realize how uptight she'd been. Her whole body relaxed with relief. But what did a drum have to do with how she felt?

'Right, so sit down and cross your legs, like me.'

She inched her way to the floor, examining him with wary eyes, wondering if he was in actual, fact King of Kooky Land.

'Good. Now take the drum.'

He held it out as she weighed it up. It was gaga, he was gaga. But would it make her feel any worse? Unlikely. So she tentatively reached out and did as she was told.

'And... off you go!' He sat smiling expectantly at her.

'But...what am I supposed to do?' Examining the wooden goblet-shaped object in her hands, Vee felt horribly self-conscious and she was glad of the dingy lighting.

Pierre shook his head at her, cross that she was so clueless. As if she'd ever mentioned drumming before! He snatched it off her and began.

'Like this...'

He tapped out a rhythm, softly at first.

She shifted around on her bum – she'd sat on a discarded piece of pasta – and fussed about before getting comfy.

'Experts believe drumming can reduce stress, lower blood pressure, conquer social isolation, boost immunity, improve psychological well-being...'

He increased his tempo and touch on the skin of the goblet-shaped drum. Vee watched, hiding her amusement because she didn't want to insult him.

'...we all have a natural sense of rhythm. It can take us back to the womb, when we'd hear our mother's heartbeat. It's affordable, accessible, sustainable...'

He closed his eyes and began beating harder, his head jogging. After a while, she found her foot was tapping along and she was breathing in time. It was eerie the way it did seem to calm her: take her to a state of being rather than feeling and worrying and thinking.

'...we are born drummers. And, yes, while you might feel foolish, it is imperative you try. Small pleasures are the key to happiness.'

Shortly, he faded his fingers out then handed it to Vee.

'Your go,' he said.

Awkwardly, she started with one hand, then stopped. This was ridiculous.

'I can't do it. I feel all creepy.'

'Try,' he said, setting a tempo with the clap of his palms. Vee's tummy rumbled. She'd eyed up some quiche for lunch and the sooner she did this, the sooner she could eat. So she got on with it. After a shaky start, all jerky like being on roller

140

skates for the first time, she managed to get into the swing.

'Good. Now let it out. Whatever it is that's bugging you.'

With her eyes focused on her hands – she dare not look up because she might burst out laughing – she thought of her earlier frustration and anger and incredibly, her fingers responded with a heavy slap. Beat after beat after beat, like a metronome, her brain worked out the challenge of coordination and finally her hands expressed her hurt. But not for long because she lost her concentration. Yet she had an inkling that Pierre had been right about its feel-good factor.

'It's ridiculous, Pierre. Nice ridiculous, I mean,' she said, looking up at him as he awaited her verdict. 'Where did you get this from? It looks exotic.'

'It's West African. A djembé, which means "gathering in peace". The top, that's goat skin.'

'Wow, you've travelled then?'

'What? No. Just here and France, really. My ex gave it to me. She got it from a charity shop two doors down. Thought I'd like it, which I did. I keep it in work for when I need to think. If someone's complained about my cheese. It helps.'

Vee laughed. 'You're a one-off, do you know that?'

'That's what she said. In fact, that's what lots of them have said. Why do people always say that?' He looked quizzically at Vee, as if he expected her to come up with the answer.

She shrugged. 'Because you're an individual. You do things your way, I s'pose. Like, you could be anywhere in the world, what with all your connections with your parents and stuff, your schooling. But you've chosen to be here, in Wales, in this little town. You stand out.'

'Yes, that's the trouble.' His shoulders dropped and a slab of sadness landed on his chops.

'What do you mean? You're great!' She said it with feeling because he was. He treated her with respect, he accepted her imperfect slapdash ways because he saw she meant well and he was interesting. Not to mention extraordinarily handsome.

'My relationships. Doomed. Always.'

'But what is there not to love?' she asked, suddenly realizing she sounded a bit fan girly. 'As in, you're fab. And good-looking. Not that I… you know… have noticed.' She gave him a sheepish smile, but he tutted at her.

'Not you as well?' he groaned. 'Everyone says that. At first.

How handsome I am. But then when they get to know me they say they just want to be friends.'

'Oh, it must be awful being so attractive,' she said, heavy with sarcasm. 'Such a disappointment on the inside.'

'But that's just it! They are drawn to my looks, which for the record I have nothing to do with, it's not my fault. Then my personality can't live up to them. People seem to think I'm some kind of Heathcliff, so when I talk about the cheeses of the future they find me dull. It's a dagger to the heart.'

'Why don't you speak French to them? That'd do for me, it's very sexy.'

'It makes matters worse. They expect more... 'down there',' he said, gesticulating to his privates.

Vee stifled a laugh.

'No. I left all that to my bastard of a brother. He plays 'ze French man wiz his baguette'. I feel British. Apart from when it comes to cheese.'

His explanation struck a chord with Vee: for hadn't she yearned for excitement because her brother was so conventional?

'You just haven't met the one yet. That's all. You will. Defo.'

'I don't think so. I'm thirty-nine. Everyone thinks there must be something wrong with me to be alone at this age.'

'Well, at least there's always the chance you could have kids, like, forever. Women like me, single and thirty, we're the ones who have a deadline. Think about that, eh? By the time I've met someone and there's the build-up and the getting to know them and meeting the parents then the proposal and the moving in... well, it could take years and it'll be too late. You guys don't have any of that pressure. That's why men run a mile from my age group – they think we're all bunny boilers with baby brains. Why not go for a younger model and enjoy their pert bodies and fresh skin? That's what my ex did.'

'The rascal,' he boomed.

'Yep. I was all ready for him to propose then he dumped me for a younger woman. And I bet he's eating banana pancakes off her belly button as we speak.'

'Oh dear, I was supposed to be making you feel better. And now both of us are in the doldrums,' he said.

'It's me, it is. I'm sorry.'

A tinkle at the front announced the arrival of a customer.

Pierre jumped up and hugged his drum as he peered out to see who it was.

His cheeks turned pink as he announced it was the electrician. 'I'm having terrible trouble with my... er... meat slicer. The switch has gone, unfortunately.' It was quite incredible how dodgy his electrics were proving to be.

Then she saw a light bulb flash in his eyes and he came over to her.

'I've got it! You and me, we're going to host a singles cheese and wine evening. We'll do it for lonely hearts and minds. That's what we're going to do. And you're in charge of it! Although, I'll have to clear it with HR first, obviously. Right, must attend to my slicer.'

Vee was left staring at his back then the wall then at her palms which covered her face: bless him and all that shite about small pleasures, but he was off his rocker and it was going to be a disaster. Just like everything else.

Chapter Fourteen

K

Cardiff City Centre

Shoe shopping. Kate just didn't get it.

Whilst the thrill of searching for a new pair sent most women into raptures, she found it too close to public soul-searching.

For every time she braved a rack of heels and flats, she felt the pressure of having to face up to who she was and where she was going wrong. Consequently, she'd developed a survival technique: whatever M&S had in dark mid-heel courts did for work, then decent wellies and trainers or beige imitation Birkenstocks were suitable the rest of the time.

Today though was wedding shoes day so she had no choice but to throw herself into the path of danger – she could hardly wear her Hunters down the aisle. Well, she could if it was up to her but even she drew the line at that.

As she entered the department store's tasteful shoe boutique, she felt momentarily dazed and wobbly as if she was a newborn foal in stilettos. Luckily, with it being a Monday morning, there were very few people to witness her wobble. Spotlights directed her eyes to shelf after shelf of glamorous styles as though she was viewing works of art. A quick scan revealed Vee was yet to arrive: if she was going to be found out as an amateur then she needed to have Vee by her side. She found a corner couch and bowed her head, pretending to check her phone so she didn't have to make eye contact with any assistants.

As a child, Mum had always picked for her: Clarks with 'extra square'. Oblivious to the concept of thinking for herself, she'd continued going for the safe option as a teenager when all the other girls were doing their best Sugababes impression in strappy Faith and Dolcis heels. At uni, she had the chance to begin to wonder what she liked out of the multitude of looks which were happening around her. Definitely not the clunky Timberlands of Girls Aloud and Britney, which would've made her skinny legs look like golf clubs. Neither Carrie Bradshaw's ostentatious skyscrapers, owing to her height, nor the cowboy boots of the football Wags that required pink hot pants to carry off. Instead, she'd veered towards a relaxed but personal style, teaming Converse with a prom dress or wedged trainers with jeans. She figured she'd have plenty of time for career heels when she went to the City. Then it all went wrong when she got back from travelling.

Looking back, how didn't her family see that she was heading for a breakdown by her choice of footwear? Who in their right mind went out in the rain and severe gales in studded dominatrix ankle-breakers or went to the shop in slippers?

The ensuing tumble to her knees had forever left its mark: scarred, she had placed practicality above all else. So she could run if she had to. But practical wouldn't work for a wedding. That's why she'd asked Vee to come: she'd judge it right. Her mother would've insisted on ladylike – which given her past she was anything but. Charlie had a thing for sparkly stuff and Kate wanted nothing to do with diamanté.

Just then, a pair of cherry-red polka dot low-wedge sandals containing shiny yellow toenails appeared by her side. The clash of colours, which shouldn't work but did, could only belong to Vee.

'Ready?' Vee said with a playful grimace as if they were about to parachute out of a plane.

'No,' Kate said, smiling, grateful to her for understanding that this was going to be traumatic. 'Whatever you do, don't tell anyone they're for the wedding. They'll make me feel inadequate for not bringing a swatch of material from my dress.'

'Good idea,' Vee said, answering in a similarly low voice, 'we don't want to blow our cover. Have you brought the balaclavas? I thought we could crawl around on our knees. Secure the perimeters. Release the hostages. Then grab a coffee.'

'If only it was that easy,' Kate smirked.

'Well, I'm excited even if you're not. I love shoe shopping. See these?' she said, tilting her foot coquettishly. 'A fiver in the charity shop. The one next door-but-one to the deli. The women who live round there are so posh, they are, that they chuck out things that are virtually brand new.'

'It helps that you have average-sized feet,' Kate said, looking down at her own pair of size eight baguettes. 'Mine are enormous and the choice is a bit more limited.'

'Drag queens manage!'

'Believe it or not, but I don't think six-inch sequinned shoes are my style.'

'You surprise me,' Vee laughed. 'So are we looking in the bridal area then?'

'No. I don't want anything ivory, cream or white. Or heels or flats or twinkly bits or ribbons either.' She held up her hands to illustrate she wanted no drama.

'Right, well, let's go and have a look for some unicorn hooves then, shall we?'

Kate took the point that she was chasing the impossible and agreed to start looking.

As they began to wander, Kate watched Vee display the attributes of a seasoned shopper by picking up and examining shoes as she went. Kate could only cross her arms and recoil at the sight of spindly spikes, perky peep-toes, fat platforms and bejewelled straps. And why, she thought, did they give shoes names? They were patronizing ones too, such as Tiffany, Cinderella and Tutu, trying to tap into every grown woman's inner little girl. As if a pair of shoes would deliver your dreams. Well, it just turned Kate off.

They mooched in silence until they'd done a circuit of the shop floor.

'Seen anything you like?' Vee asked brightly.

Kate shook her head tightly.

'Maybe you could try some on? They might look different when you're wearing them.'

Vee's tone had changed: she was doing the maternal thing, as if Kate was a toddler refusing to taste something new. She felt embarrassed, curling up to defend herself from any interrogation.

'I'm so sorry, Vee. I just haven't seen anything. I wish I had then we could just go.'

'It might help if you know what you're looking for,' Vee added gingerly.

'That's just it,' Kate sighed. 'I'm so confused. The bridal mags, which I've tried hard to avoid but Mum keeps shoving in my face, are all about "this season's must-have look", which apparently is all Poldark ruffles and buckles. I wouldn't, even if Aidan Turner was the groom.'

'Oh forget all that nonsense, it's about what you want.' Vee nodded encouragingly: from her point of view this was an accepted given. But Kate may as well have been offered the control panel to a space rocket.

'Me?' she said, incredulously. This wedding was to be endured not enjoyed.

This time Vee made the disbelieving noises. 'Yes. It's your day. No one else's.'

Kate rolled her eyes. That was exactly what it wasn't.

'What's your dress like then?' Vee asked, trying another tack, bless her.

It was hard to remember actually. 'Sort of plain. Long.'

'Let's see a picture of it then. You've got one on your phone, haven't you?' Vee asked in such a way that inferred that that's what normal brides-to-be would have on their photo roll. But she only had shots of Jack, Boris, Griff and views of the countryside.

Kate shook her head and began to feel ashamed at coming across as so uncooperative. She wasn't doing it deliberately. This was as hopeless and embarrassing as she'd feared it would be.

'Shall we just go? Get a coffee and I'll look online?'

Vee searched her face and took a breath.

'Look, I shouldn't say this because, you know, we're not long friends again...' She waited to see if she was on safe ground.

Kate nodded slightly to show she could take whatever was coming. She had thick enough skin these days, so what did it matter if Vee was going to tell her she was a nightmare? It's not like she didn't know it already.

'...but I'm wondering if you are okay with this wedding. Like, I'd say that to anyone, I'm not trying to upset you or make waves... It's just that this is going to be a day you look back on forever. You need to be sure you're doing the right thing.'

Her friend's eyes burrowed into hers, trying to work out if she had hit home.

'I do love him,' Kate blurted out, defensively, not sure what Vee was getting at.

'I know! That's not what I meant. I'm talking about the details. Are they what you want?'

The thump of the question hit her right in the throat.

Neither Mum nor Dad had ever suggested it was 'her' day – they'd insisted on paying and so they, or rather Mum, had had the last word, choosing a smart Cardiff hotel's 'Orchid Package', with chair covers and choice of colour bow and ambient lighting to match the theme. Jack had tried to challenge the booking, but when he'd put it that they wanted somewhere more intimate, Mum did her passive-aggressive act: crying that she'd only wanted the best for her daughter. With fresh regret, she remembered how she'd taken her mother's side to shut down the discussion: she'd learned long ago that a peaceful life meant giving in.

Kate stared at the shelves of shoes and saw nothing but herself shuffling up the aisle of some converted conference room looking down at the carpeted floor rather than at her wonderful husband-in-waiting. They'd wanted to do it by themselves: she'd imagined herself in something floaty, the hem tickled by a sea breeze, with the taste of salt on her lips. Free.

Yet that delusion now choked her: there was no prospect of changing things. Mum would go ballistic. She wouldn't dig in her heels – she'd bury them in concrete. It would be like trying to get an oil tanker to do a handbrake turn. There would be recriminations, accusations, blame and guilt along the lines of 'do you know how much this has cost?', 'after everything we've done for you,' and 'what will everyone think?' Kate gulped, feeling the despair all over again, of being controlled by a mother who was so hard to love. Who was so easy to hate.

'The thing is, Vee, and I mean this in the nicest way, but you've only just come into this situation. This is my mother we're dealing with. She's had it planned forever.'

Vee bit her lip. Then she spoke. 'Yes, of course. You're doing what you think's right. I shouldn't have said anything.' Vee coughed as if to fill in the awkwardness. 'Just going to the loo, be back in a sec.'

It took a moment for Kate to realize that Vee's retreat hadn't solved anything and didn't make her feel any better. It felt depressingly familiar. And then it came to her: with horror, Kate was reminded of herself in her mother's company. Silenced and shut down. The thought of it made her stomach twist. Here she was on the brink of a new chapter in her life, having made up with Vee and about to be married, and she was still too scared to confront things. After that scene at Mum's on Sunday too. Thanks to Charlie, Kate had realized she needed to start being honest: hadn't she said as much to her mum that day?

The tangle of her secret had been threatening to suffocate her, but Charlie had shown her the way to hack it down: to own it, declare it and therein find freedom.

Coming to, she felt her face wet with tears.

Anger swept through her, then sadness: of being in this position again. Of believing things were improving only to be proved wrong. Her eyesight glazed, she felt Vee's arm around her and movement. A blur of lights and counters, smells and voices.

Then they were in the sunshine, passing people and buses, stopping only when they came to the sweet scent of grass. She breathed in and felt her lungs expand with the wide open space before her. They were in the grounds of Cardiff Castle, where ancient trees gave refuge from the city centre hustle and bustle.

Slowly returning to normal, she looked at Vee, who passed her a bottle of water without passing comment or pushing her to explain herself.

Then the words began to pour.

'It's my mother. The "keeping things together". The brave face. The lies.'

Vee was deep in concentration, her eyelashes blinking as if she was beckoning Kate's words, as if to say 'you're safe here'.

'I've had enough.'

This isn't the time nor the place, her mother's voice said in her head, but when and where was? Here, now, it felt right. The truth wasn't bubbling up as she'd thought it would; instead it was flowing around her body, calmly, cooling her, soothing her.

'I had a breakdown shortly after I came back from Thailand. I remember the flight home, thinking I was ready to start work in the City, so relieved to be going back to normality. The excitement, the relief, they came over me like a huge tide.'

Kate felt a shiver, like a muscle memory. Vee's face was etched with concern.

'I had a month before I started my job. I thought I could just get myself ready quietly. But the sense of expectation from my mother was enormous: she was on at me every second to find a flat, choose the right suits, research the markets, all of that. Fail to prepare, prepare to fail. I couldn't cope with it.

'My behaviour became erratic: I was unpredictable, overspending, under-eating, drinking too much, taking risks, sleeping around, and the buzz I got from it made me believe I was really living. Mum thought I was trying to hurt them, they couldn't see I was going loopy. They said it would end in tears. It did. I was marched to the doctor, who referred me to a psychiatrist and she said I was suffering from a combination of panic disorder and depression. She gave me pills but I didn't take them, I thought it was all nonsense, that I just needed to get to London.'

Kate hadn't spoken of this for years. Now she saw that Vee's reappearance in her life was for this very reason: to unburden herself, to make peace with her past. She fixed her with her eyes: she needed to say this straight.

'My mental health got worse. I got pregnant. I didn't realize at first. I thought I was missing periods because I was a bag of nerves up in the City. My job, it was all fourteen-hour days, terrific pressure, learning the ropes in banking and the partying, or the covering up my anxiety, continued. One weekend, when I went home, Charlie made me do a test. I was fourteen weeks pregnant. It was too late in my mind to have a termination.'

Saying it out loud, Kate had always thought the earth would crack open. But all she could hear was the rippling of leaves. The world hadn't ended.

'Mum slapped me round the face when I told her. Dad went berserk at her. I closed down. Everything stopped. I never went back to London. I was given anti-depressants but I refused to take them because of the risks to the baby - they were minimal but in my head they were enormous. And I wanted to punish myself, I guess. The midwives monitored me with home visits but the hormones made my depression even worse. I spent the rest of my pregnancy inside, refusing to go out unless it was necessary.'

'Oh, Kate...'

'I remember the beeps and the lights in hospital, the ferocious contractions. Giving him away. It was Mum's idea...'

Vee gasped as Kate paused to let it soak in.

'She sorted all of the legal stuff. I was in a haze for months. Suicidal. Drugged up on anti-depressants because I was hit by post-natal depression by then too. Then gradually, I came out of it. I had counselling, the tablets eventually helped. Getting my job at the estate agent gave me a new focus. Then I met Jack, came off the pills, and finally understood how to love and how to be loved. I felt safe.'

'What about...the father? He wasn't involved?'

'No. There was never any point.' There was nothing dishonest about this.

'So where is the baby now?' Vee asked quietly.

'I still see him,' she said, feeling the swell of love at the memory of his soft skin and bed hair. 'I always have done. Mum didn't approve, never has, but if I hadn't had any contact, I would've ended it all.'

'I don't understand,' Vee said.

Kate looked up from her fingers and stared her in the eyes. An explosion went off inside.

'Charlie. She'd been trying for a baby for a while. They had tests. Tom was infertile. My nephew. Griffy,' she said, 'he's my son.'

'Oh,' Vee said, dumbfounded, her face agog.

'With my blessing, while I was pregnant, my sister and her husband applied for a special guardianship order giving them the same parental responsibility as me. I was unable to look after him. My head was in bits, I was incapable.'

The words hung in the air but there was no thunder, Kate realized. Only love.

'The wedding shoes,' she added, feeling barefoot and blistered, 'I can't walk in the footsteps of the person my mother wants me to be anymore.'

'Does Jack know?'

'Sort of. He knows I gave up a baby. Just not that it's Griff. We told no one, we agreed. I kept it from him, from everyone, out of loyalty to my sister. But it feels wrong now.'

'And Griffy?'

'He knows he had a, what we call, tummy mummy, someone who gave birth to him - just not that it was me.'

'Oh Kate, what are you going to do?' Vee whispered, reaching to Kate to hold her hand.

'Be honest. Take responsibility,' Kate said, tears flowing. 'Tell Jack. Cancel the wedding. Sit down with Griffy and Charlie to tell him, not to bring him back to me because that wouldn't be in his interest but just to be honourable. And watch my relationship collapse around me,' she said, running her hands through the grass as if she was wiping her hands clean, 'but at least I'll be able to live with myself.'

Chapter Fifteen

M

London

'I… think something's…' Dad said, stuttering, over the phone, 'I… it's…'

'Dad? What's the matter?' He sounded really weird, not with it, absent. Murphy was frightened and began to look up and down the street frantically for a cab.

'I… don't…' He could hear his father's confused mouth opening and closing and a strange muffled sound as if his tongue was floundering.

'Have you been on the piss?' Stupid question. It was almost six o'clock on Mam's birthday. She would've been fifty-five. Dad would've been in all day, with the curtains closed, knocking it back. But he didn't sound drunk, more unstable.

He flagged down a Hackney and jumped in.

'Are you in any pain?' Murphy's heart was racing. 'Paddington, mate,' he said to the taxi driver.

'I'm not… er… all that… clever. But… no… pain.'

'Don't move,' Murphy said, 'I'm on my way.'

Fuck, fuck. Fuck. It was going to take three hours to get back, if he was lucky. Who the hell was there? The warden at the flats would've clocked off at 5 p.m. He had no emergency number. The only person who could get in was the cleaner. Unless… His stomach went full Mario Kart crash. He was going to have to ask Vee.

She'd left her number on a thank you scrap of paper when she'd stayed. He'd let it remain on the coffee table for a few days, undecided whether to chuck it or make a note of it. It was like a game he'd played with himself: if he threw it away, then he could just put her reappearance down as chance. If he kept it, it'd mean he'd be tempted to see her again. Maybe when he was next down in Cardiff. Just for a drink or whatever. He resisted admitting to himself that with her he'd had the happiest night in ages: because if he did then he'd be admitting his way of life, his existence without her, was somehow lacking. Hollow.

Eventually, he caved in and typed it into his phone. After that, his fingers had itched to text her. To say he'd heard a Pulp song and it'd reminded him of the time she'd thrown up on the dance floor of TJ's in Newport. Or he'd seen that *Twin Town* was on, her favourite film, and did she know? He went from wanting to punch himself in the head to shrugging because they were sort-of mates again. Simple as.

Now, as he found Vee in his contacts and pressed 'call', he was grateful at least that he had a valid reason to ring. There was no one else he could rely on to help, not geographically anyway.

'Hello?' she said.

He could hear music in the background.

'It's me,' he said. Then when he realized she wouldn't have had any way of knowing it was him, she didn't have his number, he added a quick: 'Murphy.' Even in these circumstances, he winced at his clumsiness.

'I know!' she said, which made him feel forgiven. 'You all right?' She sounded pleased to hear from him. The tune in the background was from one of those quiz shows. He remembered it from Mam, she'd watched it right up until the end in the hospice.

'Yeah. Actually, no. Listen, are you free? Like now?'

'Er…' She was walking somewhere, away from the telly '… yes, why?' She sounded suspicious.

'It's Dad, he's in a bad way. It's Mam's birthday.' Straight to the point, no messing.

'Oh, shit. Right, fine. What do you need me to do?'

Thank God, she got it.

'I'm on my way to Cardiff now, but could you go and check on him? His cleaner's got a key. I'll text her to say you're coming, text you their addresses, they're both in Llanedeyrn, near my old house. Get a cab and I'll give you the money.' There was no time for p's and q's.

'I'll go in Mum's car. It'll be quicker.'

'Vee… look, I don't know what state he's in. Maybe take

your dad? I'll ring an ambulance now, tell them you're coming. All right?'

'Yes. Course. I'll call when I'm there.'

'Okay, cheers. Oh, and Vee…'

'Yes?'

'Thanks a million. I owe you one.'

'No problem. Speak later.'

Then he dialled 999, explaining there'd be someone at the house shortly. Pulling up at Paddington, he dashed to Platform One and got on the train with three minutes to spare. No seats, so he jostled his way past the students and suits to the area between the buffet and first class because if he needed a wall to lean against, it'd at least be less grubby there.

Then he spoke to Orla, to tell her not to worry but he was on the way to see Dad, who'd sounded out of sorts. He was sure it'd all be okay but he had a meeting in Bristol tomorrow anyway. 'Light a candle for me, yeah?' he asked her, feeling bad he'd miss their annual ritual when they'd have pie and mash and remember Mam.

His insides twisted when her voice went shaky, but he promised everything would be tidy. Get Phil over, he'd said, there was some lovely grub in the fridge, some monkfish that he'd got in to cook for Ruby tomorrow – he didn't tell her that bit – a bottle of nice white, a posh pudding too. Have a party for Mam, he'd said.

Then he gripped his phone in his slippery hand, wired with the worry, and waited to hear from Vee.

As the London grime faded, as his head lolled to the train's rocking, as the white noise of passing trains and wind rushing through the crack of the door window, his breathing returned to normal. But the lurch in his stomach remained. He saw kids bouncing on trampolines in terraced back gardens and remembered how their yard had been cemented: Mam knew Dad would never look after a lawn. She'd put pots out to make it nice and some gravel, but the bastard cats of the neighbourhood treated it as a litter tray.

More gardens, with washing flying like kites and cats asleep on the tops of sheds. Then a barbecue in another garden, a bloke in an apron with a can and tongs, a bunch of adults and loads of children running around. Orla and him never had friends over. It was too risky if Dad got in pissed. Vicky was the only one who'd come round for tea, making a fuss of Mam's cooking, which to be fair wasn't bad. There was no need to explain to her if they heard shouting. She'd just turn the music up or start talking a bit louder, usually to Orla as if she was trying to take her mind off it. How Vicky understood, he never knew. Only that she did. And, even now, after all they'd been through, he was thankful for that.

The suburbs gave way to industrial parks, all Pizza Huts and PC Worlds, warehouses and car showrooms. Places where, inexplicably, people went on Sundays. He had a strong signal here, *come on, Vee, call.*

Then, shit, they were in the countryside where there was an intermittent service at best. Fury as the wifi on the train was lagging. *Think calm thoughts, keep it together, son*, he told himself as he stared at the words No Service.

Be positive. Vee was on the case. Vee. He didn't want to do that fate thing but... Jesus, Orla would rip it out of him if she knew that he was even going down that path. But... how come he'd been able to ring Vee for help? Why had this happened at this moment? Because Dad could've had a funny turn any time before now. It was luck, that's all it was, pure chance. Yet it still made him feel weird: not just that he was able to rely on Vee but that there was no one else he could've relied on.

Suddenly, there was a flurry of beeps and buzzes in his hand. Three missed calls, all Vee, new voicemail and four texts. Where did he go first?

Voicemail. *Please, God, let Dad be all right*, he found himself thinking. Yet how many times had he wished for him to disappear? Did this make him a hypocrite? Or did it mean he was capable of compassion? Forgiveness – he'd considered it. Breaking the cycle, Orla called it, but it was so hard when any memory he had of Dad being more interested in him than the bottom of a can were so old they were on Betamax. Most of the time he was closer to cutting him out of his life.

'You have three new messages. To listen to—'

Get on with it, he thought, jabbing the number one, and returning the phone to his ear.

'He's all right.'

Murphy's head dropped to his chin. Thank fuck. But the way she'd said it, with gravity rather than relief, suggested there was more.

'It's a suspected stroke.'

Oh, Dad.

'His right arm is a bit weak.'

Maybe that'd stop his drinking, he caught himself thinking.

'He's gone to the hospital. We're heading up there now. We'll wait there for you.'

He felt a frenzy of anger: Dad had been so selfish, drinking his way through life, he was to blame for all of this. If this didn't teach him...

'He was a bit rambling. He said he'd been to the cemetery. Said he loved her. Took some wildflowers.'

Murphy stopped. His Dad, the soak, who never mentioned Mam, he'd gone to see her. And he'd taken her favourite flowers, the one's she said reminded her of Ireland. The revelation made his head spin all the way until his cab pulled up outside the University Hospital of Wales in Cardiff.

Taking the stairs two at a time, he arrived at his father's ward panting but then took cautious steps to his father's bed, preparing himself.

Then boom, all of the emotions at once as he saw his grey face staring into space. Vee, who was sat beside his dad, stood up, her eyes tender, and came forward to touch his arm, which made him shaky inside, and his hand gripped hers tightly.

'He's okay,' she said before she melted away from his vision because he could only see his father.

It caught his breath, the sight of his dad so helpless. What got him the most was a strand of hair that was sticking up at the top of his head, like he was a child. The anger Murphy had felt was gone – instead his heart was pierced with pity and pain for the old bastard. But where he expected confusion, Dad just looked blank. Gathering himself, he went to him and stood in his eyeline.

'Dad,' he said, quietly.

'Hello, son,' he croaked. His eyes were watery, vacant. 'You just got in from work?'

'Yeah,' he said, hoping it was a turn of phrase and not a sign that his dad was out of it. 'How are you feeling?'

'Okay, a bit... whatyoucall...' he said, his breathing laboured.

His eyelids, like crepe paper, fluttered then shut. He was in his pyjamas, which Vee had thought to bring.

'He's been nodding off a lot. The doctor said it was normal,' Vee said.

He turned to her, his vision trailing lights. 'You can go, now? You've done enough.'

'You sure?' He nodded. 'I'll catch my dad on the way out, he's nipped to the loo.'

'Vee. Thanks.' He felt weak and impotent, unable to put into words his gratitude.

'He's really confused, just to warn you. Like, he thought I was Kat when I got there,' she gave a small smile and a shake of the head. 'Asked if I wanted some breakfast…'

Murphy felt his guts cramping at her suggestion that he was talking total shit. The fucking irony of it.

'…Anyway, see you soon.'

But he couldn't look at her. Instead, he pinched the arch of his nose until the pain brought tears to his eyes.

*

Mikey's parents' house, February 2008

Kat's throbbing head drags her from the black death of sleep.

She fights it, keeping her eyes shut, not ready to confront where she is. Because she knows from the familiarity of her dry, battered mouth, her aching thighs and her nakedness, that it won't be good. His body is radiating heat next to her, but they're not touching; it feels deliberately that way, like they're opposing magnets. It's quite a feat considering they're in a single bed. She's on her side facing away from him, her nose an inch from a greasy wall, but she can still smell the sourness of his sweat, and hers, which has soiled the sheet.

Her fingertips feel something shiny just above her. She opens one eye and in the gloom she can make out a Blu-tacked cover of Time *magazine. It's a mock-up of an iPhone containing the words 'Best Inventions of 2007'.*

Kat plays a game of denying who he is: if she wishes hard enough then there's a chance that the flashbacks of last night, which come to her like blows from a hammer, might be all jumbled up. That actually, she blacked out before the end of the evening; perhaps she went home with another guy from the pub.

There's more damning evidence, with a Pixar poster of Toy Story and a ripped out photo of Steve Jobs. Shame and disgust kick in as what she knows deep down is true.

What the fuck has she done? As the wrecking ball swings towards her, she covers her head with her hands and moves her legs into her stomach. But how can she protect herself from the violence when she is the author of her own hurt?

But it feels as if things are happening to her, as if she is being swept along. Like last night. After a week or so of putting it off – she didn't want to see anyone, just drink Dad's posh wine, sleep and recover from the nightmare of her backpacking ordeal – she finally met Mikey. In The Albany, an old-fashioned local pretty much equidistant from their parents' houses. They'd catch up and she'd give him Vicky's letter.

She thought the reckless feelings she'd been having, the ones which come out of fear rather than excitement, would have been deadened by the quiet. But the pub was jumping from a darts match and after her first pint of cider she began to feel the rising. The panic about her job: she can barely concentrate on reading a paper, how is she going to manage reports and figures? The mess in her mind: from drinking and sleeping till lunch. Mum going on, endlessly, about getting herself dressed, reading the business pages to prepare for the City because 'there's a recession on the way, you do realize', finding a place to live in London, to take her make-up off before she goes to bed. Dad just clears his throat when Mum is on one, then he goes off, leaving Kat feeling like she's being eaten by a lion. She's seen a doctor, Mum made her go, and a psychiatrist. Panic disorder and depression, the psycho said from her swingy chair over a box of tissues. The palpitations, nausea and trembling were classic signs of anxiety and her behaviours a result of masking her symptoms with drugs and alcohol. Blah, blah, blah. But pills aren't going to change that - Kat flushes them down the loo to make them think she takes them. What she really needs is to get the hell out of here, away from her mother, away from Cardiff.

With all of that going on, Kat had kept on drinking to drown it out. Mikey had matched her pint for pint, he was fine at first but then his layers fractured the more he sank.

He was supposed to be going to London to start a new job, the Apple place, she thinks he'd said, but he had to turn it down because he's just found out his mother has ovarian cancer. He was feeling wretched, torn in two, wanting to leave home, fulfil his dream but unable to because his dad was throwing himself into the whisky. Orla was flying at uni so it was down to him. His mum's in the hospital, recovering from a hysterectomy. His voice had splintered when he told her she'd collapsed in an office the other day with a duster in her hand.

A tear running into the pillow, Kat remembers the exact moment when she felt a surge of bitterness and anger, which she'd known would end her up where she was now. He'd cried, saying he'd missed Vicky so much and how he wished she was here with him: she'd understand. There was no way he could visit her now, but he couldn't wait to see her when she got back in three weeks' time.

Jealous and offended that he doted on Vee not her, she felt

herself curdling. Then he began attacking Kat for wasting her opportunity – why was she getting so wrecked when she had a future ahead of her? He'd go straight to give anything to go. But he was trapped here. She was 'a silly cow', he'd said. Kat had back-pedalled then, claiming that maybe she did have mental health issues after all, that's how desperate she was for his sympathy. But he'd had hysterics. 'Mental health issues? My arse. You know what your problem is? You don't realize how lucky you are. You've got everything, but it's not enough.'

She laughed it off but the spite took over. 'Have you heard from Vicky then?' she'd asked, imagining the letter in her bag burning to ash.

'I'm waiting til she's sorted in Cambodia. I'd rather speak to her over the phone if she can get a number for me to call her on. It'd be shit to say I can't come on an email.'

'She won't mind,' she'd said, with innocent eyes, 'because when I left her last week she said she was going to catch up with this bloke, Conor. He'd tried it on with me and I tried to tell her but, you know...'

His head had jerked up then and he'd attempted to focus his eyes, to understand the implication.

'What do you mean?'

'Oh, she was obsessed with this guy. They were friends, really close...' He breathed out, long and hard. 'I'm sure she's probably forgotten about you going anyway.'

'But she was dying for me to visit...' His eyes had gone like charcoal, all splintered and hard.

'Yeah, well, I think she sort of changed while we were away. She was critical, like I'd be having the best night and she'd always want to go back early. Or I'd make friends and she'd get all insecure. I dunno why... She sort of betrayed me. I guess that makes two of us.'

He'd nodded slowly for a good few seconds and then got up, grabbing his coat. She'd followed suit, suggested chips, because she hadn't eaten since, well, probably that morning. He'd shrugged but then let her slip his arm through his and they'd ended up back at his. Their mouths had bruised each other, their hands rough. Silent functional awful sex. Leaving only the taste of regret.

That memory makes her want to throw up: Kat needs to get away. She slides down the bed and grabs her clothes off the floor, slipping her mini-dress on first then picking up her bag to finish off getting dressed in the loo. Down the stairs, she creeps, unaware of the time, hoping it's so early that no one is up.

But as she reaches the bottom of the shabby stairs, his dad calls out. He's at the end of the corridor, in the lounge, in his seat which gives him the perfect view to catch her leaving.

'Morning, Kat!' It's a cheery hello. Only one a father of a son could make. Like she's proof he isn't batting for the other side.

'Oh, hi, I was just...'

'There's bacon going if you want a bap?' he says, kindly. Christ, her parents would be chasing off the interloper if this was at their place.

'No, no thanks. I've got to go. Thanks but...' She gives him a weak smile then flees.

The rain battering her cheeks, she scrabbles around in her bag. The letter. She takes it out and watches the ink bleed. Then she throws it in the first bin she passes. She can't go any lower. That is it – she'll never be part of their lives again.

Chapter Sixteen

V

Cardiff City Centre, June

'This place is mega fancy,' Vee said, her nerves from eating out with Murphy numbed by her third drink, as she looked around the former bank vault, which had been converted into a restaurant below Cardiff's city centre.

'Lush though,' she said, just to clarify that she wasn't being judgey. Because Murphy had brought her here to The Potted Pig as a thank you for helping him out with his dad.

Bricks, low-hung lights and a bar dedicated to thirty varieties of gin could've meant it was a bit poncey, but the people didn't seem overdressed. Maybe because it was a Wednesday night? Like her, they were in jeans, although theirs were probably not from Peacocks.

'Nice atmos, amazing food – my belly pork is tender as – and this G&T, well, it's so unusual, tastes all orangey, like a Terry's Chocolate Orange. It has to be one of those artisanal creations.'

Mikey almost choked on his steak. And then he started to laugh his head off in giant gasps which shook his shoulders. Just like he used to. In school. Round hers. In pubs. A pang of the past slapped her cheeks and then the present gave her another for good measure.

'What?' she said, as he wheezed to a standstill, 'what?' She felt a bit worried then, that she'd let the side down with a mention of Chocolate Oranges, as if he was sneering at her because it was something 'common people' ate. A pang of antagonism struck, as if he was too urban for such talk. God, it was so annoying that she could walk around feeling like she wasn't a bumpkin, that she'd lived a bit, but in his company he made her feel like a square. This was the trouble, this was why she had been reticent about coming to this place with him. She'd have been happy at Pizza Express. Their new friendship was like some complicated dance routine: she'd try her hardest not to tread on his toes, avoiding insights based on their past, and then he'd stamp on both of her feet.

'Put your lip away!' he spluttered, catching her defiance. 'I'm not laughing at you,' he said, getting his breath back, 'I'm laughing because you pronounced it "artis-ANAL" not "arteeeesanal". You've just stuck up two fingers at everyone stupid enough to go to cereal cafes and play centres for adults! You're quite right!'

'Well, I didn't do it deliberately,' she huffed. 'Although I do know you say keen-wha not quin-oah.'

'Who cares?' he shrugged. 'It's brilliant. Artis-ANAL.'

Then it struck her. 'I've been saying that at least a hundred times a day at the deli! It is quite funny, I suppose.'

'Funny? It's hilarious,' he said, wiping his eyes which glistened like chocolate cheesecake, 'I'm going to start saying it like that. It's proper funny. God, I haven't laughed like that since...'

Suddenly, his face crumpled into sadness then and he pushed his plate away. The strain of what had happened to his dad was plain to see. It was a hideous situation: the man who hadn't given a shit about his son was now relying on him. Was this a good time to ask about him? She wondered because she didn't have the right to intrude, not anymore, and while they were on good terms, they weren't where they had been. He'd said his piece at the start: his dad was on the mend. Needed R&R but the stroke team was doing all it could to help with physio. Then he'd skirted it and she'd got the message. Yet she suspected there was no one else who understand the back story. If he didn't want to open up, he'd let her know, she thought.

'How's it going then? With you?' she gambled, cautiously.

He rubbed his face with his hands and sighed. He fixed his eyes on her, looking as if he was debating whether to fob her off or not.

'Pretty fucked up,' he said, which didn't tell her either way. 'He's had to move in for a bit.'

Right. Now she understood. Vee whistled a deep note

through her lips. That was why he had bags under his eyes.

'Yeah. It's okay. He's sleeping loads and he just watches telly and stuff. But he's different. They call it emotionalization – changes in the brain. So I'd never seen him cry, not even at Mam's funeral, he was like a slab of rock. But now he blubs at the drop of a hat.'

She didn't interrupt, he seemed to be unloading, in the flow.

'He'll be able to go home at some point but not for a while. There was nowhere else he could go. He leaves taps running and forgets to eat. I think he'd just drink himself to death if he was left alone. I have to watch him like a hawk, he's still craving booze, I let him have a hot toddy before bed, but that's it. I've got a carer coming in to help because I can't be there all the time.'

'Is that who's there tonight?'

'Yep. She's good as gold. Does the showering and stuff.'

'That must help. It must be hard when…'

'…when he's done fuck all for me. I know. Orla says it's a chance to mend our relationship.' He grimaced. 'But I dunno. I feel so angry and resentful… and sorry for him.'

'I guess that's natural.'

The waiter appeared, offering pudding, but they both declined, and Vee felt a pang of disappointment the night was over when Murphy asked for the bill.

'Shall we go on for a nightcap?'

Vee was briefly elated that he wanted to stay with her until she saw his face of desperation: it wasn't her he wanted to hang out with per se, it was just because he didn't want to go home. He wanted to suspend time and delay reality. But she didn't blame him.

'Go on then, but it's my treat.'

'Okay, well, how about we cab it over to Roath, then you're near home?'

'Deal,' she said, grabbing her cardigan as they got up to climb the stairs back into the early summer twilight.

'I feel quite pissed,' she said as they walked to the taxi rank.

'Yeah, I do too. I've had a good night, you've cheered me right up.'

Vee felt a squeeze in her heart: they'd got their footwork right after all.

'It's nice, isn't it? That we can do this,' she said, feeling it was okay to say it without fear.

He gave her a cynical look, one she knew of old, that said he completely agreed with her. She nudged him to show she got it. And then she remembered there was a Jarvis Cocker tribute act coming to Cardiff next week! He'd seen that too and she felt so comfy by now that she asked if he wanted to go. Without hesitation, he agreed, they'd go together. It felt so great to have a plan to go out because she was starting to get sofa sores from all the telly. What's more, it was a perfect arrangement for the both of them, here under duress but that didn't mean they had to suffer it before the rest of their life started again.

'Are you missing Hackney?' she asked, as they waited in line.

He scratched his chin. 'I thought I would, actually, but nah, it's good to get away every now and then…'

'What about Orla, your mates, your girlfriend?'

'Orla will be loving the place to herself. My mates, there's not so many, just colleagues really, and Shell isn't my girlfriend anymore. I was sort of seeing someone, Ruby, but we've let it go because I'm going to be up here for a while, I reckon.'

Vee felt a jolt of shock that he'd jumped from one girl to another in a matter of weeks then some satisfaction that he was single again. But why? It meant nothing to her. It must be because it made her feel less alone.

'What about you? Do you miss Brighton?'

'I did, massively, at first. It was home for years. But when I look back, I wanted to move to Hove anyway, it's a little more gentrified. Less scabby. I think I'd grown out of Brighton. Or maybe got boring.'

'What about your ex?' He kicked at something on the floor – he wasn't really interested, he was only asking out of politeness.

'I miss being loved,' she said. 'Loving someone. Not him so much anymore. I can see now I was living according to his rules and I'd lost myself. If that makes sense…'

He gave an ambiguous nod – she doubted he'd ever had his head in the clouds when it came to a woman.

'Anyway, it's nearly us for the cab, so where do you want to go for a nightcap? How about The Heath? We can go outside, if you're dying for a fag?'

'I'm cutting down. Dad's not a great advert for it, to be honest.'

'Oh, that's great. You do know no one smokes anymore?'

'I do, Vee, I do. What about the Roath Park Pub? That's not bad.'

That didn't appeal to her, it was a bit chainy. Then it was their taxi. As she stepped inside, it dawned on her just where to go. She looked back, smiling, to him at the door, his body preparing to double up so he didn't hit his head on the roof. He might be all buff and bang on trend, not to mention handsome, but he was still as gangly.

'The Albany! she said, grinning. 'Like old times! When you, me and Kate would make a pint last an evening!'

It felt fabulous to bring her up in his company – she'd never tell him about Kate's baby, she'd barely got her head round that one: the misery she must've felt every day ever since she'd had to give up Griff. Vee hadn't stopped thinking about what Kate had been through: it certainly explained the fleeting dark clouds which Vee had seen cross her face. She'd been texting her every other day to check on how she was doing and she'd come back with apologies that she'd dumped it on her and that she was fine, she was building up to telling Jack. Clearly she felt guilty at having shared her secret with Vee before him: how much she wanted to tell her that she hadn't blamed her. It was easier to confess to someone unemotionally involved. Instead she had simply offered her the chance to talk any time. It struck her then – perhaps a night out with old friends would do the job? Because she never found out why those two lost touch. She could find out then!

'Tell you what,' she said to Murphy, 'we'll have to get Kate out one night – we see each other every now and then. She got me my job, actually, forgot to say.'

Murphy had been about to get in the cab, but she saw his body pause. She leaned across from her seat to look at his face but his relaxed expression had become ashen, like granite.

'Actually,' he said, 'I'm… er… Look, I just feel knackered, it's come on like a pile of bricks. I think I just need to go to bed.'

'Oh, right,' she said, unable to read his face because he was resting his arms on the frame and the door, his head out of sight.

She told herself off for feeling a bit disappointed although she too could do with going home.

'Course, you must be with everything. No worries at all. See you, maybe, at the gig then next...'

But he'd shut the door. As the cab pulled away, she realized what she felt was foolishness. She'd misjudged the mood and she'd read things into his behaviour: as if they had promise. It reminded her of those feelings she'd had when she'd been away, when she'd felt a glow from just thinking about him. When she'd almost certainly been on the way to telling him she wanted to be together. He'd obviously pulled out from going on to the pub with her because it had been too much too soon: they'd had a nice meal and that was that.

She could see she'd read it wrong by the torturous look on his face as he stared at her until the car had turned the corner.

Chapter Seventeen

K

Penllyn just outside Cowbridge

With every step she took in the cool shaded woodland, she counted down to the end.

The end of her love story with Jack, their blissful home, their easy peace; the end of life as she knew it.

Through the vertical blind of trees, there was a glade of meadow where the sun shone down in its full glory. For Kate, it represented where she had to go: to leave what on the surface was a safe and blessed twilight and emerge into a naked clearing where she would be at the elements' mercy.

Yet this cocoon with Jack was built on deception: she had not been truthful to him about the most important thing in her life - that the son she gave up was Griff. By admitting she had not been honest, even though it was for good reasons, for Griffy's sake, it would cast doubt on her. She would not be the person he thought she was.

Beyond, there would be pain and consequences but at least she would not be lying anymore – her conscience would be almost clean. Because it was unbearable: once it had come out with Vee, then she had felt it at her surface for every second since. Fighting to be free.

It could've have been so easy for a second eruption, but she needed the right time, the right place to tell him: she wanted to kill him kindly, give him space to react – to pace and stamp and cry. He could do that here below the thick canopy of leaves beyond the stile which led into their cottage garden. Oh, what she would've once done to stop this from barging in on them: he'd given her everything she'd never had: love without judgement. But if she kept the secret, it would slowly asphyxiate her and ruin their relationship anyway.

Jack didn't deserve to be a victim. Today, she would liberate him. Honesty was kindness. He wouldn't see it like that at first, but in years to come when he was married and happy, he might believe he had had a lucky escape, barely a month before they would make their vows. That his love had saved a damaged woman. But he would have time, aged twenty-seven, to have another life.

She didn't believe there would be anything more for her after him. She would focus on her son, no doubt he would remain her nephew, he wasn't hers to take away. She couldn't scoop him up only for Charlie's heart to break. The person who needed stability was Griff. Kate's version of the future was to be as close to him as she was now: he would be the man in her life, upon whom she would dote. The rest of her time would be spent working and pursuing her interests. It wouldn't be adventurous or fulfilling but it would be honest.

She stopped to breathe in the earthy scents of moss and bark, to listen to the snapping of leaves and twigs as Boris bounded towards her, to watch insects fly in the dusty early summery morning air. To take in this one last moment of perfection before it all came tumbling down.

Jack came up behind her and put his arms around her waist. She shut her eyes and savoured their final act of intimacy. His warmth, the comforter of his embrace, his fingers smoothing her stomach: his innocence which she was about to destroy.

'There's something I need to tell you,' she said, speaking the words which had been waiting for the last seven years. Twisting so her face looked up to his, she saw him frown slightly in concern, that one look crucifying her because it showed how much she was going to hurt this lovely decent man. She pulled away to hold his hands between them before she dropped them and took a seat on the trunk of an old fallen tree.

'It's going to be difficult for you to hear it.'

He squeezed his eyes and rubbed his chest, as if he was bracing himself.

Jack took to a tree stump to support himself, barely a footstep from her but what felt like a chasm. The light was hazy behind his head. He had been her angel, he would remain so forever.

'I've kept something from you and if it had no bearing on us now, I would never speak of it. But it does and this is not a way of reliving any guilt: how could it be?' She could not wish away her own flesh and blood. 'Only regret that I have kept it from you.'

He nodded in a contained manner, but she could see his breath heaving with dread. She didn't want to put him through any more.

'Griff,' she said, softly. 'He's my son, Jack. He's the baby I gave up.'

She swallowed and saw Jack through blurred eyes dip his head. There was only birdsong and the ripple of wind for a long time, a soundtrack incongruous with her annihilating announcement.

Her hands trembled as she awaited his reaction: she felt relieved of her burden but it was replaced by anxiety at the transfer of its weight to his shoulders.

His foot scrunched at the earth, his hands went up to his mess of baby curls and then he looked up at her, his chin quivering.

'Of course he is... his eyes. They're yours. His nails, they're exactly the same shape too. His running around, his energy...' He was gulping now. 'How didn't I guess? Why have you never told me?' he said, hurt bleeding from every pore. 'Why wait until now?'

'I was afraid. That you'd leave me.' She sobbed because the irony was plain to see.

'How do you know I would've? What am I? The judge and the jury? Casting judgement, unable to understand?'

'You're the greatest thing that's ever happened to me,' she said. 'Wonderful and true. I've made it dirty.'

'This is absurd,' he said, 'What you've done is put me on a pedestal and assumed I couldn't handle something complex.'

It made her feel cruel, as if she had underestimated him.

'I intended to say, before you met Griff, but I was in too deep already. Knowing I'd found the love of my life.'

'The panic attacks... that's why you had them again, when you'd seemed to have put them behind you.'

'Yes. Seeing Vee again brought that time of my life up again. But when you said I had to deal with whatever it was that was troubling me, that you could live with it but you were afraid I couldn't, that's when I knew I needed to say something. Before the wedding so that you wouldn't feel tricked or deceived. I'm telling you now so that you can start again. But please know that I never wanted to keep anything from you: I wanted to protect him, we all did. You've made me happier than I've ever been. And I don't want you to go...' A sob burst from her, '... but I know you will want to. You won't be able to trust me again.'

'I don't have the right, but may I, er, ask who the father was, is?' Jack said, with apologetic dignity, looking first at her then away so that he wasn't observing her discomfort, which made her jaw clench.

'I... I... it's too...' Kate tasted blood as she wrestled with herself whether to go forward. She didn't want to admit who because he was dead to her and if he was named then he would be present, reborn, haunting her all over again. Yet if she didn't, or couldn't, it might be seen as another cover-up or worse, that she was claiming to be dealing with this but failing. What she needed to get across to him was that it didn't matter who he was because she'd never once seen him again. 'It was a mistake, it's water under the bridge, it's not important...'

'No, no, of course.' So reasonable, so decent. It was killing her to even think of the father in this moment – he'd caused enough trouble and she didn't want him anywhere near them now. Jack was wonderful, she didn't want him tainted.

'I'll tell my mother and father that it's off. The wedding. I'll move out. Or you can. It's up to you. But Jack,' and her voice caught, 'I will always love you.'

He stood and began pacing. Then quietly, he spoke.

'Your mother,' Jack said, stopping to double over. 'Your bloody mother,' he shouted, hitting the floor.

'I know...' she wept.

'No, that's just it,' he said, strangled, 'you have only realized half the problem. It's not Griff, Jesus. I love him like blood, it must be because, Christ, he was yours. Is yours. He isn't the issue here. You didn't tell me because your mother has controlled every inch of your life and you have let her. You were brainwashed by her, so afraid. That is what you need to address, Kate. Her. That's what I can't understand. The wedding, how you've let her get her own way. It was my day too, but nobody ever thought to consider my wishes. I wanted the happiest day of my life to be about us. Not her.'

'I'll tell her now,' she said, desperately, her heart rising that there still may be a chance. 'I'll go there now. It's Sunday, she'll be home. I can be back by lunchtime. I promise. If we can stay together, I'll do it now.'

'But do you feel it, Kate?' he implored, then shaking his head because clearly he didn't believe she did. 'That's what I need to know. Do you see that you are still enslaved to her? Do you see that your happiness hasn't ever depended on me or Griff but on her? You cannot keep bowing to her for the rest of your life.'

'I won't. I'll sort it,' she said, stepping towards him, her fingers in a clawed spasm of excruciating self-hatred.

'I need some time to think,' he said, turning his back on her. His shoulders jerked up and down as he let it all out.

'Of course,' she said, wanting to touch him, groping the air with her hands but backing off, frightened she would break him. 'I'll go to Charlie's,' she said. 'I'll go back to the cottage now, pack a bag. However long you need, if there's a chance…'

And then she ran as fast as she could, because out in the clearing, she could begin to be free again.

Chapter Eighteen

M

Cardiff City Centre

'I'm going out, Dad,' Murphy said, crouching down to check he'd understood. It was hard to tell because his eyes were vague. At this time of day, even though he'd only been up since 11 a.m., the tiredness would come like a rising tide.

'Melanie's here. I'll be back about midnight. She's going to stay in my room. Okay?'

Dad stared at him vacantly. 'Have you told your mother?'

Murphy rubbed his temples and counted to ten because it would be so easy to shout. His dad was a pathetic sight, with tufts of hair sticking up where he'd missed with the Brylcreem and there was a stain of curry on his shirt, which Murphy had made worse by rubbing at it.

'The football's on tonight. The Champions League thing,' he said, hoping he'd said it right because he knew fuck all about it. He checked his watch. Shit, he was already late.

'1971. When Cardiff City beat Real Madrid one-nil. At home. You weren't born yet. Your mam and I had just met. I turned down a ticket to go courting with her. Twenty-one I was, she was sweet sixteen, fresh off the boat from Ireland. That family of hers, well, I'd have sorted them out if she'd let me. But she never saw them again.'

Sixteen? Mam had got here at sixteen? She'd always said twenty-one. Murphy was torn between wanting to know more and having to go. *Shit, Dad, why did you have to do this now? Why not earlier when I sat with you, when I got you a pork pie and tomato, just like you'd asked. But you didn't say a word. Just ate and burped.* This was becoming a thing, his talking of Mam.

Little moments of what their life had been before it'd gone wrong. How did it happen? If he left now, he might miss it and he sensed this might be why his parents had fractured off into their own directions, leaving Orla and him in a wasteland of brittle love.

'What had happened to Mam? Why was she here at sixteen then?'

His dad wiped his damp eyes and stayed silent. Then just like that he snapped out of it.

'I need a piss,' he said, shuffling himself to the edge of his threadbare wing-back which Murphy had got a man with a van to bring over so he'd be comfy.

'Tell me about Mam,' Murphy said, grabbing his wallet off the side.

'I can bloody manage, Michael,' his dad shouted, waving him away, creaking to his legs and groaning without inhibition.

The door had closed on his memory: Murphy felt it as if it had been slammed in his face. He popped his head round into the kitchen.

'I'm off, Melanie,' he said. 'Help yourself to anything. Dad'll ask for a nightcap, just give him a small one.'

'Will do, love, have a good time,' she said, tidying away the dishwasher stuff. 'Expect I'll be asleep when you get back. That dinner was lovely, thanks.' She gave him a warm mumsy smile, which got him every time because it reminded him of his Mam on a good day.

He didn't know what he'd do without Melanie. She'd been a carer for years; you could tell by the way she never flapped. Over a cuppa, she'd make him see he was allowed to have feelings of exasperation and anger – 'it was perfectly normal' – but just think how confused his dad was too. She'd done the impossible, this supposedly unremarkable fifty-something woman with a stoop, and made him more patient with the old bastard. People like her were the bloody heroes, not his generation of entitled millennials who'd grown up thinking they were special. And if it wasn't for Melanie, he wouldn't be going out to meet Vee now.

When she'd texted in the week to ask if he wanted to go to that gig, he'd thought no. Every time he had heard Vee say Kate's name, it was like his brain had shut down. How could he get involved with Vee when there was classified information between them? Yet he felt doomed – because every time he backed off, the pulling towards her would return. He had no one else he could stand to be around when his days were filled with worrying about Dad and trying not to get cross at him for muddling up breakfast and dinner or feeling dreadful pity when he did his buttons up wrong.

Vee was the only one. His efforts to block her out only worked partially, because she would feature in his dreams. Always her, laughing, taking him somewhere, her fingertips brushing his.

Then when Melanie had caught him stirring salt into his tea, she'd told him he needed time away from Dad. If he didn't, the resentment would creep in. So, yeah, he'd replied, he was up for seeing Jarvis Cocked-up, where he was heading now.

It wasn't far to the Tram Shed – he did a quick walk through the tired backstreets of Riverside and Grangetown, seeing not the litter and for sale signs but the stoic silhouettes of buildings beneath a vibrant orange sky. Thinking it was good enough to get outside, he hadn't realized how housebound he'd felt in Cardiff compared to his 'hardly home' situation in Hackney.

A few lookylikies wearing black-rimmed specs and tweed suit jackets hung around outside the venue but most of the people were just normal. It made him feel like he didn't have to look cool, like he did in London.

When he went inside, his spirits went tequila when he saw her. It was proof of how lonely he'd been. She looked like she was up for a good night: she'd dressed up a bit. Not for him, of course. But for the occasion: all rockabilly with her hair up and fifties bandana, a black and white polka dot shirt, turned-up jeans and a red pair of lips.

'Hiya!' she sang, her eyes wide, happy and vibrant. She held out a bottle of beer for him. 'I'm off tomorrow, so cheers! Had a swift one before I came out!'

Ah, so that was why she was so buzzing. He was shocked to feel a bit of a downer that it wasn't about seeing him but the fact she could have a night of it without work in the morning.

'Wicked,' he said, as she clinked the neck of his drink on hers – it made him stop as if it was an act of intimacy.

Jesus, Murphy, he thought, *it's not as though you've been in solitary, is it? Calm yourself.*

'Sorry I'm a bit late. Dad.' That's all he needed to say.

''S'all right. Only been here ten myself. Mum dropped me in but the traffic was awful. Jarvis is on in a sec. Fancy going up to the balcony? Get a good view then.'

As they went up the stairs, she began to talk, looking back at him every other footstep, stopping every now and again to make a point, to throw her hand in the air or do a face. The chat came easy, she was filling him in on stuff, he didn't hear all of it because of the music, but he felt his cares slipping away.

They were in position just in time for the lights to fall. Vee grabbed his arm and his stomach flipped, but then the floor did look as if it was moving from up here: the crowd was jumping in a dizzying murmuration as the fairly spot-on Jarvis, waggling his finger and angling his legs in cords, launched into 'Disco 2000', the song of their youth.

He stole a look at Vee, just to make sure she was enjoying herself, and his eyes rested on a lock of her hair which hung long down her cheekbone. He followed its path and saw how it touched the exposed skin on her chest.

He took a shaky breath, something was happening. Maybe it was the release of stress. And his ribcage was thudding – was it from an echo of the past? That deep longing he'd felt when she was away? It was the most intense friendship he'd ever had – no wonder it was coming out, being here, now with the music transporting him back to the days before she went away. It had to be like a muscle memory, easy to recover after previous practice. Or was it from the bassline?

The boys, they'd say it was because he hadn't had any lately. Orla, she'd make out it was meaningful with a knowing look. Yet it wasn't that kind of feeling.

Throughout the night, not even a load of Pulp covers could stop him from being so aware that she was next to him. Perhaps it was just because it was a big thing to get used to, having her around. That was the complicated bit – everything else, how they communicated, was effortless.

What did it mean? Did he need to worry?

The trouble was, when the gig had ended and they'd had a few more beers, her arm seemed as if it was meant to be in the loop of his.

'Murph, Smurf,' she giggled, as they walked back into town, and his grin ran up and down his body. 'I don't want to go home yet! Vodka, I want. Shall we get some from the shop and get drunker in Roath Park?'

'What, like we're seventeen again? You puke and I carry you home?' It wouldn't be the worst ever ending to a night out, to be fair.

'Yeah! Come on, town is full of wankers,' she said, as he got elbowed by a pissed girl as they joined the swarm of Cardiff's Saturday night revellers. It wasn't even ten to eleven and there were casualties everywhere. 'I don't want to queue up for hours to get in somewhere shit and then sober up before I've even got to the bar.'

She had a point. He couldn't face that either.

'I've got some voddy at mine. There's a roof terrace. We won't disturb Dad then. Fancy that?' It'd just come out, saying that, so easy and he felt self-conscious as if he sounded desperate.

'I don't fancy it,' she said, which made his stomach lurch until she added, 'I bloody love it!'

He swung her round the corner of Westgate Street and up to the flats which were in the shadow of the Millennium Stadium.

'I didn't realize you lived here!' she said, gazing up at the huge Victorian four-storey building. 'I thought only judges and MPs and lawyers owned these places.'

'Yeah. A few do,' he admitted, letting them in. 'I'm on the second floor.'

Inside his flat, it was all quiet with Dad long asleep and Melanie getting some shut eye, so he tiptoed in to get the booze, two glasses and a throw. It could get chilly up there after a while even on a nice June night like this.

Vee hung back, thank God: she was on the right side of making loud drunk shhh noises. Then he took her along the hallway, through a door and up some metal stairs to one of the best views in Cardiff. He felt a mixture of embarrassment and pride at her extended 'oh my God' as she went to the edge to peep out over the heads and cars, buses and cabs across town, from the twinkling trendy office blocks and illuminated arch of the stadium to Cardiff Castle and City Hall's dome which were lit up like Christmas trees. Like a kid, she waved down then span around and skipped through a few tables and chairs to a vast rattan day bed which the residents' association had chipped in for.

'This is amazing, Murphy!' she said, lying back and resting her head on the cushion. 'It's so quiet up here.'

'Apart from that siren.'

He walked over and hesitated at the bed: he didn't want to barge into her space. But she was lost in the sky and so he joined her, settling down as far away as he politely could, putting his arm beneath his head.

'And I can see the stars.'

'If you block out the orangey glow from the lights.'

'Mike… Murphy, I've just had the weirdest déjà vu. To that night before I left. We were star-gazing then.'

His heart almost stopped at the memory of their hug.

'Almost nine years ago,' she said.

He didn't dare breathe. He didn't want her to go back because he would follow her.

'Remember… that was when I asked you to be my back-up man? How blinking rid-ic-ulous!' She laughed and he shut his eyes as he recalled how he'd tried to resist her suggestion. He'd told himself then he hadn't wanted to be tied down but now he knew it was because he'd never wanted to be her second best. To not be her first choice.

And as his father was sleeping a couple of floors down from him, he found himself wondering if all he'd been doing in between that night they made their pledge and now was drifting to avoid anything that would ask difficult questions of him. It struck him that all he wanted was to belong to her.

'Mad we're still here, now, isn't it?' she said, her voice louder, which meant she'd turned to look at him.

He fought the urge to face her but failed: there she was, across from him, her eyes searching his and he felt himself being sucked in, falling.

'I wish we hadn't lost touch, you know,' she said.

He knew exactly how she felt. This conversation, the one he'd been avoiding all his adult life, was going to happen. But he couldn't do it now because he wanted to hold onto this moment.

Then he felt her hand brush his and he couldn't help it, he was done for. She rubbed his scar with her finger as if trying to heal him. He shifted over, not breaking eye contact, wary to see if she didn't want this. But she was looking at him with some kind of need, mirroring his and she rolled into him and their bodies came together in a moment of sheer bliss. Murphy wrapped his arms around her and held her into his chest, the top of her head nestled in beneath his chin. Nothing but their hearts beating: his was calling to hers and he didn't know what the fuck was happening but it was the most beautiful and pure hug of his life.

As if he'd found the missing piece.

*

St Mary's Church, Cardiff, November 2008

The tears won't come. Even when he thinks of Mam down there, alone, in the freezing ground, dressed in her Sunday best and her pretend pearls.

He turns away from the freshly dug earth covering her grave to face the biting wind which whips his chops. At least he can feel that and the grit of the soil in his palms. But beyond that, there's a vast nothing, a numbness that goes on and on.

He sniffs, wondering if it's the beginning of emotion. But it's only from the cold. He's made of ice and his feet are blocks as he walks to Orla, who's weeping in her boyfriend Phil's arms. Mikey didn't bring anyone. He's seeing a girl at work who's on the rebound, it won't be permanent, he can never find one who fits.

Across crunching grass and gravel, they go to the car, where Dad's already waiting, his knee jerking, his nose red. A battered silver hip flask is in his shaking hand, already near-empty, he can tell by the way he has to tip it high to get a drink.

For fuck's sake, he's going to be legless before the cling film has been taken off the buffet.

The motor starts. It feels like they're in a giant airless coffin, travelling in silence, bar Orla's juddering sobs, beside him: Phil is in the front, so she tucks her head into Murphy's neck. Her mourning veil, Mam's one, is scratchy on his skin but he can bear that. They hold hands as Dad stares straight ahead the whole journey, just as he did in St Mary's and in the graveyard.

It doesn't hit him when he enters the house either: that Mam's not around. She was in the hospice for the last weeks, so it's not a shock.

He left for good in March, before he found out it was cancer, went to London, sleeping on Orla's floor in her student hole, eventually getting his chance to start at the Apple store when a position came up. It's everything he wanted: people into the same stuff as him, quick minds and fast fingers. He's doing well, better than actually, on the Genius bar now. In the nights, he's working on an app, it'll take him forever to get it right, a game of some sort. The App Store only opened in July but one-hundred million were downloaded in the first sixty days alone. That's the future, right there. His life is miles away from here in this room where a handful of people stand talking quietly and give him sympathetic looks.

Mam didn't have many mates; the church lot got dumped long ago. A few from her work, Dad's drinking pals, a couple of neighbours and a middle-aged woman he doesn't recognize. She was at the mass too. Turned up late, by herself. Hovering now by the table, ready to hoover up her share.

Murphy opens a can and stands with Orla at the fireplace. There's chit-chat of the priest doing a lovely funeral and wasn't she a lovely lady, all that shite.

Mam's friend, Siobhan, who did cleaning with her, is in charge. Mam told her what she wanted and fair play she's done it to the letter. She knew Dad would be incapable. Intoxicated. There was no wake, Mam didn't want people tramping dirt into the house while she was still in it. But there's a vase of wildflowers and a good spread of sandwiches cut in triangles, cocktail sausages and a tea loaf.

The woman he doesn't know comes towards him. Something familiar about her hair, black with silver streaks, and golden eyes.

'Hello there,' she says, softly in an Irish accent. 'We haven't met. I'm your—'

'They don't want to know who you are,' Dad says, lurching in.

'Dad?' Murphy says, looking at him. He's got spit at the corner of his mouth and he's already taken his tie off. He looks ready for battle and this isn't the place.

'I didn't tell you lot about Bernie for you to come.' Dad is jabbing his finger in the air which is thick with musty suits and hairspray, what Mam called lacquer.

'Please…' The woman looks as if she's been stung by a wasp. 'Brynmor, not today.'

Murphy hasn't heard anyone call him that for years. They know each other, of old.

'Don't you come in here telling me what to do in my own house.' He's gone white now.

Murphy can see people looking and he knows Mam would be losing it if she was here. 'Dad, come away. Leave it.'

He stands in front of him, holds up his arms and shuffles him out into the gloomy hallway.

'Calm it, Dad.' Sometimes this works, taking him out of a situation. 'You need me to make a speech? I'll do it if you need, thank everyone for coming.'

His father dips his head, breathing hard. Which way is he going to go? Come on, Dad, do the right thing, for once.

But he pulls his spine up and steps towards Murphy.

'This is my bloody house,' he says. He's close enough for Murphy to smell his sour breath. His eyes are bloodshot and a lock of his hair has come loose. 'No one is telling me what to do.' Full of menace and fury.

'Course not, it's cool.'

Dad's sizing him up and Murphy waits, willing him to pull himself back from the fire.

Suddenly Dad shoots out his hand and puts it round Murphy's neck, pinning him to the wall. He's much stronger than he's ever given him credit for and his grip is tight. Murphy knows the old man isn't going to kill him, but even so he shits himself because it makes breathing hard. He wants to throw him off but he can't, like he just wants it over with. He can't fight his father at Mam's funeral.

'You get that woman out of my house. Now.'

His hand falls and he stands there shivering as Murphy backs away, sucking the air, scared not by his father but by the demons in his head.

Into the room, the woman sees him and the situation and she gets her handbag. Orla has her mouth open.

'I'm going,' the woman says, picking her coat off the stairs, fumbling to get it on, to get away. 'I didn't mean any of this,' she says, slipping out. 'I wanted to pay my respects. Because times have changed.'

What the hell does that mean?

Orla is in the hall now, still with a gob like a bucket.

'Who was she?'

'Mam's sister…' Orla whispers it like it's a secret.

'Jesus.' They've never ever met any of Mam's family. It was never discussed. It was just the way it was. 'Bad people,' Mam only ever said.

'Brigid. She said she came to represent her brothers. One's in America, the other in Ireland, too ill to fly. She flew in this morning. That's why she was late.'

Murphy clutches his neck which feels sore. Swallowing hurts and his head is going off on one.

'Did she say why we never met her? Any of them? Why Mam cut them out?'

Orla's eyes, usually the colour of flames, have gone rusty.

'Problems in the past was all she said. Then you came in. What happened with Dad?'

Murphy cranes his head into the room and sees him slumped in his chair, his knuckles white round a bottle of whisky.

'Nothing.' He's not going to tell her the score. He picks at a bit of peeling floral wallpaper. It's bumpy underneath. Woodchip. Like that Pulp song.

'I wish Vicky was here,' Orla says out of nowhere, her lip wobbling. He knows exactly what she means. She'd make it all all right, dilute the tension. Why didn't he just knock on her mam's door last week? He'd gone there after Mam died, his hand was about to bang the knocker. He was sure Vicky would come if she knew what had happened. But then he'd thought, what if she didn't? What if her mam told her and then she stayed away? It was better not to put himself through that.

'Well, she's not,' he says, grimly. For the best because he couldn't face her after what he did with Kat. He has to shut this down because Orla knows nothing of that night – she'd been at uni then, oblivious. He doesn't know where Kat is – she could be beneath the rubble of the banking crisis for all he cares. For any thought of her reminds him of what they did, how they abused each other because they were fucked up without Vicky - now they're forever contaminated by it. Even if he wanted to build bridges with Vicky, that night would always be lurking in the background.

And then as Phil appears with a pork pie and puts his arm around Orla, Murphy points to the bathroom and walks in a blur through the kitchen to the back and locks himself in and sits on the loo and finally his shoulders begin to heave with sorrow.

Chapter Nineteen

V

Murphy's roof garden

She was in his arms, breathing him in, unable to believe it was happening.

It was the cuddle of her entire life. Yes, she'd been drinking and yes, she had longed for someone's touch since the day she'd walked out on Jez. Yet she didn't feel drunk on booze now: the vodka was untouched. She was drunk on Murphy. But at the same time, completely sober.

Opening her eyes to the darkness of his body, she checked to see if she was rotating, seasick, but everything was still. It was impossible that this clarity was happening now when she was at her most wonky: when her life was in limbo. It had to be just a fleeting calm amidst a storm. But they'd been lying here for ages now, silent. Neither of them had pulled away in awkwardness, neither of them had cracked a joke or made excuses. There was just their shared warmth, their breathing in unison. Her face was tucked into the smooth skin of his neck and he smelled so good: salty from the gig but natural, his own personal scent which was masculine and earthy. She could feel his deep reassuring pulse against her cheek and his hands caressing her back. Smoothing strokes which became more intense squeezes every now and again. Her right hand was up against his chest: the thin fabric of his T-shirt barely concealed his muscular form which had a smattering of hair. Her left was wrapped around his waist, her fingers tracing the sinew of his back, and their legs were entwined. The only way they could be any closer was if they were as one: the thought made her pelvis ache and she wondered if his did too.

Where had this come from? The night had been fantastic, as if all of their sins had been forgiven. Murphy had turned up a different person and they had got on so well. She'd gone out determined to have a good time, to go nowhere near the danger zones which had muddied their other recent contact. No expectations, no needing to heal herself, their relationship – she had had enough of the analysis. If he began to back off as he had done, as he'd always done, then she would accept it. She couldn't force him to do anything. So what was behind the change? She had to know.

'This is...' she whispered, uncertain but unable to keep it within.

'I know,' he said into her forehead, his lips touching her skin as if it were a kiss.

'How has this...' she said, giving him permission to return to himself. To bring up their past.

'Dunno. Truly.' He sounded as spellbound as she was.

And still they clung onto one another. Happiness but also desire was flooding through her. Could she trust herself to cope with whatever was going to happen if it were to happen?

The feelings she'd had for him would come back stronger. Who was she kidding? They were already here: this was why she had got back in touch with him. She knew then that she had always been in love with him. Always.

She anticipated suspicion: was he a player? Was he doing this because he was vulnerable? Were they using one another? She discovered she just didn't care: she only wanted to be next to him like this under the orangey sky.

Her thoughts translated into movement as her right hand reached up his neck, and his followed, their fingertips exploring what they had always seen but never known. She rested her mouth on his skin and allowed her breath to communicate her longing. He moved just an inch, as if he was giving himself to her, exposing his throat, unguarded, and she pressed her lips into his neck. Still she needed to know if this was right for him.

It was. He rolled his chin up and stroked her back. *Further*, she thought, *go further*, and his hand went lower, lingering on her hip. Then it was on her backside, motionless, waiting for a signal. It was intoxicating, their slow movements both teasing but innocent because this was uncharted territory for them both. They moved a fraction, telling one another they were consenting, and so she kissed his neck once, twice, and his breathing became heavy. Again she nuzzled him and his hand around her back pushed her into him all over.

Pulsing everywhere, she led her lips upwards as he dipped his head until their cheeks were touching. His eyelashes brushed her skin and his lips crept to hers. And then their mouths were tantalizingly close. She waited to hear a voice telling her it was wrong, they were friends, that this would lead to problems, but there was nothing.

The anticipation of years and years came to an end in a split second as their lips met and Vee forgot all of the things she had been desperate to know.

Only this moment mattered.

Chapter Twenty

K

Cowbridge

Kate saw her reflection in the window of Fromage and it confirmed what she knew already: she looked as if she'd been dragged through a jungle backwards.

Her hair was wild from the blustery wind and she had the tell-tale signs of break-up make-up – almost cried-off mascara and barely there foundation from all the nose-blowing.

But then what did it matter? She was hardly game for the deli's Summer Singles Cheese and Wine Night. Only here for Vee, who'd been frightened it would be just her, Pierre and the beardy bloke who, she said, smelled worse than his beloved Époisses de Bourgogne and wondered why he was alone in this world.

But by the looks of it, Kate thought as she walked in, a fair few, around twenty, had turned out. It occurred to her that it was busy enough for her to walk straight back out again but too late, she'd been seen.

'Kate! You came!' Vee said, weaving through the still-self-conscious throng. Initially flushed with excitement and nerves, her face had changed to deep concern by the time she got to Kate. 'How are you? You really don't have to be here, you know, you must be feeling awful. Go, really. Don't stay here for me.'

'I owe you,' Kate said, not just for the shoulder when they'd gone shoe shopping but for every other way she'd wronged her.

'You don't! Seriously, if you're not up to it then-.' Her kindness was so innocent, so unconditional that Kate had to work hard to keep herself in check.

'Stop! I want to be here, for you.'

'Really?'

'Yes. Now go and circulate, your public awaits! We'll chat later.'

Vee gave her 'if you're sure, you're sure' look before Kate waved her off to start the proceedings. Only for Pierre to pop up by her side holding out a glass of red. Did he know about her and Jack? By the way he grabbed her into a bear hug, it was an obvious 'yes'. Either Jack or Vee would've told him - and while she was touched, she didn't want tonight to be about her woes.

She managed to squeak 'I'm fine' into his chest before she was saved from tears by Vee tapping her glass to begin the welcome and explain the format of the evening. Groups of four would spend ten minutes at each table, where wines and cheeses were paired up for their enjoyment; Pierre and Vee would move amongst them, answering questions. Then a mingle before proceedings ended at nine o'clock. Romance optional. And then they were off.

Kate did the rounds half-heartedly, with a smattering of small talk, letting the others in her group do the chit-chat: after all, she wasn't here looking for love - it would forever be out of bounds judging by Jack's dignified replies to her texts to ask for space while he considered their future.

There was Aled, a trendy BBC Wales thirty-something in a shirt buttoned all the way to the top; Stuart the red-faced trainee fishmonger from two shops up, drinking far too quickly; and, hang-on, wasn't that silver-eyed beauty of a brunette beside them that electrician who'd been here that day she'd met Vee?

She was Beatrycze, spelling it out when Kate asked her to repeat it, 'just call me Bea', who had come to the UK ten years ago from Poland where one in four people - including her - were unemployed. 'Electrics, I always love them, since I was a kid, but was no place at home for lady sparkies. Good money here, so I come and I can live without my parents and so I stay.'

'And you're single?' Kate asked before she could stop herself. Because here was a gorgeous and intelligent woman who could've turned up in her boiler suit and still be head and shoulders above everyone else.

'Of course! I see the sign for tonight when I came here to fix his lights. He say they flickered then poof, but all he needed was new bulbs. Has happened quite a lot lately what with one job and another.' A huge grin and a wink that told Kate all she needed to know – Pierre was inventing jobs to get her here and Bea was playing along!

Talking of whom, he appeared by Bea's side, concentrating on everyone else but this beguiling woman, as if he would explode if he locked eyes with her.

'Wine and cheese, the perfect partners,' he began. 'Astringents are rough and dry in the mouth, while fats are slippery. Having them together balances them,' he said, groping the air with his hand.

'Is maybe all about the, how you say, "mouthfeel", the way it sits on your tongue,' Bea said not suggestively but it sounded indecent now that Kate knew there was something going on.

Pierre looked up from nosing his glass. His frown fell in a facial landslide and his eyes went from impervious rock to sticky toffee pudding.

'Fascinating,' he said, breathily, as Aled and Stuart clocked their attraction and started talking rugby leaving Kate to feel like a prize gooseberry.

'Tell me, do you have oscypek? Is my favourite.' My goodness, how could she make cheese sound erotic? Kate thought, searching for someone to come to her rescue. She caught Vee's eyes and widened her own which Vee answered immediately.

'Are you okay? You've done so well lasting until now, go if you need…oh, I see!'

Vee had followed Kate's slight nod to the right towards Pierre and Bea and a smile broke out on her face, contagious as it moved to Kate's mouth.

'Blinking heck,' Vee whispered. 'Fast work! Come with me a sec, I've got to get some more wine.'

'Anyone you like?' Kate asked as they went into the stockroom, trying to keep the mood light because she was managing to enjoy herself despite everything.

'No,' Vee said, her back to her, as she retrieved some bottles. Then she sighed, turned around and revealed, 'Not here anyway', as a twitch of her lips became a soppy grin. Which she then tried to rein in out of empathy for Kate.

'Sorry,' she said, shaking her head, 'Crap timing.'

'Please…don't apologize. It makes me happy that you're happy.' And she meant it because Vee deserved something good, someone good. Just because Kate was black and blue

190

form losing the love of her life didn't mean everyone else should suffer. 'So who is he? Because it's quite sudden!'

'Kind of,' Vee said, shyly, 'But still, unexpected.'

Kate was intrigued as Vee's beam came out again.

'I don't want to say any more in case I jinx it, but it's… it's blown my mind, to be honest. And it might just be because we're both in weird places and we're kicking against where we are.'

'He's nice though?'

Vee's eyes drifted off into space. It was bittersweet for Kate: she remembered feeling that way when she'd got together with Jack, when he'd completed her.

'Yes. Very.' She gave a sloshed smile. Then immediately she apologized. 'Sorry, sorry. God, here I am not even asking how you are…'

Her ever-threatening tears came and she gave a sudden sob. 'Battered, broken.'

'Oh, love, it must be so hard.'

'It's awful,' she said, with a shivery voice, 'to have lost him. Us. Our future.'

'Has he been in touch?'

Kate shook her head. 'He's the type who needs to hide in his shed. I've messaged him but he wants to be alone to work things out. It makes me feel helpless but I understand.'

'Does your mum know? And Griff?'

'Not yet. I'm just giving myself a bit of recovery time before I have to tell her. Probably in a couple of days. Then Charlie and me will sit down with Griff.'

Vee reached out to her then. 'You did the right thing, you know.'

And there it was. The reason why she was in this position. Why she was pillaged and plundered but why she wasn't on her knees. Why her misery wasn't all-consuming. Why she had been able to get up, get dressed and get in the car to drive over here. Because living with Charlie had brought her under the same roof as Griff, where she could watch the very best thing that had happened to her. As much as she needed Jack, loved him with everything, her son was her lifeblood. The way he jigged when he was offered ice cream, his sleepy eyes when he claimed he wasn't tired. She would move out as soon as something came up at work; she was on the lookout already. A flat somewhere quiet but near a playground and a cafe where she could take him. But Charlie, her husband Tom and Kate had discussed late into the night how they would nurture their son, how Kate would be there as a second mother without having to be ashamed.

Kate's spine straightened and her shoulders went back as she spoke. 'I can live with myself now. I might be down, but the truth is beautiful.' A calm washed over her. 'If Jack doesn't come back to me, then I will survive.'

Vee hugged her with all her might and they returned to the tasting session with a variety of bottles to keep up with demand. A happy chatter rose above the background of world music – Pierre's choice obviously – and there were a few couples who had retreated into corners to get to know one another better.

She looked for Pierre to see how his coupling was going. But he was by the door, talking to someone outside. Bea was doing her best to engage in conversation with another man but her eyes were flitting back and forth to Pierre. She hoped something would come of it because Pierre was a lovely man: she'd seen him lose himself over and over to crazy women whom he was drawn to but let him down. He was too wonderful to be treated badly again. But she had a feeling about Bea, no lady friend of his had ever shown so much interest in cheese before.

Vee had returned to her group so Kate felt it was time to slip away. She found her mac and then manoeuvred her way around the edge of the room, her head down, not wanting to be asked 'going so soon?'.

But when she reached the door, when she looked up, the question didn't just come at her, it pinned her to the spot.

Jack was standing there, barring her exit; unintentionally his body filled the frame.

'I was just going if you wanted to come in,' she said, looking him right in the eye because she had done her apologizing. But that didn't mean her heart wasn't swirling with love. And her stomach churning because he'd turned up for a singles' night, hoping he had turned up to support Pierre in the way she'd been here for Vee.

'I was here to see you, actually' he said, backing out to give her room to leave the deli.

So this was it: he would tell her now that he had had a good think and he thought it would be best if they went their separate ways.

She nodded, ready to take it.

'I think we need to formally cancel the wedding,' he said.

'Yes,' she said, as concrete poured on her soul.

'And, um, if it's okay with you, maybe we could go to tell your mother together if you haven't already?'

His decency that she wouldn't take both barrels alone was breathtaking.

'Thank you,' she said, 'but I'll be fine. It's what I need to do. To stand up to her. Really.' By this, she wanted him to see that she understood what he had meant when he'd told her to take on her mother, rather than laying herself prostate at his feet in a last bid to win him over. It was obvious it was too late for that.

'No, I'd like to. Because... I've been in the shed and Boris agrees with me...' he said, earnestly.

Here it came, the noble end and she steeled herself, thinking of Griffy.

'...that you and me should cancel the wedding. And start planning our own happy ending instead.'

His eyes were watery now and he was holding out a hand to her.

This was absolutely the opposite of what Kate had anticipated and she was dumbfounded, silent. She couldn't let herself believe it: if she'd had more than one glass of wine she'd have thought herself drunk.

And then he was bending down on one knee, looking up at her, smiling.

'Will you marry me, Kate?' he said. 'On our terms? No one else's?'

Stunned, she gasped and blinked and sized up this magnificent man gazing up at her. It couldn't be real. But he was waiting. For her.

As the reality swept through her, Kate's pulse began to boom in her ears.

'Yes,' she whispered, then louder still because there was no room for ambiguity. 'Yes, yes, yes!' she said, throwing herself into his arms as he stood up, 'I'll never keep anything from you again.'

And as Jack spun her round, she saw a carousel of faces and heard a chorus of cheers from a standing ovation outside the deli.

Chapter Twenty-One

M

Cardiff City Centre

Murphy actually caught himself whistling as he got ready.

Fucking hell, he thought, stopping with one leg in his shorts, *this is embarrassing. This is mental. This is… amazing.*

Falling on to his king-size bed like a cliché, he thought he'd been on the cusp of it with a couple of girls but he realized now that he'd been nowhere near. Not even close.

Sighing, it was as if he'd been walking around with shades on the entire time – but since his kiss with Vee, the blinkers were off and the world wasn't dark and nasty. It was bright and in technicolour with surround sound. Like a film. Too good to be true. Then insecurity seemed to multiply like a parasite, feeding on his happiness.

This was how it had been since Saturday night. Huge ups and skydiving downs, wondering if he had made a massive mistake. Taken advantage of her. Or allowed himself to be manipulated. Got himself in deep shit. Opened up old wounds. Walked into a mess which was only going to get messier. How was he going to handle the Kat situation with Vee? Ignore it? No, he would have to tell her eventually. And it would not end well. Better to nip this in the bud now.

But, but, but… He was happy. Fucking on one. Buzzing. It was the lamest, naffest counter-argument ever. Too simple, too uncomplicated, too clear and too pain-free. Yet that was the bottom line.

When he thought of their kiss, their hours of kissing in the darkness, it turned him on in every way. Just her lips on his, nothing more, which in itself told him just how different this thing with Vee was to everything else he'd had. His mind replayed the scene, having trouble doing up his shorts because he was feeling himself stiffen at the moment when the hug turned into something more. The long, slow night ending at dawn when, flushed and smiley, she'd gone. He'd snatched a couple of hours of sleep, enough to stay on some kind of dopey buzz for the rest of Sunday. As if he was walking on the moon, chilled.

His T-shirt on, he puttied his hands on autopilot and did his hair, remembering how he'd worried about whether he should message her or not, to apologize or make a joke of it. Normally, he'd leave it until the girl contacted him. But he couldn't stop himself. Nothing major, just a few pings along the lines of needing a roast to get him through the day, feeling tired, and trite shite like that. But she'd been on his exact wavelength – moaning about her parents asking where she'd been all night, as if she was a teenager. Then the exchange of messages about maybe catching up…

He laughed at how he'd tried to play it cool with the woman he'd known since she was a girl. The to and fro of 'could do…', 'wicked, free Wednesday? My day off', 'yeah, Roath Park?'

That was where he was heading; Melanie was on her way, Dad was up in his chair, watching daytime crap until the racing started.

'I'm off now, Dad,' he said. 'You sure you'll be all right? Melanie will be here in a minute.'

Dad turned his head to him. 'Might go and get the papers later.' He was lucid now, the confusion came and went, he'd learned.

'Great. The exercise will do you good.' The doctors had all said Dad needed to push himself. The brain was a muscle like any other. 'And it's a lovely day.'

Murphy threw up the sash window and sniffed the air: it was sweet and summery. Like Vee. This was how it was with her: she was everywhere. He couldn't wait to see her.

So he left, stopping off at the shop, wondering if he should get some fresh bread and cheese, but what if she was sick of the sight of it from the deli? He eye-rolled himself for being what Orla would call 'sensitive to a person's needs' and settled for some beers and posh crisps. There was a cafe at the park if they wanted anything else or they could get a take-out.

As the bus pulled up beside the park, he saw her. The familiarity of how she stood, alert but relaxed, ready to move, with one hand on her hip, the other checking her phone, looking up and around her. But there was also the unfamiliarity of who she was now: how he'd always known what she was thinking but that was before they'd crossed a line. Friendships were all about opening up, but when it was more than that, you kept a hold of your feelings until it was safe.

Suddenly he realized this was the challenge: how he'd be able to protect himself. Because she didn't know everything and it sent him into a spiral just as his feet touched the pavement. What was he doing here? He was going to hurt her because the ugly would have to come out. Fuck. Fuck.

'What's up?' Vee said, smiling coming towards him. 'You look like you've sucked a lemon.'

See? She could tell from the set of his jaw and he hadn't said a word yet. This was the worst thing he'd ever done, getting involved with her. What was he going to do? He could make up an excuse, yes, that's what he'd do.

'Just work,' he lied, feeling the blow of betrayal so soon into this.

'Oh, right. What's happening?' she said, her face crestfallen, instinctively withdrawing from his personal space. Thank God they both had sunglasses on because it'd kill him to see her hurt – and she'd see his eyes were cold.

He walked off, towards the path which ran around the lake, feeling a bastard.

'Just stuff.'

'Oooo-kay.'

Silence apart from the hissing of wild geese and swans which behaved as though the park belonged to them.

'I'm not stupid, you know,' Vee said. Bollocks – she'd seen right through him. Of course she would.

'No, I know…'

'Like, just because I don't spend my life staring at a screen doesn't mean I'm not able to listen to your technical woes.'

His heart stood down – he thought she'd been about to start on the deeper issues between them. There was relief, then the realization that she'd disarmed him yet again. And he was a bit stressed out with his latest project.

'Right, well, it's complicated, you know? So I design apps,

yeah?'

'I've got that bit already,' she said, sarcastically, getting him right back.

He couldn't help but defrost a bit. 'I'm having to rewrite some code, it's long, boring, heavy-going, I've got to incorporate testing feedback.'

'Who's the client?'

'Can't say. Breach of contract. But it's a massive American company, relaunching its iOS app.'

'Lots of pressure then?'

'Yep. FaceTime meetings at stupid o'clock so it's convenient for Pacific Time and for the office in Tokyo. I should be in London doing it, helps being with the others at Kode, ideas and specifications and stuff.'

'Wow. I thought I had it bad having to keep on top of the Stinking Bishop.'

He laughed, she was good at defusing the bomb.

'But it's not just that. The bigger issue is that the language is changing all the time, you've got to keep up to date. Then it's the corporate crap too.'

'Could you go back to doing games? What was that one you did again?'

'Smash The Suburbs. Was a sort of zombie game.'

'And?' Oh, she was going to make him tell her.

'It was set on a new estate where the brain-eaters came out of conservatories and got shot at by the heroine.'

'Heroine? A girl? Wow,' she said, impressed and thankfully not dwelling on the setting.

'Yeah…she was a punky gun slinger.' Named after you, Victorious, he didn't say. 'Anyway, games are in the past, and what I'm doing now seems to be heading that way too. It all just feels a bit… wrong. Basically, I'm having a few doubts about my direction.'

'In what way?'

'Like, with Dad being ill, it's made me see there's a health market there, or something for the elderly, because the population is ageing and living longer and…' He had to check himself – the , words had flowed from nowhere, he hadn't even known this idea was in his head let alone talk to colleagues about it – and it was all pie in the sky, he'd done no research. How was it all coming out of him? '…I'm talking out of my arse, aren't I?'

'Well, there's those fit band things, and they track heart rates and steps and all that so, no, it's not you talking out of your arse at all.'

Shit. She was right. Not in any technological way but in her understanding of where he was heading. She'd got it out of him and given her support. Backed him.

'You're wasted you are,' he said. 'What are you going to do with your life then?'

It was her turn to draw down the shutters.

'Oh you know, perfect the art of serving artisANAL cuisine.'

'Come on, there's got to be more that you'd like to do.' Don't joke about it. For once. Talk to me about your dreams - I want to know what's going on inside your head.

'Once I wanted to be a teacher. But it didn't happen. I let myself be persuaded.' By a man? he wondered, feeling an anger that whoever it had been had stopped her from contentment.

'You can train, can't you? They're always looking for teachers.' He sounded so unlike himself - upbeat, positive.

'Just train,' she scoffed. 'You make it sound so easy. It's money that I haven't got.'

'Get a loan? You could ask your mum and dad, couldn't you?'

'I could but I wouldn't. Why should they pay for it?'

'Well, someone else then... like me...'

Jesus, he'd been going to end all of this just five minutes ago and now he was offering his cash. '...you could pay it back when you've got it. When you start earning.'

'Oh God, no, I couldn't. Thanks but... no. I've got to sort myself out. I'm thirty, for God's sake!'

'They might have bursaries or whatever they call them, grants. It might be worth checking out.' He so wanted to help her.

'Why bother though?'

'Why bother? Because you'd be the best teacher ever.' He had his shoulders hunched, his arms splayed because this was a no-brainer. She was perfect for the job. And she was perfect.

'Really?' He could tell by her suspicious frown that she was waiting for a punchline. That's how they did things. But that was before this...

'Yes,' he said, smacking his fist into the palm of his hand.

'You're a doer, you see the good in people, you bring out the best in them.' He had the urge to shout it out loud, beat his chest and even jump up and down!

Still, she didn't believe him. She screwed up her face, lifting her sunglasses to inspect him. 'Really? Do I?'

This was it: the question he had to address. Would he be her cheerleader, not just as friends but as a team? As a couple. As lovers and partners. Or would he step away, avoid the inevitable pain...He pushed his shades to the top of his head. His gut was talking and he wouldn't silence it.

'Yes, Vee,' he said, 'you do. Mam always said you were special.'

And then he couldn't stop himself: she looked so lovely with the breeze tickling her hair, her sweet rosy lips, her freckled shoulders bare. He moved towards her, staring deep into her eyes.

'Victoria Anwen Hope, you make me want to be a better person.'

And then they kissed.

*

University Hospital of Wales, Cardiff, December 2008

A crack in the peeling magnolia ceiling slashes a crooked wounded path to the hushed voices beyond the tatty curtain.

'This will do her no good.' Mother is hissing. Harsh and direct while Kate lies there sagging, deflated and haunted, dreading the moment, whenever it comes, when she is to surrender her son.

Mother suggested the arrangement as soon as she found out 'to save her career'. It was a terrifying, revolting concept. But as Kate's belly grew, her helplessness and fear deepened her anxiety - she was too young, too unprepared, too weak to bring up a child alone. The midwife and consultant had told her that medication would help: untreated depression in pregnant women presented a bigger risk for children's development than antidepressants. She would be able to go out, meet other mums-to-be and see that an unplanned pregnancy could be a source of joy. But Kate refused - she didn't want to engage with the world and fill the baby with drugs. Then they offered her a space in a special unit to make her see she would survive if she had help - they had to make every effort because the best scenario was always to keep mother and baby together. Kate only wanted to pretend it wasn't happening. She didn't want to bond with the baby because she didn't want to keep him. So when Charlie caressed her bump and sat with her for hours as she swung between mute misery and primal wailing, unable to function and too unstable to face motherhood, giving up her baby to her became the only solution.

'Nothing is going to make this easier for her,' Charlie whispers. 'She wants to do it. And it's best for the baby too.'

Even now when the crunch had come, when she'd kissed her own son fresh from her body, she remained convinced of her decision - it was about the baby, giving him security and love. And there was no one better than her sister and Tom to do that. No matter how hard her instinct wanted to resist it, to claw out the eyes of anyone who would take him away.

Kate turns to see him lying in a plastic see-through cot next to her bed. It takes her breath away: so delicate, so helpless. A white hat with a little pom-pom gives way to a downy olive face, luxurious eyelashes and a puckered mouth. His tiny fist pokes out from beneath the waffle hospital blanket, revealing a little-too-big-for-him white babygro. His chest rises and falls quickly and then his brow knits in a flash as something passes over him. It's a look she's seen before in his father.

Kate gulps and finds herself filling up and flooding again, oozing grief in her blood. She closes her eyes and feels every cell spasm. She is a mother but not a mother. The vessel who gave birth only a few hours ago. No drugs, no intervention – the overwhelming, contorting fever of delivery was the trial she had to suffer.

When a night of pain fanfared in the most glorious moment, when this creature was placed on her naked chest, red and waxy, bawling with fury. She kissed his wet scalp then passed him, fighting herself so hard, to Charlie, her birthing partner. Both cried their hearts out. But not for the same reasons. Kate, for giving him up. Charlie, for the joy of receiving her child, for promising Kate she would give him the world. Baby Griff, whose name, suggested by Kate, was picked from a shortlist drawn up by her, Charlie and Tom.

Charlie handed him back to Kate so she could cut the cord. That was all it took for him to search out her dark plump nipple and take his first suck. A reflex, an instinct, something so simple in this turmoil. Kate and Charlie stared urgently at each other: what to do? They had agreed bottle-feeding, Charlie would be able to bond from the start. But now he was latched on, how could they pull him off? Frantic eyes and tight throats. Kate tried to assess things: would breast-feeding make it harder? That she would find it impossible to give him away? But there was nothing worse; there were no degrees of this torment. The fact she wouldn't be his protector was all there was. And they were doing this to give him the best start – it had to begin surely with her milk?

'We can make up our own rules,' Charlie said, her chin dented with emotion. 'Just a few days if that's all you want to or can do.'

It was Charlie's gift to her.

He knew what to do straight away, drawing the goodness of her colostrum, nuzzling into her breast. The midwife warned that her milk wouldn't come in for thirty-six-hours. 'The baby will get hungrier and hungrier, his cries will stimulate the production of milk in your body,' she'd said.

Charlie and Kate had kept him their secret for a few precious hours before surrendering to their mother and ringing to tell her he had arrived. By the time she swept through the ward, Griff was on Kate's breast mother and Mother was horrified. She'd wanted the baby to be taken off Kate straight away.

'Mum, Kate is going to be part of this forever,' Charlie says wearily because neither of them have had any sleep. It's barely past seven a.m. and Kate cannot drop off because she fears her baby will be gone. This precious moment when he remains her property will end.

The curtain swooshes back and Mother's face is taut.

'Katherine. How long will they keep you in? Because the sooner we get out of here, the sooner we can...' She rolls her hands forward. 'Your father will pick you up.'

Kate looks away from her, hating this woman, this child snatcher. She knows her mother thinks this will all be over when they leave the hospital but for Kate it will never be over. In a blister of spite, she prays she is told to stay here in hospital so she has more time with her son.

'There's no rush,' Charlie says, sitting at the edge of the bed, taking Kate's hand in hers. 'The midwives said we need to let Kate recover. And establish feeding. I can introduce the bottle later on.'

Their mother leans in to them. 'You think it'll be that easy? Babies become attached. Neither of you wanted anyone else when I was...'

Kate is sickened that she drank from her mother's breast. She can't imagine such tenderness.

'We want to try. For Griff. Kate will do the feeds, I'll do everything else. The midwife says we can gradually switch to a bottle.' Switch mothers, Kate thinks, that is the brutal fact of the matter. But she will do anything to have him with her just for a while.

Mum takes in a deep breath and runs her ring fingers along her eyebrows.

'You're making a mistake.' Then she throws her hands in the air. 'All right, all right. But Charlie, you and Tom have to come to our house. Where I can keep an eye on you.'

Make sure I let him go, Kate thinks, tumbling and rolling and fearful of what comes after all of this. If there is anything ever

202

again.

Chapter Twenty-Two

V

Murphy's flat, Cardiff City Centre

Two weeks they'd been together. If you didn't count the seventeen years beforehand.

Yet that was the point: dating your best friend was, well, The Best, Vee thought, staring dreamily at Murphy in the early morning light creeping through his white shutters as he slept beside her on his enormo bed. He was on his side facing her and the soft sheet cascaded down his ripped downy stomach: the urge to run a fingertip from his cheek to his hips was overwhelming. But she didn't want to wake him, so instead she looked around at his stylish mix of antique and modern furniture, pinching herself and blinking hard to prove to herself she was here. Which was delightfully silly because of course she was: it was meant to be.

Vee had stayed over last night for the first time: his flat was gorgeous and cool and all to themselves because his dad was having a trial run at living by himself again. He'd planned to cook but they'd ended up horizontal and ordered in noodles instead.

Pointing her toes at the memory, they'd had 'almost sex', both of them intuitively wanting to work up to it, to enjoy the discovery of their bodies, but it was only a matter of time before it spilled over. Because this situation, this whatever-it-was, seemed to have a will of its own. It was effortless, but that wasn't to say they were like boring marrieds: knowing one another meant there was no small talk or awkward silences yet the new dimension to their friendship, or dare-she-say-it relationship, was thrilling. Not because it was illicit – it felt right, Christ, so right, she thought, squeezing her buttocks – but from the headiness and stomach-twirling of being able to touch one another – naked, NAKED! – and of the tension it created. It was intense in a way she'd never known. The shift magnified everything as if they were walking through a hall of funny mirrors. God, it was bloody fantastic. She could feel it everywhere, like jingle bells, the adrenalin forcing her awake, despite her tiredness, just to watch him sleeping... Then, some kind of hymn starts up, it's his alarm, she realizes, not proof they're in heaven.

'What you smirking at?' Murphy said, his big brown eyes laughing as he stretched an arm over her. But from his lazy smile he knew she was simpering.

'Am not,' she said, poking out her tongue, suddenly self-conscious of their heart-stopping attraction. It was as if they'd unscrewed a bottle marked 'chemistry' and sniffed, drunk and bathed in it. To think it had been there, bubbling under all this time. Mind you, maybe it was only so intoxicating because they'd waited so long.

The last fortnight had been so different from every other honeymoon period that Vee had had with a man. Not that that stretched beyond a couple of school boyfriends, her uni ex and Jez. It was because their compatibility was already proven and they trusted one another. As for loyalty, they may have had a blip – an eight-year blip admittedly – but they'd come back together. And then there was all the stuff they knew about one another – their parents, their friends, his preference for red sauce, hers for brown. They knew what they were getting themselves into.

Yet the beating of her heart wasn't a pedestrian rhythm – it was a hypnotizing throb of drum and bass proportions. Because she was only finding out now he had lovely hairy legs – that holiday in France, they'd been physically adolescent – and he had a delicious dark dot of a freckle just to the left of his right hip.

'You got the kettle on?' he asked, pulling her towards him, which made her shiver.

'I'm the guest, you do it.' Then recognition of the music...'Coldplay! This is bloody Coldplay!' she squawks, 'After all you ever said about that band!'

'What?' he says, her insides flipping as his hand slid from

her clavicle through the middle of her breasts to just below her waist.

'You hypocrite!'

'It's Paradise,' he said, kissing her shoulder as the music soared around them.

She should've been laughing at him but the way he said the title of the track made her quiver.

'Paradise…' he said again, now a whisper. On her belly. His hot breath making her even hotter.

'It is.' She surrendered then, moving her hand slowly down his chest, through the hair of his groin and onto his cock, making him groan. Overcome by his desire for her, she had to let him know she felt the same. She moved closer still, wrapping her leg over his hips, pushing him into her, realizing what was forever meant to be. Them and only them, their bodies making the physical form of their love which had been between them for years. Feeding off one another's intensity, they fell into a twilight of their own, tumbling and soaring as they moved to a unique rhythm which Vee had always known. To touch the parts she had never touched before was all consuming: and as they came together, Vee felt completed, whole.

Spooning afterwards, flushed by the step they'd taken, Vee reached her arm back to him to ruffle his hair. 'Coldplay, indeed.'

'News just in: I don't care any more, it's a good song and it's you and me.'

She felt his lips on her wrist as she began to play with the soft tufts on his head which had grown in since they'd bumped into each other on Barry Island.

'You're reaching boy band status,' she said. 'With this hair.'

'Less of the boy, I reckon, now,' he said. 'Not a kid anymore.'

She heard a crack in his voice: he had something to say. It didn't worry her because what could he tell her that she didn't know already? Instinctively, she took his hand to her mouth and kissed his scar. 'Mmm?'

'Yeah. Like… this… it's happening.'

'Yep, sure is.'

'And I want it to, you know?' He wanted her reassurance. And she felt the requited thrill that he'd admitted it first.

'I do, Murphy, I do.' Relieved, liberated to be able to show she'd been thinking the same.

Then a big breath.

'There's some stuff I need to say...' She rubbed his hand, which was tucked round her waist and she nodded. 'Before we go on because it's important and I wish I could park it. Like, it isn't a big deal because we're past it but it's always been on my mind and...'

He was going to express exactly how she felt and she was so glad.

'When you went away, I missed you so much.'

'Me too,' she said, echoing him.

'But I've always wondered... what happened?'

'I know, me too, ever since we lost touch.' She turned her head to the side to kiss his cheek. They were beyond ruining this now, they had sealed their love and she was no longer afraid of knowing where it had gone wrong because now it would be eternally right.

'No, I mean "what happened" what happened?' There was a different tone now, a vulnerability, which made her face him because she wanted to see he was safe with her. Then she realized they needed to broach this because then it could be put away or all time.

'I don't know,' she said, 'I thought we might... that you'd come to see me and we'd... but then I guessed the letter had put you off, that I'd got the wrong end of the stick. But, we're here now, eh?' She smiled.

But his face frowned, his eyes clouded.

Suddenly, she lurched inside: what was going on?

'Letter?' he asked, confused, 'Do you mean the emails because I thought you were going to email me when you'd got to Cambodia to say where to fly to but I never heard anything.'

'Not the emails, no,' she said, lightly, because surely he knew. 'The letter... I gave it to Kat to give to...' Murphy was shaking his head. '...oh my God...Didn't you get it?'

'No.' He whispered it and his eyes searched hers, going back and forth, as if he was looking to see if she was lying.

'The letter,' she repeated, to show it had been real, 'I remember what it said word for word...' She'd never forgotten it, how could she when it had been the first time she'd acknowledged her feelings for him? And what she'd taken as his rejection had seared itself onto her soul, that, she realized now, was why she'd abandoned herself to Jez, because she'd felt the real her was so worthless after Murphy had ignored her declaration.

'I said "I might give you a promotion from back-up man", that "the more people I'd met and the more places I'd been made me realize how special you were".'

There was absolutely no recognition on his face. She felt panic rising.

'That "I'd always known you were special but being at home made me think that was how it was in the big world but it wasn't – everyone paled in comparison to you."'

Feeling the terrible disappointment again, she relived the hope that had been dashed.

'I didn't exactly spell it out, to try getting together, but I said "if you're single then we could see what happens". Then I did a dramatic joke, you know, to back-pedal, "If I'd got it all wrong, then feel free to never contact me again". That's what I assumed happened.'

Please, tell me that's what happened, she pleaded inside, because she hated this possible new version of events because it made her feel unsteady.

'But what about Conor? You loved him.'

Now Vee was wounded at the accusation over someone she barely remembered.

'Conor? I didn't love him! I loved you!' She'd said it and she didn't care. She felt desperate. 'How do you know about Conor? He was just some bloke, Kat and I fell out after she tried it on with him when she knew I liked him.' Her breathing shallow, she was questioning his eyes now.

'Kat,' he said, in a tiny voice, looking up to the ceiling. He turned his head to her and a tear was moving through his stubble as if it was lava tracking through rock. 'I never got the letter,' he began, touching her then recoiling, a grimace coming to his lips. 'The night I saw Kat, when she said she wanted to catch up, I'd been in half a mind to see her because I'd sort of left her behind. And you'd said she had turned into a nightmare, I was on your side. She'd be going to the City, she'd treated you badly, I felt there was no point. But then I went, for old time's sake. I was lonely. I wish I never had.'

'Why? Why didn't she give you the letter?' she said, knowing as soon as she'd said it he was the wrong person to ask. 'Why do you wish you hadn't seen her?'

She felt a sickness in her throat now, nausea at Kat's betrayal and a dread of something coming which was going to change everything.

'Because...' he said, scrunching himself up, 'I... we were drunk... we ended up in bed.'

'No. No, you didn't...' Utter torment as her heart broke in two.

Murphy began to nod over and over as he began to cry properly.

'How could you?' Vee was up now, looking for her clothes, wanting to get out of there.

'Mam was ill, Dad was—'

Excuses. She never ever thought Murphy was the type. Hurt welled up in her chest and she started sobbing as she got dressed.

'I'm sorry,' he said, getting up and kneeling down at her on the end of the bed. 'It was nothing. It was just anger and I was so unhappy. Mam was dying and Dad was drinking himself to... to this, where he is now.'

Vee had heard enough. Once again she'd been in fantasy land. Once again she'd suspended herself for a man, allowing herself to be swept up and rolled over. She wasn't going to do this, she wasn't going to let herself go down this path again.

She jeered, 'When are you going to stop blaming your parents for everything?'

Then she covered her mouth with her hand in shock at what had just happened. She'd attacked him in the worst possible way: going for the jugular by attacking his upbringing. His most private of insecurities, the basis of who he was and how he defined himself. It had just rolled off her tongue without her even knowing it was there.

Just like that, Murphy had grey bags under his eyes, as if she'd punched him and the anger momentarily subsided to sorrow.

'Please, Vee, it was a long time ago. I love you. I always have.'

He loved her. It should've taken her even higher. But this wasn't some romantic confession: it was a poison arrow. If she didn't move quickly, it would pierce her heart.

'Please forgive me. I thought you didn't want me.'

'So?' she hissed. 'I thought you'd abandoned me. I didn't go and sleep with one of your mates, your best mates.'

'People make mistakes,' he said, his hands in a position of prayer.

Yes, she thought, walking out, slamming his front door, cantering down the stairs and out into the morning air, and her mistake had been to think she could mend their rift.

But it was done. Seventeen years. Two weeks.

Within seconds he'd texted her.

The past is in the past. Please. M x

Trembling, she deleted his message. He was right: she should've left the past alone.

Chapter Twenty-Three

K

Pentyrch, North of Cardiff

'Well, this is lovely, just the four of us,' Kate's mother Pam preened from behind her menu. 'Isn't it, Jonathan?'

Her father dipped his head to give a nod from behind his glasses – forever silent, never contradicting his wife. He coughed then returned to perusing lunch across the table. Weary, that's how he looked, Kate thought, wondering just how he'd survived forty years of marriage to her mother.

Kate had deliberately picked a public place to break the news to them that their wedding, or at least the version her mother wanted, was off and instead, still quite unbelievably, she and Jack would have it their way. Mother lived by the rules of public appearances: manners and saving face were all. Especially here in The Pineapple, an ancient stone inn north of Cardiff which boasted a gastro chef and well-to-do diners, a couple of whom her father knew from the surveying industry. That had settled Kate's nerves because mother would never overreact with such a prestigious audience. And even if she didn't accept it, Kate had turned over a new leaf: Jack had given her a second chance she never thought she'd have and she was not going to let that go, especially for her mother.

Jack put his hand on Kate's thigh and she turned to him: he was absolutely radiant from a shower and a shave in the home she'd moved back into straight away. Squeaky clean and ruddy, complete with a shirt which always made her smile because it was so unusual, he looked the essence of wholesome goodness. Their relationship even better now, she didn't need to be afraid with him by her side because his intentions were always honourable and true.

Their reunion after his 'proposal' had begun with her promise to tell him everything: she had explained who the father was, how he had no role in her life and that she finally felt free of the torture from carrying her secret alone. Jack had accepted it without drama; how could he judge her for something so many years ago when she had tried her best to live with it? And he saw that she would never make him sit in the back seat of their life again when it came to her mother.

'I think I'll have a salad,' Pam said, giving Kate a knowing smile, expecting her to follow suit because of 'their figures'. She was so happy to deprive herself, to look the martyr – it inspired Kate to show Jack she meant business. That she was not just doing it to spite her mother and impress Jack but because she finally she felt able to make her own decisions. Okay, it was only a meal but it was a start.

'I'll have the Welsh burger with Perl Wen cheese on a brioche with chips,' she said, feeling empowered as her mother's gaze turned sour.

'Not long until the wedding!' she trilled, feeling her pearls, then brushing a lapel of her trouser suit. 'I make it...' pretending she had to think when she would know to the second, '...so... today is June the fifteenth, which makes sixteen days to July the first.' In other words, 'not long enough to shift those calories', even though Kate was as svelte as she'd ever been. But she would change – she already had. Instead of going running to beat the demons, she'd sat with Jack and confronted them and it had worked.

Recalling the pep talk she'd had with him in the car on their way, Kate ignored her mother's barb. 'Jack? Dad? What about you?'

'Steak. Rare. With everything. Onion rings, fries, roasted veg, the lot,' Jack said, rubbing his stomach and grinning.

'Fish, for me, dear.' Her father received an approving smile from her mother: Kate was done with anger but not sorrow as she pitied him for dancing to her tune.

They repeated the scene when the waiter appeared, complete with commentary from Pam. Every occasion Kate had eaten with her, she had felt her mother's judgement. Today she had decided it wouldn't touch her. Her outfit said the same thing: gone were the tailored trousers and smart blouse, which constricted her. Instead she was in a soft cotton wrap dress which emphasized her femininity rather than covered up the body that had given birth.

'So, you said you wanted to talk to us, Katherine,' Pam said, taking a sip of her wine and performing a shoulder squeeze because it was naughty to drink at lunchtime. The timing was incredible: she said it just as Kate was swallowing her wine and she couldn't react with a firm 'yes'. She'd tried to put her on the back foot, wanting to take control, to force her into a stifled nod.

But Kate found the strength to make her wait. Not to say hesitation and fear weren't on the edge of her vision but she had learned for herself what cruel taskmasters they were.

'Yes,' she said, boldly. 'Jack and I, we've made a decision about the wedding and—'

'A decision?' Alarm ripped across Pam's face and she looked at Jonathan, who was expressionless.

'Let me speak.' Kate heard a quiver in her voice and she gritted her teeth, determined to see this through. Jack put his doting arm around her seat and then she knew she had nothing to be afraid of.

Pam's lips thinned and Kate saw her begin to tap her wine glass with a blood-red nail. It was like a bomb ticking.

'We would prefer to get married our own way,' she said, looking her mother then father straight in the eyes. 'We will obviously cover any cancellation charges incurred, along with the flowers, the band etcetera.'

Pam gripped Jonathan's hand. 'Cancellation? But you can't.'

'We can and we will.'

'Jack? What's she talking about?' Pam gave a pleading look, begging for him to backtrack, to say Kate was having one of her episodes as if she couldn't make her mind up for herself. Her mother seeing this self-expression as 'mental illness' because it broke the mould she had made for her daughter.

'It's a joint decision, Pamela. Jonathan. We're very sorry that it's so last minute but we feel the organization and the planning went awry a long time ago.'

'We understand you will be unhappy and we apologize for how you feel but it's our day,' Kate finished.

'This is ridiculous. It's all paid for. I just don't…' Her

mother pinched her nostrils to show how emotional she was. Then she produced a tissue from her sleeve and gave her final offer of doe-eyed persuasion. 'Jack, dear, can't you…?'

'We want it to be what we want,' Kate spoke, wanting to show it was done. 'It's a celebration of our love and the way we want it, well, it's more us, isn't it, Jack?'

He smiled. 'Brighton bandstand. We've booked a new date. It's not a Saturday, it's a Thursday, July the thirtieth, but then we were lucky enough to get a slot as it is.'

Jonathan was now being ordered to say something, but his jaw was set, as if he was too cross at Kate to speak. She was so used to his impotence, she pushed on.

'You're invited, of course you are. Along with Charlie, Tom and Griff. Jack's mother will be coming. A few friends. We originally wanted it to be just us and the dog, but we want to share it with our loved ones.' Kate felt the penultimate weight fly off her shoulders. She'd get round to the subject of the final one in a minute.

'What will people say?' Pam said, looking around to make sure no one could hear their conversation. 'It's terribly embarrassing. And the dress? That beautiful dress!'

'We don't care what people say, Mum,' Kate said, this time gently because she was about to let it all go. 'Just as we don't care what people will say about Griff.'

Pam took a sharp intake of breath.

'Jack, I take it, knows, does he?' she said in a low growl.

'Yes. Everything. And soon Griff will too.'

'Jonathan. Please…' Pam said, her face sunken, defeated.

Her father played with his knife and then placed it down very carefully. Kate had seen this all before. He would remain silent, let his wife do the talking. He didn't care and—

'Pamela. Will you please stop.'

His voice was quiet but there was an unmistakable warning in his tone.

Aghast, Kate had never heard him speak to her mother like that. She had lifted her chin in defiance. There was tension in the air – Kate held her breath, waiting, not knowing if there would be a showdown or a capitulation.

Her father adjusted his fork. His hand was trembling. But then incredibly her mother dropped her eyes and stared at her lap.

Was this surrender?

Again her father spoke. 'Pamela, this is what I've been trying to tell you over so many years. So many years.'

Her father, speaking out? It was inconceivable that he had ever tried to have words. It was astonishing he was doing it now in public, in front of Kate.

'It's time to stop all of this,' he said, now softly, 'Katherine is an adult. She has made her own choices. You have to respect them.'

Pam's shoulders drooped and her father placed a hand on Kate and his wife as though he was trying to complete a circle. Close the chasm that had kept them apart for so long. His tenderness, his strength, just when she had needed it most just when she'd thought he had completely abandoned her, made Kate's throat sore.

'Katherine,' he said, his eyes meeting hers. He drew breath as if this would be the one and only time that he would try to unify their family. 'Your mother and I, we had very little when we were young. Your mother never had the opportunities you had. Her parents... I can say this, Pamela, can't I?'

Her mother held a hankie to her mouth. 'I've tried my best, that's all I've ever tried to do.' It was as if she was convincing herself.

'Your mother had a very hard upbringing. Her parents were, are—'

'Are?' She had always been led to believe they had been a sweet couple who had passed away, her grandfather going, quickly followed by granny who died of a broken heart, when her mother was newly married.

'Still alive. Or at least we haven't heard otherwise. In North Wales, they retired to Rhyl.'

Kate's head was spinning. 'But why didn't we see them?'

Her mother shook her head as if she couldn't bear their mention.

'I'm afraid it was simply neglect. They were very religious, your mother received no support. Our wedding... they didn't come because I wasn't Catholic. It hurt your mother very much, it still does. After that, we cut all ties.'

Kate's insides went to mush. No wonder this wedding was of such importance to her. And her father had been walking an impossible tightrope of emotion.

'When you and Charlotte were born, she would say she would die fighting for you. She would never turn her back on you as her parents had. She still would.'

'Oh, mum,' Kate said, her chin trembling, knowing she would do the same for Griff, 'that's why you pushed us.' It all became clear: her mother had turned her own neglect on its head, not wanting Kate or Charlie to feel unloved. Instead she had become controlling and fearful – rationing her love just as her parents had. And the awful, awful thing was, her mother was still trapped.

Kate wanted to get up to hug her, console her, forgive her. But she could only do that if her mother conceded that Kate had the right to follow her own path. Otherwise it would be history repeating itself. The anguish was intolerable.

'I'm ready to go, Jonathan,' her mother whispered before composing herself. The smile was back on and she began to fuss with her handbag.

'Mum,' Kate said, reaching out then pulling her arms back in, unable to work out how to behave because she wanted to save her mother's face.

'I'll call you later,' she said, brightly, plastic. A small sniff was swallowed and she was on her feet. 'Jonathan?'

He nodded and picked up his blazer. He took a step towards Kate, kissed her cheek and then held her eyes with his. They were apologetic, serious. They said 'you have Jack, Charlie, Griff and me – your mother has only me'.

At last comprehending his terrible anguish, Kate let them leave without a scene.

For a few moments, she stared at her napkin and began to twist it until her fingers hurt. She felt ravaged by how damaged her mother still was. Unable to be maternal.

Then Jack's hand was on hers, pulling her fingers free.

'I'm proud of you,' he said, lifting her chin, 'And I'm sorry you had to learn about your mother like that. You've done the right thing by not backing down.'

Kate looked up into his clear blue eyes and felt his love.

'It's a generation thing, I guess,' she said, feeling the shock waning, 'I expect no one ever showed her affection. Griff, he'll never suffer that.'

'No,' Jack said, 'he won't. Listen, I need to go to the gents. Shall I cancel the food?'

She gave a weak laugh. 'We're making a habit of that, aren't we?'

'Well, let's break the habit. Let's stay and see this through. Think about the wedding. Work out where we can stay, book a hotel. Think about a honeymoon... if we've got any money left once we've paid off the now not happening wedding of the year!'

Kate let out a loud laugh, releasing her stress. It left room for a renewed hope for the future when she had once believed she wasn't entitled to one.

As Jack crossed the dining area, she felt a surge of joy that they would be able to lead a simpler life from now on. That didn't stop her praying the ping coming from her tote bag would be her mother, paving the way for a reconciliation, but knowing it wouldn't be. Not yet. One day perhaps now that there was a reason for her mother's behaviour which gave her an insight towards understanding her. Although it wouldn't be her life's work, she wouldn't allow it: from now on she's putting Griff, Jack and herself first.

Finding her phone, she saw it was a text from Vee! She must have a sixth sense, Kate thought, feeling so excited to be able to tell her of her liberation.

> Hi, how's it going? Need to chat to you. In person. When are you free?

Strange, there was no sign-off and Vee was a serial text kisser. She had probably been disturbed by a customer in the deli.

But Kate was too happy to analyze it. She replied straight away, revealing a plan she'd wanted to speak to her about. What was the harm in doing it in a text?

> Hi! Such timing, have just told mother we're cancelling the wedding to do it our way! Anyway, I've found a flat that's right up your street, you said you were craving you own place, it's cheap but cheerful, no pressure! Do you want to meet there tomorrow in your lunch hour? Will text address in the morning if you fancy it. X

Then she switched it off because when Jack came back, they could start their new beginning undisturbed.

Chapter Twenty-Four

M

Mikey's flat, Cardiff City Centre

All he had to do was click on 'submit resumé'.

But Murphy's arms remained crossed as he stared at the cursor poised on his screen.

He was ninety-nine per cent sure about it. Everything pointed towards it. Even the rain which was battering his sash windows in the lounge. The hammering sound spurred him on: there'd be no wet Wednesdays in Santa Clara Valley, California. Hot, dry and three hundred and thirty sunny days a year would suit him fine.

The old him would've come out in an itchy red rash just thinking about all that Californian UV. But Murphy wasn't that person anymore. He'd let down his guard, just as Orla had told him to do, to let in the rays of love. He'd tried, but it hadn't worked. Vee had gone. It'd be sunglasses all the way from now on, son.

Coffee, that's what he needed, he thought, getting up from his stainless-steel table, imagining himself in his element, ordering soya skinny caps in American delis and cruising to work in some fuck-off truck. Grids. The roads were like grids there, everything was laid out tidy. If he worked hard enough, he'd forget he'd ever had a messy life here.

Rubbing his eyes, they were sore from straining over his Mac for hours, compiling his CV, making sure his application ticked every box and more. One more read-through, he just needed to do that, then he would start chucking it all over the Silicon shop. This job though was the one he wanted. Human factors software developer at Apple's HQ in Cupercino.

Designing software that 'intuitively meets the needs of the user in health, fitness and biometrics'. Being part of the leap into 'healthcare wearables'. It could be technology that detects heart problems or makes diagnoses – an area unknown but one which would help people.

Ironically, his interest had been sparked by Dad's stroke and inspired by Vee.

His hesitation now though wasn't to do with Dad. He'd done his bit for him, nursed him back to a semi-decent standard of living, trying to stay on the wagon. Got him to a place where he could go back to his flat, where he was coping thanks to Melanie. Nor was it to do with Vee. She'd made it clear she wasn't going to look back. He'd rung her phone off the line, sent messages and emails but she'd never picked up. She'd disappeared from Facebook. He'd even gone up to the deli but the boss said she'd gone out on a delivery, even though the van was parked outside.

She loved him, he knew it, but he couldn't make her trust him.

Wrecked, he was. He'd been on his knees since she left that morning. After two weeks together, when he'd glimpsed how it could be, how love had changed his everything, it had all come crashing down. He'd been stupid enough to open up. If only he hadn't mentioned the past. And what if he had received the letter? They could've avoided all of this and they might be blissfully happy. But that was a pipe dream. Kate had seen to that. And he had toyed with the idea of finding her and asking why. But he knew deep down it was because Kate was damaged, just like him. Now he was just bones, filleted like a fish. When before he'd been so alive, head over heels twenty thousand leagues under the sea in love with Vee. He still was in love with her. The only way he could deal with it would be to swim off and come up for air thousands of miles away. Put the Atlantic and the Pacific between them.

No, the reason he was double-triple-checking himself was Orla. When he went, which would happen because he was skilled up and determined enough, he'd be losing the one person who'd never let him down.

He knew she'd be gutted, but he also knew she'd say to go for it. Because she was okay, she'd always been okay. The sadness would come from his side: he'd made it his duty to protect her, when in fact she didn't need it – he'd invented it for his own protection, to keep him human. He'd always feared he'd go over the edge without her.

Yet what he'd learned from this whole mess with Vee was that he had to grow up. If he couldn't do it in his relationships then he'd do it at work.

That was why it was so important he got a job in the emerging technological healthcare area. Ditch the nerf gun brigade, who'd bring their toys in on Fun Fridays. Do serious work with the very best people in his field. The pride of making the modernistic Apple Campus his place of work. In Cupertino, one of the wealthiest, healthiest, safest cities in the States. Driven to achieve in a team, lunch in the iconic Caffe Mac on site, grabbing a free apple on his way back to his department, going to one of the beer bashes, where co-workers were given beer and snacks on the house. In his spare time, he'd get into the outdoors – bike and hike in Santa Cruz mountains – shop at the mall, find himself a neighbourhood bar. Early nights and early mornings. Go clean.

He had to reinvent himself as an adult.

A gob of coffee, then he was back at the table.

The drumming of the rain and his fingers moving to the keypad. If he couldn't have Vee, this was what he had to do.

Submit resumé, click.

*

Brighton, February, 2009

'Isn't this incredible?' Jez says, spreading his arms wide through a fug of patchouli smoke.

No, this is the least incredible thing ever, Vee thinks or at least tries to as a heavy techno bassline assaults her brain.

But Jez hasn't seen her curdled grimace because he's in an elaborate man-hug with a bald bloke in a top hat, velvet blazer and, yes, obviously, pierced nipples.

'Brother, sister, we're so glad you're here. I'm Top Hat,' he semi-shouts as two stoned girls come forward and Namaste Vee with prayer hands. The rest of the room is comatose in jumpers on manky beanbags, oblivious to the sunny winter Brighton morning outside, which is hidden by patchwork blankets across the windows. Anarchic graffiti covers the walls and the floor, well, the bits which she can see that aren't covered in ashtrays and plastic bottles of cider.

'Welcome to our commune!' Top Hat says, swirling around laughing, dancing off with his high priestesses of dilated pupils, forgetting they've turned up.

'Let's find our space, yeah?' It's so cold in here she can see Jez's breath. He gives her a lovely reassuring smile then picks up his rucksack, grabs her hand and leads her out into a hallway. Thank God he's here with her because she's finding it hard to see the bright side of this.

Down the corridor she can see a kitchen where an old stand-alone cooker heaves beneath a pile of saucepans. They go up the first stairs, treading over someone skinning up, and try some doors, finding more people as they go: some chanting, others shagging. Vee's fingers recoil into the sleeves of her cotton hooded top, bought from a blisteringly hot market last week in Sihanoukville. She'd thought it would be fine for the British weather but when you're in the midst of Cambodia's sweaty heat you can't truly imagine how five degrees Celsius feels. Like spikes of ice up your nose. But her body isn't just withdrawing from the temperature – it's from the *filth, which covers this decaying house like dust. She gets a sight of a grubby avocado-coloured bathroom and again she's thrown by the difference in what she'd expected – a decent hot shower and a hairdryer – and the reality. If she bathed in there, she'd come out dirtier than she went in.*

Shuddering, she goes up the next flight behind Jez and they walk into a large attic which is halved by a purple batik throw hanging from the ceiling. Jez pulls it aside then nods.

'Here, this is us!'

Vee peers round and sees a sunken mattress on the floor. Mercifully, the rest of their half is empty – no surfaces for more grime.

Jez falls onto the bed and puts his hands behind his head. 'Home!'

Vee lets her long blonde hair fall around her face to hide her disgust. Home? Hardly! This isn't how it was meant to be. They've had the best time: inseparable since they met on the white sand beach of Sokha, him juggling fire, her collecting glasses for a bar. Except she didn't realize one of his tricks was to eat flames and she thought he was alight and chucked water on him. 'Oh, fuck me, I'm so sorry,' she'd said, brushing his thighs down with her palms. He thought she was hilarious and says he fell for her then and there because she was so unlike anyone he'd met before. They've shared a hammock every night for the last year in Cambodia. And it's the real thing – they've known other couples who've split up when they've got back from travelling. They can't deal with real life. But that isn't going to happen to them. Practically married – eek! she wouldn't say no to the idea – they've helped to run a guesthouse for the last six months, delaying coming home as there was nothing to rush back for, dealing with difficult backpackers, running housekeeping and the cafe. They could've fallen out, it was really stressful when some of his mates from Laos turned up and wrecked the place, but they've never argued. He's just so intuitive and committed. This won't be forever, living here, he'll have a plan, she knows he will.

'Hey, what's up, rarebit?'

'Shitholes abroad, I can deal with. We only slept in them. Spent the rest of our time working or on the beach. But this...'

Jez's face falls into concern. 'We agreed we wanted to try a commune, yeah?'

'A commune, yes. Not a squat. I was thinking somewhere

222

more…'

'Comfortable?' Jez raises his eyebrows as if she's being a bit middle class.

She knows he's only teasing but the accusation unsettles her because she's not like that anymore: she's seen the world. Poverty, first hand, where public services are only for the rich. She swore she'd never take central heating, a full fridge and her dressing gown for granted ever again. Not that she's even close to that yet. Unfortunately. This was not what she had planned when he'd sold her the idea of moving back home, starting a life together.

'No, not that,' she implores. 'More educational, you know, like we said, ideas and people on rotas, working together, cooking, growing veg.'

'How do you know that isn't happening here? You're judging them.'

He's right. Although Top Hat doesn't look like he's on top of anything apart from a drug-induced high.

'Communes are supposed to be financially solvent co-operatives, places of equality, non-hierarchical. There was that one in Wales I told you about, which is self-sufficient. Low impact, wood-fired kitchens, home schooling—'

'Do not dwell in the past, do not dream of the future, concentrate the mind on the present.' Jez does meditation fingers then tucks a loose brown dread back into his ponytail.

'Buddha wouldn't say that if he had to carry around his own loo roll in case someone nicked his,' she says, making him laugh. But she's serious. A little voice asks her if she can make this work… but no, she puts her foot down, because she is committed to Jez. And where else would she go seeing as Kat and Mikey have moved on.

'Hey, this is the beginning, who knows what we can achieve here? Brighton, it's where we should be. For my art, for your…' He wafts his hands around to find the word. '…journey.'

'Teaching, Jez. That's what I'm going to do.' Saying it out loud gives her some relief. Because she loved volunteering at the local school in Sihanoukville where the disadvantaged kids lapped up the chance to learn. In her bag, carefully rolled up inside a tube there are drawings and paintings they made her when she left. She'll stick them up on the wall in here to remind her of what she needs to do - her way to get out of this rank pit. 'I can't wait to enrol,' she says, forgetting her surroundings. 'I'll unpack and then we can go and look for jobs and I'll see what the score is teacher training-wise.'

'Chill, rarebit, chill. We have all the time in the world.' He gives her his sexy eyes and she feels herself softening. But she's not doing it on that mattress. Her sleeping bag is easy to get at, so she pulls it out of its case, unzips it and lays it down where she joins Jez.

'I really want to be a teacher, you know,' she says into his chest.

'I know, rarebit… one day.' He kisses her neck and his lips give her the warmth she's been missing since they landed at Gatwick this morning. The warmth she had always craved after Mikey left her so cold. When Kat had frozen her out. Jez had fixed her when she was broken. 'There's no rush. Let's just settle in here, we can live off my trust fund for a bit. I need you anyway as my muse…'

Ooh, she thinks, liking the sound of that, inspiring his art, posing nude but in a tasteful way. A whole body of work devoted to her. His mouth on her belly button, playing with her ring, convinces her that she's been working so hard that she can afford to take a bit of time off.

'Let's enjoy the now,' he breathes on her skin.

'Mmm,' she murmurs, trusting him that they have all the time in the world.

Chapter Twenty-Five

V

Cathays, Cardiff

Vee hesitated before she buzzed the intercom of the old grey stone building in the student part of Cardiff.

The street in Cathays made her itch: it was grubby, littered by cartons from the takeaway next door and old newspaper which performed death throes in the wind.

Kate was already here, her car was squeezed into a residents' only space – it was down to Vee now.

She could walk away from all of this, just as she'd done with Murphy.

Still in ruins from finding out he had slept with Kat when she'd supposed to have handed over her letter, Vee wasn't a fountain of tears and woe: it was worse than that. Deep, in her bones, like rocks, dragging her down. She had lost part of herself to Murphy, again, not just her heart but her soul.

To think they had reached a beautiful place: this was the torment of her situation.

Ignorance had been bliss. Would she still be with him if she'd never found out? Yes, undoubtedly. Forever she would've revelled in the magic that after all that time, they'd come back together and fallen in love. How it had been meant to be. La la, bloody la.

Who was she kidding? Finding out later down the line would've been worse. Thinking back now, both Kate and Murphy were guarded whenever she brought up the other's name. How did she not pick up on it? As for forgiving and forgetting, could she accept people made mistakes, as Murphy had said? Process the hurt and put it behind them? Maybe that was what love was: to be grown up, to say 'okay, what's done is done, let's do now'.

But what they had, what they had had, was soiled. The trust had gone.

She had no choice but to disentangle herself from both of them. However painful it was proving to be.

Pierre had offered her time off – he was on a high from his friendship with Bea, who would come in every day 'just to see if Polish cheese here'. Vee suspected Pierre was withholding it to make sure he saw her. But no, she had done her damsel in distress thing with Jez: she would get through this, she wouldn't surrender to it. Because she had decided she would never put a man or a friend first again. That was the lesson she had to learn, to fulfil herself. Throw herself into this awakening, which had come to her in grief.

Her saviour would be teaching, that was what she had wanted to do all along. And so she had started researching grants and post-grad courses, working out if she could afford to live away in a house share and study in a new city, away from here where there were too many memories of betrayals. It would be tight but an evening job and Pot Noodles might do it. The course to qualify was only a year – she could cope with that, and afterwards, she could apply like mad for jobs. It was a sacrifice worth paying – and she longed to leave, to run.

Of course, Kate knew none of this – Vee had agreed to come to this viewing as a means to an end: of getting them both together without the potential for an audience, somewhere empty where they could unload.

Weighing it up on the doorstep, she decided to face Kate – to get the answers which had been in her head. To find out if all of this effort she was putting into their friendship was out of guilt, cunning, or both. Because she couldn't believe Kate was all bad. She never had. And she was intrigued to see what Kate thought would appeal to her with this flat, because she had described it as 'perfectly you'.

She pressed the button of flat 2a, her heart pounding. Waiting to be buzzed in, she did concede that this grand building with arched windows and an unusually large communal garden was appealing. When the door clicked, she went into a cool parquet hallway where a spiral staircase, which looked original, took her up onto the second floor.

The door was wide open and she went in, taken by the light which made it seem larger. She was immediately disarmed: it did feel very her. Quirky yet comfy, and, she realized, full of potential. But she had to stop those thoughts because she wasn't here as a client.

'Like it?' Kate said, with her eyebrows raised in hope, as she appeared from the kitchen. 'It's an old school. Converted into flats. You used to want to be a teacher, didn't you?'

Vee's stomach dive-bombed at her insight.

'It's small. Bijou, we call it. Bedroom, through there, bathroom, kitchen and this is the lounge. Great connections, cheap and the city centre's just a walk away.'

It was the first time she had seen Kate in action in her work environment. The patter came easily to her, she looked the part, smart-casual in a blue linen shirt dress with a drop-down necklace from which a silver heart-shaped locket hung. Her hair tumbled down her shoulders, unstraightened with big kinking waves. The tired gaze had gone: she was relaxed and fresh, as if she had ironed out the creases from her reunion with Jack and cancelling her wedding. Vee acknowledged coolly she was about to take it all away from her.

'You were right. It is quite me,' Vee said, smiling at the irony that Kate knew her so well and yet she did the very thing that she knew would hurt Vee the most.

'Well, it's the least I can do,' she said, beaming.

Yes, it is, Vee thought, feeling her face harden.

'I owe you because if it hadn't been for you, I'd never have taken on my mother and— Are you okay? You look...'

'I'm not here to view the flat, Kate,' Vee said, suddenly tired of lies.

'Oh, right. What's up?'

'You and me.'

Kate felt for the windowsill behind her as if to steady herself. 'In what way?' she said, shaky.

Vee had considered how to say it: a tirade was unnecessary but neither could she be apologetic. Directness was the only way.

'The letter.'

She waited for it to sink in, for Kate to understand. She flinched and shut her eyes.

'Why didn't you give it to Mikey?' Vee said, her voice

wobbling.

Kate began to shake her head as though she was refusing to go back. But Vee was insisting.

'Because he was The One, Kate, you knew it, you made me wake up to it. Then you ruined it. Just like you did with Conor and travelling. Why?' She was higher pitched now as her emotions were freed.

'I'm so sorry, Vee, I am,' Kate said, walking towards her. 'There's not been a day when I haven't felt the guilt in my heart. Believe me.' She clutched her chest as her eyes welled up, but Vee could not stop, she was immune to her sorry.

'Why did you do it? That's what I need to know. Because you had everything.'

'Because I...' Kate seemed to be assessing her explanation. 'Look,' she said, her shoulders crumpling, 'I could say I did it to prevent you from heartache, that I had tried to save you, because Mikey was so very dark when I saw him, not at all the friend you thought he was.'

'Don't you think that was my right to find out?'

'Yes, yes, I do. I could say I tried to protect you, but... I didn't care. About you, about him. About myself. It was an awful mistake. I was ill. I was... how did you find out?'

'Murphy.'

The colour drained from Kate's face.

'We were seeing each other.' Vee almost enjoyed the revelation: to say, yes, you won, ultimately, but I had him for a while.

Kate held her head in her hands.

Vee felt a stab of victory, as if she'd taken some kind of revenge. She went for more. 'I thought, this is it, it was worth the wait for him. We had just made love for the first time and then he told me. Hoping we could move on. But it's tainted now. He said he loved me. But it's over.'

Kate made a guttural noise from deep within.

Just then, a toilet flushed and Kate leapt back up straight, sniffing back her tears, wiping her face with the fingers and backs of her hand.

'Who's that?' Vee said, looking around, unnerved by this interruption. Surely there wasn't another viewer here?

'Aunty Katieeee,' came a voice. A child's. Jumping feet.

'It's Griff,' Kate said, quickly. 'He threw up yesterday but

228

school won't let them go back for forty-eight hours in case it's a bug. It was nothing. He was right as rain within five minutes. Charlie had to go in to work. I was able to bring him with me… he has his iPad…' Then she added, 'He doesn't know anything yet' as a warning, just as Griff landed with a leap into the room.

'Hi,' he said shyly to Vee, going to Kate.

He looked up from under his shaggy fringe straight at Vee.

And then with a frightening clarity, as if she'd been confused by an optical illusion and it had made sense, Vee saw it. The jut of his chin, the colour of his hair, skinny legs and a pair of cheekbones.

'Oh my God,' Vee said, backing off, feeling the floor sliding as Kate held up her hands and widened her eyes which were screaming at her to not say it, to save this little boy.

Her chest heaving, Vee understood he didn't need to find out this way however Kate had behaved - it wasn't his fault.

But with her face, Vee asked if it was true: if he was Murphy's son?

She expected Kate to crumble.

But instead, she pulled Griff to her body, kissed his head and then gave a firm nod.

Vee got it: with that gesture, Kate was saying she didn't care how this innocent had come into the world, she was proud of him and she loved him with all her might.

This was too complicated a battle to fight, Vee thought. There was never any 'Murphy and me', never.

'I have to go…'

'Griffy, have a play, will you?'

''Kay,' he said, taking her mobile and plopping himself down in the square of sun on the floor.

'Murphy doesn't know,' Vee whispered by the door.

'No. I… I'm so sorry,' she said, looking over her shoulder. 'It was so long ago…'

But excuses were no good.

'You have to tell him. You know that, don't you?'

'Yes,' she said, with inevitability, 'Please… forgive me.'

It was far too early for that, impossible to even go there.

'If you want to make things okay, Kate,' Vee said, feeling cold and shivery, as Kate hung on her word, 'you have to tell him. I'll text you his number.'

Then she left and Vee found herself crying for Murphy's

ignorance.

Chapter Twenty-Six

K

Charlie's house, Lisvane, Cardiff

As Kate hugged Charlie, she felt the oceanic flow of their love, strength and unity passing between them. Their mother's skewed devotion had never manifested itself emotionally or physically; this was how the sisters had filled the gap, depending on each other for touch and support.

This was why Griff's place in their lives was to be celebrated, Charlie had said last night in the comfort of their smart Victorian semi in the leafy suburb of Lisvane as they'd prepped today's chat with their little boy.

'He saved you and I,' she'd told Kate. 'We were given someone to love and to cuddle.' They had cried together, holding hands, as Kate had relayed the scene in the restaurant where she'd found out the reason for her mother's distant determination. 'This is why Griff needs to know he has two mums, that wherever he turns he will never want for love. And, Kate, you know, you gave me the greatest gift of all, motherhood.'

And this bond was what they shared now in each other's arms in Charlie's hallway.

'Ready?' Charlie asked Tom, who was wringing his hands in a sign of his own personal apprehension. Although he wholly agreed with telling Griff of his true beginnings, he had admitted that however selfish it made him, he was afraid of losing his son to an unknown quantity. Kate and Charlie had applauded his bravery to speak that out loud, but yes, it was different for him. The sisters were blood: not in competition for Griff's affections but driven by the same need to keep him safe: Kate had given him up to the next best person. And she would never take him off her sister. But when the father was told, which Kate was dreading but could no longer avoid as she had done for so long and hoped to keep doing until Vee's demand, there was no knowing how Murphy would respond.

There in Tom's clean-shaven pinched face was his concern: Murphy's involvement could affect his relationship with Griff.

Watching him nod that he was ready, Kate felt the terrible responsibility of dragging her sister and brother-in-law into this. For it would be her fault however Murphy reacted. The fact she'd hidden it from him for seven years. Mikey, well he had been loyal up to a point – but Murphy was a mystery: she feared a legal battle. Yet if Vee had had the capacity to fall in love with him, did that mean he was different now? That he would tread lightly and form a bond which didn't threaten anyone but enriched Griff's life.

The repercussions began to claw at her skin: Charlie reached out to both her and Tom with her hands, having read their minds. 'Let's do this, and this only, now. One step at a time.'

'I'll go and get him,' Tom said, so decently, looking warily up the staircase before he sighed and regained his composure. He rolled up the sleeves of his rugby shirt and took the steps, asking 'where's that little monkey of mine?'

'We'll be in the lounge,' Charlie said to him as they went in to the large room which was a shrine to Griff. The back third was his den: a personalized gaming chair faced a PlayStation where he'd thrash his dad at FIFA. French doors went out onto the garden so he and his friends could dash out when the whim took them. A bookcase featured kids' classics and canvases of his art hung on two walls. The rest of the lounge may have been 'for the grown-ups' with its huge, deep sofas and wood burner, but still the surfaces were stuffed with photos of Griff with grandparents, of him blowing out candles and on holiday. Charlie and Tom had given him the very best, what Kate had been unable to give. There was always a lump in her throat when she saw the single picture on top of the mantelpiece of his sleeping newborn face: it had been taken in her arms, but now she looked at it with new eyes. He was coming back to her. They had it all planned.

Charlie sat on the sofa in 'her seat' beside a circle from

Griff's body, where he would curl up with her after his bath. Kate crossed her legs on the floor so she would be at his feet and Tom would be on the other side of Griff, protected by them all.

They had researched every which way to handle this: Charlie and Tom had friends in paediatric mental health whom they'd turned to and Kate had devoured official websites, family message boards and reams of conversation threads, working out the best way. They'd all come up with the same conclusion: be positive about the situation, keep it simple, be prepared for either a lot of immediate upset or a minimal reaction later followed by tears, anticipate questions he might have – and most of all, show him how much he is loved.

'Boing, boing, boing,' Griff said, bursting in with pogo bounces.

The last moment of his ignorance, Kate thought, aching for his innocence. Yet it didn't have to be the end of his world: they were focused on making sure it would be a blossoming continuation of the stability he'd had.

Charlie would take the lead because she was his mother – and would forever be.

'Come here, boingy boingy,' she said, making a playful grab for him, which made him shriek.

Griff darted over with his arms open and started chatting away about Minecraft and servers and mods and all sorts of technical computer stuff which he seemed to understand innately. Murphy's son, right there, Kate thought, before she berated herself for the lazy assumption: all kids were into that and actually he loved sport, unlike his father. Looks-wise though, there was no mistake. Her blue eyes, but the rest, the shaggy brown hair, the bold lips and the set of his shoulders, were all his.

'We want to have a family chat, all of us, okay with you?' Charlie said, wiping his fringe off his forehead as he fidgeted with a loom band on his wrist.

'Can I have some crisps?' he said, shifting around, unable to keep still.

'Later!' Tom said, his face bright, concealing his turmoil. 'After! You've only just had pizza!'

'Come on, Griffy,' Kate said. 'Mum and dad and me, we want to tell you something really fab, it won't be long. I'll get you smoky bacon straight after. Deal?'

'Deal!' He punched the air and beamed.

'So, Griffy, you know we've told you about your tummy mummy, the mummy who grew you?' Charlie said, evenly.

'The one who couldn't look after me,' he said, factually, reciting from his account of his beginning.

'That's it. Well, she's a bit better now.'

'That's good.' His empathy was a new thing, he was growing up. Then his brow furrowed. 'She's not taking me away, is she?'

Kate's heart flipped at his naked fear.

'No, of course not. You're ours, we're yours. We love you very much and we'll never let you go. Okay?' Charlie was emphatic, undramatic.

He accepted it without question and relaxed.

'Good. You said she was really nice, didn't you?'

'Yes. She's wonderful. She loves you very much.'

'How do you know?'

'Because you're so wonderful!'

He crossed his eyes and laughed. Kate held her breath because she knew there was to be no beating about the bush. It was coming and her stomach tensed.

'The thing is, what we wanted to know is how would you feel if Aunty Katie was your tummy mummy?'

Griff looked at Kate then at Charlie then at Kate again. Waiting, his reaction was being formed: he opened his eyes wide.

And then the relief as the words toppled out of his mouth.

'That would be... epic! Aunty Katie, she's awesome,' he told Charlie, then to Kate. 'You're awesome!'

Kate smiled and she felt it with her entire body.

'Well, it's true! How fantastic is that?' Tom said, putting an arm around him.

'Do I have two mummies then?' He looked up at his father, eyelashes blinking with concentration to clarify things.

'Yes! Isn't that cool!' Tom said, ruffling his hair.

'It is!'

Tom looked at Kate now: it was her turn.

'Mummy will always be your mummy. I can stay as Aunty Katie if you want or mummy number two or—' She touched his bare knee, feeling her own flesh and blood, marvelling that he was even more beautiful today now that there was no more pretence.

'How about sausage head?' Griff said, hooting as they all joined in laughing.

'Whatever you like,' Kate said, her eyes watering from happiness at his acceptance, her lungs bursting with her rebirth. Her heart screamed for him to come to her, to cuddle her and let her breath in her baby, but she contained it: they had agreed to let him lead the way.

Then he chewed the side of his mouth. She could see his mind working away.

'What about my dad then?' he said after a while.

'Well, I'm your dad,' Tom said, 'like mum is your mum. The dad who made you, you can decide later if you'd like to meet him.'

Kate admired his courage, which he used to hide his pain.

'Is he a rugby player?' Griff asked, suddenly animated, his face lighting up. It would kill Tom every time he thought of that, Kate knew.

'No,' Kate said, firmly. 'He's just a normal person.'

'What's he like?' he asked.

'Oh, he's…' Panic, the one moment of it, stormed in. What could Kate say about him? He'd been one of her best friends, he'd gone through some rough times, Kate had turned him against Vee. He doesn't even know you are alive. It's my fault, I was ill, it made me do things I shouldn't have done – but thank God for you, my darling…

'He's nice.' She would never badmouth him to Griff. She would never make him out to be wonderful either, until he proved otherwise. The three adults paused, hoping this would satisfy him.

Griff scratched his ankle and gazed up at the ceiling.

'Okay.'

And just like that, Kate knew, he was done.

'Any questions?' Charlie asked, kissing his forehead.

'Can I have my crisps now?' he said, pulling away, moving on to the next thing.

'Yes!' Kate said, unable to stop herself just this once, needing to smell his sweet scent, tickling him as he collapsed onto her. Her son.

'If you ever want to ask anything, ever, just ask,' she said, studying him in her lap.

'Uncle Jack? Is it him?' Oh, the gallop of her heart revealed how perfect that would be.

'No. But he loves you as if you were his.'

'Okay, Griffy?' Charlie said, measured, wanting to show him she would stay and sit and talk all night if he needed it

'Crisps!' he shouted, over it while the rest of them still trembled.

'Yes, all right!' Tom said, wiping his eyes, hugging his wife.

Griff cocked his head and clocked them all, each sniffing and trying to keep it together.

'Why are you all crying? You should be happy. I am!' His hands were out wide, as if he was informing them night followed day.

'We are!' they repeated, one after the other.

'Because we're even more epic now. I have two mums and two dads, well, three if you count Uncle Jack, and that beats everyone, everyone including Lily in my class who has two mums and one dad. Dad, want to play FIFA? Bagsy I'm Barcelona!'

Then he shot out the room, leaving Kate to marvel at his understanding, his simple shrugging at the facts without baggage or complication. That would come, no doubt in his adolescence, but at least he would look back on this moment in his life and remember the love.

That is what she clung onto as she considered her next move. She'd lost Vee yet again, but she could make amends: one last person needed to know.

Chapter Twenty-Seven

M

Cardiff Bay, July

Murphy bit his nail and ripped it off with a savage tear. A sharp pain then blood, glinting red in the morning sunshine as it oozed up over the exposed skin of his throbbing finger.

Why the fuck had he done that? he wondered, sucking the tip, tasting bitter iron then pressing it hard against his palm to stop the bleeding.

A pitiful distraction, it was, doing nothing to stop his pounding anxiety.

He was waiting for Kate: the thought made his guts writhe like a pit of serpents. While it was a hot July day, the hairs on his arms stood up from the fear. His eyes, hidden behind shades, scanned the waterfront for her. Would he recognize her after all this time? He hadn't seen her since that night. Not even the morning after because, out of shame, he'd played dead until he'd heard the front door click. Afterwards, she'd never contacted him and he'd never contacted her. But the sickness from that morning had stayed with him right up until now.

Since then, he'd known he'd never be lucky enough never to see her again. Life punched you in the balls like that. He'd carried that lurking dread of bumping into her for years: yes, it had subsided when he'd got to London but it was always there. Then when Vee had come back, he'd felt it acutely, stabbing him every now and again, but he'd been so wrapped up in her that he'd kidded himself, pushing it out of his head because he'd found her. Now it possessed him entirely. But strangely he accepted it: because it had caught up with him. Like it was a fair cop. Anger, too, there was that, finding out that Kate hadn't given him Vicky's letter. What if he'd read it and he and Vicky had had eight years together and all of this could've been avoided? But what ifs were worth jack shit. He'd thought about telling Kate to do one when she'd messaged 'we need to talk'. He hadn't even been surprised to have heard from her. Somehow, pointlessly, he hoped it would mean that Vee would forgive him: if he could show he could face up to things, then she might let him love her. It was worth it because without her, having had her, was like walking on broken glass. But in his heart of hearts, he reckoned it was over. She'd cut him out completely. All he had of her now was the memory of her next to him, her energy charging him, soothing him.

A deep breath then: he was a man, he wanted to get this over with. The air settled him a bit and from his metal table and chair he took in the waterfront of Cardiff Bay. Shiny and sleek, it was impossible to see how it had once been derelict wasteland. Beautiful, it was. Big open spaces, a wide plaza full of kids scooting and dogs chasing the wind. He savoured it sadly. It might be the last time he was here. Because he would leave, that was almost certain, there was nothing to keep him here. He'd had a couple of phone interviews with American companies interested in his applications: one offer so far depending on the visa stuff. Nothing from Apple as yet – that hadn't stopped him cramming posts on websites by anonymous employees, who revealed the mad questions, technical issues and brainteasers they were asked during the mammoth selection process. But actually, he found he didn't care now, as long as he could get out of this country.

A sip of his espresso burned his throat as he saw her. Kate was heading towards him along the boardwalk, her face checking every person sat outside the cafe. She walked differently, not stumbling and pissed like the last time he remembered, but with grace, appearing capable, grown-up. He felt queasy at the thought that he'd slept with her, so he crossed his legs to anchor himself.

Finally, she clocked him with a stare, a shifty fiddle with her bag betraying the nerves beneath her composure, and then she was at his table.

Murphy's mouth was dry, so he took a sip of his coffee.

She raised her sunglasses and stuck them on top of her head.

It was brave, that. Like a peace offering. But he couldn't do the same. Not yet. He needed to wait and see what she said.

'Hi,' she said, pulling a seat back to join him, dropping her bag, tucking her hair behind her ears. Moving naturally, not rigid like he was.

Guarded still, he nodded. 'Hi.'

She waved at a waiter, who came over and she ordered green tea. She was one of 'those', cleaned up obviously in natural fibres. No make-up, or hardly any, free of the troubled torment of her early twenties.

His body went into fight or flight mode but somehow he managed to wait for her to talk because she had been the one to start this.

'Thanks for coming. I appreciate it.'

He shrugged his shoulders and drank again. She sat herself up straight and then swallowed, preparing.

'Murphy, there's something you need to know.' No beating about the bush, no small talk, he could cope with that. She stared right at him, the hoods of her eyelids creased now in serious concentration. It disarmed him. Completely.

'Right,' escaped from his mouth because he understood this was going to be important. An apology, he expected that, because why else would she be here? Or maybe she'd spoken to Vee and it was part of some deal to set things straight.

'I want to apologize. For the way I behaved. The letter.' Her eyes bored into his, needing him to see she meant it. He took off his sunnies to show he was listening. Because all of that shit from the past, despite what she'd done and how Vee and him had nearly made it, he just wanted the turmoil to be over. Now she was here, unconfrontational, he could see that his finger-jabbing fantasies of how she'd fucked him over wouldn't happen. What was the point anyway when he would be leaving?

'It's all right,' he found himself saying, looking at her then at his lap and blowing out of his cheeks, feeling a weight off him. 'It's time to let it go.'

'It is... and it isn't.' Kate stopped to clear her throat.

He felt like a tortoise as he pulled his head into his neck, wondering what she meant.

'The thing is...' Kate rubbed the end of her nose and blinked hard.

Prickles of alarm went off all over Murphy's scalp. What

was it? What was she going to say?

'The night we spent together, when I came back from travelling…' She looked at her palms now.

'Yeah?' he said, holding his breath, feeling his frown.

'I fell pregnant.' She raised her face to his but he was thrown because she didn't look upset.

Murphy's heart though was banging. Pregnant. Shit. Immediately, he felt sorry for her, that she'd had to go through with a termination by herself. No matter what had happened between them. 'I'm sorry,' he said, feeling inadequate, impotent.

'Don't be,' she said, which was odd, and she had a shine in her eyes. 'it was, it is, the best thing that ever happened to me.'

'What do you mean? How?'

Stoic, she looked. He'd seen that in Mam.

'I should've told you, I know, and I was going to. But I wasn't well, depression, postnatal problems—'

Murphy felt himself paling at her language, which suggested she'd had the baby. Fuck.

'Postnatal? You mean, you had the…'

'Yes,' she said. 'You have a son, Murphy. He's… wonderful.'

Her eyes weren't afraid. But inside he was going mental. Confusion, disbelief, the fucking unbelievable fact that he was a father and had been for… how many years? Seven. And he hadn't known it. And oh, he covered his face with his hands and breathed hard, then the screech of metal against the concrete floor.

'I'm a dad?'

Blurred eyes as he saw Kate had moved closer.

'Yes.' She was examining him as if he was a patient. She'd come to terms with it, she'd had years to, but he was all over the place.

'I just can't… it's so hard to… take in.'

A shot of fury and helplessness and desperation. 'Why the fuck didn't you say? Why the fuck didn't I know?' He searched her face for answers that he already knew.

'I was ill. We were young. It wasn't the right time for you or me.'

He knew this, but still. 'But I wish I'd known.'

His shoulders sagged and he heard a sob, his own. The days and weeks and months and years that he'd walked this earth, not knowing he had a son, that he was a father.

'I'm sorry. I made an absolute cock-up of it all. I can only apologize.'

'But where's he now?' he asked, feeling an urge to look around just in case he was about to be unveiled in some *Surprise, Surprise* thing. 'What's his name?' He didn't even know his own child's name.

'Griff. He lives with my sister and her husband. He's got my surname, Charlie kept hers. I couldn't look after him. Charlie couldn't have kids, so I gave him up for her.'

'You gave him away?' he gasped unable to comprehend how someone could do that but knowing Kate could've done nothing else because she was ill. His heart was in two now – one half cracked by the lies, the other by the horror she must've been through.

'I was very depressed when I was pregnant. I wasn't well, mentally, when we...Expecting made me worse. Then once he'd gone, I was put on medication. I'd always resisted it before, stupidly, but that was the depth of my illness. I felt suicidal so I gave in and I thank God I did because it began my recovery. I had therapy and then things improved a great deal. Charlie and Tom, her husband, they brought him up, beautifully. He's such a gorgeous boy. We've only just told him. That he's mine. He's dealt with it very well. Accepts it. He thinks he has three dads now, including my... Jack.'

'Does he know about me?' Murphy felt a desperate need to hear if he was, would be, a part of his life. Because now that he knew, he'd have to see him. He knew he loved him already.

'He knows he has a father who isn't Tom.'

'What, well, can I meet him?' He shook his head at the image of them being introduced. Trying to catch up on seven years. Never having touched his skin. He'd never contemplated fatherhood before - how could he when he'd been put off by his dad's neglect? So Murphy was staggered to find his mind now accepted it as fact - he was a dad and he would do his best in spite of his upbringing.

'We can discuss that once it's all settled down. Of course. If...'

And there it was. The look in her eyes, the first time she'd shown any real trepidation. It was like a hammer on his skull because she was doubting him: wondering if he would be a negative influence in her boy's life.

Fury grabbed him by the scruff. She was judging him on his father.

'Just because I have a shit dad doesn't mean I would be.'

Kate shut her eyes from the force of his blow.

'No, I know,' she said. 'My mum, it's the same thing with me, history doesn't have to repeat itself.'

He felt the anger breaking up, melting.

'Vee?' he said, weakly. 'Does she know?'

'Yes. She guessed. I'm ashamed of it all, the way I've handled it.'

Of course, Vee wasn't stupid. The game was up - now he had lost her completely. 'Look, I'll do my bit. More than that, I need to see him.'

'Yes.'

'Whatever it takes. All of it. It sounds so lame and I'm not going to go through it all, because you've all done the work, but I can do it too. And money, God, I'm a prick for even saying it, but… you know. Anything. Tell me, is he happy? Have you got a photo?'

It was a big blurt but he couldn't stop it.

'He's the happiest child I've ever met,' she said, taking her phone, tapping in her passcode and handing it over.

Happy. His child. He'd take that, he realized that he'd be miserable forever if his son could be happy.

'Go to photos, there's an album, it's called Griffy…'

Gasping, he saw him. Big brown eyes like his, thick eyelashes, lips like an angel, chestnut hair which was shaggy, just as the style he was growing. All legs and bruised knees and skinny and pulling faces and posing for the camera.

He loved him, he knew it. Just like that.

'Does he like school? What does he like doing?'

'He loves school,' Kate said, smiling. She lifted an eyebrow which said 'unlike you'. And he found the edges of his mouth turning up. 'Very good at maths…' Like her. 'But imaginative, writes funny stories about robots. Plays rugby, football, loves swimming…'

He had a whole life going on that Murphy was unaware of. It was cutting him up.

'…but Minecraft, computers, that's his thing.'

He looked up.

242

'Must be in his DNA,' she said. It was a minor acknowledgement but it made him dizzy.

'When's his birthday? When was he born?'

'December the twenty-first.'

It hit him hard. His Mam would never have seen him had he even known. She'd died in the November. 'I wish my mam could've held him,' he said, knowing it was useless.

'Regrets,' Kate said, 'I've got more than Frank Sinatra.' She said it without humour. 'But you know something, Murphy, it's taken me this long to see that acceptance is ultimately contentment.'

'Vee,' he said to Kate, looking down at his hands and at the nail which had already begun to heal. 'She came back into my life. Into yours. And without her I'd never have known.'

'You can either be cross about it or you can take it with gratitude.'

His father, he'd be over the moon at being a grandad – probably say 'thank God because I always thought you were a poofter' – and Orla, well, she'd love bomb that kid. The swell of emotion was threatening towards positivity.

It was like the photos of his son: he'd seen a version of himself. A genuinely happy one. But the problem was, was he capable of it?

*

Ibiza, September 2009

'Oi, Midas!'

Mikey tuts from his bobbing pink lilo and keeps his head on the pillow. He's not going to grace that piss-take which the boys have come up with because 'everything he touches turns to gold'.

'What you having?' Now that he will answer. He pushes his neon green Wayfarer sunglasses onto his brow and squints through the dazzling Ibiza sunshine to see Hugo at the villa's terrace bar. They've only been up an hour – the other three are still in bed – but Hugo's already on something, he's chewing like mad. Charlie, probably. It's so common here, that if you ask for Coke somewhere, you have to clarify you mean the drink. He isn't into it, he's tried it once but it wasn't all that: sort of seedy, and when the others are on it they think they're fucking Sorted Simons when all they're doing is talking shite.

'One of those retro cocktails, with an umbrella and flamingo ice cubes,' Mikey says, 'or a lager. Whatever's going.'

Knowing it's shallow but unable to help himself, he admires his forty-eight-hour mahogany tan which begins on his toes all the way up to his chest. He's never had one before – he didn't know he was capable of it, always hiding from the UV in his jeans. But then that's been the story of the last eighteen months, denying Kat's existence and hurting from Vicky's rejection, waiting in vain for her to come back to him: he's gone from lonely despair on Orla's floor to thousand-thread count sheets. Headhunted by a former Apple guy, he was taken on by Kode, an app development company in Islington. He's got his own office, they call them 'labs' because they're a bit like that, you know, up themselves but then it does feel like they're at the frontier. And they're making money, shitloads of it. They've all got old-fashioned school-type desks, there's a jukebox in the loungey area, 'the reloading room', and they have dress-up Fridays, when everyone wears three-piece suits. He's got a moustache, an ironic handle bar, which he waxes for effect. The weird thing is everyone thinks he's cool because he sort of appeared under the radar. Like they ask his opinion loads and he's seen as a sort of enigma. It's embarrassing, but they pile it on him. The work is incredible. Mobile first, desktop second, that's the thinking there, making apps which are intuitive for top brands. He does the prototypes, native for everyone, bespoke, fulfilling the brief, usually of functionality and style. It's a different world: he never has to buy his own dinner anymore. It's like Club bloody Tropicana, drinks are freeee. All because of Steve Jobs. Murphy remembers he almost cried when he heard he was having a liver transplant in the summer. It made him think of Mam. And Dad's drinking. But you've just got to get on with things. Like Apple, pressing forward with its awesome iPhone 3GS. It's rumoured there's a tablet coming next year. That's why desktop is dying. Mobile is the future.

Even better, his app is almost ready to go – the latest effects make Smash The Suburbs a bit of a laugh, slaying zombies in golf slacks on a new-build estate. He's gone out on a limb with his main player, a punky girl as opposed to the gun-toting bad boys everywhere. Yeah, Orla said she looks like Vicky, but that's a coincidence, that is. She's faded from his mind big-time, he's come to terms with her disappearing act and life is busy enough to forget her. Especially with all the interest he's getting from women. He doesn't want to become a playboy but it's hard resisting when good-looking clients cosy up to him. But he usually ducks out, he's no good at relationships so he heads to the gym because he's started working out, it helps him focus. Anyway, as soon as he's done, he'll submit Smash to Apple to see if it'll make their App Store. He doesn't expect anything – it'll be one of ten thousand they receive each week. Christ, the suburbs are as distant now as his misery: he can't get over how he's made it. Working out, working hard and now the reward, a few lazy days and large nights.

He settles back with his palms knitted behind his neck and takes in the view. The infinity pool seamlessly becomes the Med where super yachts are anchored. This place is a palace in Cala Jondal where it's too expensive for the lager louts.

He wants to cool his feet in the water so he peels his legs off the scorching plastic inflatable. It reminds him of the seats in the family car, where him and Orla would sit baking, supposedly on holiday, their thighs sweating then near-tearing when they moved to reach for the pop and crisps passed through the window while Mam and Dad were in the pub.

He couldn't be further from that here in this five-bed villa with its *Bang and Olufsen* speakers. It's all sliding glass doors and white walls, tasteful, on trend. Every room is a double en-suite, each with a flat-screen TV, and the communal space is amazing – a shaded rooftop chill-out zone, a disco area and tables and chairs inside and out so you can eat wherever takes your fancy. Low-lit night-lighting too for what they call ambience. There's hospitality too, so if you want a car or a boat, you just click your fingers. But the best bit is getting VIP tickets to the clubs. It's part of the deal sorted by his workmate Hugo, who's a professional wanker. In the nicest sense of the word. Cafe Mambo last night for sundowners and then Pacha tonight. They're also going to Space and Privilege.

Beautiful people, massive dance floors, the best DJs. Obviously, it's all total turd, he thinks as he slides off the lilo for a dip before he swims to the edge of the pool.

There's shaky white tiles, bent rays and music pumping beneath the surface. He comes up for air, its heat searing his lungs, and he laughs when he sees an umbrella poking out of the rim of his beer.

'There you go, Midas.'

He springs himself up onto the side and offers Hugo a 'salud'. The icy bubbles have a party all the way down his throat. He sparks up a fag knowing where he's found himself is all surface, course it is.

But while he blows smoke rings into the bluest of skies, he realizes he's at least slain a few of Mikey's dragons. And found a happiness he had convinced himself would never be his. He'll never tire of this. Never.

'I've told you, lovely boy,' he says to Hugo, 'it's not Midas. It's Murphy.'

Chapter Twenty-Eight

V

Roath, Cardiff

'Mum, Dad, tea's up,' Vee called, placing a tray on the garden table – the new one from Homebase which her parents had finally settled on after weeks of price-checking and pondering.

'Lovely,' Dad sighed, creaking to his knees from where he was weeding the border. Then he helped Mum up with a playful pull, pretending with a groan that she was a dead weight.

'Cheek!' she said, flicking him with her pink floral glove. Vee watched as Dad laughed then held her tight, kissing her nose.

Their faces were glowing from hours out here. Under a beating July sun, they'd worked side by side since lunch; Vee had peered out at them from her bedroom window now and again when her eyes had needed a screen break from the task of working out her finances and her plans. Whether they were chatting or silent, they'd always known where the other was, in tune, in love. Just as they'd always been. As a kid she'd sneered at their obsession with the lawn: its cut and condition, colour and cultivation. If it had been up to her, she'd have paved it all or gone for Astroturf because it was so bloody high-maintenance. All of it was, the constant watering of pots and deadheading and all of that pointless repetitive shit. But now she got it: it was their relationship right there. They understood they had to invest in it to reap the benefits. And they were happy just to be together, that was all there was to it, not needing adventure to prop up their marriage. What they had was beautiful: they were so lucky to have this because it didn't happen for everyone. It wasn't going to be that way for her, she was accepting this now, relationships weren't her thing, clearly. Instead she would find happiness elsewhere. It was time to leave, head back to her life, which had been on standby ever since she'd got here four months ago.

'Lovely cuppa,' Mum said, wiping beads of sweat off her forehead with the back of her hand. 'Look at the state of me!' she said as Dad picked a blade of grass from her hair.

'Another hour and I think I'll open the bar, love,' Dad said, slurping from his mug and sighing with pleasure.

'Ooh yes, a nice cold glass of white for me. Will you have the same or a beer?'

'A can of lager will do it for me, love. A quick sit then we'll get on with it, finish the weeding.'

'Yes, love,' she said, joining him. 'I'll need a good soak in the bath after this.'

Their patter, their routine filled Vee with warmth: she decided now was the time to tell them.

'I'm going, by the way,' she said.

'Where to? And what time will you be back?' Mum said. 'Because we could have a barbecue tonight, couldn't we, Bob? It's nice enough, I could do a salad if Victoria gets some burgers and what-have-you from the shop.'

'Well, I didn't mean I was popping out. But I can.'

'A steak, I want, Victoria. Get me a nice juicy one.' Dad rubbed his hands at the thought of it.

'I'd like a bit of pork, myself. A nice chop.'

Vee rolled her eyes at them with amusement, savouring their patter, knowing how much she'd miss this. It was hard to believe she'd hated moving back but her parents had turned out to be the perfect remedy.

'What, love?'

'Mum, I meant I'm leaving. Not yet, got to save a bit of money and get my application in, but I'm going to be off.'

'Application?' Dad raised an eyebrow and Mum leant in.

'To become a teacher. I don't know where yet, maybe Manchester or somewhere.'

'Well! That is something to celebrate!' Mum said, getting up to give her a cuddle. 'I'm so pleased for you!'

'Fabulous, love!' Dad held up his cup for a cheers.

'You could at least look a bit gutted that I'm going!' Vee joked. Sort of. Because as much as she needed her own space, it would've been nice to hear they'd miss her.

'Of course we are! But we never thought you'd stay here, did we, Bob?'

'No, never. You're young yet. It's right that you should go. Our Gavin, he's different to you. Sensible and a homebody.'

'But you... life's too boring here for you!'

They might as well have said she was the unreliable, flighty sibling who had no direction. It crushed her a bit. And after all this, the being dumped when she'd been ready to settle down, then finding Kate and Murphy...

'Love? What's up?' Mum was at her side, digging out a tissue from her bra, holding it to her as Vee found herself crying.

'I tried, Mum, I really did.'

'You've got a life to lead, I'm sure you'll find what you want to do.'

'But I have. The teaching. That's what I want to do.'

Dad and Mum swapped knowing glances.

'What?' Vee said, before realizing they were doubting her. 'You don't think I'm going to do it, do you?'

'It's not that, love,' Mum said, visibly squirming.

'What your mother means is that you have lots of ideas, always have done, and you get excited by them then—'

'Oh my God. You think I'm a waster. A loser.'

'No, no, no,' they chorused.

'It's just that you were going to do this before, weren't you, love? And you're working in a deli and, well, you haven't done anything recently about working with kids, you know, volunteering, getting some work experience...'

Vee's jaw was on her bloody lap. 'You don't think I'm capable of doing anything decent in my life, do you?'

'It isn't that, Victoria,' Mum said, looking earnest now. 'It's just that you haven't found your calling yet. It's hard for women your age these days—'

Vee shut her eyes - she knew what was coming. The whole career, babies, mortgage thing.

'It wasn't like that in my day. We met, fell in love, got married, had you two. There weren't the choices you have.'

A surge of something, was it a scream, came from deep within. She felt the throb of her heart and a rising pressure in her throat: something was coming. 'I wish I didn't have all these choices,' she said, not knowing where this was going, 'I wish I had someone to keep me here. I had it. For a few weeks and then…'

'Oh, love, talk to me. Who was it? Was it that Pierre? I thought you might have had a thing for him.'

'Pierre? No!' she baulked, before whispering 'Murphy' because it felt stupid and childish.

'Michael?' Mum said, astonished. 'Michael Murphy?'

'I better get the wine now, love,' Dad said, getting up and patting Vee on her shoulder as she began to sob.

'Yes,' she said, in a small voice because she was embarrassed about it all. A mad fortnight that had torn her apart – of not falling in love because she had always loved him but of finally realizing it with him. Cruel, it was. She had to move on.

'Why didn't you say?'

'Because I suppose it was too good to be true. Another week or so, I'd have told you. But it was so surprising. Like, we clicked, Mum. We've always clicked, but there was more. It was like seeing you and Dad together.' Once she had pitied their relationship, labelling it as sad and boring, but my God, she knew that what they had was all she wanted.

'Does he know all this?'

'Yes but it doesn't matter.' As her dad appeared with wine and glasses and left them to their 'girl' talk' so he could get some meat for the barbie, she explained the whole story, of their first kiss to finding out he'd had a fling with Kate and they'd had a child. Then she waited for Mum to tell her, yes, now she understood why Vee had to leave to start over. It was the only thing to do. She couldn't be friends again with Kate, not after all the deceit and lies. And Murphy, if she saw him again, it'd finish her off.

'You know, people make mistakes, Victoria. Ones that they can spend the rest of their lives regretting…'

'Oh God, please don't tell me that you had a wild affair with the postman when Dad was once away at a conference or that you caught him in one of your dresses and make-up. I've had enough of people revealing their secrets.'

'There's no skeletons here,' she said. 'Your dad would never fit into my dresses anyway. He's going on twelve stone! I'm still the weight I was on our wedding day, eight stone twelve!'

'So how come you're so forgiving? How come you've always been good at listening and not judging?'

'Because I believe people are human. I have nothing that you'd call "exciting" that's happened to me. I've been very fortunate. Your father's the same. But that doesn't mean I can't empathize with what people go through. All I know about, and I thank my lucky stars, is being happy. Making the most of what we have. Enjoying the little things in life. Love and hope. That's why I think you should forgive them both, Katherine and Michael. Because you were a different person when you got back in touch with them. You were rock bottom and then you met up with them and you seemed happy. I never saw you like that with Jez. I never said because who wants to hear that? I just hoped you'd realize he wasn't right for you. It happened, and it broke your heart, but you wouldn't go back to your life in Brighton, would you?'

Vee needed no time to consider the question. The thought of being back with him in his flaky circle, wanting to please him, made her shudder.

'No. Definitely not.'

'Do you know something? I always thought you and Michael had a spark. And I wondered if one day your paths would cross again. Because he's a rough diamond, that one.'

'Did you?'

Mum nodded. 'Life isn't a bed of roses, Victoria,' she said, pointing at her garden, 'so you've got to hold onto the things and the people who make you happy. Who, if you'll excuse my French because this wine has gone straight to my head, will hold up an umbrella if the shit hits the fan.'

'Mum!' She'd never heard her swear before – and it brought Vee out in a smile.

'There you go, I'm not such a stick-in-the-mud after all, am I? Now I'm going in to change. Have a quick bath. Radox, I need. Put something clean on. You have a think.'

As her mum groaned up to standing, Vee turned her face to the sun to catch the last rays before it descended behind next door's conservatory. Mum's talk had really rung some bells. She had found her happy with Murphy and she was determined to become a teacher. They were the facts.

It hadn't been a fling with Murphy. Her desire to go to training college wasn't on a whim. She had invested in herself and she was more settled, more self-determining. More grown up. Hold onto your happy and accept shit happens, that is what

Mum had said. Vee found herself repeating it over and over to herself as the early evening began to sigh.

And then she worked it out – if she applied to study in London, then maybe she could have both: she loved Murphy and Murphy loved her.

Her friendship with Kate though, she didn't know if that could be saved.

wasn't going to give one but this was what he had hoped for from the moment he'd understood his father drank more than all the other dads. That was two decades of willing him to do it, raging at his addiction, feeling alcohol came first. It was momentous and yet he couldn't show it because that would heap the pressure on his dad. He would never jeopardize it.

'Right.,' was all he said. He studied him and saw he was clean-shaven, his hair was Brylcreemed and even his shoes shone. Melanie, that was who was behind this, he was sure of it. And what a job she was doing. But again, make no mention of it, son.

'Brought you some shopping,' Murphy said, holding up a couple of bags.

Dad took a suspicious look at the Waitrose branding. He'd see it as complicated poncey food. But Murphy wanted him to eat quality stuff, not cheap crap and he wouldn't turn it down.

'There's sandwiches if you like. Melanie left them for when I got back. She's cutting her hours.'

Oh, shit. Why? She was doing him so much good.

'On my ask. I need to start doing things for myself again.'

Jesus wept, who was this man standing here pretending to be his father?

'If it's the money… you don't need to worry.'

His dad ignored him, pointed at the fridge and beckoned him into the lounge. It looked like ham salad… on brown bread. Wonders would never cease.

'Help yourself,' Dad said from his chair.

'Cheers.' But he wasn't hungry. He had something on his mind, why he was here.

Dad picked up the phone and pointed it at the telly.

'That's not the remote…' It was like a kick in the stomach, seeing him still a bit confused.

He threw it on the occasional table and sighed.

'It's not easy this,' he said.

'You're doing grand,' Murphy said, flinching then, waiting for a verbal slap.

His dad turned to him and stared. And smiled. Murphy had a shiver. What was he smiling at?

'Your mam used to say that. "Grand".'

'Yeah,' Murphy exhaled, taking the weight off his feet on the two-seater.

'It was all grand, for a while, you know.'

Murphy held his breath. Dad still had moments like this, when he'd drift back in time then abruptly end his story, leaving Murphy hanging. A patch of light glowered on the wall, as if the sun had been turned up. The clouds were parting.

'The baby. That's why all this happened.'

His pumping heart, like the clappers it was, what baby?

'We met at the railway. She was the sweetest thing. Fresh off the boat. Troubled eyes though.' He looked at the wall as if he was narrating a black and white cine film.

Please tell me everything, Murphy thought, *please don't stop until you've told me the whole thing.* He had to know what was behind his parents' promising start which ended in acrimony.

'The baby. Left Ireland in disgrace, pregnant. A farmer's son's boy. Brought shame on the family. That's how it was in those days.

'Couldn't get it sorted there though so she came here. Had it done. Couldn't go back. We met and three weeks later, we were married. But she never got over that termination. Guilty as hell.'

An abortion. His poor mam. There could've been another brother or sister for him and Orla if she'd kept the baby - he would've been the middle child, not the eldest with all the responsibility and expectations that came with that. Maybe his entire life would've been different. Dad wouldn't have turned to the drink, Mam would've stayed sane, perhaps his and Orla's innocence could've lasted longer than it had. Maybe Mam would've lived longer and she would've got to meet her grandson... But no, there was no sense in thinking this. It was a different era: pointless looking at it through twenty first century eyes when morals and religion didn't dictate the rules. His heart ached as he thought of Griffy - that had he been conceived decades earlier - he would have been terminated too. The pain of that led him to acknowledge his parents' pain. How good of him to take her on, as they would've thought of it back then, and to stick by her. It was a shock to learn he had a good side. And to see they had tried to keep tragedy at bay but it had caught up with them. His father was only human, after all. And he could forgive him that, he could. The tragedy they endured which, in the end, defeated them, showed they were only human.

'Then we had two of our own,' his dad said. Murphy felt as if he should stop him - he clearly didn't know where he was or who was with him. But he was paralyzed by the moment.

'She had you first,' he said, turning to his son. Shocked, Murphy saw a very real presence in his eyes and they were deep, not flinty and brittle. 'Then of course Orla. We were so happy for a time. But the darkness, it came back to her. That bloody church of hers, she asked for forgiveness, she'd say, but God wants me to suffer. Her moods... she retreated and I hit the bottle. If I could have my time again, son, I'd do what I'm doing now. Go sober. I'm sorry I didn't do it earlier.'

Was that an apology to him? To Orla and Mam? Or an expression of regret to himself? Probably the latter and it was bitter-sweet: to have given it the elbow was outstanding but look at what he'd missed out on.

Then Dad took a sandwich and began to eat hungrily, dropping salad cream down his front. Murphy leapt up and handed him a tissue from his pocket. He was on his knees, dabbing the mess and then it came. Tumbling out like a whispered confession.

'Dad... I'm a father... I've got a son I didn't know I had.'

'Nice sandwiches.' Oblivious, Dad was, but the dam had burst within Murphy.

'That night, she came back, you saw her leave in the morning...'

'Lovely ham.'

'She got pregnant. I only just found out. He's seven. He looks like me. What am I to do? I was going to leave. Vee, I love her but she... Like, I just don't know what to do. I've got a chance to go to the States. Dad, help me.'

Murphy looked up and saw his dad's head had lolled forward, his hand still clutching his lunch. Fast asleep, worn out. Murphy wanted to cry: he felt so alone, unable, incapable. His energy deserting him, he fell onto his haunches, supported by shaking knuckles on the floor, barely able to stop himself face-planting the carpet. 'Help me,' he said as the sobs came, forcing his forehead down towards his thighs. 'Help me.'

And then there was a buzz in his trouser pocket. And he knew it was her. Their connection, he couldn't forget it. The day he was put beside her in the classroom on his first day of school, when the jocks wolf-whistled and she wrote a note and passed it to him: 'acting like dicks won't make theirs any bigger.' The sassiness of that brain had him there and then the way she tucked her lovely hair behind her ear with her fuck-you finger. The night before she went away when she said she'd never meet anyone and asked if he would be her insurance policy: how he'd considered then to tell her she was everything to him but what could he offer at that moment to a girl who wanted to escape? He was convinced that what they had was a one-off but what right did he have to tell her? He wasn't such a prick that he'd clip her wings. The stillness he felt on Barry Island when her eyes, watery from the wind and raw from tears, reached out to him, locking him in. And the ecstasy of skin on skin, making them as one. Her shoulders, his to kiss, the shiver as he tasted her breasts, her hips, her thighs… Something he'd never dared to dream of because he'd needed her consent - she was so special, so precious. Real. Their connection, it would always be there.

Reaching for his phone, he was all thumbs, fumbling to unlock the screen, then he read her message.

> I've made a mistake, Murphy. Is it too late? I'm going to London. Will you come with me to start again? XXX

He couldn't believe it. His head fizzed and pounded, whirled and yelped. The consequences of his life were colliding now and he didn't know which way to turn.

Is it too late?

He thought of his father who wished he'd done something earlier to save his marriage, his wife, his kids, himself.

If he didn't make the right decision now, Murphy realized, he'd end up like him, living life with a shit load of regrets.

Chapter Thirty-One

V

Brighton

Deep breaths, Vee told herself in the ladies, as she teased the tilt of her polka dot saucer-shaped fascinator from drunk-at-the-races to c'est chic in the mirror. *Just because you're in Brighton, it doesn't mean you're going to see Jez.* He was what he called 'an east end boy', never venturing west towards the ball-achingly bourgeois and gentrified area of Hove. His studio was in the quirkier Kemptown, his playground was the bohemian Laines and if he went on the beach, it was the nudey one near the marina. The one where Vee had felt self-consciously lacking in piercings on her privates.

Even if he did drift this far up the seafront he wouldn't come anywhere near a posh bar like this one. Christ, she'd given it a swerve for the entire seven years she'd lived here: the drinks were too expensive and it was too touristy. Thank goodness Kate suggested it as a meeting place for the wedding party - it was close to their B&Bs and over the road from the bandstand, well-placed for those in heels.

He wouldn't recognize her anyway: she looked so different to the scrotty girl who'd left in February. Scrubbed up now, her hair was pinned back, she wore wedges and a spotty black and white tea-dress and her face featured expert swooshes of eyeliner, peachy blusher and red lips.

Yet under all of that, Vee could see the stress on her face. For all of its cosmopolitan ways, Brighton was small enough to bump into someone unexpectedly. Those sorts of coincidences were part of its magical charm, she'd once thought. Now it felt like a practical joke, as if someone was lurking with a banana skin.

Remember why you came, she thought. *To prove you could. To show Kate that you were true to your word of forgiveness when they'd made up nearly a fortnight ago and apologized over and over together, accepting her invitation to the wedding with grace. That you're a grown-up now.*

Still her breath quivered slightly but then it was chilly in here.

Into the bar she went, pinching her bolero closer to her chest in the air conditioning. Outside wasn't much better considering it was July, but she'd seen days like this here when a sea fret would come in, cover the world in white and then melt as the sun – and the people – broke free.

At a table in their finest were Charlie and Tom plus Jack, looking adorable in Welsh kilt regalia, complete with sporran. 'The next best thing to shorts,' he'd said. Boris was dozing on the floor in a bow tie. In the comfy chairs were Jack's mother in conversation with Kate's, who was in full martyr mode about her attendance, but 'these are the things we do for our children'. She'd cracked in the end, of course she had: she was too much of a control freak to not be in on the action. Then best man Pierre, aka Monsieur Bond in DJ, was racing around, Bea by his side, checking the time and hurrying up everyone's drinks.

As page boy, Griff was with Kate and her dad. Vee felt like crying at the thought of her friend having her son with her: that was what Vee had taken from her chat with her mum. Kate had been through hell and back and Vee didn't need to punish her for it. Kate had asked her to be maid of honour, but Vee didn't want to barge in on the intimacy before the ceremony: and anyway, it'd make her feel like an old spinster. What she'd learned during this journey these past few months was that she was brimming with experience now rather than regret. And what better way to show she'd learned from everything – that she could make peace with the past. Just hopefully it wouldn't include Jez.

'Drink up, chaps!' Pierre called, hustling them to gather their things. 'The bride's ETA is twenty minutes. Vingt minutes!'

Vee's mouth flopped open - he'd spoken French, out loud! Pierre caught her surprise and winked. Zut alors, she thought, he must've found his va va voom with Bea.

In the street, they behaved like sheep, allowing him to direct them to 'cross!' in a break in the busy traffic and following his march into the Victorian bandstand. Only Vee lagged behind, inspecting this city she'd called home with new eyes. On the drive here, with Kate and Jack, she had been nervous about how it would feel to return. She had feared memories at every corner: from the sweeping Downs and glorious Pavilion to the street art and markets. But as she'd watched from the car window, the hairs on end came not out of sadness but realization: their life had all been about him. The walks were always so he could take photographic studies for his art, the eateries his choice. How could she have lived like that? she wondered, joining the wedding group now.

Sunflowers adorned the ornate white edging of the roof while green deckchairs complimented the colour of the proud columns through which the sea lay grey and still. In the distance was the eerie silhouette of the West Pier, destroyed by arson but not beaten, commanding and proud.

'I bring bread and salt, Vee,' Bea said as they gathered.

'Didn't you like the breakfast? I thought it was lush!' The B&B was one of those old fashioned ones, with eggs and bacon. Possibly not to Polish tastes.

Bea rolled her eyes from beneath her floppy cream wide-brimmed hat: she looked like a seventies film star as her brown hair styled in waves sat on a dark blue pashmina over the bare shoulders of her green flared jumpsuit.

'Is Polish tradition to have bread and salt at wedding. Bread so the couple may never know hunger, salt to cope through the difficulty of the life.'

'From Fromage?' Vee giggled.

'No. Waitrose,' Bea winked. 'Don't tell him. Hey, Pierre look nervous. He take this very seriously.'

She was right: he was craning his neck to look for the bride, trying to take in the registrar's words and checking again and again he had the ring. Anyone would think it was his wedding! Maybe that was what he had in mind. The thought hit Vee in the heart quite out of the blue. The thought that she might never get to have this, what she had longed for with Jez. Yes, it would've been a disaster in the long run, she'd have worked it out eventually that she wasn't being true to herself, but still, it hurt. Because she had texted Murphy days ago, asking him if it was too late for them to try again and he had replied saying he needed time. He didn't know where he was going – he had an opportunity in the States, a child in Cardiff and a life he wasn't living in London. His head was screwed. She understood but it had crushed her, it still did, that their love was destined to remain complex, unconsummated. Because she couldn't – and she wouldn't – compete with America or Griff. To have waited all this time to have tasted such happiness only to have it snatched away was unbearable.

'I'll just go and keep an eye out for Kate,' Vee said, faking a smile. She needed a moment away to compose herself.

She took a spot on the pavement and looked up and down the road for Kate's rickshaw, which she'd hired as a bridal car. But it was hard to make out much through the fog. The sound of the engines, tooting horns and lurching buses helped to drown out her emotions. People walked past her, not batting an eyelid at her dress – this was Brighton.

Then her heart stopped. It was the way he walked, the loping style of the favoured, with no money worries and an inner confidence from good schooling. The outline of his shoulders looming in the mist. Clutching her hands to her chest she fought to breathe again as he sauntered towards her. She wanted to run, but her feet wouldn't move. This person, who was in and out of view, bobbing in between people's heads, was so similar to Jez it set off a rushing train of thought: the dreads had gone! He'd changed, he looked older, more adult...had he seen her?

He was getting closer, big shades hiding his eyes, but his chin was the same - certain, held high...the boom in her chest filling her ears. The speech she'd always dreamed of delivering came to her: she'd moved on, she'd gone back to the suburbs and, actually, it was full of adventure. Not full of 'experiences' but emotion and meaning, friendship and learning. How a few days with the love of her life had been richer than the years she'd spent with him.

It would inspire an apology, he would express his regret at how he'd treated her, that things had gone wrong for him and his girlfriend. He'd made a mistake, he wanted her back...

Closer, closer, he came, and her breathing became quicker until he was just a few steps away and she felt a pull and her hand lifted towards him. Just as she saw that it was a stranger. And he was passing her, oblivious to her agony. After everything she'd been through, to find herself vulnerable again because she'd thought she'd seen him felt a betrayal. Here she was supposed to be over the rejection, having worked out that her happiness depended on her and not a man.

Weak, that's how she felt, beaten as if the last few months had meant nothing.

'Vee!'

The shout stopped her. She swivelled round and saw a yellow rickshaw chug to a halt at the kerb.

'Kate!' Vee ran towards her as miraculously the sun came out.

She stepped out, captivating in a graceful ivory gown which skimmed her figure as it flowed to the floor - but just before it did, Vee saw a flash of gold...Kate had only gone and chosen flip-flops, which showed she had found her way! Vee clapped her hands in awe – and, oh, her father in tails was taking Kate's arm and Griff was jumping for joy by their side.

Murphy's son. The sight of him, a mini Murphy, in waistcoat and shorts, it was enough to bring her to her senses. Because this was real - this was where she was at, not in the past where she'd lived a fantasy with Jez, but right now. With Murphy, she'd had something solid: tarnished, chipped and worn, yes, but wondrous for its flaws and character. Gulping at what she was losing but grateful she'd at least tasted it, she flung an arm around Kate. And then Vee felt a vibration in her clutch bag. Tutting at the timing, she covered her friend in kisses.

The buzz again. Who on earth...Kate had noticed it too: she raised her eyebrows to say Vee had time to see who it was.

Quickly, ready to silence it, she opened her bag and saw it was him. Murphy was calling.

Vee panicked. What was she supposed to do?

'You okay?' Kate said. 'You look like you've seen a ghost.'

That was one way of putting her vision of Jez.

'Murphy's ringing...'

'Oh God, no way. Answer it, go on. I'll wait for you.' There was no hesitation from Kate.

'No! It's your wedding day!'

'Look, I've got ten minutes to spare. Please. It's important.'

Vee shut her eyes, bit her lip and made a quick prayer. And then she swiped her phone. Just as he rang off. Disappointment, despair and fear rushed through her: what had he been going to say?

'Phone him back!' Kate waved her bouquet of sunflowers at her.

'What if it's bad news though? What if he's leaving, going to America, and that's that? Or he's going to stay in Cardiff when I go to London? It's going to ruin today. No. No way...' She looked mournfully at the screen and was about to put it away when there was a third buzz. 'Oh no, he's left a voicemail.'

Kate grabbed her arm. 'Vee, you need to know.'

'But it's your day.'

'Listen, everyone can wait. I'll stay with you for as long as you need. Dad, go and tell Pierre that I'm here but just having a few moments with my best friend.'

He took Griff with him, leaving the two of them on the pavement.

'I was going to turn my phone off. I wish I'd turned my phone off. Why didn't I? Then I'd be unaware and we could just go in and celebrate you and Jack.'

'Well, you didn't and you aren't and we will.'

Kate was looking at her pleadingly.

'No. I can't. Come on, let's get you married.' Vee began to pull Kate towards the bandstand and the now emerald sea, wanting to blank out the thoughts running wildly around her head. But Kate was resisting.

'Vee, if it hadn't been for you, I wouldn't be here now doing this, my way, with my son. You gave me everything. It's time you let me give something back.'

A rift formed in Vee's defences as the words caressed her heart.

'Don't be afraid,' Kate said, reading Vee's mind. She looked up at her: their bond was evergreen. Despite everything. 'I was scared. But you showed me the truth is beautiful. Whatever it is, we'll deal with it.'

Vee was nearly there, holding the phone, weighing it up. Then it came to her. 'It's his birthday,' she gasped, 'I completely forgot. He's the unlikeliest summer baby. He should've been born in the dead of winter. His birthday. Shit.'

'Okay... so...?' Kate didn't get this bit.

'We made a pact, the night before you and me went away. If we were still single by the time we were thirty then we'd get together.'

Kate put a hand to her mouth. 'He's thirty today! Vee! Do you think he's going to…'

Vee didn't know what to think.

'You won't be able to concentrate if you don't listen to his message. And you've got a reading to do! I need you with me.'

Vee nodded then she called her voicemail.

The ringing took an age to pass. The woman droned on and on until the recording kicked in. There was a pause. She could hear his breathing, his turmoil. Kate was staring into her eyes, waiting for a sign.

'Vee,' he said, 'It's me.' He sounded serious, contained. It wasn't going to be good. 'I've come to a decision. I can't come with you to London. I want to help bring up my son. I'm staying in Cardiff. I didn't want to waste any more time, we've wasted too much already and-.' She ended the call. Click. That was it.

Her chin crumpled. Shaking her head at Kate, she was numb.

No tears came because she had known all along.

Kate moved towards her and put an arm around Vee's neck, the other around her back. 'Oh, Vee, I'm so sorry.'

'At least I know,' Vee said into her hair, hearing the waves and the seagulls and the traffic and life continue on without her. 'At least I know.'

Kate's hand was there to soothe her but Vee felt cold and distant. Trying to process this even though she had expected an unhappy ending. Seconds passed in a daze until her phone went again. Murphy. Why was he pursuing her like this? It was unbearable, a sore that would never heal.

'Take it,' Kate said, backing away to give her space. 'Take it!'

So she did, just to get it over with.

'Vee, did you get my message?' he asked, with urgency. 'Where are you?'

'Brighton,' she said, wooden.

'I know that! Where exactly because I'm here, I've-'

'Here?' She swung round, her eyes searching, sweeping the hustle and bustle of heads and shoulders, moving in a complete circle, as Kate understood what was happening and joined the hunt.

'He's come for you, Vee!' she said, gasping. 'I didn't think he would…'

'You invited him?' Vee shrieked, dropping the phone from her ear.

'Not as such,' Kate said, carefully, 'I thought about it and if it was me, I'd have been desperate to see Griff, so I said Murphy could come, not to introduce them properly, not yet, but to breathe the same air as his son...and you because...you two, you're made for each other.' She held out the palm of her hands to show she meant no harm.

Vee looked up to the sky and blew out of her cheeks. Overwhelmed, all she could go with was her instinct: Kate hadn't been underhand. This was her final peace offering. And Vee was going to grab it with hungry fists.

'Where are you?' she pleaded, back to the call, scanning the prom.

'I can see you!' he said and she could tell he was smiling. And she was twirling, trying to pick him out from the masses.

'Because I can't live without you, Vee. Didn't you hear the message?'

'I did, but it was too much, losing you...' Desperate now, needing him.

'You didn't listen to the end, did you?' Amused that he knew something good that she didn't and he couldn't wait to explain. 'I said in the message, to stay in Cardiff, to do your training there. And stay with me.'

It was all too much - his sincerity was in no doubt, it was her hearing she didn't believe.

And then she saw him: a flash of his hair, his cheekbone, his chest and her legs began to move of their own accord, taking her to him as they blindly stashed away their phones and dodged men and women and kids to be reunited.

She'd seen an apparition earlier but this was true: breaking into a run, wanting him to be hers. Vee smashed into his body and buried her face in his neck. His warmth like fire, his strength squeezing her tight, his musky smell and his lips, pushing on hers.

'Did you mean it?' he said, eventually, holding her face with his hands. 'Did you mean it when you said we should get together if both of us were still single when we were thirty? Because I'm thirty now. Today.'

'I haven't got you anything!' she wailed, realizing instantly that this wasn't the point. She was distracted by his skinny grey declared she'd study in Cardiff because there was no way she was going to lose him, this wonderful man who had put his son first even when he didn't know how Griff was going to take to him. Talk about responsible, amazing, incredible and bloody epic. He'd grown up and she wanted to grow old with him.

The next day she jumped on the 08:25 back from Brighton and turned up here, with a stonking hangover, and fell into his arms – then asleep in his bed for twelve hours. The morning after he told her how beautiful she was when she was sleeping. He'd watched her into the early hours. She almost died from the romance of it – until he said he'd even found her dribbling cute. Vee has been here ever since. They love one another deeply, tease each other remorselessly and give support unconditionally. They're loved up and sickening in other words. But it's not been all running slo-mo through a meadow.

Murphy had a wobble in the days after Kate's wedding, leading up to his first meeting with Griff, wondering what, if any, his role would be. But he needn't have worried because his son loves computer games and that's how they've bonded. It's not a father-son thing, more like an uncle-nephew.

Kate and Murphy, who've found their way because they both love Griff, will never be his proper parents – Charlie and Tom will forever be that. Griff is just chuffed that he gets more presents.

Vee had an interesting time at college, falling pregnant three months in. On the day she graduated, she gave birth – almost in a cab, he was that quick. It was like he was desperate to arrive, as if he'd been there forever waiting for them to sort their shit out. Murphy was there at the birth, cross-eyed with love, sobbing at his perfect skin, as pure, as his mum would've put it, as the head on a pint of Guinness.

They named him Jarvis Bernard after Mr Cocker and Murphy's mum Bernadette. The good thing about Jarvis is it can't be shortened, like theirs - it might reduce his chances of an identity crisis, that's the aim anyway.

Murphy took time out to look after Jarvis so she could apply for jobs and it took a while but she got there in the end. He's left the company in London to start up his own business, producing health wearables and apps, which Vee thinks is fabulous albeit complicated. As for Apple, he has no regrets - he was offered an interview but he wasn't even tempted. That's not to say he doesn't have the latest iPhone. But everyone's got to settle down sometime, he always says, even Jarvis Cocker: 'Look what happened to him - he ended up doing the voiceovers for Sainsbury's ads.'

All of it means this flat just isn't practical anymore. Ha, they thought they'd be the coolest parents in the world here, living it up in the centre of Cardiff – having a baby wouldn't change them. As if! They both worked that out five minutes after they first attempted to get the pushchair up the stairs.

Vee blushes when she thinks that Murphy sold his London pad for enough money to buy a six-bed mansion. But they unanimously decided to stick to a three-bed semi, one room each for them, Jarvis and Griffy, with an annex Murphy can use as an office, so he could help Orla and Phil with a big deposit. This place they'll rent out, probably to some whizzkid. As for marriage, she's found out that it's not that important in the scheme of things. Murphy is keen but they agree right now, the holy trinity of a home, family and friends is more crucial.

So yes, they're heading to the suburbs. They regularly shake their heads at themselves, that they spent their lives trying to escape the boredom only to be returning of their own accord. At least they're safe in the knowledge they're still their wonky old selves with their own unique version of domestic bliss. Even Kate's mum Pam has got on with it although she is still clinging to the belief that as far as everyone knows, she has a nice, normal family.

'So your new place!' Kate says, when Vee appears with a tray of drinks. 'I never really thought you'd go for it when I sent you the details.'

Vee thinks of the new-build estate which backs onto fields, on the edge of the countryside where there are waterfalls and horses, woods and hills. Murphy and her went to see it 'just for a look, to rule it out' and played a game over several days to see who would admit loved it first. She cracked before he did, she's never been any good at holding things in. The thing about it is the convenience of living close to Murphy's dad and her parents while also being in the catchment area of a good school.

'What's not to like about suburbia?' Vee says, thick with self-deprecation. 'Nah, I can't wait. Mum's had a look. She says there's room for a conservatory. But that is so not happening. Well, not yet!'

THE END XXXXXXX

We hope you enjoyed this book!

For an exclusive preview of Laura Kemp's *The Late Blossoming of Frankie Green*, read on or click the image

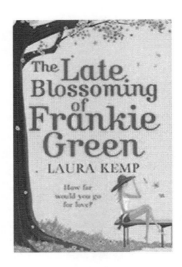

More addictive fiction from Aria:

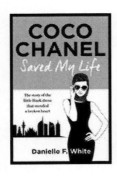

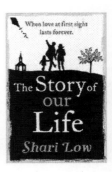

Find out more
http://headofzeus.com/books/isbn/9781784978877

Find out more
http://headofzeus.com/books/isbn/9781784979560

Find out more

http://headofzeus.com/books/isbn/9781784978242

Acknowledgements

Lizzy Kremer – There are around one hundred thousand of them poured into this book but when you want to find the words to express your love, respect and gratitude for somebody it can be difficult to find the right ones. My go-to when it gets like that is humour - glittery tits spring to mind, Lizzy - but she deserves more. Having picked me and nurtured me, Lizzy made me see what it was to dig deeper. She is my motivation: it's all about repaying her belief, loyalty and direction. TBUM is for her.

Clare Bowron, thank you for your incredible insight and direction, which changed everything.

The Aria Team: Caroline Ridding – Top bird, boss and mate. How lucky I am to have you – your energy and enthusiasm is unrivalled – cheers!

Nia Beynon – Oh! You're magnificent in every way. The Yes Woman who works until it hurts.

Blake Brooks – M&P extraordinaire – let's do promo tattoos and Lovehearts!

Yasemin Turan – Skillz all round, lady.

Jade Craddock – A simply amazing editor: how do you do that thing when you know what I want to say and put it in a comment on your notes and I go 'oh, yeah! that's exactly it'?

Next, and say no more, The Readers – Without you, nada, nothing, zilch. Thank you so very much - and keep in touch, I love hearing from you and reading your reviews.

Authors – The kindest cuddliest cackliest gang in the world, even to small fry like me, particularly Milly Johnson, Lucy Diamond, Miranda Dickinson, Amanda Jennings and Tosh plus the RNA crew.

Bloggers – Bloody diamonds, the lot of you! Thank you to the library on the moon and back for your support.

Twitter – Love my feed for news and views and scraps and laughs. Plus Tanni's plugs!

Facebook – I apologize for my lame updates. It's procrastination.

Instagram – No better place for positivity, hilarity and touching snapshots from everyone's lives.

Mum, Dad, Jamie and Paddy – For your excitement and belief. And Tesco runs. My secretary, Ollie, who is excellent if he gets a dog biscuit.

And finally, Jo, my eternal back-up woman. That one long-term friend who saw you at your spottiest and still loves you.

About Laura Kemp

LAURA KEMP lives in Penarth, Cardiff with her supportive husband, gorgeous son, playful dog and ancient cat. Writing to Laura is compulsive. With 15 years journalistic experience and several successful books to her name, writing is her escape and her love.

Find me on Twitter
https://twitter.com/Laurajanekemp?lang=en-gb

Find me on Facebook
https://www.facebook.com/Laura-Kemp-374265565994740/

Also by Laura Kemp

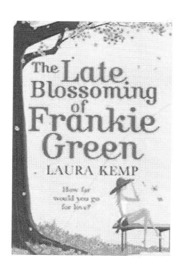

Find out more
http://headofzeus.com/books/isbn/9781784976996

Visit Aria now
http://www.ariafiction.com

Preview

Read on for a preview of *Whatever Happened to Vicky Hope's Back Up Man?*:

Frankie Green's happy ever after is put on hold when her childhood sweetheart husband complains things are boring in bed.

When he asks for some space, she sets out to win him back by getting herself a sex education.

Little does she know that her hilarious, tender and embarrassing journey of enlightenment is going to change everything…

A story full of humour, heartache and happiness, of friendship, coming of age and overcoming insecurity.

Can't wait? Buy it here now!
http://headofzeus.com/books/isbn/9781784976996

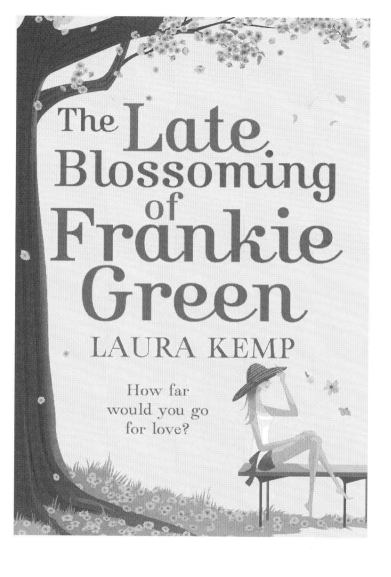

The Late Blossoming of Frankie Green

of

LAURA KEMP

How far
would you go
for love?

One night in May...

Frankie

Frankie shivered as she waited for Jason to unveil his surprise.

'Keep your eyes closed,' he said, rustling about with something as his movements shook the king-size bed.

With a smile on her face, she couldn't believe that after fourteen years together he still made her all tingly. In fact, tonight was the tingliest she'd ever felt, she decided, as a wand of fairy dust sprinkled excitement on her toes, which raced all the way up her bare body. Except for the bits covered up by her new matching white M&S underwear.

It was their first wedding anniversary and they were in the same posh hotel room where they'd started life as Mr and Mrs Green.

Soon they'd be making love in their familiar way, his body on hers was all she desired. The girls teased her for having only slept with one person but she was so relieved she hadn't had to kiss any frogs like they had – and still had to. But his muscular weight was the measure of their love; it was solid and secure and, secretly, she wanted to feel possessed by her man. Just as she had done at lunch when he led the way to their table overlooking Cardiff Bay's glorious waterfront. Their hideaway was only ten minutes from their house in the city but she saw no need, and had no desire, to go anywhere else.

'This way, Mrs Green,' he'd said, guiding her to her seat with his lovely old-school manners. She had a glass of pink fizz, her favourite, while he had a bottle of some fancy lager, one he hadn't tried before, then he'd tried to persuade her to try some chorizo. But she stuck to her trusted bangers and mash followed by banoffee pie – the exact meal they'd had for their wedding breakfast.

The only fly in the ointment had been when she'd brought up starting a family next year. A cloud had crossed his usually cheerful face. He didn't think he felt ready, he'd said, taking her hand and squeezing it affectionately. 'I just want to enjoy us for a bit longer, there's so much fun to be had. It was a big enough deal to get married, wasn't it?' he'd said, smiling his irresistible smile.

She'd felt bitterly disappointed, not because she felt broody. After all, they did have masses to finish in the house and she honestly had nothing to worry about because she had years before her biological clock started ringing. But because that's what couples did, wasn't it? Domestic bliss equalled the patter of tiny feet. She was tired of her hairdressing clients asking when she was going to have a baby. On the plus side, Frankie was flattered he still prized her company and didn't want to share her after all this time.

They'd met in the first week of college: he was her first and only boyfriend and she loved it that way. She was forever his Tinkerbell, the pet name he had given her from day one, owing to her long blonde hair, blue eyes and her figure that back then was a perfect hourglass, but was now a tad plumper thanks to her love handles. He was the only one for her. He was perfect, with his boyish good looks and easy-going nature. He was positive, kind, generous and...

'Almost ready, Tink,' he said, from his pillow. She beamed, hearing the thrill of anticipation in his voice. What was he going to produce? A piece of jewellery, maybe, or some lingerie? Whatever it was, she would adore it because he knew her taste was simple but elegant.

There was the muffled sound of fabric then a click. It was all too much for Frankie so she peeped through her eyelashes. And then she wished she hadn't. In the place of the box from Tiffany's she'd been hoping for was a fluffy black handcuff attaching one of her blindfolded husband's wrists to the bed railings. He'd used her scarf, her best flowery one in fact, to tie round his head to hide his eyes. Inside her head she screamed 'Oh my God' but she was so horrified, the words wouldn't come out. Instead, her eyes nearly popped out of her skull.

'Frankie? Are you there?' Jason said. 'Say something! What do you think?' he asked, as if he was showing her a new T-shirt.

'You... look like a hostage,' she said, aghast at how the blindfold made his crew cut and stubble seem like he'd been taken captive. Wincing, she knew this wasn't what he'd intended. It was a good job he couldn't see her face, which was contorted with shock and disgust. Kinky sex had never appealed to her – whenever she came across it in magazines, she'd flick past to find the romantic questionnaire instead. Mum had given her a copy of *Fifty Shades of Grey* and while Frankie had soaked up the love story, she was bewildered by all the equipment.

Jason's laughter turned her stomach now. 'Come on!' he said, 'I'm your slave, do whatever you want to me.'

She ran through her options like a shopping list: lock herself in the loo? Say she had a headache? Or have a go? But what was she supposed to do to him, specifically? Cover him in whipped cream and call him Margaret?

'The only thing I think I'm capable of, Jason, is tickling you,' she said, wincing at her cluelessness as her fingers wiggled. 'I'm sorry. I'm just confused, this is so out of the blue.' She pulled his mask up onto his forehead so he looked like a camp Rambo; she needed eye contact. That way they could be honest, which was how they'd always operated. But while his big brown eyes usually shone with warmth, now they were hurt.

'I was just trying to liven things up,' he said, staring down. Then, after a pause, he added, 'Because…'

'Because?' she asked, warily. What was going on?

'I dunno, things are a bit, you know, predictable in bed, that's all.'

'Oh,' Frankie said, touching her face as if his words had slapped her cheek. She smarted from both the shock of his confession and the naive shame that she hadn't realized he'd been unsatisfied when she thought they were a flawless fit. 'You never mentioned it…'

'No,' he said, meeting her gaze with embarrassment, then looking away again.

A chill snaked its way around her heart as she waited for him to elaborate. But he remained quiet, pensive.

'We're okay, aren't we?' she asked nervously, searching his troubled face for a smile. Because they did it twice a week, which was 'very good' according to the experts. And Jason always seemed content afterwards. 'Oh, God, is it because I've put on a bit of weight over the last year? It's just because I'm so happy, that's all.'

'No, don't be silly, you're perfect,' he said, reaching for her hand then placing it down softly on the duvet as if it was porcelain. 'Maybe that's the problem. You're too perfect.'

'What? I don't understand,' she said, wishing – no, praying that he would leap up, yell 'joke!' and they'd have a laugh then clean their teeth together, like they did every night. But he was silent. It was a very bad sign. There was no denial, no 'everything is fine'. This was even more worrying than the sight of him trussed up. 'Jase?' she asked, her heart running up her throat with fear as the bed tilted and she lost her balance.

'I love you, you know that, don't you?' he said.

'Yes,' she replied in a tiny voice, with her heart now in her mouth, terrified of what was about to happen. This was how people started talking when there was a heartbreaking and life-changing 'but'. When bad things happened and they became defining 'before' and 'after' moments. Like the time Mum told them she was leaving. She pushed the memory of her parents' split out of her mind; she was anxious enough already and didn't need to think of that too. This wasn't supposed to be happening to her. 'What is it?' she said, panicking. 'Because whatever it is, we can put it right. We're in love. We're together forever, like you always said, remember?'

But, oh, Frankie's fear mounted as he failed to answer her. It was a pathetic sight as Jason sighed heavily, unlocked the handcuff and threw his mask to the floor. He turned his back to her, sitting on the edge of the bed, bent his head and rubbed his eyes with the heel of his palms. Then he spoke. 'Don't you ever wonder what else is out there, Frankie? Don't you wonder if we got together too young and we missed out on stuff? Like, we needed a change but we thought the wedding was the next step instead of being brave enough to live a little, then settle down. Don't you ever wonder that?'

Inside, she screamed, "No, never" – but her voice let her down. She wanted him to stop – how much more could she take? – but she could see by his drooping posture that he wasn't finished.

'Ever since we got married, I've felt sort of numb. Lost. As if everything's a grey blur. I even went to see a doctor, thinking I had something wrong with me. But there wasn't. I knew then I wasn't happy. And it's not fair on you to carry on. Because I can't. Not like this. I'm so, so sorry.'

His words were clearly well-rehearsed which was the most hurtful thing of all. He'd obviously been waiting to tell her. This wasn't some spur of the moment thing; he meant it.

Panicking, she stalled for time. 'The doctors? Why didn't you tell me? We tell each other everything.' He just shook his head. 'We can sort it out,' she pleaded, desperate now. 'We know each other inside out.' Jason's shoulders began to shrug as he broke down.

She reached out to him, trying to steady him yet he remained aloof. 'Please, Jason, tell me you're not giving up on us?'

'I can't... It isn't.'

Frankie hugged herself, feeling pain at the charade of their marriage, at how differently they saw their futures. 'Oh, God, no,' she whimpered as the tears came. This time, he turned around and embraced her and they hung onto each other, seeking a comfort that was impossible to find.

'I wish I didn't feel like this,' he offered. 'I never wanted to hurt you. I love you so much, Tink.'

She moved back from him, her breathing quickening. 'You're talking as though that's it. It can't be, you can't just announce all of this as though it's your thing. It's *our* thing.'

'I just feel overwhelmed,' he said, 'like my whole life is planned out. It's not that I want to travel the world or anything, I just feel hemmed in. I need some time... Some time out.'

'So go on holiday, do a climbing course, learn to fly, maybe that's all you need,' she said, madly trying to convince herself that was the answer. 'If it's the baby thing, we can wait for a few years,' she said over-brightly, as if it was the most reasonable offer going.

'I don't feel as if I'll ever be capable of being responsible enough for fatherhood. I need to sort my head out. Away from...'

'Me,' she whispered, 'Away from me.' She felt nauseous at his retreat. 'How have we gone from being happily married half an hour ago to this? How did I not see this coming?' she wailed.

Even as she said this she began to make a mental list of all the times he'd worked late to avoid coming home, the appointments he'd made up to get out of choosing new kitchen tiles, and the excuses he'd come up with to prevent any plans taking shape. Frankie had translated all of them as signs he was preparing to feather their nest as their marriage headed towards its next phase of parenthood. She'd thought all those extra hours at his dad's scaffolding business and refusing to go on holiday this year had been about him preparing for the future. But it had been his escape. From her. She wept as she registered that everything she thought was true had been pulled from under her and was now out of reach.

Her vision swimming with tears, she felt the terror build. 'So what now then? Because you seem to have it all worked out.'

'I think I should move out, give us both some space. So we can work things out. If we can.'

It was all too much to take in.

'Is there someone else?' she asked, eager to lay the blame elsewhere, convincing herself if it was just a quick fling with another woman then it could be overcome. Failing that, she could find a reason to hate him.

'No, of course not, it's not about anyone else, it's about me. And you.'

'If it's the sex thing, I can change, I can,' she said, knowing but not caring that it was a desperate and hollow plea.

'I'm so sorry, Frankie,' he said, suddenly looking exhausted.

It was over. She could see he'd made up his mind. Frankie felt herself tumbling off the edge, grabbing empty fistfuls of air. Freefalling, she was losing everything she'd ever wanted. The love of her life, her best friend, her soulmate, her future, their past. Terror took its place. She was going to be alone, without him. She didn't want to let go, she wanted to hold on, but he was out of reach. If only she could handcuff herself to him now.

Two Months Later, a Tuesday Night in July...

Frankie

A plump pink blob which curled slightly at one end appeared beneath Frankie's nose and she wanted to cry. How was she expected to put that in her mouth?

She looked at Letitia, who was nodding encouragingly at her.

'Go on, babes, try it,' she said. 'It's a bit rubbery, it is, but I guarantee, the "pulpo" is totally lush.'

Frankie gulped and turned to Em, who was prodding it with her fork.

'Cephalopoda mollusc. Among the most intelligent and behaviourally diverse of all invertebrates. The scientific Latin name of octopus derives from ancient Greek, which translates as "eight-foot".'

'That doesn't help, to be honest, Em,' Frankie said, holding her throat. 'Can't I just start with the patatas bravas or those ham croquette things, because this is my first time trying tapas and, you know, I need to work up to it.'

Over the table packed with exotic dishes, Letty pouted her Spanish genes; she was all crimson lips, with flashing eyes. She finished off by tossing her señorita mane of black curls with a bare shoulder, peeping out of a stunning, and, by the looks of it, expensive black pencil dress. Then she broke the spell with a brazen cackle which revealed her closer Valleys girl roots, which were all heart and gob.

This had been Letty's idea to get Frankie back out there and broaden her horizons. She'd resisted her invites for weeks, preferring to stay in with the girls because she'd wanted to hide from the world. And, privately, she'd thought, on the off chance, that she'd be there if Jason appeared at the door of their marital home, where she remained after he moved out. But then she'd run out of excuses – and Jason hadn't come back. Reluctantly, she had realized her friends only wanted to help. Even so, she still felt the fear, staring down some tentacles.

The restaurant was smack bang in the city centre, fifteen minutes away for all three of them, albeit from different directions. Frankie was from across the river in the busy and cheerful suburb of Canton where she was born and bred, Letty was living it up in the boho-chic area of Pontcanna while Em called the shiny redeveloped docklands of Cardiff Bay home.

To Frankie, Viva Tapas was all exotic and low-lit, with clattering pans and hisses of steam where the chefs worked in an open-plan kitchen-diner. The stainless steel set-up was very dramatic, but she could never live with something so stark and clinical; the wooden units of her kitchen made her two-up two-down in a quiet cul-de-sac homely and safe. Well, they had before Jason had gone. The heavy wafts of sherry and garlic were atmospheric, but she found it a bit overpowering. It was boiling in here too, not helped by the raging heatwave which had wilted her top-knot on her walk into town.

She pulled up her top, regretting the adventurous neckline which made her now feel exposed. Thank goodness for her comfy pants and bra, which held her in nicely. Scratchy undies might look nice but they weren't soft enough, which was was why she had stuck to the same style for the last ten years. When you'd found a formula that worked, you stuck with it.

But in here it felt a bit dangerous. This was the problem with going along with Letty's daring ideas. Not that she meant any harm; she was incredibly loyal, just a bit overwhelming at times. At least Em was here, the sensible buffer to Letty's boisterousness. Frankie pitched in somewhere in the middle – it had always been like this.

They'd met in their first week at secondary school when Em and Letty moved into Frankie's neck of the woods. Floyd and Em had arrived from London for their dad's work while Letty's mum had left the Rhondda for a new start after Letty's dad had gone out to buy some milk and never come back. Frankie, who had been split up from her primary school mates, didn't know anyone in her class. So the three of them had bonded immediately when they discovered they all had distinctive names.

She was Francesca because her mum thought it was classy,

while her dad liked it for being the female form of his favourite singer, Frank Sinatra. Em was Emerald Good-Fellow, thanks to her hippy parents, who were in their crystals phase when she was born, and among the first to double-barrel their surnames for equality reasons. Then there was Letitia Cox, christened after her Spanish granny but called Titty – amongst other things – by the boys. Poor love. How they'd wished they'd fitted in like all the other Rebeccas, Samanthas and Rachels. From that beginning, the threesome had loved one another fiercely. And Frankie had no idea how she would've coped if she hadn't had them over the last two months post-Jason.

There had been the initial deep depression at finding herself alone for the first time in her life. That meant a few days moping in her pyjamas at Dad's, where he'd let her talk and howl, all the while trying to get her to eat. She'd been so low she'd even accepted an invite to stay over at Mum's, which she had spent her childhood trying to avoid: her mum tried to help but couldn't quite keep it up. After five minutes of being allowed to analyse the breakdown of her marriage, she'd been told to 'shush now' because Corrie was on.

There were sudden bouts of crying when flashbacks of happier times hit her at the checkout or the wheel of the car, and one infamous night when Em held her hair back as she was crouched over the loo after too much to drink indoors.

Then anger struck, when she'd bagged up his belongings and cleared the cupboards of his cereal and mugs. A brief stint of numbness too, when she'd cut hair on autopilot, deflecting sympathy with a wave of her scissors. Now, she was living with it; the 'acceptance' phase, the magazines called it, which meant her grief was less raw. Yet she still held onto the belief that she could win Jason back. He just needed time, she was convinced of it. One day they'd look back and see it as a blip. They still spoke or texted every day or so. Did he ring out of guilt? Partly, she suspected, but they loved each other. And he always picked up, no matter what time she called him or what insult she'd slung at him in the last call. He was also still her husband – in dark moments she wondered for how much longer – and fundamentally a kind man too. Even though he was sleeping on his brother's sofa, he still paid half the mortgage. It kept the hope alive. Only this afternoon she'd replayed her dream of him coming back to her, saying he'd made a mistake and 'could they start again?' Where and how they would begin, she still didn't know. But she would make it work, it was all she wanted.

After much soul-searching, she realized she *had* had her head in the sand; that was undeniable, otherwise she would've seen the break-up coming. Frankie couldn't be someone she wasn't. And she'd never want to be. Yet she conceded, at the age of thirty, she needed to loosen up and live a little. That Jason hadn't been talking entire rubbish and maybe she should've tried to make things more interesting. Which was why she'd agreed to taste something with eight arms – or were they legs?

'Look, babes, I understand, you're a bit scared,' Letitia said, warmly. 'But you need to come out of your shell.'

'I like my shell,' Em said, staring matter-of-factly through green eyes. She nodded to confirm it, making her poker-straight red bob swing until it fell quickly back into precise place.

'This is about Frankie, remember, not you,' Letty said, wagging a red-nailed finger at their friend.

Frankie didn't want this to be about her at all, so she changed the subject and asked how they both were.

'Busy. Tired. Annoyed with Floyd,' Em said, referring to her big brother to whom she had offered her spare room for the night, after his landlord had sold his flat. That had been six months ago. 'He's lovely but he's noisy and messy and he still acts like he's fourteen.'

Frankie nodded sympathetically, knowing how larger than life, six-foot-enormous Floyd could be. She could imagine Em accusing him of making her neat flat look untidy just because of the way his limbs sprawled when he sat down. And he'd fill the place with his personality too.

'The other day,' Em continued, 'for no reason whatsoever, he tucked two mangoes in his vest and announced he was "a lady". He's thirty-four, for goodness sake.'

Letty stifled a laugh which Em ignored, looking downcast. 'Work is mental too.'

Ah, that was the real reason for her peaky pallor. It meant so much to her. Of the three of them, she was the career woman. If they'd been in *Sex And The City*, Letty would've been Samantha because she was sex-mad and she worked at a glitzy public relations company, Em was Miranda the lawyer (minus the girlfriend), and she was sensible Charlotte. With no fourth gang member, Frankie had considered christening her sleek black psychic black cat Carrie courtesy of her white paws, which she imagined to be Jimmy Choos. Until *she* turned out to be a *he*. So it was Leonardo di Catprio instead after her favourite actor.

'It's this weather,' Em said, now animated. 'Did you know, a rise of just four degrees from twenty to twenty-four Celsius means sales of burgers increases by forty-two per cent? Make that ten degrees, as is forecast this weekend, and you're looking at three hundred per cent more barbecue meat and fifty per cent more coleslaw. It's not just getting the supplies, which everyone is fighting over, it's finding the space too.'

'Well, I never knew that!' Frankie said, in awe of her friend's important role. Frankie's idea of an emergency was her hairdryer breaking down. Which actually wouldn't ever happen because she was capable enough to have a spare. Two, actually.

'And it's all to be done in this heat. It's making me feel ill.' Em was too pale to enjoy anything beyond spring and autumn.

'What about Simon? Have you seen him lately?' Frankie said gingerly; it was always a gamble asking about Em's private life. But she wanted her to know she was interested and ready to listen, to show she wanted to pay back her friends' support and relationship talk wasn't taboo. After all, he was the only bloke Em had mentioned in forever.

'No,' Em said in a clipped voice. 'No Simon Brown news.' She always referred to him using his full name, it was one of her quirks and it was charmingly old-fashioned.

Then she went silent. But she was fidgeting with her hair, double-checking the top button of her white crisp shirt was done up, and the slightest flush of pink came to her cheeks. Frankie ached for her – it could only mean she was still besotted. Yet she didn't dare point it out – she'd been the one who'd 'had it all' but look how much of a fantasy that had been.

Frankie waited until Letty had finished ordering more wine – and flirting with the waiter – then turned the spotlight on her. She always had something, or more accurately someone, happening in her life. 'What about you and that Aussie, the personal trainer? Or have you moved on?'

'Come to your senses more like,' Em tutted, referring to the awful fact he was in a relationship and had a young kid.

Frankie prayed she'd stop there. Both her and Em had made known their disapproval, there was no need to drag it up again. Letty shifted in her seat for a second. Frankie knew she felt terrible about it. But did she feel terrible enough to have called it off?

Letty, who spoke like a bottle of shaken up Coca-Cola, launched in. 'It's just sex. And yes, I know I said it wouldn't happen again but I'm only killing time before I meet someone. There's nothing in it. Just keeping the motor running.'

Em arched a cynical eyebrow.

'Honest to God, I mean it!' Letty said, defensively, but with vulnerable eyes. 'Why does no one take me seriously?'

'We do, we do,' Frankie said, knowing that this was Letty's greatest insecurity. In work and in love, Letty yearned to be seen as more than a pair of boobs – admittedly, she did have great ones. But she'd been treated badly by blokes and had never had the break to become an account executive at the public relations company where she was secretary, so it was a raw nerve.

'Give me some credit, I'm hardly going to fall for a man called Lance Boddy, am I? A man who named his gym The Boddy Shop! I mean, how naff is that?' she said, laughing, throwing her hands in the air like a flamenco dancer. The trouble was, Letty had form. 'I could fall into a bucket of naked men who had 'boyfriend material' stamped on their heads and I'd still come up sucking my own thumb,' Letty had said the last time she'd been dumped, that time, by a model. She just didn't like run-of-the-mill guys. But why did that mean they treated her so badly when she was so fabulous? It was all very unfair.

'Twenty-first-century fitness is about being lean and smart. But he makes it sound like he's a rescue centre for old bangers!'

Just like that, Letty covered up what she considered to be a show of weakness with humour. It was how she dealt with things. Underneath, Frankie knew that Letty was just like her and Em, wanting her own special someone.

Then two pairs of eyes flicked towards Frankie. It was her turn. 'Right, well, I'm not bad, you know. Jase came round to collect some stuff the other day, that was awful. But lovely too, just to see him,' she said, feeling her chin wobble. She paused. It was no use, she couldn't keep it in. 'I still want him back, I still love him,' she admitted, crumbling, feeling a relief at letting it out. 'Like, I miss him every day, so badly. The bed is too big without him. I feel like I'm rattling around the house. My heart jumps every time I get a text or the phone calls. I see shadows of him everywhere.'

Letty got up to give her a *cwtch*, the Welsh word she used for a cuddle.

Em went into problem-solving mode, as ever. 'You need a project,' she said. This was classic Em – hand her a situation and she would try to fix it. 'Something to keep you busy. Distracted. You can't waste your time wondering what will be because it might never happen. Get on with things, that's the only way. Talking of which, I'm starving. I'm going to start.'

Bless Em, but she could be so blunt and it only made Frankie feel worse. Letty clocked her despair. 'There's nothing wrong with keeping the faith,' she said kindly. Thank goodness for Letty's soft side. 'But I also agree with Em,' she added, making Frankie groan.

'Distraction is good at a time like this. And I know just the thing – going on the rebound can work wonders.'

'I didn't mean that sort of distraction,' Em said, stopping to frown, before she carried on loading her plate. 'I meant exercise or an evening class or something. Not the kind you do with your PT.'

'But it could make Jason see sense, you know, make him jealous, and if it doesn't then at least Frankie is getting some practice after what he said,' Letty added.

'I am here, you know,' Frankie coughed, feeling a sting from the mention of Jason's boring-in-bed comment. It had been a serious blow to her confidence.

'Oh, I'm so sorry, babes,' Letty said, with genuine concern, 'We didn't mean to make you feel bad… Now, are you going to try some of this octopus?'

'In a sec,' Frankie said, hesitating.

'Well, let me just take a shot of it first. I'll put it on Instagram, I will,' Letty said. 'Bit of a crop and a filter… and there… boom. It's on my feed.'

Frankie didn't get why people shared photos of avocados and sunsets but she guessed in Letty's circumstances it helped her to see the positives when she was struggling to find any. Then, no more time-wasting, it was over to Frankie.

She took a breath to prepare for her Bushtucker Trial. Unfortunately, Ant and Dec were nowhere to be seen to save her.

As Frankie raised her fork, Em launched in with one of her

'interesting facts'. 'Did you know reproduction is a cause of death in octopuses and males can only live a few months after mating?'

That was it. With her stomach churning, Frankie's hand dropped to the table with a clunk. Playing it safe seemed far more tempting right now than living a little.

Wednesday

Em

The next one-hundred-and-twenty seconds are going to determine the rest of my life, Em thought.

As she sat on the toilet seat behind a locked door during her morning tea-break, she could hear echoes of footsteps marching past the ladies'. It was usually her clip-clopping purposefully on her way to human resources, the canteen or the manager's office. Instead, due to an act utterly out of character, she could soon be waddling her way down the corridor. And then, worse, barefoot and stranded at home.

Once more, it took her breath away when she thought about that night. After hiding her feelings for five weeks, six days, twenty one hours and twelve minutes, she'd finally been able to let her head clock off and her heart start the night shift. His shy smile, his delicious lips, his considerate question: if she was really sure? The fact he didn't laugh when her name badge poked into his chest. How they melted into bed yet she felt as if she was flying a slow-motion loop-the-loop.

She didn't believe in magic but that was the word that kept coming to her as she recalled Simon Brown's touch. Looking back, it had all seemed so inevitable and – now she could admit it – it had felt like that in the build-up too. Yet hadn't she always said fate was nonsense and that free will and hard work got you through life?

It had been the most frustrating and bewildering thing that had ever happened to her, she thought, as the digital numbers on her watch counted upwards. She and Simon Brown had instantly clicked, something that very rarely happened to her. She knew she was geeky – her brother Floyd had nicked all the touchy-feely genes and she'd been left with a better understanding of details and numbers than of people. That's why she'd been so surprised by their friendship. Simon Brown had come from his small store in Bristol, where he was assistant manager, to her mammoth one for a six-week secondment shadowing her. It meant they were together every day, including breaks, when he would ask questions and listen to her answers. They occasionally touched, her guiding him with an arm to look at something in the warehouse or him reaching out to ask for an explanation about stock control. Each time she felt an electricity race through her, as if she was being rebooted. But she told herself 'stop right there' when she began to yearn for more. It was unprofessional. And he wouldn't see her as anything more than a colleague, she was sure of it.

Yet he was different – men in his position were usually cocky know-it-alls, round here they said blokes like that 'thought they were chocolate'. But Simon Brown respected her. At his leaving do, he said as much in his speech.

Then as easily as he took off his tie and rolled it neatly to fit into his pocket on the walk across the industrial park to TGI Friday's, he'd told her he'd really enjoyed working with her – in fact, what he meant was he'd *really* enjoyed it and… After that it all fell into place, as if it was the most natural thing in the world. They found a booth and spoke all night, oblivious to the party people leaving as soon as they'd realized there would be no raucous piss-up. She'd asked if he wanted a nightcap at hers – a Scottish whisky from her Highlands hike last year, which turned out to be his favourite Scotch. Sexual encounters had been few and far between for Em – she wouldn't sleep with just anyone. Not that she was given the option. There had only been two others before Simon Brown: one from school, the other someone at university. But sleeping with him had been a revelation, a wonderful one, because it was sex on a different level. Physical had met mental.

Then, the morning after, came the excuses. Again, remembering it as she perched on a white plastic toilet seat, Em felt her heart respond to the hurt – the pain of having fallen for someone who didn't feel the same. And her insides lurched when she considered how things were supposed to be. She'd decided long ago she would get married, have two children, a boy and a girl, with eighteen months between them, unless she was lucky enough to have twins. But when Simon Brown walked away, he took her hope with him. She'd clicked and dragged the file marked 'life plan' into the trash can.

Seeking calm, she looked at the floor tiles between her

polished court shoes; the sight of straight lines and right angles usually soothed her. But not today. She was so desperate not to be pregnant in this situation that she apologized to any god who might be up there for being an atheist. If he or she could possibly help her out, she'd definitely reconsider religion.

Returning to her default strategy, she rationalized her situation. Statistically, she was very unlikely to be expecting. She'd Googled it last night and a study on unprotected sex suggested the chances of it leading to pregnancy between a young couple on any random day was five per cent. And having taken the morning after pill, the probability was reduced to almost nothing. Her aching boobs were not a definitive sign because she always had that at her time of the month.

On the other hand, she was late. Very late. And just like her mind, her body ran like clockwork. Unfortunately, there were no figures available to support Em's belief that things like this didn't happen to people like her. But she simply wasn't the type. That's why she'd put off doing a test. That night had turned out to be her first and last one-night stand – quite unintentionally because she hadn't expected it to be a one-off – she was simply too averse to risk-taking.

For heaven's sake, I'm deputy store manager, she thought. Started as a Saturday check-out girl, joined for good on a graduate scheme and hand-picked for the future manager programme. The boss was due to announce his retirement any day and she was sure to take over.

But she knew this line of thought was hopeless. Since when did a sperm and egg check with their owners that conception was convenient? She stared at the test in her hand, willing it at first to hurry up, then wishing she had forever. This just can't happen, it can't… Oh shit, it just has, she thought, as the word 'pregnant' appeared on the stick. There was no ambiguity. She'd spent more on the digital variety rather than the two-lined version because it presented the facts in unarguable plain English.

Em felt the colour drain from her face as the tears threatened. She looked up, blinking hard, trying to force the emotion back. Logic, where are you? she begged, clearing her throat in a bid to regain control. So she started with the facts.

I am thirty-one and single, she began. I have a good job, a pension and my own flat. I've never had a meaningful relationship – the closest I've come is with this man who didn't want to be with me. It took until Simon Brown to find someone I really liked, therefore it is unlikely I will meet anyone suitable again soon. The kind of man who likes quirky American box sets, trekking in the hills and making culinary wonders with leftovers from the staff shop. The kind of man who doesn't care about looks or tiny breasts or freckles. The kind of man who is not just more mature in years – say, thirty-seven, like him – but in experience and approach.

Face it, Em, she told herself, he made it clear that he was sorry, so so sorry, but they could never be together. He has moved back to his store, an hour away, and he has commitments. You know what you have to do.

Em stood and felt her shoulders pull back, assuming her management pose. She opened the cubicle door, threw the test in the bin, washed her hands then brushed down her suit. She noted with satisfaction how her work face reappeared, revealing nothing of her turmoil.

With a deep breath, she went out into the corridor and made her way down the stairs and through the thick plastic curtains which marked the divide between staff only and the shop floor. Head up, she thought, as she swept into the public arena, scanning the shelves for gaps and checking the gondola ends were brimming with this week's special offers.

Right, she thought to herself, recalling the first thing on her mental to-do list, I need to have a chat with Gary the produce manager about some very unsatisfactory wonky carrots.

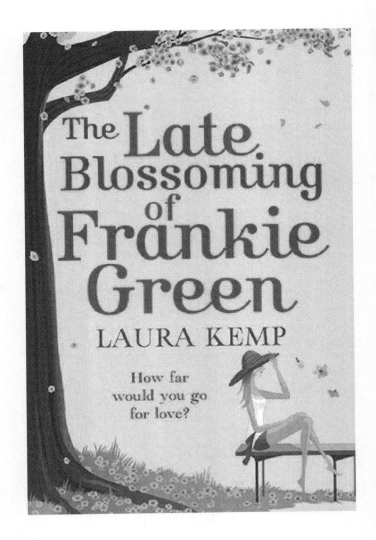

The Late
Blossoming
of
Frankie
Green

LAURA KEMP

How far
would you go
for love?

Become an Aria Addict

Aria is the new digital-first fiction imprint from Head of Zeus.

It's Aria's ambition to discover and publish tomorrow's superstars, targeting fiction addicts and readers keen to discover new and exciting authors.

Aria will publish a variety of genres under the commercial fiction umbrella such as women's fiction, crime, thrillers, historical fiction, saga and erotica.

So, whether you're a budding writer looking for a publisher or an avid reader looking for something to escape with – Aria will have something for you.

Get in touch: aria@headofzeus.com

Become an Aria Addict
http://www.ariafiction.com

Find us on Twitter
https://twitter.com/Aria_Fiction

Find us on Facebook
http://www.facebook.com/ariafiction

Find us on BookGrail
http://www.bookgrail.com/store/aria/

Addictive Fiction

First published in the UK in 2016 by Aria, an imprint of Head
of Zeus Ltd

9 7 5 3 1 2 4 6 8

A CIP catalogue record for this book is available from the
British Library.

ISBN (E) 9781784977009

Aria
Clerkenwell House
45-47 Clerkenwell Green
London EC1R 0HT

www.ariafiction.com

Printed in Great Britain
by Amazon

35534967R00185